I Am Sam

James Durose-Rayner

Clink
Street

London | New York

To Jon Sammels, legend

1970 was his time and Brazil was the football.

The season prior to the World Cup he had been his club's top scorer in Europe and had just scored a sublime winning goal in a major European final, giving his club their first trophy in 17 years.

Possibly the most cultured football player of his era had just hit his peak and firstly the World Cup and a then a new season beckoned.

Robbed of international honours – partly due to Sir Alf Ramsey's deluded loyalty to lesser players who had served him well in 1966, and partly due to the fact that no Arsenal players would ever figure in any of Ramsey's squads – he watched on as England floundered in Mexico and a new type of football was born – his type of football – dynamic one and two touch possession football, skilful ball control, 40-yard passes and powerful outside the box shooting.

His time was truly here.

After being ostracised by sections of the crowd for the fact that they didn't understand what he was trying to achieve, or for just being a player ten years ahead of his time, the expectation he had of the 1970/71 season was that his club could go onto greater things and that finally he would be accepted as the type of player similar to those that had graced the

Estadio Jalisco in Guadalajara – however what he didn't anticipate was that after scoring two goals in a pre-season match in Sweden, his world would be turned upside down as he broke his ankle and would be out until 21st November.

What he came back to was a league not focused on playing like the Brazilians, but a league solely focused on how to unsettle their system. He had returned to a league where aerial bombardment was king.

Daily Mirror
21st December, 1971

written by Frank Taylor

Do you realise that the First Division championship is being won by an aerial bombardment?

Look what happened on Saturday. Jack Charlton of Leeds headed the goal which destroyed Everton. Two of Arsenal's three goals, which humiliated Manchester United at Old Trafford, came from headers. Both teams are topping the table by airborne assault.

Soccer now belongs to the big boys. If you haven't a six ft plus goalkeeper, centre half and centre forward, you have no chance of lifting the League championship – as Leeds, Arsenal and Spurs are proving.

Denis Law confirmed that view when he said: "If you can't go through or round a defence, the only way is over the top. This leaves the players such as Johnny Giles and Billy Bremner of Leeds, Bobby Charlton of Manchester United, Sammy of Arsenal and Charlie Cooke of Chelsea working like slaves in midfield, either shoring up the defence or serving up the ammunition for the big fellows to administer the kill.

I put this proposition to Harry Catterick, the Everton manager, still smarting after that Charlton header which beat the League champions.

"Quite true," he said. "Every club is looking for the big fellows at centre half or centre forward. Look what's happening to Manchester United?

"I now believe Arsenal will pull off the League championship because they seem to have mastered this English style better than any other club.

"Leeds played some great stuff last season but at the moment there is a hint of desperation about them, perhaps because of their unhappy experience last season.

"As for Spurs, I think that for entertainment and expertise, they are the best side in the country. But alas, they appear momentarily to have gone off the boil.

"The easiest ball for a defender to play is the chip into the penalty area, but it is bringing results where teams haven't tall, dominating defenders to deal with it.

"But how much longer the public will stand tor this 4-4-2 formation I don't know."

Contents

Chapter 1
The Me Show,
starring Me

A taxi dropped me off at my girlfriend's flat off the A503 Forest Road in Walthamstow about 10:30pm only for me to be greeted by all my worldly possessions strung across the small lawn and railings. Obviously something had been bothering her, which was made apparent when an iPod docking station came flying out of the window, and hit the bullseye, consequently splitting open my head. I thought her seeing blood gushing from my head would have helped calm the situation down, but the fact that a 32" flat screen followed it out of the window chalked off that theory. I had chucked my lot in with Nicole and now I had nowhere to go. My house over in King's Cross had been rented out on some lease which I never really wanted to happen. Emily had supposedly been trying to get it back on with her husband so that was a no-go and Sooty and Libby certainly didn't want me at theirs – and now this. I picked up what I could and checked into a hotel around the corner from the office on Euston Road and sent a text over to the letting agency to call me 'as soon as'.

My thirty-six years so far had been littered with a succession of failed relationships, a few maxed-out credit cards, a brand new car which was costing me a fortune to run, a business which in my mind was about as successful as

Lesley Ash's lip implants, but which in my business partner's mind was quite the opposite. My wife was the only one
who understood me and even she didn't understand me, and
apart from paying her two grand a month mortgage she had
just recently saddled me with over three and a half thousand
quid's worth of maintenance payments for my two kids,
which supplemented her part-time job in Sainsbury's quite
nicely, especially as she was now knocking off the manager,
who was five years younger than her. He also drove a rag-
top Mercedes, which was probably the sole reason behind
my vanity purchase of a Maserati, which was costing me
another fifteen hundred quid a month on a PCP and about
the same in parking tickets and fuel. I tried not to think
about it and then spent the rest of the night thinking about
not thinking about it and by the time the traffic on Euston
Road woke me up I'd managed about two hours' kip.

I got into the office to be greeted by Faranha, a nine-
teen-year old Asian girl with a western mentality and legs like
you wouldn't believe. 'Rule One' had been instilled from the
top down by my business partner, which was basically 'No
diddling the staff', which was something that I really, really
had tried to adhere to, and which lasted exactly three days,
before I played my ace card and offered her a lift home, only
to get stuck in traffic for three hours on the North Circular
on my way up to South Woodford and get walloped with yet
another traffic congestion fine as I had to drop a violin off in
Clerkenwell – don't ask! That put me off her a bit. That and
the fact that I have a set rule when it comes to women. They
have to be less than five foot four, blonde and have nice legs
and small feet. Oh yeah, and they have to be intelligent –
the latter one of those requirements being the most obvious
reason why I usually got dumped. In this instance Faranha's
parents had taken one look at me and hated my guts and I
spent the next three weeks checking under my car for incen-

diary devices, especially as her brother had a big beard, did quite a bit of twitching and mentioned the car quite a few times. It was a bit unnerving really.

"BSkyB have just been on the phone," she said on my arrival into the office. "They want either you or Sooty to phone them back."

My business partner was also my best friend. We had known each other since we were kids and went to the same school and through University together, and six years ago we kicked up this 'thing', which had recently been hanging around my neck like a ball and chain. I wanted him to buy me out but he thought things were great how they were. He would do. He had a great life with a wife who had a great job, two kids that loved him and lived in one of those big stucco-fronted houses a few tube rides away in the posh part of town. It pissed me off that he always seemed to get on. My stucco-fronted house on Frederick Street, which had been costing me another four grand a month, currently had a family of Russians residing in it for the next eight months, which should have partly-offset the mortgage by them paying me rent. Then there was the ten percent that was being skimmed off the top by the letting agents. That was if I actually got paid any rent at all. As it stood I currently owed the letting agency a few months of that ten percent. Sooty's house had been handed down to his wife after her uncle died. When my uncle died all I got was having to listen to a full hour of Roger Miller at his funeral.

"You're in early," he said as he walked into the office and slung his proverbial bowler hat on the rack.

"We've had Sky on the phone," I replied.

"I know," came his reply. "One of their bods called me last night about us doing some programme about the World Cup."

Another pile of shite, I thought.

World Cup year was always garbage, especially when England were in it. It was generally a case of dragging a few corpses out of the wardrobe to talk about Sir Alf, why Greavesie didn't play in the final and that fucking Russian linesman.

"It'll be interesting," stated Sooty, smiling.

"Yeah, about as interesting as the Beckham Bore-ography we did," I replied.

"That was good," he argued.

"You what? He's the most boring man on the planet," I said.

"I like Beckham," stated a grinning Faranha as she passed him a coffee.

"You would do," I replied. "And that thing he married is a right sour-faced old cow – every time I see her she looks like she's sucking a lemon."

"I think she's great," said Faranha.

"You'd think she'd be happy with all that money," I added, still shaking my head.

Our business was a small sports media company that put together programmes to fill TV slots and that made DVDs, with our speciality being football. Sooty and I were always destined to go into business together and as kids we had always talked about it. I was the outgoing one with the big ideas and he was always the level-headed one that supposedly held me back from doing something stupid. Our original business ideas were pretty rangy, and covered anything from being rock gods to living in the wilds out in Saskatchewan where we could work on our idea of a type of fantasy football with pretend clubs and players that we could patent; setting up a sports or music magazine; doing exactly what we were doing now; and managing Stoke City.

Everything went tits up when he got accepted at University, and not to be outdone I followed suit and ended up saddling myself with a load of courses that precipitated boredom at best and suicide at worst. Have you ever read Balzac? Well take my advice, don't. He's more boring than David Beckham.

Managing Stoke City was our ticket to get the hell out of there, however we may have got a nice letter back from the chairman, but we didn't make it for an interview. It was a shame as we couldn't have done any worse as the idiot they hired as he ended up getting them relegated. We had some great ideas, and put them forward to the board as eloquently as we could, but it wasn't to be. I'm sure with us in charge they wouldn't have fared any worse and I'm sure we wouldn't have been turned over 0-7 at home by Birmingham City.

Sooty got out of University with some nice degrees; I got out with more or less the same as I went in with. It was a right waste of time. Football and music had been our life, but we were as different as chalk and cheese. He liked Leeds United, I liked Arsenal. He liked Meat Loaf and I liked anything but Meat Loaf.

"How can you listen to a fat bloke with long hair who looks like a pig?" I used to ask him.

"He's great," he always replied.

"You said that about Darren Anderton when he signed for Leeds," I reminded him. "And then you spent the next two seasons praying that they got shut of him."

"He wasn't a bad player," Sooty replied. "He was always injured … and he had a massive chin."

I agreed. I certainly wouldn't have signed him. There's nothing worse than having your team full of ugly players. I remember looking in wonder at an old Panini football sticker book and seeing a sticker of Kenny Burns of Nottingham Forest.

"His dad used to chop firewood on his face," my dad had said, looking over at me reading the old sticker book.

And Graham Baker of Southampton wasn't much better. He looked like an escapee from Rampton. Ask anyone – no one likes ugly players in their team. The mugsmashers will tell you that they loved Peter Beardsley. That's a total lie. I was told that Kenny Dalglish kept him in a cage and only let him out for ninety minutes on a Saturday and when he scored nobody ever wanted to kiss him. There was hell on when he got out one night.

We were once asked to do a 45 minute slot on 'Maradona – The Hand of God' and we set about interviewing Beardsley. I may as well have been interviewing Pak Doo Ik. I was lost at 'Hello' – It was that bad we needed subtitles.

I sat behind my desk and checked my one hundred or so emails, the majority of which were porn-based although there was an interesting one from a Nigerian prince who wanted to rest three million of his dollars in my bank account until next Friday. I looked over at Sooty talking to Ginge, who I'll get to in a minute, and sent his bank account number and sort code over to the said prince.

Next up – the kid we called Ginge. How can I describe him? I had no idea as to how he came by the name of Ginge as his parents were from Ghana. He's a great kid and a stone-wall Arsenal supporter, however the only players he ever wants to talk about are other coloured players. He was devastated when Arsenal sold Alex Song and threatened not to renew his season ticket – if he ever had one at all, as he did have a tendency to embellish the truth.

We had needed an extra body in the office and we advertised for an assistant camera man and a general dogsbody and he was the result of the said advertisement. Twelve and a half quid an hour may look lucrative up on Tyneside, but in London it's classed as slave wages and the amount of applicants that either turned their noses up, or in two cases bollocked us for it was unreal. In the end it was either Ginge or this intimidating Eastern European with the skinhead who spoke about as much English as Peter Beardsley.

The BSkyB request was fairly basic, and as we thought, was a purely case of dragging Bobby Charlton and Nobby Stiles out of their coffins. There was never anything better than getting us in the mood for another glorious failure than listening to the Class of '66 talking about how they did it. Sooty and I had sat through every game of that competition about five or six times and we both had the same mindset. It was a shit competition, with shit teams playing shit football and we were lucky. The strange thing however is that BSkyB wanted us and three other companies to sort of 'tender' for it. This, I had not come up against before. Generally we could make a nice earner from a project like this, at worst around one hundred grand and at best around half a million, especially with DVD sales.

"I can't do another fucking re-run of '66," I said.

"'66 was great," said Ginge. "We won the cup."

"We?" Sooty replied.

"Yeah – England," he said.

I shook my head and just smiled.

"I'm English – I was born in Hackney," he said.

"Jesus was born in a stable but it don't make him an horse," Sooty replied.

"Anyway you were shouting for Ghana at the last World Cup," I said.

"I wasn't," he replied.

"You were," I said. "I remember you writing to Arsené Wenger to go out and buy Andrè Ayew or whatever his name was."

"I didn't," he replied.

"Yeah you did," I stated. "You even sent it recorded delivery – I know because we paid for it."

Ginge was your archetypal Arsenal blogger. Arsenal need

a forward – buy Demba Ba, Benteke or Bony. Arsenal need a beast in midfield – buy Pogba or Yaya Toure. In Ginge's mind it was a simple case of 'buying black' because it was well-documented Wenger liked Africans, hence the reason why Benteke had been publicly whoring himself out after committing himself to both Aston Villa and Paul Lambert after his nine million pound transfer – initially stating that his move 'had been a dream come true' but who was now apparently pleading for Wenger to rescue him from his 'hell'. Strangely though, Wenger didn't fall for the egg under the hat and sort of took the stance of Alex Ferguson. Wenger had recently had his hands burnt with Gervinho, who had been his bargain basement alternative to the man he really wanted – Eden Hazard.

Ferguson had had his burnt after he had chucked a couple of million at Eric Djemba Djemba – a player so good they named him twice, and after running the rule over him he had decided that the money would have been better invested letting the Nigerian prince who had recently emailed him requesting funds to sink his country's first aluminium mine.

It is strange I should mention Gervinho as his agent contacted Sooty the other year requesting that we do a 60-minute DVD of his client, with his client being guaranteed twenty thousand quid up front. After Sooty had told him where to go we had a discussion about it.

"We could probably stretch it out to sixty minutes if we put all his step-overs and misses in it," I said. "Otherwise I reckon we'll be struggling to take it out to nine minutes."

Some football players were absolutely stupid and had no concept of reality.

We mulled over the details of the 'tender documents' which BSkyB emailed us over and at their remit. Basically they wanted some great story of England and the World Cup and I immediately knew that the other media companies chasing it would go for 1966. Us? Not a chance. However we needed an angle, and this would come via a strange source.

I'm sort of putting it over that we were a set of amateurs and struggling to keep afloat with some dodgy staff. That was anything but the truth; apart from Faranha who handled the reception and doubled up as a P.A to me and Sooty – we were all football mad. Everything revolved around football, and both Sooty and I could give a summary of almost any player from any generation, and our video archives were absolutely chock-a-block with matches, edited highlights from Match of the Day and such and literally thousands of interviews. We truly lived football.

Our other two members of staff were Fred 'Nerk', who ran the camera and the cutting room and a girl called Abi, or Abigail, who did the editing and marketing. Fred was another Arsenal nut case and lived somewhere over in Holloway. He was about our age and was supposedly happily married with about ten kids. Abigail was another which Rule One had applied to and which had also been strictly adhered to. She fitted within the profile of all my girlfriends, however the fact that she batted the other way made her a no-go area. Both Fred and Abigail were really great at their jobs.

I copped a light lunch with Sooty at a wine bar around the corner from the train station and we did a bit of brain storming, which carried on when we got back to the office and which resulted in us trawling through YouTube – firstly to re-live the 1986 World Cup and then the 1990 World Cup and the missed penalties. In between that, we picked up on a spat on TV between Malcolm Allison and Alan Mullery that I hadn't seen before, and its content referred to the 1970 World Cup and the fact that whilst Mullery thought he was brilliant, Allison thought the exact opposite, and basically described him as a one-paced carthorse who ought to be put out of his misery. We suddenly had an angle.

The 1970 World Cup was well before my time, but the football was good and it was in colour. The fact that it was a World Cup was inconsequential, as England had always been shite, and this shite going out to Brazil this summer would, in my mind, fare no differently.

I trawled through the archives and noticed that both the BBC and ITV were jockeying for top billing in the battle for viewers, and the fact that ITV had Malcolm Allison was sort of offset by the fact that the BBC had had Brian Clough.

What an era to be alive, I thought.

We have very few characters in the game nowadays as the majority of viewpoints have been purposely suppressed, by not only the FA but by the times we live in. If I had a house to go to I would have watched the lot, but I did not.

I sent a nice text over to Nicole which she reciprocated with a "Drop dead u bastard."

Ours was never going to be a 'Love Story' starring me as Ryan O'Neal and her as Ali Macgraw, however I never really thought of her as being the violent type. She worked in the marketing department of some company that sold safety gear. I couldn't really elaborate on what she actually did, as I never thought to ask. Paul Merson had been one of the guest speakers at a 'Christmas Do' her firm had laid on and I had managed to get an invite – a bit wrong really – but there you go. Merson was rehashing all his stories about being on tour with Arsenal and his coke addiction and I had copped her on one of the top tables and went over to speak to her. Her parents lived in Bristol but she was now London-based and I asked her for a date. Armed with my Maserati, Armani suit and around two grand cash on the hip I easily won her over and managed to ponce off her for five months until yesterday night. Relationships are always great at the start. It's a getting to know you stage which sort of goes, 'Do you like this? Do you like that?' and sort of culminates with 'Can

I put it in there?' or in my case 'Have you got a couple of hundred you can spot me?' neither of which I have to add are truly great lines.

"You going back to Nicole's?" Sooty asked.

"I fucking doubt it," I replied.

"What have you done this time?" he asked.

"To be honest, I'm not really sure – I know of about half-a-dozen things which could piss her off, but I'm a bit unsure of which one it actually is."

Fred Nerk offered me a bed for the night, but kipping in his rat hole full of kids wasn't really what I had in mind, and the chance of Abigail offering me a bed was as likely as Abou Diaby claiming the Ballon D'Or. In fact I had a better chance of Abou Diaby offering me a bed for the night, her kipping over at Fred's and Fred winning the Ballon D'Or.

At seven bells I knocked off, got my car out of the underground car park and drove into Walthamstow to find out how much Nicole actually knew. To be on the safe side I parked the car out of bowling distance and rang her buzzer.

"What do you want?" came her reply via the intercom.

'Somewhere to sleep' would have been an honest answer, but I couldn't really say that. A lie would be the safest bet, so I laid on a couple of nice 'loving lines' down the wires.

"Is that it?" she asked.

I hadn't really anticipated that, so I sort of went over to the car and contemplated sending her another nice text, but before I could, she opened the door to her flat. She looked good – she always looked good. I don't know what I was thinking of. She was generally great – she never really argued with me that much and I more or less always got what I wanted. Then another thought hit me – she may have looked great but I was a bit wary of the expression on her face and the fact she had her hands behind her back. I generally got loads of smiles and was generally referred to with terms of endearment such as 'sweetheart' and 'honey', however that face I was staring at was still in 'U-bastard mode'.

"Are you okay?" I asked.

"Who the hell is Emily?"

Mmm. That was one sixth of those half-a-dozen things that I knew would indeed piss her off. I needed a great lie to offset this, but at that point my head was a shed. If you could have put Nicole in a mirror it could have been Emily staring straight back at her, but whereas Nicole was twenty-four, Emily was thirty two. Eight years was a long time, and looking at Nicole it could be what she could be facing if what I thought she had behind her back was to sort of end up in mine.

"Which Emily are you on about?" I asked.

"Why, how many are there?" came her quick response.

"Emily who's married to Freddy's cousin, and Emily who's married to my mate at Sky."

Notice how I tied both Emily's up with a power word – 'Married'?

"Apart from that I don't know any Emily's," I lied.

"Who's the one who looks like me?" she asked.

Mmm. I was really hoping that that Emily wouldn't be brought up. "Benny's wife," I lied.

"Oh," was her reply.

I liked 'Oh's. 'Oh's smarted of indecisiveness and mistakes. I could always do an 'Oh'.

"Jump in the car and I'll drive you over to theirs if you want to meet her?" I asked, hoping like hell that my fake-pressuring would offset her suspicion.

"That iPod split open my head," I added, trying to change the subject.

"Good," she said. "You deserved it."

I didn't want to ask 'What for?' as I wanted to keep her away from the Emily line of interrogation. As it turned out, one of her workmates had seen me somewhere with Emily, who she happened to sort of know her through her job in marketing – ten million people in London, and there's actually someone who knows someone. I couldn't believe it. I thanked the lord that I'd changed her number on my phone when I was invited in after a thirty-five minute stand-off, as the first thing on Nicole's agenda was to trawl through my phone. Fortunately I now had Emily down as 'Abou Diaby'.

Chapter 2
Dad

The next morning we had our first meeting with BSkyB's Assistant Head of Sport, or his assistant's assistant rather, and it was myself and Abigail who were present at the meeting. I let Abigail do the talking at this stage; she was a million times better at it than me, as I either got bored or tended to repeat myself. The guy taking the meeting appeared a strange one. Despite what Lenny Henry says the TV industry is generally made up of minorities such as gays, ethnics and social worker-types, and this Herbert was all three of them rolled into one – and he had one hell of a twitch and a stammer which was as equally as good, and which, if you weren't expecting, gave you one hell of a shock. I was just glad he wasn't giving me a shave. He had either had some form of stroke or his mother had dropped him on his head as a kid. He kept wanting to say the word 'inconsequential', I have absolutely no idea why because he continually struggled with the 'c' and its following vowel, and he had me incessantly trying to mime the word for him.

"Thank god that's over," I said as we walked down the corridor.

"I think it went well," replied Abigail.

"Really?" I said, slightly unconvinced. "Are you sure we even met with the right person?"

I phoned Sooty to let him know what was going on, and he kindly let me know that the police had been round with a warrant for my arrest.

"What?"

"They wouldn't tell me anything," he stated. "They left a phone number though."

Apart from the odd traffic offence I never ever broke the law and the only thing I could ever be accused of is being a 'dick'.

I rang the number they had left and it turned out that the Russian family who were not paying me rent to live in my house at King's Cross were doing some kind of online scam and using my name – which was nice of them – and some detective had been trailing me for the last three weeks. Regardless of what I said to them, they still wanted me in for questioning and they pissed me off that much that I got Faranha to call the firm of solicitors that dealt with all our legal stuff and copyrights. I have to tell you now that any confidence I had in this going away was immediately offset by the sight that would greet me when I got back to the office. I had some heavy set trainspotter-type bird in a flowery blouse, some crimpolene skirt and a pair of rubber Crocs waiting to go fight my corner.

"Hello," she said holding out her hand. "I'm Finola Barclay."

I took her into my office and gave her a brief summary of what the copper had told me on the phone, as well as the details of the ignorant useless bastards who paraded as my letting agents. I wanted a clean sweep. This to go away and the Russians turfing out of my house.

"And while you're on with it can you sort me a divorce?" I asked.

She jotted a load of stuff down as I tried to keep my gaze away from her footwear. I hated women with big feet as much as I hated Crocs or flip-flops, however it was as if she wanted me to see them, and every time I positioned myself further around my desk in a bid to decontaminate my view, she seemed to shuffle her chair further around – sort of following me. What possessed women to dress like shite was beyond me. Okay, she was a bit on the chunky side, but she wasn't that bad looking. A couple of weeks on Ephedren, a good scrub, a haircut and some decent clobber, and she wouldn't look half bad. I was trying to debate what size shoe she was, but it was hard to tell. With my women I generally drew the line at size fives and below. She definitely had to be a seven or eight. All the time we were in conversation, all I was thinking about was the size of her feet. I was sure I was going round the bend.

When I eventually turfed her out of my office I had a natter with Sooty, who told me that Libby had summoned me over to theirs for dinner. I didn't like the sound of that. Libby was everything in a woman that I neither liked nor wanted. She was tall, dead bossy and had big feet, and that being the case, the last place I wanted to be was at their house just to be told off.

"I've got something on," I lied.

"No you haven't," Sooty replied.

"Then can I fetch Nicole?" I asked, knowing full-well that Nicole coming limited the chances of me being bollocked by Libby.

"Why, would she come?" he asked.

That was an interesting question, which really deserved an answer, so I sent her a text. We had sort of made up – however my idea and her idea of making up were poles apart. My idea was basically for her to let me back in, whereas her idea was that she wanted to be part of my life and for us to do things together and for me not to shag around. Basically the same as what my wife had wanted, however I was not the type of person that wanted to sit in every night holding hands and watching Coronation Street.

My phone beeped and I got a "Yes plz x". Her mood had changed.

"She's coming," I said. "But do me a favour – tell Libby not to be on my back all night."

I looked over at Ginge and Fred Nerk who were checking what footage the ITN archives held on 1970. We particularly wanted footage of the ITV World Cup panel.

"How are you two doing?" I asked.

"Okay," replied Fred. "But it's going to be expensive if we start requesting this lot."

He was right on that score, and it was a pity we couldn't just download the clips or rob the footage off some other DVDs. We also needed an angle which we could draw some gritty narrative.

"You got any ideas?" asked Sooty.

"Loads," I replied. "But at the minute they're all shit."

That was my job as part of this firm. Sooty handled the legal side and accounts and I handled the creative, but at this moment in time my creative spark needed igniting. It was a pity Malcolm Allison was dead, he would have been great to interview. I got Faranha to get me a meeting with Alan Mullery and the first thing that came back from his agent was a request for details of what his fee would be. I'd seen Mullery play, but to be honest apart from the goal versus West Germany in 1970 and a goal of the season on Match of the Day I had never taken that much notice of him. All I knew was that he looked like some armed robber out of 'The Sweeney' who used to play for Spurs.

Dinner at Sooty's was about as eventful as I thought it would be, and I spent the majority of the evening trying to stay out of the way of Libby's discerning gaze. Nicole was great though, and she kept Libby's mind occupied, so much so that I was only referred to as being an idiot three times. She looked good as well, and even more so when standing up alongside the huge athletic build of our female host. Sooty had always had a penchant for the manly looking bird – and Libby? Well she was hardly in the discus-throwing category but she could have easily been a 400m hurdler or a tennis player. We finished dinner and sat on the sofa and my worst nightmare happened – we had to watch a video recording of both their kids in a school play and then some footage of their holiday in Hawaii. At around eleven bells I was about ready to slit my wrists, but Nicole explained that she had to attend some board meeting at eight o'clock the next day and therefore averted any impending doom.

"Thank god for that," I said when I got into the car.

"Aw, they were really nice," said Nicole as she put her seat belt on. "Libby really thinks a lot about you."

"She might think a lot about me, but believe me – it's all shit thoughts."

Nicole smiled. "She treats you like a younger brother."

I refused to get into any further conversation and I knew that I wouldn't have to go to their house for at least another couple of months.

We got back to the flat, but not before we had called off at some late night deli and wine bar and had some proper food and washed it down with a bottle of wine.

The next morning I copped a phone call from 'Abou Diaby' on my mobile. Emily had just dropped her husband off at Heathrow. He was working away in Hannover and it was basically a question of 'Did I fancy meeting up for a drink?' which translated into 'Did I fancy bollocksing my life up even more than it was already?'

As stated, Emily could have been Nicole's twin sister, and was possibly the nicest woman I had ever known. She had great taste and was forever telling me how brilliant I was. I didn't really know what she actually did, but from reading between the lines she was a marketing director with some firm in North London who manufactured hats, walking sticks or whatever. I'm not exactly sure what it was, but I know it was something pointless. She had a great smile and laugh and was one of those women who would do anything for you. Nicole was similar, but whereas Nicole would give me a resounding 'no' to certain requests, Emily would always give me a 'yeah' or 'okay then'. If truth-be-known I could have easily married her if it wasn't for the fact that she was already married. A bit of a shitter, that!

I spent the morning downloading the back pages from the newspaper archives of summer of 1970, and in particular any interesting snippets regarding England's World Cup team, when something slapped me in the face. It was a kind of spat from Alf Ramsey regarding a London-based freelance journalist.

"Maybe Mr. Mardell should mind his own business instead of other people's," Sir Alf had candidly stated. "If politics is what he specialises in, maybe he should stick to his speciality. As for my speciality – it is, and always will be football."

I was never a big fan of any one in football who talked overly posh, and Alf Ramsey was exactly that. He was not quite as posh as Garth Crooks, but then again Garth was either the Duke of Edinburgh's secret love child or he just stuck a pool ball in his mouth when he spoke. Whatever it was, it annoyed the hell out of me.

If you ever speak to Jimmy Greaves, however, he will tell you how Ramsey changed international football by shaking up the F.A. Pre-Ramsey it had been a case of a selection committee comprising a set of pompous asses who decided on the England team. He made me laugh describing his 'Dear Greaves' letters that he received to announce his inclusion in the next squad of players for the forthcoming England game.

I know I'm an Arsenal supporter, but I do like Greavesie. He was and always will be a breath of fresh air.

I eventually found the piece of news that Ramsey was referring to in his spat, and although it was just an opinion, back in the summer of 1970, an opinion was the last thing Ramsey had wanted to wake up to. It appeared that this Mardell guy had spoken with a few top managers and they were all of the same mindset: that Ramsey had overlooked certain players in favour of some of his old boys, and the ones who were being initially singled out were the Charlton brothers, Nobby Stiles and Martin Peters.

I managed a lunch and a drink with Emily around one o'clock, and she gave me a bit of news which I certainly wasn't expecting. She was fourteen weeks pregnant and it was mine, and to make matters even worse the husband wasn't aware of it – yet. I got back into the office with the crap that I had just been saddled with, along with a great pile of paper and accompanying .pdf documentation on a flash drive, when Sooty explained that BSkyB wanted us in for a second meeting. I shouted Abigail in and between the three of us we constructed a game plan. We had several angles, all of which I knew would make better viewing than anything that the other media companies could knock together. I was often called conceited, not least by my wife, girlfriend and Libby. You could chuck Sooty in there as well if you wanted, but I knew what I knew. Media is something that needs to attract viewers, listeners or readers. To do that you have to make it firstly interesting and secondly compelling. Listening to Bobby Charlton waffling on didn't fit into either category, but I liked the sound of this Mardell guy and what he had to say.

Chapter 3
The Intervention

Arsenal were the most frustrating team I knew, and they had just been spanked 3-0 at Everton, and struggled like hell to break through against one of the most mediocre sides we had played this season, which had Ginge clamouring for the Wenger to sign Lukaku.

"He's not the solution to the problem," I stated. "He would add a problem to the problem – the main problem is Arsené Wenger."

Me trying to talk football with Ginge was pointless. I knew exactly what I saw and that was a set of talented individuals who lacked the guts for a fight and had no trust in the manager. Why should they? The winter transfer window passed without incident and all we were given was a Swede with a bad back, when we should have had our front line and midfield bolstered. By not doing anything it gave Wenger the option of overlooking the enigma that is Nicklas Bendtner and playing his eighteen year old 'towel boy' from Auxerre, who if I am honest is about as useful as an ashtray on a motorbike, and then watch him pass on deflective post-match comments to the press after we had watched his new project ponce about in front of goal, missing loads of chances and giving the ball away when we were 0-1 down against Wigan in the semi-final of the FA Cup.

I had liked Wenger when he first arrived, but like anyone who knows football, I think he will always be found wanting when push comes to shove. He had done a great job of shifting on a load of the deadwood – this is the deadwood he bought I hasten to add – and replacing them with decent players. Our current weak links were the goalkeeper, the fact that he didn't rotate the team and the fact we needed a top defensive-minded midfielder and a world class finisher, which brings me on to Luis Suarez. I was amazed at how many of these so-called Arsenal fans didn't want him at the club, along the fact that Wenger had insulted the hell out of Liverpool by firstly offering a pittance, and secondly by offering a quid over the alleged release clause. If he would have gone in with a bid of, say, £55 million he would have been taken seriously, but he didn't and we were left waiting to drool over a cumbersome and gangly teenager from the French second division, who had been out of action half the season with a rare and contagious disease which only coloured players whom Arsenal sign from Auxerre get. Me personally, I would have cut our losses with Diaby and paid him off as in reality even when he's actually fit he has only ever had three good games for us – and against Tottenham his statistics are rather damning to say the least, and is something that I don't think many people have really picked up on. The player Arsenal currently need is sort of out of favour in Munich. Javi Martinez is what is needed and £35 million would get him. Arteta has lost a lot of mobility and Flamini is limited. Ramsey and Martinez would be a fantastic backbone, with the latter taking very few prisoners. Arsenal need a couple of nasty bastards in there, not some flaccid garlic eater who hasn't got the balls for a fight.

Whenever Arsenal lose or play shite it generally sets the tone for the week, and on taking the kids back to the wife I copped an earful for having them watch the match with me in the pub. The kids were the two things I missed more than anything. Like Emily they both thought I was great, but young kids are impressionable and my plastic lifestyle often looks brilliant from the outside, when in reality it is not. As with Sooty and Nicole I failed to tell them about the future addition of a new brother or sister. As a rule, I tended to leave things until the very last minute – that way, I get as little nagging as possible directed at me.

My wife Jeanette was a gold medallist when it came to nagging and the sound of her whining voice was enough to drive a man insane. And I had just endured thirty-five minutes of it and I didn't even live with her. A couple of 'bye-bye dad's' were followed by a drive into Walthamstow, and to a girl-friend who decided that the day I had the kids would gen-erally be the day she advertised her sheer discontent of all things me.

I can do without this bollocks, I thought and kept my fingers crossed that the family of Russians living in my house on Frederick Street would soon be evicted so I could tell Nicole the next time she kicked off to 'Go bollocks', which was to be sooner than I thought as 'Abou Diaby' had called me while I was in the toilet and Nicole ended up answering it.

"Who's this?" Nicole had asked.

"Emily," came the reply.

Well that was fucking it, Nicole lost the plot and I was homeless again. But at least Emily's bloke was out of the UK. I drove over the river into Greenwich, which was the last place I really wanted to go, especially in this car, and I spent half the night looking out of the window at all the street robbers and rapists pacing up and down the street.

"Come away from the window," Emily said. "You're making me nervous."

"What do you live here for?" I asked.

"It's not that bad," she replied.

"Not that bad compared to what?" I inquired.

It was a shit hole up in parts of King's Cross, but it was nothing like this. I hated the place, but I had few options open to me. Emily insisted that her being pregnant could be 'dealt with', but I immediately saw my own two kids and knew then that if the same had been discussed with Jeanette then those two adoring faces I had look at me each weekend wouldn't be there now. There was no way I would sanction a termination, but it was her body, and that being the case it was her shout.

Emily was always happy and I more than enjoyed her company, however there was no way on earth that I could stay at hers. Today had been a really crap day, which was not helped when the alarm sounded on my car and I went outside to see some coloured kid running off with my mobile phone.

"What did you leave it in your car for?" asked Emily.

"It's caused me enough bother today," I replied.

I rang the police who sent someone around and I got arrested on the spot as there was an outstanding warrant on me for internet fraud, which had not been sorted as the fucking idiot solicitor I employed was more concerned in earning bigger money through my potential divorce than the two minutes it would have taken her in clearing my name. I ended up spending the night in the cells over at Eltham Police Station until the copper dealing with it could come and fetch me and take me back over to King's Cross. I made a call to Sooty who informed our solicitors, who immediately sent the fat useless cow over to get me bail. I was anything but happy, but she did tell me that the Russians would be out of the house by the end of the week, which was about eight months quicker than I'd anticipated. As it was, they had already vacated and stripped the place bare.

I finally got out of the police station with absolutely no apology whatsoever and was met by Sooty who took me back down to Greenwich to retrieve my car. If I was being honest I would say that I was cracking – I had just about had enough.

I looked at Emily and got a smile as I climbed in the car and drove it away. My phone was retrieved some four hours later via the GPS tracking system but in the time it had been out of my hands it had managed to rack up around twelve hundred quid's worth of calls to some mobile over in Somalia and I noticed that a load of photos had been wiped.

That should please Nicole, I thought.

By the time I got in to work on Monday morning, I found out that the guy we had originally met at BSkyB regarding the 'World Cup Special' had been removed from his post. I could certainly understand why, but it meant that we were in limbo to how we currently stood. This was Sooty's department and I left him to go over and sort it, as in the meantime I had the letting agency on the blower threatening legal action regarding something to do with 'breach of contract'.

Something must have snapped inside me and me telling them that I would go over and torch the place to the ground wasn't my best move and was followed by a visit from the same idiot copper who had just released me, and as I was on bail pending further inquiries I got locked up in the cells again. I couldn't make this up. Everything around me was in freefall, and it was made a thousand times worse when there was talk of remanding me in HMP Pentonville. Fortunately our firm of legal people sent a proper solicitor to act on my behalf and by half past five that night everything had been quashed and I was a free man. A free man to go where, I hadn't a clue. I rang Nicole who told me to 'Go fuck myself" and I phoned Emily who said she had an appointment at the local abortionist at the end of the week and 'Please could I not phone at night' as her husband was back.

I paced the poop deck a few times whilst in thought,

before putting my cap in hand and calling to see my soon to be ex-wife. I don't know why it did, but it all came out. She who thought she knew everything about me was speechless. Well, for a few minutes anyway. She twitched a bit like the man we had seen at BSkyB before calling reinforcements in the guise of Sooty and Libby, which I certainly didn't want, but which I got. And I had to tell them the same story I had told Jeanette. It seemed easier the second time around, and the bollockings I got away with at dinner the other night I got in triplicate by Libby this time around, and she tore me to shreds prior to her putting me back together again.

"You can't go on like this," she said as she sat across from me. "You have to have some order in your life."

I woke up the next day to two excited kids in the bedroom. My little girl thought it was absolutely brilliant that I was here and my little lad kept on asking, "Are you going to take us to watch Arsenal in the mucky pub again, Dad?"

Jeanette didn't say much but she did make me some breakfast and I sat at the table with the kids, who thought it great that I was sat there with them, and I watched them both smiling, eating their breakfast and chatting. Bearing in mind the crap I had given them and their mum, they seemed happy. I offered to take them to school, which was the least I could do, and after dropping them off I called to Frederick Street to see what the state the Russians had left the house. It wasn't as big a shit tip as I thought it would be and it would take around a week to clean it up and paint it. Well, at least that would be something to occupy my mind.

I got into the office to be greeted by a smirking Sooty. "How did it go last night?" he asked.

"My options were extremely limited," I replied.

"I wouldn't have told her about Emily," he said still smirking. "That was a really bad move."

I had to get it off my chest, but what I didn't know at the time was that Jeanette had gone over to see Nicole at the place she worked, and they had both met up with Emily. Prior to my honest and naked appraisal of my life, none of these three really knew each other. By the time five o'clock came I knew there was something up when I saw Nicole's face at my office door. Mmm. I never knew something so pretty could possess such a stern face, and by Christ did she dish me out a bollocking.

"You got her fucking pregnant?" she roared, whilst I did my level best to keep the noise to a minimum by closing the blinds and standing in front of the door. Not that it did, however.

"You know she's on about keeping it," she added.

I didn't go in for big arguments and confrontation. In my opinion it was much easier to let them get on with it and me walk away, but this time I felt that I had started the cleansing process, so it would be best to keep it up. Facing my problems was never something I was good at, but starting a 'project' is always the hardest part.

"I love you Nicole," I said. "I always have."

That wasn't a lie and it stopped her in her tracks.

"What about this Emily?" she asked.

"I sort of like her as well," I said.

"Well you can't have fucking both of us," she snapped, shaking her head. "So what now?"

"She reminded me of you," I said rather stupidly.

"Yeah and I reminded you of her," she snapped before candidly adding, "She even reminded me of me."

"You do look alike," I admitted.

"Where do you fucking even dig them up from?" she then asked rather nastily.

She sort of calmed down after that and explained that

my ex-wife, wife or whatever – Jeanette – was concerned about me and *she* had thought it best to get things out into the open.

"You reckon?" I said. "It's probably more to do with giving you both a bit of what she had."

From reading between the lines the upshot was that Nicole still wanted me, which was a strange one. At times I could never really figure out women – especially the women that clocked on to me. Nicole was young, petite and extremely good looking. So why on earth would she want me? I brought absolutely nothing to the table and was the most shallow and conceited git on the planet – well, that was, according to Libby's candid description of me last night.

However there was still that big fucking black dog to overcome in the guise of an unwanted pregnancy, which Nicole suddenly re-remembered and she then proceeded to ram that down my throat like she was loading up a cannon. This one was a strange bollocking, and from what I could work out, she wasn't exclusively pissed off that I had had the affair with Emily, but more to do with the fact that she didn't get a baby. I may have read it wrong – shallow I may be, stupid I was not.

"What are you saying?" I asked. "That you want a kid?"

She stood there with her arms folded and said nothing. Well she did, but at that moment she was fairly quiet, then she hit me with something that made me look quite normal.

"I see you with your two children and I see what a great father you are," she said. "I feel left out – I've always felt left out."

And then she started crying.

Mmm. This was a strange one. I preferred a violent confrontation rather than this, as at least I could have walked away from that.

What should I do? was my initial thought.

Patting her on the shoulder with a 'There, there' was a bit Victorian. I could have given her a hug and that could have ended up with me taking a winder, so I offered her a chair and she sat down.

"So what are you saying?" I asked. "That you want to get married?"

"Don't be fucking stupid, you idiot," was her apt reply.

"Then tell me what you want," I said.

"I don't know – you've messed everything up."

She eventually left and I was still no wiser, but now I had a light at the end of the tunnel which was my house, and when I left work I did an appraisal of the work that needed doing and phoned up a guy who Ginge claimed to know who was a decorator-cum-odd job man of sorts, and within half an hour he was stood next to me. Like his mate, he was a second generation African who let me know straight away that he was both an Arsenal supporter and that we should have done that DVD on Gervinho.

"He's tearing it up at Roma," he said.

"And ask yourself why is that," I replied. "Italian football is in the shitter."

I could talk all day about Arsenal and football in general, but most African Arsenal supporters have the same agenda. They only like other Africans and it wouldn't be long before I was asked my thoughts on Alex Song.

"We should have never let Song go," he said.

See?

"He was lazy, slow and petulant," I said. "It was the best business Wenger has ever done."

"Look at all his assists," he replied whilst checking out the woodwork and writing stuff down in his little book.

"You could have got as many assists as him if you played in the same team as he did. All he had to do was boot the ball to Van Persie."

"Van Persie is shit," was his reply.

I explained what I thought, and which was that Van Persie was a player who knew he was carrying a team which was full of dead wood and which had loads of holes in it, one of which was Alex Song.

"Wenger likes to serve up what we think is a smoked salmon buffet with the Beluga caviar, but he can't resist sticking a dog turd in there – the main reasons players such as Fabregas, Nasri and Van Persie left is that they could see the future, and that future was being lumbered with the next Emmanuel Eboue or Manuel Almunia or Alex Song – For all the good we had, we had equally as bad."

I knew Arsenal and football inside out. Football is a relatively simple sport to dissect, and I knew from watching a game what was good and what was bad. Sooty is the same, but more recently with the goings on at Leeds he didn't seem quite as opinionated.

"Two thousand quid and you supply the paint," he said.

"Nice one," I replied.

I made my way to Jeanette's and had a couple of hours with the kids and I reflected on what Nicole had said.

"Are you wanting to stay the night?" asked Jeanette.

"If it's okay," I replied. "The house should be habitable soon – I've had a guy come and price up some work."

"Have you thought any more as regards your conundrum?"

I had, but it was not for public consumption as the last time I let my mouth run away with me she went and spewed out the lot to the two main characters in the 'show'.

"Why, what would you do?" I asked.

"I'd marry Nicole – she loves you."

I couldn't believe how simple she made it sound.

"The other one cheated on her husband, so that tells you everything you need to know," stated Jeanette before shaking her head and telling me what I already knew. "I can't believe how much they look alike."

I bathed the kids, watched a bit of telly and I took them to bed and told them a story – one of the rather tall stories my dad used to tell me about Tarzan and King Kong, leaving out the fact that *his* Tarzan used to work down Barnburgh Pit and *his* rather gory and racist description of King Kong eating all the Africans.

I then drove over to Walthamstow where I managed to have a heart-to-heart with Nicole. I told her that it was true that I had been horrible to her and I apologised.

Chapter 4
Fast Eddie

The next morning I left Jeanette's house early, leaving her a note which sort of told her thank you for letting me sleep there for the past two nights and that I had thoroughly enjoyed being with the kids – and get this – and that I would always love her.

I had no idea why I put that but at 7:10am my phone beeped through a message which said "Thanx x."

Although I had been a total shit with Jeanette, I had always provided for her and I had always loved her, and there wasn't a day that went by when I didn't think about her and at 8:30am I had my phone beep through a message from her which said. "You callous bastard."

Slightly unnerved, I plucked up the courage to call her and she told me she had just received word from our firm of solicitors that I was filing for divorce.

"I meant exactly what I said in the note," I confirmed. "The divorce thing is just bad timing and was something that was brought up last week when I was mad, and which I had forgotten about."

There was a short silence.

"If I could change things I would," I said, which sort of shocked me because it was a really brilliant thing to say.

"Really?" she asked.

"There's not a day goes by when I don't think about you or the kids," I added. "That is me being honest."

There was a short pause of silence which was followed by, "You've always been great with the children."

I had heard that said quite recently.

There was a bit of dialogue which culminated in me saying, "If you want – just rip it up and we can keep things how they are. I'll do whatever you want."

I was becoming untouchable. This being nice and honest thing was great, and I text Libby to tell her thanks for her intervention and I gave her a "x" which is something I never did as she generally scared the shit out of me.

In the meantime I had work to do and me and Abigail read through a load of reports that I had acquired from the press files; however, the only ones that seemed to interest me were written by this Mardell guy. He was as acerbic as Desmond Hackett, as erudite as Hugh McIlvanney and as witty as Keith Waterhouse, but from what I could see he also appeared to know his football. He was also the journalist who broke the news on the death of Jeremy Thorpe's wife Caroline Allpass in June 1970.

I ran a Google check on him and found out that there was an Eddie Mardell on a town council up in the north of England who had an email address under a photograph of him. I sent an introduction email to him stating that I hoped that he was the same man, along with my mobile number, and ten minutes later I had a call from him.

Our line of business follows footballers. All the public like to follow their idols, but as stated, most footballers are thick as shit, and eighty per cent of them pretty much possess Ladybird book intellects. Journalists are a lot different. A journalist tends to know his subject matter. If the BBC report on, say, the Iranian embassy siege, they don't have an Iranian terrorist relay the story, that have a journalist, and this Mardell guy wasn't just a sports hack – he had been a fully-fledged political correspondent and analyst with both *The Times* and *The Financial Times,* but who had been black-balled surrounding statements he made surrounding the Conservative party and in particularly, Enoch Powell.

"It wasn't much different to what it is now," stated Eddie. "The Tory party were afraid of Powell as they are now with Nigel Farage – however Powell was a Tory, and Farage is not. If Powell had got to power, he would have helped changed the face of Britain as we see it today. He was an extremely educated individual living what was, in his case, in the wrong time – but saying that, is there ever a right time?"

I knew little of politics – it bored the hell out of me, although Sooty and Libby could talk for hours on the sub-ject. Me – I preferred football. After I had got off the phone to Eddie, which was after a good fifty minutes, I had a word with Sooty and gave him my thoughts. Eddie Mardell was in London throughout the whole World Cup and foresaw the implosion of England along with the current government, however that was only a small part of the story.

"He could be full of shit," I said. "But it's certainly an angle that needs looking at."

I jumped in the car and shot up A1 (M) and a few hours later met this Eddie Mardell character in the Red Lion public house in a market square a few miles east of Doncaster.

It was apparent that we were mirror images of each other and whereas I had been born in the wastelands of South Yorkshire and moved to London in search of the streets which were paved with gold, Eddie had made his journey in the opposite direction.

"I loved London," he smiled whilst pouring a bottle of Holsten Pils into his half pint glass, "However, I was made an offer I couldn't refuse."

"What, did Alf Ramsey put a horse's head in your bed?" I asked, sipping at my white wine.

"I chased the money as opposed to the career," he said. "Don't do what I did. Build your house out of bricks rather than sticks."

Eddie had sold his soul for thirty pieces of silver, and had been recruited by the National Coal Board after the strike of 1972 to work as their chief political analyst.

"I was always a diehard Tory, but there's little difference between any one of the three – it is just a case of who has the nicest face wins," he said. "Labour dropped a major bollock with Gordon Brown – there is something very unhealthy about his smile."

"Do you rate Cameron?" I asked.

"Not especially – it's like footballers today compared with the Class of 1970. Okay they are much better and fitter, but they lack the character of yesterday's men. I think money has done a lot of that – I mean how can a club justify paying Rooney three hundred grand a week, or in Arsenal's case paying Abou Diaby around twenty million for three decent games, only one of which they actually ended up winning."

"Don't you like him?" was my obvious question.

"He's okay when he's fit," Eddie replied. "He just doesn't fit in with Wenger's system and half the bloody time he's either caught in possession or about as mobile as a lamp post. He should never have left the French league."

"So, you follow Arsenal?" I asked.

"I certainly like Arsenal, but for my sins and just to frustrate the hell out of me I sort of follow West Ham."

"They are a poor side this year," I said.

"They were a poor side when they were actually good," he replied. "I was only watching the '64 cup final the other night – I can't believe how crap they were – I must admit we looked a lot better on the day and even then Preston should have beaten us."

"West Ham did it in '66 for the country," I winked at him.

"Pele getting crocked did it in '66 along with a dodgy Russian linesman – our side in '70 was a load better and even then, Ramsey left much better players at home."

"I read something along those lines," I replied.

As the evening ran into night, I booked a room and stayed over and drove back to London the next day. After Eddie had staggered home after his seventeenth bottle of Holsten, I had taken a phone call from 'Abou Diaby' – it was Emily's turn to piss in my ears. She had told her husband of the surprise package waiting to burst out into the world in 22 weeks' time.

"He wasn't really that happy about it," Emily had said.

"I think he'd be flashing his gnashers and handing out the cigars even less if he knew it had been conceived in a Travel Lodge off the A406 North Circular with his wife handcuffed to the bed and me as the delivery boy," I nearly said, but my new-found honesty hadn't yet stretched that far. However it was true what Nicole had said – Emily certainly wanted to keep it. There was another angle, which I neither liked the sound of nor anticipated – and that was 'He knows it's not his'.

Oh dear!

The husband was a rather big bloke and that being the case, meeting him to stick my hand in the air and admit 'It was me' was the last thing on my agenda – There was certainly no way on earth this would ever make my list of 'Things to do'.

"I do love you," I told her.

"I do you," she replied. "But we are a bit all over the place aren't we?"

I didn't know about 'We', but I certainly was.

"It's weird how me and your girlfriend look alike, isn't it?" she asked.

It was a coincidence, but I was sick of it being said.

I got stuck in traffic coming into London and Sooty phoned me to tell us that we had got the gig from BSkyB, which I was sure of anyway, and that Nicole had been at their house a couple of hours last night – her main remit was wanting to be convinced by them that I could change.

"She really loves you," stated Sooty – his voice sounding somewhat surprised.

"And?" I replied.

"It's just a bit of a shock hearing some woman saying nice things about you."

"What – she was saying nice things about me?" I asked.

"It covered about thirty seconds of the two hours of conversation," Sooty explained. "It was certainly worth waiting for."

I phoned Nicole and had a twenty minute conversation on hands-free whilst I watched on as some paramedics shovelled up a cyclist off the tarmac on Edgware Road who I think had been hit by a bus. The police were on the scene and there was quite a lot of pointing at the bus, so I surmised that is what happened.

Nicole had had time to think about Emily being 'with child' and this was phase two of the interrogation; and as that was the case, it was time for the 'where and when' line of questioning, with a further line of questioning aimed at the intricate details pencilled in as phase three of the operation, provided the answers to those from phase two were acceptable. If you follow that, that is?

I had met Emily in a very similar way to that in which I had met Nicole, but in this instance it was a business meal to raise money for a good cause – a local Hospice, and the guest speakers were Tommy Smith, Norman Hunter and

Nobby Stiles. I had clocked her straight away and I'd had a brief conversation, which covered subjects such as what she was wearing to the deployment of the 'false nine' and the fact that Matthieu Flamini was a more silkier and more athletic version of Nobby Stiles, which told you everything you needed to know of the latter.

That was met with a bit of disquiet at the other end of the hands-free, however that was soon to be rectified when I told her that I had met her a few days later at a sushi bar off Wardour Street and we had gone back to my mate's flat and had consummated the relationship. Even though I failed to mention the details, which again strangely included hand-cuffs, straight away I knew it was a bad move and I took a mega-bollocking. Not for the fact that I had given her one at Bondy's flat, but for the fact that I'd never ever taken Nicole to a sushi bar.

"Okay, I'll take you tonight," I said, trying to diffuse the situation.

"You don't even like fucking sushi," she said.

"Look, I have admitted I have acted like a total wanker," I said. "I am trying to sort it out."

"So what is *she* doing about the *thing*?" she asked.

Mmm. This was another one of those loaded questions when no matter how I answered it, I would take some form of bullet.

"Truth?" I asked.

She answered in an affirmative and I then proceeded to inform her of more impending doom. I hated being the bearer of bad tidings, it was a truly crap job. I had pissed her around for the past five months and now I was making her suffer even more. I loved her far too much for that and stated that it would probably be best all round to end it. She immediately counter-attacked that, thinking it to be a José Mourinho type tactic, and that being the case she certainly didn't want to leave the field of play for me and Emily to get it on and raise a family.

"And she sort of wants me to tell her husband," I added.

"Why doesn't she tell him?" she asked. "She did it."

I quite liked the bit where I was expunged of all the blame, but this was the new me who'd had an intervention of sorts and who wanted to make good, and I had to take some of the flack, but just to give me some respite from the interrogation I asked, "So did you enjoy it over at Sooty and Lib's?"

"Not particularly," she replied. "I had to sit through the rest of their Hawaii video."

I pulled up in the underground car park and went into the office, where there were loads of smiles knowing that we had just won a potential five hundred grand project.

"We should get Steven Gerrard to do the narrative," said Abigail.

"Don't be stupid," I replied. "Nobody would understand him."

I then went on to explain the meeting I'd had with Eddie Mardell, and whilst looking at my notes, I reeled off some form and stated that he was with the *London Evening Times* as a freelance writer for eight months during 1970, in between moonlighting for a few other respected broadsheets – and was commanding fees in excess of two hundred quid a week. "He was a guy in demand."

"That would have him earning more than a footballer," said Fred, shaking his head.

Fred was spot on. Eddie was nearly earning what George Best was earning, however it may have been a surprise that George Best wasn't the top earner. The top earner was actually English, and he was never considered for the flight over to Mexico.

Now we had a project I would be getting in early and working late. I needed this so as to keep my mind active. We had also been asked by Tottenham Hotspur to do their club DVD for 2013/14. Coming from where I was from I never had a hatred of Spurs, and this being the case I was quite friendly with a lot of people around the club, supporters included. I thought they had bought very well in the summer and thought that they could push for the title, however how wrong could I have been? I personally think Daniel Levy panicked and got rid of André Villa Boas far too soon – it is just a pity the Arsenal board aren't as forgiving.

I had it from the horse's mouth that Emily had sort of confirmed to her husband the fact that the package definitely didn't belong to him and he was currently MIA, with her thought being that he was staying with his even bigger mate. I relayed the information to Nicole, who was now a bit pissed with me as I had told her what I had told Jeanette, that if she didn't want the divorce to go through, then I wouldn't pursue it. From the outside it may have looked like I had three women jockeying for my attention but in reality I had none. They were just jockeying to knock the other jockey out of the race.

"Why did you tell her that?" Nicole had asked.

"I don't know – I just did," I replied.

I wasn't lying; it was just that I didn't want to hurt her.

There was a quiet at the other end of the phone and then I hit her with what Jeanette had actually said.

"She said I should marry you," I said. "She said you love me."

"That's very fucking generous of her," came her blunt response.

It was. Jeanette meant it. I think?

Seeing as Emily was now without a husband, the traffic on my mobile phone was hotting up and in the space of half an hour I had received a shed load of "I love U's" and smiley faces from 'Abou Diaby', who was insistent that I meet him, or her rather, for a light lunch in Covent Garden. I hated the west end as much as I hated Manchester United. It was always busy and not unlike the majority of the Manchester United fanbase, full of Asians with David Beckham haircuts who still thought the boring git played for them. I was trying to unjuggle my life but I kept getting the fucking balls handed back to me.

After forty minutes of sweating my bollocks off on the tube and wading through pedestrians standing about watching other idiots doing the exact same but painted silver and gold, I caught sight of Emily waving. I immediately put my sunglasses on to avoid detection from anyone who may know me and I dragged her inside the first restaurant on hand, which happened to do a nice line in goats' cheese, which was the last thing I wanted to eat.

"What are we sitting inside for?" she asked. "It's lovely outside."

That was a daft question that certainly didn't deserve an answer, but being as I was now trying to be a responsible adult I gave her one, which started with the fact that I didn't want to be seen by her husband and get my head kicked in and which ended with the fact that I didn't want to be seen by either Nicole or anyone else that knew me.

"Okay," was Emily's answer.

Emily was always nice and agreeable and I watched on as she stirred her Perrier water and lemon with a straw. She was both mesmerising and beautiful, however as soon as she kicked up the conversation of babies and prams, I knew where it was leading and that being the case I pretended to check my phone and made the excuse that time was pressing and that I had a load of work to do, which wasn't a really a lie, it just felt like one as I didn't want to be there. Well I would have, if she'd have stopped rattling on about that particular subject. As it happened, I ended up staying and as we walked out into the sun and I have to say she looked radiant in her white dress and backless shoes.

Unfortunately around that time Nicole had just taken a phone call from one of her mates stating that she had seen 'Nicole' with me in Covent Garden and tried to catch our attention with an overzealous "Cooee" and a series of waves.

I had wondered who the idiot was who had been flapping around like a seal outside the shoe shop. As it transpired, Nicole had been nowhere near Covent Garden and Emily had been mistaken for her. The phone call I received from Nicole I certainly wished I hadn't, as it was anything but pleasant and if I could have separated the verbal content from the screams I am sure it would have been very menacing. I had also dropped a bollock mentioning to Emily that I had a vacant property as she now knew once all the loose ends were tied, we could be one happy family. The thing was, so did Nicole.

The way I navigated my life was extremely complex, bordering on kamikaze, and after work I nipped over to Jeanette's which went down like a lead balloon as the kids were at her mums and she had her boyfriend there.

He seemed smaller in 'real life' and if I am honest a bit on the weedy side. I had only seen him the odd time in his car. I then wondered when I was in my car, did it make me look bigger? Jeanette mentioned to me going over to her parents to see the kids, however that was something I was definitely not going to do. I nipped around to the house to see how far Ginge's mate had got on with the painting. Not only did he possess a stoop and a set of choppers like Emmanuel Adebayor, he appeared as lazy and useless as him too.

"You haven't done much," I stated.

It turned out he had locked himself in the bog for the last four hours.

"How did you do that? None of the toilets have got locks," I stated.

"I took the handles off to paint them, didn't I?" he replied. "I couldn't open the door after I'd shut it."

I could have easily imagined Adebayor doing something like that, although he would have to be in an offside position at the time. Fair play to him, he stayed until about ten o'clock to make up for lost time and he wasn't half bad at painting. Well, he knew more about it than football.

In between watching him paint and listening to him tell me about his past life in the suburbs of Paris and – of all places – Scunthorpe, I had a visit from Nicole, who had calmed down considerably if we can take away the initial finger in my face until she realised I had got a decorator in. By the time 'Frasier had left the building', Adebayor had earwigged the fact that I was basically a womanising tosser who had a wife and two girlfriends, the other one of which was having my kid, and I was up to my eyes in debt, the latter one of which really grabbed his attention.

"I will get paid for this, won't I?" asked a confused Adebayor, who became even more confused when he saw what he thought was the same woman come into the property half an hour later with a completely different mannerism, wearing completely different clothes and having a completely different voice. He never said it, but I knew he was thinking it.

I was just glad that Emily hadn't come at the same time as Nicole had been here, however she dropped some news on me, which I certainly didn't like, and which described more impending doom. Her husband was indeed going to kick my head in as she had not only told him who was responsible, but she had gone into great detail of the hows, whys and wheres.

I have no idea why she did that, but she did, and all she said in response to me shitting my pants in fear along with asking, "Why the hell did you tell him that?" was, "He asked, so I told him," which was followed by a shrug of her shoulders as though she had just given him an account of the weather outside.

"I bet that pleased him," I said.

"No," she replied, as if still weather forecasting. "He still says he's going to beat you up."

All the while Adebayor was digesting this, he had become so engrossed in the shit sandwich I had just been served that he had managed to paint the same patch for the past ten minutes.

That night I would have asked Emily to stay over but the only bed I had available wasn't fit to let a dog lay on, and that being the case we stayed in a bed and breakfast around the corner, which had a bed in a worse state than the ones the Russians had left me.

The information which Emily had furnished me with came true around 1:15pm the next day, give or take a couple of minutes, when an irate husband battered the hell out of me outside our offices in full view of around a dozen people, none of whom did anything to stop it. That was London for you. I don't know which hurt most, the five stamps on my head or the kick I had taken in the stomach – and I have to state that he was very professional at the way he went about distributing the beating. I knew two things – one – he had obviously done this before, and two – I didn't fancy it happening again.

I met Eddie Mardell off the train at around five o'clock and by then the swelling round my right eye was creeping over the top of my sunglasses. It is horrible getting beaten up but it is even worse getting beaten up in public, and feeling the pain I was currently in made me dead glad that I'd had sex with his wife twice last night. I say twice but the first go only lasted about nineteen seconds. Saying that, the second one wasn't much longer. For as eloquently-spoken and amiable as she was outside of the bedroom, at the other side of the door she was anything but.

Eddie was as gregarious a character as you could wish to meet, and Sooty and I took him to The Emirates where Arsenal came from a goal down to beat his team West Ham 3-1 with some absolutely cracking goals. We then went out for a dinner and a drink, and a drink, and a drink, which culminated in him shifting around twenty bottles of Holsten with a snifter of brandy to see him home. When the cab dropped me off at Frederick Street, the sight which greeted me was of Nicole dressed in a white leather jacket and matching skirt holding a vanity case.

"Evening," I smiled as I descended from the taxi as happy as a pig in shit. "Arsenal won."

I hadn't been expecting anyone, not least Nicole. Inside the house Adebayor had cracked on with the painting and it was looking quite nice again.

"You know what you said the other day?" she asked.

I didn't know what I had said today, never mind the other day, so I asked her to enlighten me. She found a place to sit and commenced to explain to me in a matter-of-fact way about 'us' and 'marriage', which was going quite nicely until she brought up her nemesis and the fact that her mirror-image had a visit pending by the stork, and then it got a bit messy when she noticed that I had a bit of a black eye and I informed her of my thirty second meeting with her husband in which I took a thirty second beating which included the delivery of around twice as many kicks and punches.

"Didn't you hit him back?" she asked.

"I may have headbutted his shoe a couple of times," I replied, "But outside of that – no, not really." It's a bit hard trying to deliver a punch when you're on the floor and some-one's stamping on your head.

It wasn't a bad visit by Nicole, and I braved the bed which didn't look that bad when I introduced a sheet and a couple of brand new pillows, however I was as edgy as hell thinking that I may get a similar visit from Emily. Sex was good. It wouldn't make it into my 'top ten' but it was quite nice, and to show that I was appreciated she gave me a couple of 'thank-yous' after I hit the bullseye at the second attempt, after the first failure – which lasted slightly longer than the steamy nineteen-second failure of yesterday night. I was beginning to get dead crap at sex and maybe I had a bit too much on my mind.

At seven o'clock the next morning, Nicole left the house more or less as Emily arrived. Fortunately they missed each other by around five or ten minutes, but it did nothing at all for my nerves. I couldn't go on like this. To make life more interesting Jeanette phoned to tell me that the kids would like to see me tonight and that we should talk. Unfortu-nately whilst this boring conversation was taking place I was flat on my back in bed whilst Emily was searching for her bullseye. Then she found it, and not only did my recently arrived African decorator hear it two flights down cleaning his brushes outside, so did Jeanette.

"What was that?" she asked.

"Nothing," I lied.

"Have you got somebody with you?" she asked.

It was easier to go back to lying than telling the truth as just recently all the truth had given me was loads of bollockings and my head kicked in by an unhappy, albeit estranged, husband.

Eddie was in the office before I was. Seeing to Nicole and Emily was a really time consuming business and I was abso-lutely knackered.

Chapter 5
Eddie's Tales – Take 1

I was in the Red Lion Hotel in the centre of the town and this young man came in and everything sort of stopped. It was like one of those scenes in a Western where a guy in a big white hat stops off at some one horse town and enters the saloon.

I could have said that he was around 6 foot tall with blond hair, however the easiest way to describe him was that he was a nailed-on ringer for a young David Beckham. That aside, he was wearing what looked like a two-thousand pound suit and possessed a smile that lit up the room.

"Eddie?" he asked, before coming over to shake my hand.

You couldn't help but like him.

"I can't believe how much you look like David Beckham," I said.

He never said anything.

"Has no-one ever told you?" I asked.

"Never," he replied.

I had been a freelance journalist in London between 1967 and 1971, covering both politics and football, with the latter being something of a hobby, but something that began paying me a damn sight more than my day job of quoting politicians – as well of getting me into a lot more bother.

The next thing I knew I had woken up with one hell of a hangover.

My wife Pauline had told me how drunk I was when I stumbled home. About twenty-odd times if I recall rightly.

"So what is he wanting you to do?" she had asked the next morning as I drank my tea whilst she did her damnedest to make sure I heard the clink of every pot and every pan. "Some TV programme?"

I nodded.

"It sounds a bit far-fetched to me – I mean, who would want you?"

"Thanks," I acknowledged. "And I love you too."

"Well it is – how old are you? Sixty-nine?"

Whilst she continued to rejoice at the sound of her own voice I checked my phone and found much to my delight that he had reserved me first class tickets at Doncaster train station.

"There you go – he wants me down in London," I grinned.

"When?" she asked.

"Now," I replied. I loved it. I was a man in demand.

I'll give Pauline her due in that she tried to throw every obstacle in my way to stop me going down, however there was no way on earth that anything was going to make me not go down.

"What about Dawn?" she asked.

I knew I would get hit with that one.

"I'm not going forever," I said. "I am coming back,"

I looked over at her and saw the expression on her face change.

"I will be back," I assured her.

When I arrived at King's Cross I found that I had been checked in to a double room at St. Pancras Hotel and later on I was whisked off over to a box at The Emirates to watch West Ham United get literally slaughtered by Arsenal, whilst being wined and dined by two of the most charismatic scoundrels you could ever wish to meet. It would be safe to say that the 'hair of the dog' did nothing to stop hangover number two and to say I enjoyed myself would be severely understating it – they were both brilliant lads.

A lovely young girl called Abigail Tyson had picked me up from the hotel and had taken me their offices on Euston Road early next day.

"Call me Abi," she said, smiling, before asking, "So what do you reckon to them?"

It certainly wasn't like me, but I just didn't have an answer and unknown to me at the time I had just boarded one hell of a ride.

On walking into the foyer I met another extremely pretty girl by the name of Faranha who shook my hand and gave me a kiss on each cheek before telling us that Sooty was waiting for me, but stated that '*he*' - the other half - was having a 'spot of bother' with some Russians, his wife and two girlfriends and not necessarily in that order.

"Girlfriends?" I asked.

"Don't concern yourself," Abigail nodded. "It's just a normal day in *his* everyday life."

Although I didn't know it at the time, a glimpse into *his* everyday life was something else, and something which was not helped by the man I briefly knew as Sooty, who came through into the corridor to greet me.

"'Did you have a good night?" he asked, smiling.

"Yeah, great," I said.

"Is the hotel okay?" he asked.

"Yeah, great," I replied.

Did you sleep okay?"

"Yeah, great," I replied.

"Well that's okay then," he said smiling. "I just wish the wife was as easily pleased."

I just looked at him and shrugged my shoulders.

"Women – they're a weird lot," he said with a serious look on his face before nodding over at Abigail. "She's the same – great looking, gorgeous figure, intelligent and she's living with Ronnie."

"Ronnie?" I replied.

"Yeah, a big butch bird off Bounds Green Road – Great at tennis, by all accounts."

Abigail shook her head, smiling.

I then got introduced to a young coloured kid called Sam who for some unknown reason preferred to be called 'Ginge', and a Freddy Nerkland, a man who I was to find out always had an opinion.

The surroundings I was standing in were – if I was being honest – really something else.

"We generally do football programmes," said Sooty. "Not the printed sort that get flogged outside of grounds by the bloke with the flat cap and dog, but those that go on telly – I have to say that just in case, as sometimes things can get misconstrued."

"Take no notice of him," said Abigail, "They're both as mad as hatters."

Around 11:00am *'he'* entered the building.

"You okay?" asked Sooty, smiling.

"Go bollocks," he replied before winking over at me.

Chapter 6
The rather illuminating story of the 'Tall Dwarf'

Eddie had ignited our interest further by mentioning some facts surrounding the 1970 ITV World Cup panel and it was this that set us trawling through ITN archives for some footage; however the footage we were looking for certainly wasn't on their website. Apparently and according to Eddie, Malcolm Allison hadn't been very forthcoming in his appraisal of Bobby Charlton and it had been wiped from one of the programmes.

"At that time I was fairly close to Mal," Eddie had said. "Man City were the sort of 'in-team' of that era."

"I thought Leeds were the 'in-team'?" I replied.

"They were," replied Eddie. "But City were as well, and the England squad had a couple of their lads in it, one of who was being overlooked in favour of Charlton."

I'd read a rather scathing report that Eddie had written about Charlton, which to be honest was putting it rather mildly. I had always thought Charlton to be one of those iconic figures in the game who was indeed a great footballer in his time, however Eddie was of a similar mindset to Malcolm Allison in that he was over the hill and bald, and him playing made the country look stupid.

I told you – nobody likes ugly players in their side. There

was nearly a mutiny when there was talk of Stiles being a starter alongside him.

"You have to remember," added Eddie, "we were just out of the 'Swinging Sixties' and into a new decade where cool and stylish was the norm and rock groups such Rod Stewart & The Faces, Led Zeppelin, Deep Purple and Paul Rodgers' Free were prominent."

He also forgot to mention that the whole of the pop charts throughout 1970 would be sandwiched by two number ones sung by the not-so-cool and stylish bearded sex predator that is Rolf Harris and the rather uncool Clive Dunn – a.k.a the dithering old corporal in David Croft and Jimmy Perry's 'Dad's Army'. And if 'Two Little Boys' and 'Grandad' weren't a fair reflection of the music then consider some of the jam on the sandwich – the Pipkins' 'Gimme Dat Ding' and the Scaffold's 'Ging gang goolie goolie goolie goolie watcha, Ging gang goo.'

I didn't want to piss on Eddie's era and just gave him a wry smile before I nipped down to ITV's head office where they kept their archives. After being mucked about in reception for half an hour by some bird with ginger hair and posh glasses, a guy came into the foyer to meet me. Now here's a story that could be interesting and which further backs up the case of Lenny Henry talking bollocks about TV not employing minorities.

The man who came to greet me I had sort of known for a couple of years. He was called Harold Tirford, however Sooty and I had labelled him the 'Tall Dwarf'. He was neither particularly tall nor was he a dwarf, however he had the face that sort of resembled a dwarf. He was a very matter-of-fact kind of guy who did a lot of hand rubbing and gesticulations as he spoke, and he also possessed a rather 'pawsh' accent. Not quite as posh as Garth Crooks, but it was posh all the same.

The other year I had been down Oxford Street with Jeanette and I'd been standing in the women's section of River Island or Dorothy Perkins or whatever when this noisy little woman barged past me with no other than the 'Tall Dwarf' trailing behind her holding about ten carrier bags. Being noisy may have been her downside, but I'll tell you this, she was as fit as hell and looked dead like Cheryl Cole – and she had a chest like you wouldn't believe. I was that taken aback I got out my mobile phone and in between stalking them through the beads and accessories section I managed to take a couple of photos of her.

I initially told Sooty, which I wish I hadn't as the first thing he did was bawl me out and said that he couldn't believe that I'd stoop so low etcetera, etcetera. You know – all the things your best mate would say. However he was more than interested in the end product and couldn't believe what he saw when I did a printout of the photos.

"Wow – how the hell did he get her?" was his primary question.

It had been nagging at me for a couple of days, so I did a search of his name on the electoral roll and downloaded his marriage certificate and land registry file and found her on LinkedIn – all the run of the mill things that a professional stalker would do.

It was doing my head in for days, and one night when I was coming back from Bondy's flat in Cockfosters she got on the tube wearing a pair of trainers, grey joggers and a belly top of sorts. After ogling her all the way down to Caledonian Road I gave her a polite, "Hello," and, "How are you?" to which she had replied, "I'm sorry, but do I know you?"

"I'm an acquaintance of Harold," I had casually stated. "I run a sports media company off Euston Road."

A bit of common ground with some discreet bragging had opened the door and by the time I had disembarked at

King's Cross and fired up my laptop I was a connection on her LinkedIn – And within two days I was sat opposite her in the coffee shop around the corner from our offices chatting over an espresso.

Her 'screeching' voice may have got on my nerves, but I have to say she looked great. Over the next week or so there was a bit of flirting over the email, when I plucked up courage to ask her 'out-out' as opposed to just an informal coffee and some boring conversation. I did more discreet bragging by picking her up in my car from outside King's Cross station and I drove her out to Essendon Country Club – a fifty minute drive just outside the M25 where I got her pissed and made a fumbled attempt at sex in the front seat of my car. As rubbish as it was, she hadn't been put off and wanted several other cracks at it. She was quite good fun for a good five or six weeks until she mentioned the fact that she had told her husband, and that is when I took two steps back. Well, three or four actually. I must have impressed her because she felt aggrieved enough to let Jeanette know that she was in love with me and in one instance broke down crying and threatened suicide.

I ended up being thrown out by Jeanette along with the privilege of having the Tall Dwarf hiding in the privet and stalking me wherever I went. It got that bad I had to tell the police and here he was now in the reception about to shake my hand – that was, until he realised who I actually was.

I got back to the office and told Sooty that it had been a stupid idea going down there and sulked for a bit. I didn't mind taking a kick-in off some big bloke in public, but I certainly drew the line of having my face slapped in the reception of ITV HQ and told to 'get out' by an oversized midget. To make matters worse, by the end of the day I had received twenty three emails from his wife's iPhone and I had heard from Adebayor that 'some bitch with big titties' had been seen pacing around outside my house. I had to give it to Ade, I had only known him a few days but he was already watching my back.

Our offices possessed a studio of sorts that had great parabolics and which we often rented out to other companies, however we would be using it to get a version of events of World Cup 1970 from Eddie, and that being the case we had the iconic photo of Bobby Moore and Pele blown up and parted into four segments along the wall, which if I am honest looked pretty good. Faranha got her mate from a make-up company around the corner to come and dust Eddie down for the camera and after fifteen minutes we were stood around scratching our heads as she'd done that good a job on him he looked like some villain from the silent movie era – so much so he kicked off and threatened to tie the make-up artist to the train tracks when he saw the end result.

"What do you reckon?" he had asked.

"Something's not quite right," Faranha had said.

She was spot on. He looked a particularly intimidating piece of manpower from most angles.

"Maybe some glasses or a hat would calm it down," Faranha had stated.

"I aren't wearing a hat," Eddie had said before requesting a mirror – and then he blew a fuse.

We eventually washed it off; I say eventually as the crayon she had been using was as hard to remove as ink from a rapid marker, and only something slightly less solvent than hydrochloric acid would shift it and that being the case, Eddie's face looked like a slapped arse when the camera started rolling.

I just wanted him to talk candidly about the era so I pre-empted him as regards the season preceding the competition, and it was immediately then that I knew we had got the right person, as not only did he talk about the 1969-70 season but he spoke about the season after the World Cup in 1966, the make up of football during those four years, and the fact that both Manchester clubs, Liverpool and Leeds were the major forces in football, with Everton and Chelsea the ones playing the attractive football; the sort of football which graced the World Cup of 1970.

He was as eloquently spoken as he was damning about Manchester United being a team in decline. "History often repeats itself," he said. "And what is happening at Manchester United now was happening back then. They were an old team who the then team manager had neglected to overhaul and had then passed it on to the wrong man."

We watched on as Fred Nerk rolled the camera and Eddie continued his dialogue. "The cracks had been papered over. Georgie Best was carrying the team and the European Cup win in 1968 was about as convincing as the one they had in Barcelona in 1999 against Bayern Munich – and four goals to one more than flattered them. I said during the tournament to Malcolm Allison that if they didn't get a decent manager who would reinvest in the team, they would be relegated within a couple of years – the team was that bad. Mal being Mal told me that he hoped I was right – it was ironic that it was Manchester City and a goal by Denis Law which sent them down."

Eddie looked over at us, smiling. "Is this the sort of stuff you want?" he asked.

It wasn't, but it was interesting all the same.

"Jimmy Bloomfield had just got Orient promoted into division two," he added. "Jimmy was a great bloke and was as good an inside forward as anyone in his era, and was convinced that Manchester United would come calling as the job he had done at Orient was nothing short of exceptional. I had got to be good friends with Jimmy and he gave me an insight into the blueprint of what he foresaw at United with him at the helm, with one of his first jobs being to wheel both Charlton and Stiles out of the door – unfortunately for both United and him, the job was given to Wilf McGuiness, who found it too big for him and who handed the baton over to Frank O'Farrell who helped paper over the cracks even more before he let Tommy Docherty take them down."

It was all interesting stuff, but nothing to really do with the World Cup until the re-emergence of the Charlton and Stiles angle.

"If Jimmy would have gone into United and immediately dispensed with Charlton and Stiles, then what does that tell you about Ramsey's inclusion of them in his squad – I said it back then and I will say it now, Ramsey was a singular minded individual and had a deluded loyalty to the players who had helped earn him his knighthood, however a lot of things can happen in four years and football was constantly changing, with one of the things happening being the dominance of British clubs in European football."

"What's the other thing?" asked Freddy.

"That once 'well thought of' players in a previous World Cup winning squad can get chucked out of the door from a less than average side," stated Eddie. "As in the case of John Connelly."

Eddie knew his football back to front and was getting comfortable in front of the camera, and after an hour we had a break and he had a drink of coffee.

"So who was Jimmy Bloomfield looking to take to Manchester United?" I asked.

"He told me that he wanted Sammy from Arsenal and young Hudson from Chelsea – or as a backup plan, Tony

Currie of Sheffield United or this young kid coming through the ranks at Queens Park Rangers."

"Rodney Marsh?" Sooty asked.

"He did want him as well," he smiled. "But it was Gerry Francis I was thinking of."

He looked at it twofold – the best way of supplying both Best and Law and the state of the Old Trafford pitch come winter, and that being the case he needed players who were both intelligent and had a wide range of passing. He also mentioned Peter Shilton as a replacement for Stepney, however Peter Shilton was a player who Jimmy would inherit when he took over at Leicester City.

Sooty and I loved this. Football was our life.

"Did you know Arsenal wanted Shilton?" Eddie asked.

We both shrugged our shoulders.

"Watch the 1969 League Cup Final and tell me what you see, and then fast forward it to the 1973 FA Cup Semi Final."

"The Leeds match?" asked Sooty.

"No, the Arsenal match at Hillsborough. Although Mee persevered with Bob Wilson it was never a big secret that he wanted Peter Shilton, it was just that the Arsenal board didn't want to throw good money at a goalkeeper, even though having a good goalkeeper is just as good as a good striker. Arsenal were the same back then as they are now. They want the players, but they don't want to pay for them, and that's why the club persevered with Manuel Almunia instead of buying a proper goalkeeper – a player who ended up losing them the Premier League. As I said – history often repeats itself."

"I thought Bob Wilson was a good goalkeeper?" inquired Sooty.

"A good bloke and a nice enough man who is Arsenal through and through," stated Eddie, "But no – he wasn't even in the top six or seven even when Arsenal did the Double. Sometimes the history books can be kind to some, yet cruel to others."

I went into my office and made a few phone calls whilst Eddie nattered to Sooty and Ginge. I picked up on the steady stream of emails coming from the wife of the Tall Dwarf. She hadn't contacted me in ages, and as she had been one of the one of many reasons why I wasn't now with Jeanette, I thought of her as being trouble. Still, we did have a decent time when we were together – that is, when she wasn't talking at me.

I went back into the studio to listen to Eddie talk some more but I was losing concentration and thinking about the Tall Dwarf's wife all the time, and in particular the first time she ever took her bra off. I was never a breast-man, as such, but I had to say that I would rank them up there with the best, although there was a downside as she hated anyone touching them – I often wondered why her husband used to fumble with his hands a lot. All that anticipation followed by frustration, I suppose.

By now Eddie was talking about a player being sold and a manager rubbing his hands in anticipation of having enough money to by his replacement with a 1966 World Cup winner. That manager was Bertie Mee.

"Mee was Alan Ball – mad," stated Eddie. "Brilliant player, but like Sammy – he was the wrong player for their system."

With my mind wandering I was playing catch up, but it wasn't a problem as Fred was picking it all up on camera.

By the time 5:00pm came my head was a shed. I was all footballed out. It was a day when World Cup 1970 would take second billing to Eddie's friendship with Jimmy Bloomfield and the respect he had for Malcolm Allison. Sooty asked if I fancied having dinner at theirs. I thought about it for less than four seconds and politely declined. Having my balls rubbed with a cheese grater seemed more appealing, especially given the fact that Nicole had had to endure the bit of the Hawaii Five-0 that I missed the other night.

Adebayor was on fire back at the house and he had done a great job; it was then he let me know about the woman with the big boobs who had been outside.

"What did she look like?" I asked.

"Like them other two you got but with big boobs," he replied.

Mmm. It definitely sounded like the Tall Dwarf's wife, but how would she know where I lived? I'd had more houses than a cuckoo since I'd known her. Curiosity took over and I ended up phoning the number that she had at the end of each of her twenty-three emails and I immediately got a reply. I had forgotten how much I had actually hated the sound of her voice. Both Nicole and Emily talked sort of quiet and posh, but as for her – she was just loud.

"Have you been around to my house?" I asked.

"No, where is it?" she asked.

Mmm. That was an interesting dual-answer, which I certainly wasn't going to elaborate on as the last thing I was going to tell her was where I lived, especially after the last time. She had been harder to shake off than a bout of swine flu, and the last thing I needed was Nicole tripping over another skeleton in my closet. Then begged the question of who had actually been pacing around outside.

"I'll be in the tapas bar on Southwark Street about seven," she said.

It was something to keep under my hat, I could always do tapas and at least I wouldn't be getting nagged at by Nicole or pressured into conversations about babies from Emily. I hung up and re-asked Ade about the woman I now knew not to be the wife of the Tall Dwarf.

"Look, man," he said. "She was just outside with some clipboard and pen."

I wish he'd have told me that before I'd rang her.

"She posted some card through the front door," he added.

Again, I wish he'd have told me that before I had rang her.

He was quickly losing any credibility I had for him with his lack of common nous when answering a question. It was a good job he didn't have my lifestyle. I picked up the card and read it. Mmm. A collections agency? I wasn't that bothered about phoning that number, but the fact that I had been ordered by Libby to not stick my head in the sand, I ended up doing what I usually would not.

"Could I speak to a Lyndsey Bracken?" I asked.

This woman was dead posh and on my first impression could have easily been either Princess Ann or even Garth Crooks's sister. It appeared my Russian tenants had taken out some loan in my name and she was just checking that I had enough value in bricks and mortar to protect their investment. In fact she was that keen to protect it that she was at the front door within twenty minutes wanting to do an internal recce of all four floors and it was then I duly noted that she looked absolutely nothing like Princess Ann nor Garth Crookes.

I explained about as many times as I'd been emailed by the Tall Dwarf's wife that I was part of some identity fraud by some Russians, which the police were looking into and I was the innocent party – and if it wasn't for the fact that she easily fitted within my shallow remit of women well worth a shag, she would have been shown the door a long time before she had got through it. Thankfully Nicole had called and on her initial thought that this femme fatale of debt collector's was some half-decent trollop I'd dragged in off the street, she had entered the fray as a woman on a mission and had duly slung her out.

"What is it with you?" she asked. "Can't you fucking make a decision and stand your ground?"

I could, but that at that moment I hadn't. Things were made extremely interesting when Nicole's nemesis turned up at the door around five minutes later, which made listening to the silken tones of the Tall Dwarf wife's screeching seem utterly appealing.

For around ten to fifteen minutes my life was an absolute hell. If it hadn't been for his morbid curiosity I'm sure Adebayor would have duly left the property, but watching two identical-looking women hurl insults at each other with regards to my shortcomings in relation to what was essentially a polyamorous relationship unsanctioned by one of the three parties, one of whom appeared slightly better (or worse) off in the deal as she had a lump of my DNA inside her, I'm sure he would have.

The embarrassment was that I was made to sit down by Nicole and made to listen to what she had to say, which intrigued Adebayor who stopped painting the upstairs landing to put another hundred layers of some paint on a surface nearest the best seat in the house. I'll give credit to Nicole, she said what she wanted – and then she broke down crying, which wasn't helped by Emily who just shrugged her shoulders, looked at me, smiled and said nothing.

"I sort of love you both," I said, which was a stupid comment which didn't help anyone.

"Can't you get it into your thick skull that you can't have two of us?" cried Nicole.

Well I could, but I didn't particularly want to and I looked at the decorator whose grin on his chops now resembled a set of keys on a piano. I really, really wanted to get out of the house.

I don't know how I did it but I escaped their clutches and ended up in some posh café that was priced accordingly.

"You're having me on?" I said as she dropped me the bill. "Eight and an half quid for a fucking coffee?"

"That's got a service charge on that, sir," she said.

"Well, take it off then," I snapped.

I was well pissed off. I was sick to the back teeth of all this confrontation, and not only was I depressed as hell, I had got Nicole sending me texts as to my whereabouts. I ended up at my wife's, or ex-wife's rather, and I had the kids cheer me up a bit by bouncing around the sofa and showing me stuff they had done at school. I needed their company like I needed oxygen and I ended up crashing out around 9:30pm and finding myself laid on the sofa with a quilt over me around 4:00am. I'd had my phone on silent and I had loads of missed calls and texts, including a couple of irate ones from the wife of the Tall Dwarf who strangely accused me of standing her up, and one I didn't recognise but which advertised itself from being from Lyndsey Bracken. In between those were a cluster from Nicole and a couple from Emily. I got up and went upstairs and gave the kids a peck on their foreheads before being met half way on the landing by Jeanette.

"Are you okay?" she asked.

"Not really," I replied and even though I had been a total bastard with her in the past I still got my peck on the forehead.

I went back to the house to find both girls camped there, which was the last thing I either needed or wanted.

"I don't want to argue, Nicole," I said. "I really, really don't."

Emily never said a lot, although she did ask if I was alright.

My problem is that if I was presented with the opportunity I couldn't say 'no' – well, I could if they were out of my shallow 'blueprint'.

I showered and got changed into another suit and left them to their own devices. My thoughts were that they would eventually clear off, or at least one of them would.

My first point of call was at Tony the Barber's to cop my weekly haircut and wet shave. Tony was a Greek Cypriot with grey hair and glasses who spoke about as much English as Peter Beardsley, and that being the case I enjoyed the solitude for the forty minutes it took for him to do what he did.

Ginge had been in the editing suite with Fred Nerk looking at this proposed Spurs DVD we were doing. Fred highlighted a couple of clips of Ettiene Capoue.

"I can't believe everyone wanted us to buy him," he said.

"I think he'd be okay in a settled side," I replied.

The thing with Arsenal supporters is that the majority are half-wits, who had been garnered along the way during Wenger's highly successful and early period of his tenure. Glory boys – I hated them. If your life is shit, go follow a team that wins things and make yourself feel better. It is what the three billion Asians who follow Manchester United do. Asking the average Arsenal supporter who he wants in the side borders on stupidity and you wouldn't believe the dick heads I've come into contact with. Even the people who run the Arsenal blogosphere aren't that bright. There was or still is some guy who runs a Dublin-based Arsenal blog who was adamant that he didn't want Luis Suarez at the club – whose only sin was that he bit Ivanovic of Chelsea and hurled a minor racist insult at Evra of Manchester United by labelling him a 'blackie'. The soon to be Double player of the year and possible league champion and golden boot winner was exactly what we needed at the club, but the blogger had an agenda.

Suarez is a racist.

Yet it's strange that we as a club have had paedophiles, alleged rapists, alcoholics, cocaine addicts and ponces play for us, none of who could lace the boots of one of the current top three players in world football.

As it was, Wenger was in Baldrick-mode and had a cunning plan up his sleeve, and we were treat with the immense talent of yet another tosser from the French league whom he handed a similar twenty-three year contract to that of his compatriot Abou Diaby, whilst all the time claiming he was free.

The Suarez bid wasn't the first time Arsenal have tried being cute, and a figure of one pound (a note back then) was handed to Desmond White, the Chairman of Celtic, when three clubs offered the same amount for Charlie Nicholas. And as Eddie had said, history often repeats itself.

I went into the office to be met by Eddie talking into the camera, which stopped as soon as I entered the studio.

"It's good this," explained Sooty. "Eddie's just being telling us a story about a kid from up our way who Arsenal were looking to sign – he'd been watched a load of times and they ended up missing out on him."

"Bertie Mee wanted the final decision and wanted him down for a trial," explained Eddie.

"They've always dithered when it comes to signing players," I nodded. "Carry on and I'll watch a run of the video after work."

I left work around 10:00pm with a copy of a copy of the content which Eddie had been spewing. I didn't know why, as the Russians had taken my TV set and DVD, and Nicole had slung the one I had at hers through the window.

I had the laptop, however even that was a 'no-go' as I had been bollocksing around with the regional codes on the software and the only thing I could now watch was

Region 1 DVDs as I was only allowed to change the settings a few times.

I therefore went on Ebay and ordered the biggest fuck-off flat screen TV I could for immediate delivery along with a DVD player and some surround sound.

Mmm. That made me feel loads better so I bought a load of other stuff until I had burned out my Paypal. It's not often I spent eleven and a half grand in a couple of hours, but I did that night and I had the bank on to me the very next day to check that I hadn't lost my card or that I hadn't been the subject of identity fraud.

"Yes – I had some Russian tenants who are being sought by the police," I said.

"Well we'll cancel this card and we'll send you a new one out as there was some recent activity on Paypal," stated the HSBC.

That was nice of them I thought, and I ended up getting half the order without actually paying for it. And I never really lied. I just never told them the truth.

I was out of the house before Adebayor arrived for his last day of painting and decorating and that being the case, he was a bit edgy and phoned me and asked if he would get paid. I told him I'd nip home in the afternoon to drop him off the money and he thanked me for that.

I quite liked him – he was okay.

Chapter 7
Eddie's Tales – Take 2

I'd been in their company literally just a few hours when I saw how they bounced off each other.

"You can't do that," I had said, shaking my head.

"You want to bet?" Sooty had replied smiling.

The other half was late in due to some domestic problems, which certainly wasn't being helped by Sooty.

"Mrs Tirford?" he asked, whilst on his mobile.

As eloquently brazen-faced as he could, and with the phone on loud speaker he delivered line after line of patter stating how her husband – Mr Tirford – had reacted to his business partner and how much he had allegedly missed her.

"I really loved him," Mrs Tirford had replied. "Even after that bloody horrible thing in the hotel."

"Horrible?" Sooty had inquired smiling. "I didn't know there was any horrible thing."

"I'd rather not talk about it," she had said.

This bit had had Sooty scratching his head a bit.

"You know you can always talk to me," he had said to her whilst at the same time grinning over at me. "But whatever you do – you can't tell him that you've been talking to me."

Sooty had been in stitches after the telephone call and even Freddy was shaking his head.

"He'll go frigging ape shit if he finds out," Freddy had said as he hit the 'camera lights action'.

My remit was to give them a look back in time and to get some background of the era. What they wanted was a preface to the 1970 World Cup, however what I gave them was something that I had not thought about in years. Sometimes things happen like that.

It was one cold November afternoon when I had got all my work out of the way and the evening edition was about to go to press as I made my way to King's Cross to meet a 58-year-old ex-pro called George Male, who had been in the Arsenal side during their halcyon years and had garnered just short of twenty caps for his country. What struck me about George was his eloquence, be it his mannerism or his dress. He was a nice guy and he had let me in at the ground floor that they – Arsenal, were looking at this kid from a mining village in South Yorkshire, who was supposedly top drawer. He had seen him a total of eleven times already, and one of those times he he'd had Jack Kelsey with him.

"He's good, I'll grant you that," Jack had said. "But he has a right chip on his shoulder."

George had been around youth all his life and had seen the changing generations and had adapted to it, which was something Jack had not. And it wasn't until George reminded the ex-Welsh international goalkeeper that he could be no different, citing the fact that he had chucked in two transfer requests at the back end of his tenure as well as bad mouthing the club in the press, that Jack gave him a confirmatory nod of approval regarding the lad.

George was as buoyant as ever when I met him and he seemed more happy sourcing talent than he ever did watching the team play on a Saturday afternoon. Saying that, there hadn't been much to shout about for sixteen years, but this year, George had assured me, would be different. However if I was being honest, I'd seen little to back up his claim and as was my duty, I watched nearly every one of Arsenal's home games for the last few seasons and the paper had even got me and another freelancer, Eric Batty, hooked up with the 'Four S' Sports travel company to follow the club's away games in Europe – the first of which was well worth forgetting and culminated in Charlie George being sent off and a one-nil defeat against a load of part-timers from Northern Ireland. To me the club ran with the same twelve or thirteen players, reliant on defence, often abandoning their short-ball style, bypassing the midfield and being overly reliant on either the long diagonal ball from the back or shoving it out on the wing for it to be lumped into the middle.

Bertie Mee had been in the press stating that the club were a couple of years behind Leeds United, but I think he was being economical with the truth. Leeds were a machine with Giles and Bremner as the two cogs in midfield, with every other man knowing their job. Gary Sprake was always considered to be their weak link, but that wasn't really true. He was erratic and sometimes came over as mad as a March Hare, but no more so than any other outfield player – however the goalkeeper was always the last man standing and the last line of defence. He makes a mistake and there's only one outcome – an outfield player makes a mistake and it's generally mopped up and forgotten about.

Arsenal had Bob Wilson as its number one. Although he could be overly dramatic, and at times looked unorthodox, he was never overtly flash. It was the worst kept secret at the club that the manager wanted a more solid replacement, and although Bertie Mee had made it 'sort of' public that he wanted Peter Shilton from Leicester, he was certainly never going to cough the £100,000 to get him, hence the intensity of interest surrounding this prodigious young goalkeeper up in the north.

From what George had told me, this young lad had just turned sixteen and had refused the overtures to play for Barnsley Boys or the Don and Dearne, the reason being that he didn't play Saturdays and that was that, and that being the case he was kept out of view from the scouts of both Sheffield clubs and the ever-growing monster that was Leeds United.

"He works as an apprentice butcher," George had stated. "He's a pretty dedicated lad."

George went on to give me some background and explained that his school tended to try and work around him and did their utmost to rearrange their fixtures to be midweek games, something which had been problematic as the nights were drawing in, hence this 3:30pm kick off on a Friday evening.

"How do the other schools react to that?" I had asked.

"I don't think they've 'twigged'," explained George. "The teacher who runs the team blames the fact that he has to work himself and that half the lads in the team have part time jobs as well."

When we arrived at Doncaster railway station we were met by Gordon Clark, Arsenal's chief scout. He was a couple of years younger than George and in later years had been responsible for bringing Alex Cropley to Arsenal from Hibernian as well as the three Irish lads – Brady, O'Leary and Stapleton. Gordon was originally from Yorkshire and had played football as a full-back for Manchester City before the Second World War. He went into management and he had spells in charge of both West Bromwich Albion and Peterborough with legend having it that as with Malcolm Allison some years later, that he had been approached regarding the manager's job at Juventus as he had helped get West Brom challenging for the title in 1960 – missing out partly due to a 'bum result' against a piss-poor Fulham side during the run-in. Gordon was the nephew of Willie Applegarth, an athlete who broke the hundred-yard dash and the two hundred metres records as well as equalling the one hundred metres record before the war.

They exchanged pleasantries and I was introduced to him and listened as they talked about the club and the fact that they were wasting their best players. Gordon was as deft in his appraisal of the club's position.

"It's simple to rectify," he explained looking over at me in the back seat. "The club don't play it through the middle as much as they should do. Don Howe knows he should make use of the midfield – especially now they're in Europe."

It was something I had been saying since I started watching them. The club generally played a standard 4-4-2 or 4-3-3 depending on who they were playing and who they had fit. Another poorly kept secret at the club was the fact that Bertie Mee thought George Armstrong needed replacing. I had watched him in the League Cup final in March and thought him to be nothing more than a headless chicken who was rash in the challenge but who gave his all, the latter of which the Arsenal supporters tended to like, which just goes to show how much the run-of-the-mill football supporter actually knows. Especially Arsenal supporters.

Mee had played footsie with Burnley over Willie Morgan for months as he had with Leicester's Allan Clarke. However while he was debating over the final formalities of the latter, Don Revie had steamed him and had decked him out in the white shirt with the number eight on the back whilst Mee was still considering his final, final offer. For a big club, Arsenal rarely acted like one when it came to parting with money. This was something that both George and Gordon were actually in conversation about as two of the club's best players had been locked in dialogue about new contracts since the summer.

"Mee has been saying that they are holding the club to ransom," George had stated.

"He would say that," Gordon had replied. "It's not like they can't afford it."

And like Jack Kelsey some years earlier, McLintock and Sammy had initially refused to sign new contracts and were looking for new clubs.

"It'd be a crying shame – Sammy would be a great loss – especially now we are in Europe," noted Gordon.

Sammy had the nicest demeanour anyone could have and as such he was very well-liked within the club – saying that, it didn't stop Alan Ball lashing out at him a couple of years earlier during a 3-1 win against Everton. Storey had already clattered into him twice when Sammy steamed into him with a tackle which took both the ball and Ball.

"It was like a pub brawl when the Arsenal lads waded in and if it hadn't been for the referee Haydn Davies – I'm sure Alan Ball would have taken a good hiding," I had said.

"So this Sammy," Sooty had asked me. "Was he good?"

"Truly brilliant," I had replied. "That game was only a couple of minutes old when he picked up a speculative ball from over the top, controlled it and rifled it past the goal-keeper Andy Rankin from just inside the area."

It was well-documented that Sammy was on his way to becoming a full international, however he was stuck within a system that just didn't suit his style of football. He wasn't part of the problem, he was just being made part of the problem by the tactics installed by the management at Arsenal.

"The thing is with football players and supporters alike," Gordon had stated, still looking over his shoulder at me whilst driving, "the majority of them are pig-thick and they don't understand what a player like Sammy is trying to achieve – he was always thinking three moves ahead when the player he's passing to can't even equate to one. He's a multi-dimensional footballer – I just wish he would be a little more aggressive and nastier."

I had always liked an educated conversation and it was interesting to hear Gordon speak. I could certainly see why he was highly thought of.

We pulled up alongside a huge plot of greenbelt on the A635 Doncaster – Manchester road and I got out to survey a football field decked out with goalposts and netting and a few kids kicking a ball about. It was hardly Arsenal versus Spurs, but was definitely Darfield Foulstone versus Thurnscoe and was as much as a local derby as you could get, and that being the case there were quite a few bodies mulling around, which were supplemented by a few cars being parked up.

"It looks like a decent turn out," I said.

"These get more watching them than we did when Billy Wright was manager," replied George rather cynically.

Through their successes in the 1930s, late 1940s and early 1950s Arsenal had amassed quite a lot of fickle and fair weather supporters that came to be known in later years as glory boys, and who, as soon as the going got tough, went on to support their second club, which was more often than not Manchester United. And during Billy Wright's tenure at the helm, the going was tough and the playing bordered on abysmal.

As a person I had a dislike of Manchester United and everything they stood for. 'Munich' had made them everyone's darling, and as bad as it was – and it was, it turned out to be the best public relations exercise ever. If Billy Wright wanted popularity he should have got shot of Ian Ure sooner and put a plane down in the Alps – he would have got 70,000 through the gates every week. However as much as Manchester United were loved post-Munich, there were hidden truths that suggested that they were no better than any other club, as some of the survivors that couldn't pull on the shirt again such as Jackie Blanchflower who had suffered internal injuries and had had his arm severed and poor Johnny Berry – these both got kicked out of their homes by the club. But amidst Georgie Best running up and down the cow field that was the Old Trafford pitch and dazzling the Stretford End – all this had been secretly filed under 'Not fit for public consumption'.

"Is that right?" Sooty had asked.

I nodded. "United like to think that they are 'the' club, but they are no better than anyone else."

Munich '58 had been present on that day too, as one of the unlucky lads to have perished that night was 25-year old Mark Jones, a central defender with the club who had been due his international call up. Mark had gone to school at Darfield Foulstone and had played on the very same field I was now standing on, and was now buried in a cemetery in the next village. The school were both proud of his achievement and sad at their loss and not a day went by when he wasn't mentioned. Football tragedies do that.

The lad we had come to look at had arrived with his mates along with a huge entourage from his school. All in all there must have been just short of nine hundred spectators here, which was unheard of in school football and if I'm honest we struggled to get a central position.

"Go on lad," a tall gentlemen with grey hair shouted over to the subject of our being there, as he caught a ball out of the air during a pre-match kick about.

John Ellis was over six foot tall, and although he was just turned sixteen he looked older than his years. George had told me that he could be the next Peter Bonetti and that he marshalled his goal with authority and was as agile as a cat.

"Why not Gordon Banks?" I had asked.

"Ask any first division goalkeeper and they'll tell you," Gordon cynically replied.

Bonetti was special, but Banks was living on his international reputation as his performances in the first division hardly smarted of consistency. Even Leicester City had moved him on as he was deemed 'not good enough'. True was the fact that they had been relegated, but it was more to do with them being a poor side in general than the fact Peter Shilton had been installed as their new number one.

The game kicked off amidst roars from the spectators on the sidelines and within two minutes Darfield's left winger, who was decked out in the Everton blue and white, had turned inside his marker and hit the deck like an Oscar-winning actress and was clutching his ankle for all to see. The referee – or a teacher from Darfield School rather – had no hesitation to pointing to the penalty spot.

"You cheating bastard," shouted one of the lads decked out in the opposing Leeds United white.

The lad may have been given a stern warning by the referee, but he had a point, and as both George and Gordon had said, it had easily been a yard outside the box if it was at all a foul.

Nevertheless it would have given us an early chance to see the Ellis kid in action, was it not for the fact the penalty taker – to the dismay of his team mates – walloped the ball a yard wide of the upright. Still 0-0.

The left winger who had miraculously recovered from his 'horrific' ankle injury again picked up the ball and darted towards the goal, and this time he was fouled and it was in the box and again the referee pointed to the spot. However, this time there was a change in penalty taker. A big guy from the back came forward, placed the ball on the spot, and glared hard at the goalkeeper who reciprocated this with a smirk. The Darfield lad let rip with a shot to the goalkeeper's left, but it was turned around by Ellis. It was a good penalty, but an even better save.

"Nice one Johnny," said a couple of his team mates as they patted him on the back.

Nine minutes on the clock and two penalties. *Not bad,* I thought, but still 0-0.

Darfield played the ball about as they searched for another opening, and as they did Thurnscoe chased it around and on gaining possession immediately lost it with their 'route-one and boot it up front' tactics. On fifteen minutes Darfield's left winger again showed a clean pair of heels to both the right back and centre half and went racing towards the Thurnscoe goal from a fairly central position before he looked up to see the huge frame of the Ellis kid come off his line, shutting off both angles to make the goal look far smaller. The winger cracked the ball with quite some venom to the goalkeeper's left, only to see him save and parry the ball out to the edge of the area. The winger, still in his stride, whipped past the keeper and turned the ball goal-ward with a tasty right foot dink towards the centre of the goal; however, the Ellis kid had just about got to his feet to sort of anticipate a near-post tap in, but rose like a panther to scoop the ball over the bar with his right hand to the applause of the crowd.

"What did I tell you?" said George, sporting a smile that beamed from ear to ear.

I would have loved an action replay, and I felt gutted that this would be the only time I would ever see that save, which was nothing short of fantastic.

The ensuing corner was plucked out of the air with

aplomb and a throw was catapulted a good fifty yards which had Thurnscoe on the attack. George never overstated anything. This kid was indeed the business.

Darfield's left winger pulled away from the right back again, however this time Thurnscoe's central defender took him out with a tackle which Ron Harris would have been proud of. It wasn't a so much a scything challenge – more of a Kung Fu kick to the throat that held up the game for ten minutes due to a slight skirmish between the two sides, which resulted in a succession of handbags and finger-pointing whilst the winger was on the floor, unable to breathe and gasping for his life. Both managers – or teachers running the two sides – brought calm to the proceedings which was followed by a bit of crowd trouble as two or three sets of parents initially exchanged a couple of blows before one of them took over and started knocking the living shite out of the other.

Crowd violence in school sport?

"It happens all the time," George had explained.

I couldn't believe it.

The game resumed but that was the last we saw of the fleet-footed left winger. He may have still been on the pitch, but the last thing he wanted at his feet was the ball. A succession of corners were plucked out of the sky by 'our boy', but there was nothing else to report before the breaking of the oranges.

The Ellis kid's father walked over to George and there was a handshake as George introduced Gordon and me. He appeared a genial guy and possessed both the look and mannerism of John Le Mesurier's 'Sgt. Wilson' character in 'Dad's Army'.

George thought the words of 'The Arsenal' would break the ice, but he soon found out that the kid's father was an ardent Manchester United supporter and had been since Munich. Arsenal were the last thing that impressed him.

However what we were told was interesting – in that his lad had managed to play in sixteen games this season and had so far let in just one goal.

"That's remarkable," George stated.

"What's even more remarkable," stated the lad's father, who we now knew was called Eric, "Is that we are only third in the league – we may have a good defence but we are lacking up top – we struggle to score."

It was exactly like the Arsenal team at that time.

To me, Thurnscoe looked like a set of cloggers, the only bright spot being this man's son.

Darfield didn't look much better, and apart from the winger that was now sort of 'running scared', there was nothing to choose between the sides.

The evening was drawing in as Darfield kicked towards the goals which backed on to a peripheral hedge, separating the school playing fields from the A635.

Immediately Ellis was brought into action as a speculative shot from twenty-five yards brought a fingertip save onto the woodwork and brought consummate applause from everyone watching. Darfield swung in a corner which was met by a bullet header and brought calmly and majestically under control by the opposing number one even though he was illegally shoulder charged 'Nat Lofthouse-style', which resulted in a goalmouth kerfuffle and one of the Darfield lads getting head-butted.

Play resumed and Darfield were continually pressing with high balls being launched into the box which Ellis kept on plucking out of the air with ease, then with less than fifteen minutes to go there was a call for handball and Darfield were awarded another penalty. I didn't see it, but both George and Gordon both said it was a 'decision bordering on criminal'.

The referee, who we learned after ten minutes was a PE teacher from Darfield School, was barracked by the away crowd and was also threatened by a big bloke on the side-lines who rather eloquently stated, "You're dead after the game, pal."

Penalty number three was on par with penalty number one, and the shot was as feeble as it was wide and I knew then that Darfield stood as much chance of winning this game as they did the FA Cup, especially when an hopeful punt up front was miscued by their defender and a Thurns-coe lad by the name of Goring latched on to it and stuck it into the corner. The contingent from Thurnscoe were going crazy. They had been under the cosh for all of the match and in truth deserved little or nothing. Two minutes later the Goring lad knocked a speculative ball on to a kid called Juddy Morris, who rammed the ball down the goalkeeper's throat before knocking in the rebound and there was hell on as another fight broke out on the touchline and the referee threatened to abandon the game.

A calm eventually ensued, but the stoppages had dragged out the game into the dark and as the white-shirted Thurns-coe pushed forward, the tricky left winger of Darfield resur-faced and raced away with the ball and threatened to score; but that was as much as he did, as Ellis came screaming off his goal line and threw his body into the ball and man at the edge of the box. The referee blew for another penalty.

"Four fucking penalties," shouted one of the Thurnscoe contingent. "How many chances does he want to give 'em?"

Both George and Gordon shook their heads. It had been a brave save which saw the goalkeeper go for the ball and get the ball. The fact that the player had gone over like a flailing princess made not an ounce of difference. A penalty it was.

Another penalty taker rifled the ball slightly left of centre and Ellis turned it over the bar. However, the referee was adamant that Darfield should score and he ordered a retake.

"It's fucking Brian Glover," shouted one of the Thurnscoe

contingent, referring to the actor who played the school-teacher in the film 'Kes'.

The penalty was retaken and again completely missed the target. Ellis lumped the resultant goal kick up front and the Juddy Morris kid flicked on a header which sailed over the goalkeeper.

0-3 was how it stayed and on trudging back to Gordon's car I heard George telling him about needing to get this kid signed up as soon as possible, and that he needed to call up the manager.

I wasn't privy to any of the conversation, however I knew from the look on George's face that it was not good news. Here was a kid that they could have signed for what was essentially peanuts and all George had was Bertie Mee wanting to have the kid come down to Highbury for a trial after Christmas.

"He's too good for that," George had insisted. "In my opinion he's better than what we have."

"Then why has no-one else come in for him?" Bertie Mee had allegedly replied.

"Because we are the only buggers that know about him at the moment," George had stated.

Mee was as frustrating a guy as Arsenal were a frustrating club. A signing on fee and £15 a week would have got the lad to Arsenal.

"What happened?" Sooty had asked me.

I shrugged my shoulders. "They never got him – Arsenal back then were like they are now. Indecisive – The manager dithered and the lad lost interest."

"I've never heard of him," exclaimed Freddy.

"You won't have," I replied.

"So what happened to this Ellis kid?" asked Fred.

"He never played professionally – he continued working

as a butcher shop on the High Street for a local butcher called Jim Sharman."

There was another 'Sliding Doors' story of 'what if' here, in that the goalkeeper who was on trial with Arsenal at the time this John Ellis should have gone down was a New Zealander who was the relation of a model from Northampton, and who had recently appeared in the newspaper and who Arsenal's enigmatic midfield schemer Sammy had thought to be 'drop dead gorgeous'.

"What happened?" asked Sooty.

"The triallist put a word in and a blind date ensued and Sammy ended up marrying her," I replied.

Chapter 8
Emily 1, Nicole 0

Although I earned plenty of money, I spent it equally as quick. It had always been a problem with me. I don't drink (that much), I don't smoke, I don't gamble and I've never done drugs – although I often dabble with Viagra; in fact if I am being honest I am quite the connoisseur. Bondy a.k.a Yusuf Elias was my Viagra man, but he had buggered off to Thailand three months ago when the police started looking for him. He let me use his flat, which while the Russians had my house was handy as I used it for storage, mainly my clothes, DVDs, CDs and some other stuff. It was always handy to get a shower too as the one in Nicole's place had been smaller than a telephone box. He told me just as long as the bills were paid I could use it as long as I wanted. I missed Bondy. He had worked in and around north London – I'm not actually sure doing what, but I knew he had to wear a suit and the building he went into was near South-gate tube station. Bondy was a café man – he knew nearly every café in and around north London and could give you an account of what was good and what wasn't. He also knew nearly everything that went on in them and every shit bag that frequented them, hence the reason he was now in Thailand. He asked me to take him some money over last month. I thought he was on about a couple of hundred quid to tide him over and I nearly died when one of his mates came round to Nicole's and dropped me of quarter of a million quid in an Adidas bag. I had nightmares for a week just in case I got relieved of it by the regional muggers. Mugging is not so much a hazard, but part of daily life around here. You tend to feel left out when other people keep on getting robbed and you don't.

I had used his flat as a meeting place for Emily, and we sort of worked it on a Sunday, Monday and sometimes a Tuesday scenario as the husband was generally over in Germany. The deceit had fitted in nicely with Nicole's timetable, and I dedicated the rest of the week to her. It had been a great few months. Emily obviously knew about Nicole, but obviously the latter never knew about the former, until the former let me know about the package and the latter and former ended up meeting. It was hardly a tangled web, and from my point of view it was at one time all quite nice and manageable. I hadn't quite envisaged getting my head kicked in by her husband or having Nicole violently attack me, but manageable all the same. I quite liked that fact I had two girls who looked the same, but who had totally different personalities.

Since I had foolishly let out my house, Nicole had wondered where I slept two nights out of the week and where I kept my clothes, as suits were another fetish of mine, and I had hundreds of them. When she had found out about Bondy's place, the first thing she wanted do was to check it out and possibly bug it. I wouldn't say she was an untrusting person, more suspicious of my comings and goings. The fact that I had been married eight years and that I had been eventually thrown out for a catalogue of misdemeanours didn't really inspire her belief. She tolerated Jeanette to a point, but she hated the fact that I kept in contact with her and that she knew I was continually being fleeced for money. The kids used to stop over in the beginning, but it was now just a case of picking them up and dropping them off, although as daft as it sounds, I was now seeing a bit more of them, which both Jeanette and the kids thought was great.

Lyndsay Bracken had recently begun a line of communication, firstly to write off the fact that it wasn't me that had bought seventeen televisions through the finance company they collected for, but some Vasily Chernobyl or something. He had used an old driving licence he had found of mine behind a cupboard and had also managed to take out Capital One, Vanquis and AMEX credit cards in my name – I've no idea how they had got one with AMEX as they had turned me down. They had bought over forty four items on credit at various stores as well as a load of shite over the internet. Ms. Bracken also wanted the names of the police officers dealing with the case plus details of my legal people. She was both very thorough and very matter-of-fact. Adebayor had told me that she had called three times in one day so I phoned her mobile, initially to tell her to go piss off and haunt another house, but seeing as she wasn't shaking me down for money she sort of came over quite alright and not half as bossy. I'm not sure how it came about but I ended up having a coffee with her at the Greek coffee shop down a side street which I frequent and where old Greeks sit around all day playing cards, drinking coffee and shouting at each other. The guy who owned the place was called Fosis, and he had a sort of moustachioed eighties porn star look about him, which was further enhanced by the fact that his shirt was always unbuttoned down to his naval to reveal a ragged chest of hair providing the near-perfect background to display his glistening gold crucifix. I ordered an espresso and a Perrier water, not so much as a statement but to rid my mouth of its taste after I had drunk it. Within seconds of sitting down Lyndsay had walked in, which caught the attention of everyone, not at least the establishment's owner who straightened up his shirt as he was tasked to make her a Nescafé. Every time I had seen her she had been humping around some bag with files in it, and this time was no different. She may have been posh, but she was also a bit on the pushy side; apart from the latter she seemed to have all the qualities my ostensible persona admired in a woman. Within fifteen minutes she had told me everything I needed to know about her, although within that short window of time I had to endure about eleven minutes of boredom as she told me about her job and the daily journey from Putney into north London and the fact that the recent spate of tube strikes, including today's, had bollocksed her timetable up.

The fact that I had a fast car parked in an underground car park off Euston Road was mentioned in my brief description of me, and was utilised to its greatest ability in getting her from the coffee shop to her flat, which was both horrible and cramped, and which was shared with some huge female with great whacking feet called Siobhan. I looked around and immediately wondered what I was doing here. Ms. Bracken's label certainly did not correctly describe its content, however the damage had been done and I had unwittingly kicked off a scramble for my affection that I had not seen since the Tall Dwarf's wife.

When I got back to Frederick Street I was met by the smiling face of Emily who was sat on the wooden living room floor, legs crossed, going through some bags of stuff.

"It's done," she said. "He's kicked me out."

I gave her an okay and looked over at a great big cardboard box and some other boxes in the room leaning along the back wall.

"A DPD driver brought them around three o'clock," she said.

"How long have you been here?" I asked.

"Since lunch time," she replied.

"You fancy anything to eat?" I asked.

The thing about Emily was her smile. It was also her great legs and arse as well – but her smile was something else. We ended up doing some sushi, which I knew would have totally pissed Nicole off, and we ended up in some bar down some side street having a couple of white wines and watching a band knock out a few indie tracks. It now appeared there had been some movement within the complex labyrinth which was my life. Emily had moved in, which was denounced with some vigour by Nicole.

"What are you saying," she screamed down her mobile. "She's moved in?"

I couldn't really lie about it as all her things were here, and since I was partly to blame for the manufacture of her separation and she was carrying a lump with my name on it I couldn't really turn her away. Plus she was nice – I mean really, really nice. I did relay that information through my reply but I must have said it wrong as I received loads of abuse which was followed by a question. "You just don't fucking get it, do you?"

I got into work to see Sooty, Ginge and Fred listening to Eddie as he ran some commentary whilst watching some monochrome footage from ITN archives that I had never seen before, and which impressed me even more when Eddie explained it.

"Is that Highbury?" I asked.

"You know who that is?" Eddie said, pointing.

"No idea," I replied.

"One of the main men at Mexico in 1970 – 'The Gunman' Rivelino," he explained.

I watched the digital seconds on the screen turn as the team in the dark shirts, who I knew to be Arsenal, tore them apart with some exquisite football which included two twenty-yard shots that were hammered home by the player they called Sammy.

"Ten years ahead of his time and everything that we lacked in Brazil," stated Eddie. "The most cultured schemer England never had."

"Really?" I replied.

"Ask anyone who knows the game," added Eddie, "And I don't mean Wengerists who've had more than half a day in football – anyone will tell you that continental or international football is different to our game in England – and that smiling young lad you've just seen put two away was part of the solution to Ramsey's problem in Mexico."

I watched it again and again. The kid was awesome and his back lift and execution in the way he hammered home the goals was second to none. He was more Brazilian than the Brazilians.

"I was once sat listening to Bob Wilson talking to Brian Cowgill, who was the head of BBC Sport during World Cup 1970 and he said 'Sammy was one hell of an athlete who could bend a ball as sharply as any South American.'"

I was intrigued. "You saw him play a lot then?" I asked.

"I did – he was exceptional," stated Eddie. "All the top coaches knew what Ramsey's problem was, but because he had won it in '66 with Charlton and co, few dared to pull him up about it. It was when the competition kicked off and we couldn't put it in the net that questions were raised – we were good at the back, yet made to look very ordinary."

He went on to explain that Arsenal were of a similar set up at the time and played an unadventurous, albeit industrious, style of football built from good foundations at the back.

"They weren't quite Leeds, but you could tell what they were doing," he added. "Sammy and Charlie George were similar types of players but like chalk and cheese – I remember them ripping a great Ajax team to shreds at Highbury and a year later watching the same two players go to Maine Road and take on a fantastic Manchester City side and do exactly the same. George was the ugly outspoken big mouth with the long hair and Sammy was the exact opposite – they were immense."

Sooty and I sat back. I loved a history lesson in Arsenal, and so by the looks of it did Ginge and Fred.

"That Ajax side had Cruyff and at the time Arsenal got to them in the semi-final, they had won the domestic Double plus had already been in one European Cup final the year prior – the year after, they did the lot and won three European Cups on the bounce – they were supposedly the best football team in the world."

He was right. The Ajax team back then boasted 14-cap Dutch international defender Barry Hulshoff, who looked a bit like the actor Matt Damon – 60-cap Dutch international Wim Suurbier, who played in two World Cup finals and was rated as one of the best defenders in world football – Velibor Vasovic, a 32-cap Yugoslavian international central defender who scored in the 1969 European Cup Final only the year before – Ruud Krol, a truly world class defender who played in two World Cup finals and was capped 83 times – Gerrie Mühren, a player who had 10 Dutch international caps and who was the elder brother of Arnold who played for both Ipswich and Manchester United – the impressive 31-cap Dutch international Sjaak Swart, who played over 600 times for the club – the enigmatic and highly skilful Johan Cruyff, a 48-cap Dutch international and three times winner of the Ballon D'Or – Dick van Dijk, a 7-cap Dutch international and one of the scorers in the 1971 European Cup Final – the dazzling 34-cap Dutch international left winger Piet Keizer – and the tragic 8-cap Dutch international Midfielder Nico

Rijnders. He collapsed on the pitch whilst playing in Belgium in similar circumstances to Marc Vivien Foe and Fabrice Muamba, and actually died on the pitch, but got resuscitated; only for it to finish his career before he eventually died at 28 years of age.

"And Arsenal beat them three – nil?" asked Ginge.

"Arsenal didn't just beat them - they annihilated them," stated Eddie. "Sammy was the best player in Europe in 1970 and top scorer in the competition for the club."

"And he never played for England?" asked Ginge.

"He was an under-23," stated Eddie. "I remember I saw him score in a three-nil win against Austria up at the Old Boothferry Park – a brilliant volley – he could hit a ball like you wouldn't believe. Every time he teed up for a shot he looked like he was going to take someone's head off."

"So why didn't Ramsey take him to the World Cup?" I asked.

"It was never said, but Ramsey wouldn't play Arsenal players," added Eddie. "There was also a rumour that Sammy turned Ramsey down to play for his home town club when he was a kid, as Ramsey was the then manager of Ipswich Town. Think about it - being turned down to play for Arsenal, and him a former player and club captain for Spurs."

He had a point. Baker and Eastham were already in the England fold, but apart from that only McNab and John Radford had had a sniff – and a sniff was all it was.

Me and Sooty had a talk and it was decided that we split the documentary.

"I reckon we do the two," said Sooty. "The one they want, and they one they don't know about – give them two angles."

I loved it and agreed. It was a brilliant idea.

"Should we get this Sammy on tape?" I asked.

"I'll tell you now," said Eddie. "If you're after a damning

appraisal – this is not the man to give you it – he's like Bob Wilson and George Armstrong before him – just a really nice guy."

"Who should we talk to, then?"

"Malcolm Allison – Don Revie – Brian Clough," smiled Eddie.

"That's handy," I replied, albeit rather sarcastically. "They're all dead."

We eventually got Eddie dusted down and sat in front of the camera talking whilst I got Faranha to get a photo of Sammy, so we could do exactly the same and break it into segments; however if I'm honest, there weren't that many around.

While I had been in the editing suite I had received a missed phone call and a few texts, one of which was from Ms. Bracken. 'Thnx for the lift. Can I C U????'

That sounded ominous and I texted her back, 'Busy at the moment with work', which had a dual purpose – on one hand it told her 'no', but on the other didn't entirely write it off. Don't get me wrong, she was really nice looking – a bit taller than I like at around 5'6", but blonde, nice legs and everything else – however the grotty flat in Putney and the fat mate put me off, and there was no way I could accommodate her at mine.

'Coffee then? Plz xx,' came the immediate reply.

I knew Bondy's place off the A111 could be a goer but I actually knew she knew where I lived. I mean she had been both inside and outside of it until Nicole had chucked her out.

'I'm not at my house in King's X – It's complicated,' I texted back.

She wasn't having any and again I received an immediate reply – '?'

'Girlfriend trouble,' I texted back.

That was a mistake, which turned into a phone call and had me having to endure a sixteen minute conversation, which culminated in the fact that I'd pick her up from their office on Grays Inn Road and take her over to Cockfosters at around 6:00pm with my 'get out clause' being that I had to be back at the office by 8:00pm as I had a lot of editing to do.

By the time 6:00pm came I was bollocksed. Eddie had been brilliant and Faranha had finally got some half decent photography of Sammy from a match that never was – Snow-bound Highbury in December 1967 where Arsenal had been winning against Sheffield Wednesday 1-0 until the match was abandoned after 48 minutes. All the same, we had split it into segments and the kid looked great – in my humble opinion he looked a bit like Kaka – 'Arsenal's First Brazilian'. I liked it. I liked it a lot.

I made the pickup and was around a minute or so behind time. She looked good and I knew she had gone to a bit of effort as all the make-up had been newly applied and she was wearing a short dress, which screamed 'rape' and that no-one – I mean no-one would ever dare wear for the office.

"You look good," I commented.

I got a smile followed by an account of her day between the time it took me to get out of the traffic and over to the flat, which in truth shocked me a bit, in that their firm took over debts and then stuck a premium on them and then hassled the hell out of home owners by turning up at their door with a court summons plus an extra-extra premium to pay for the said summons. To me it seemed very dirty.

She wasn't impressed by the fact that I'd taken her to a flat, which to her only meant one thing. Well, even to me it only meant one thing. After forty-five minutes of pissing around I managed to do the deed and if I'm honest it wasn't much to write home about. I didn't tell her as such, as it may have hurt her feelings, but she'd certainly have to work a lot harder than that to keep me interested. It was about as interesting as driving a Vauxhall Corsa when you've got a pair of Maseratis parked on the drive at home. Both Emily and Nicole were brilliant. Both handled different, but you knew the drive was always going to be fantastic.

"Will I see you again?" she asked.

"Not if I see you first," I nearly said.

The journey was quiet as I dropped her off back in King's Cross. I generally enjoyed new sex. New sex can be one of a few things, but it's always great to have something that's 'new'. What I just had had looked very good – a bit like one of these new houses on a shiny pamphlet, but once you were there and inside it, there was nothing much to shout home about.

I went back into work – did a bit and got on to Frederick Street about 10:25pm, and there was Emily smiling to greet me. This was a Maserati. Okay, it's got a bit of baggage in the boot, but you know it'll kick up first time, purr like a cat, and when you boot the thing it will give you the ride of your life.

"Nicole's been 'round," she said, still smiling. "I told her you were at work."

"What did she say?" I asked, not really wanting to know the answer.

"Not a great deal," she replied. "Basically can you get your things from hers – and that you need to talk – and that you're a shallow and conceited prick – sorry about telling you the last bit."

"But you still love me?" I smiled.

"I'm very easily pleased," she replied, smiling.

"You're not that easily pleased," I said, before adding, "Fancy nipping out?"

I told her about this twin project we had on at work as we walked to the bar on the side street that had the indie music playing the night before, and she actually seemed interested.

"You should do a bit of this," she said whilst sipping at a white wine and pointing at the band. "You never know – some of these may make it."

She then proceeded to tell me about another twin project which ended up being rolled into one about a pair of revivalist bands off America's west coast. She spoke and spoke and everything she said appeared interesting.

"It won an award," she said, smiling. "It was really good."

She was referring to a documentary by Ondi Timoner on the once-promising American rock bands The Brian Jonestown Massacre and The Dandy Warhols, and the friendship and rivalry between their respective founders, Anton Newcombe and Courtney Taylor.

"How's your work?" I asked.

"You're not interested in what I do," she smiled.

She was right – I was shallow.

I went to bed that night happy and content. Well, seemingly happy and content, as I really needed to get shut of the bed. It was starting to stink.

I woke up around six the next morning to find Emily at her laptop, working. By all accounts she had some presentation up at some hat or walking stick exhibition over at Kensington Olympia. That was until she told me differently, and what her 'real job' entailed.

"Wow," was all I could muster up. I should really take more interest – which is another thing Jeanette had always kept on ragging me about.

I looked at the holes in the kitchen units where the two ovens used to be and the gap where the washer and fridge and freezer used to sit, and which were more than likely now in some other Russian's house. I made a coffee and sat at the other side of the breakfast bar watching her tap away on her keyboard. I had to get something out into the open.

"I've got the kids coming over tomorrow," I said.

She lifted her head and just smiled. Nicole would have never done that. And that was another thing I wasn't relishing – having to go over to Walthamstow to be bossed around and shouted at.

"If you've got your children coming over you could do with getting them somewhere to sleep," she said, smiling.

Mmm. I'd forgotten about that.

I got up and rummaged around in my jacket pocket and pulled out my wallet which contained a few notes and a load of plastic, half of which were maxed-out. I put two on the breakfast bar and said something I didn't realised I'd said until I'd said it.

"There's about ten grand on those – maybe if you're staying you might want to fill those holes in."

She lifted her head, acknowledging what I'd said, which I hadn't realised I'd said until I'd said it, and asked, smiling, "Are you sure?"

I thought so, I thought.

I went into work and saw a load more uploads from the ITN archive on the editing suite, and I poured myself a coffee and watched them. I have to tell you, sometimes my job was the best job in the world! There was nothing like watching Arsenal beat anyone, but beat a team with Cruyff, Krol and Suurbier in it was something else. Sooty had managed to get the Ajax game of 1970.

My pure bliss took a turn for the worse when I received a call from Nicole. I was pencilled in to go pick my gear up from hers at six bells, which was followed by a text that I hadn't read, which had been sent late last night and was what I understood to be a demand from the wife of the Tall Dwarf.

It stated, 'Meet me – Charing X Rd – bookshop – 1pm.'

It was a fairly vague demand as I hadn't a clue where.

The morning passed by with Eddie on camera talking about various aspects of World Cup 1970 behind the segmented Bobby Moore and Pele photograph, before being moved onto another angle where the segmented photograph of Sammy was positioned. World Cup 1970 was interesting in that we had everything and expected everything, but then in one mad moment had lost the lot, with everyone stating that Peter Bonetti was at fault and therefore made culpable for the fact that we went out of the competition.

I had heard the story and read the press clippings but I had also remembered something that Bob Wilson had said. "Peter Bonetti was beaten by a shot from Franz Beckenbauer and by a header from Uwe Seeler, which I have always regarded as a fluke – a fine save from Gerd Muller from five yards out when we were winning was conveniently forgotten."

Bob Wilson is a man who will always give you time – always. A total Arsenal man. I remember writing to him when I was a kid. I couldn't get my head around the fact that Arsenal didn't compete in the UEFA Cup (what was the Fairs Cup) in the 1973-74 season after coming second in the league. It had been on my mind for ages, that and how the hell we managed to throw the title away and get humped by Leeds 1-6 on the last day of that season. Bob took time out to write back and explained the 'one club per city' rule at the time.

"Bonetti might have saved Beckenbauer's shot. On most days he would have done because he was a brilliant goalkeeper, but to blame him or be equivocal about his performance is most unfair," Bob had added. Like I said – Bob Wilson is a truly nice man.

I had watched the footage quite a few times by now, and Eddie had stated it and restated it. "If Ramsey had picked a proper squad capable of playing continental football and breaking down these two banks of four, we would have walked it."

Eddie sort of got pretty animated every time he mentioned Ramsey, and he hated talking about 1966 as much as I hated listening about it.

Going into the 1966 World Cup for Arsenal ended in a 0-3 mauling by Leeds United, who were going for the league in front of just over four and a half thousand supporters – however going into 1970 World Cup Arsenal had just dismantled and hammered a very capable Anderlecht side, who were one of the dominant forces in Belgium and European football, and 3-0 in front of a packed house at Highbury to lift the European Inter-Cities Fairs Cup, which just goes to show how things can change in four years.

Eddie always went on about history repeating itself time and time again – it was without doubt his favourite saying – and in this instance we had it sort of repeating itself, but the exact opposite.

Another thing was similar in history repeating itself: there had been no Arsenal players included in either the 1966 or 1970 World Cup squad – there had if you count George Eastham, who was in the 1966 World Cup Squad and labelled as playing for the Arsenal, but he wasn't really, as he had lost his place to Sammy and was between clubs, with Arsenal waiting on Stoke City coughing up the agreed £35,000 for the 30-year old.

"Don't forget that Ramsey had been a Spurs player," stated Eddie, "And that being the case he loathed to include any player from Arsenal."

A lot of stuff Eddie had been saying made sense. If I was manager would I play, say, Danny Welbeck of Manchester United? I mean I absolutely hate Manchester United. A definite 'no' to that, however it's more to do with the fact that he's perhaps the most underwhelming England striker since Emile Heskey – and Heskey only got the gig because he was the only player that would kiss Rooney when he scored. Saying that Welbeck is definitely a Wenger-type player, but that may have more to do with him looking like Omar Williams than him actually being any good.

The rather demanding text that had been sent to me by the wife of the Tall Dwarf had been elaborated on further, and I put some sunglasses on so as not to be recognised and walked into this fusty smelling bookshop on Charing Cross Road and through into its rear. It was like something out of one of those old Harry Palmer films with Michael Caine – where he sort of meets the agent from behind the iron curtain and exchanges the suitcase of money for the microfilm. I walked up the squeaky wooden staircase and on to the first floor, which was absolutely full of books, absolutely none would of which would ever interest me. My phone beeped a message through as I walked around the wooden floored room. I had gone into the wrong frigging book shop, and to add insult to injury some fat surly looking bitch in a brown cardigan accused me of sneaking in to do a bit of pilfering. I don't know why she assumed that. I could have bought the full contents of the shop for fifty quid, and that being the case, I told her so.

On walking into the correct location of our rendezvous – Foyles bookshop – the Tall Dwarf's wife appeared immensely pleased to see me and wasted no time in pulling me into a discreet corner and whipping open her blouse to reveal her most prized babies amidst a short sharp intro from the trombone section of Herb Alpert and the Tijuana Brass, and duly requested immediate impregnation by trying to unbutton my flies. I literally had to beat her off with a big stick to get her under control. She was fucking insane. There were even people in the shop at the time – it was dead embarrassing.

Even more so when she chased me out into the street. She had to have been on something.

Eddie appeared well impressed when I told him about the ordeal.

"That never happens to me," he said, shaking his head.

"It's only ever happened to me the once," I replied.

I could see Eddie's mind was ticking away at what I had told him, and a minor panic set in when I noticed the upsurge in traffic on my mobile phone. In the space of 45 minutes I had received eighteen texts from the wife of the Tall Dwarf, which ranged from standard kisses and smiley faces to the quite dirty and disgusting, through to the completely deranged and unhinged.

"You've got to let the police know," said Sooty, smiling.

"I let them know last time and all they did was laugh," I replied, shaking my head. "I have to admit – she's never acted like that before."

After work I made my way over to Nicole's, where I knew I was in for some form of arse kicking; however I was proved wrong. She had newly applied make up on and everything else which she knew I liked.

"Well?" she asked.

I always hated it when she gave me one of those 'Well?'s, but I hadn't seen her for a couple of days so I let her off.

"Are you okay?" I asked.

I got a few tears and we ended up in bed and by the time I'd got home I'd received a couple of nice saucy texts to tell me how much she had enjoyed it, and just to make sure Emily wasn't left out, she sent her one as well. I felt a bit horrible about that, but all I got off Emily was a bit of a blank expression which followed a peck on the cheek, which nearly culminated into another special love, but she told me that I'd have to go take a shower first. I was running dead low on Viagra so I popped one from a card that I'd nicked out of Sooty's desk so that by the time I had had a shower, I was firstly dead happy and then drooling like a cabbage. They were blue, but they certainly weren't frigging Viagra and I felt like I'd had an injection of morphine or something. It sort of wore off after a couple of hours, which to be honest was a good job as I had a both an irate husband and a totally unwanted visitor at the door who initially tried grappling with me but totally failed and just ended up sort of holding me and trying to shake me. It appeared that the stinking Tall Dwarf had obviously gotten wind of the fact that his missus still had a 'thing' for me. I was extremely fortunate that the punches he threw were about as good as he looked. That was twice in two weeks he had attacked me. I eventually gave him a belt around the ear hole, kicked him up the arse and told him to piss off.

"Well, that was interesting," smiled Emily.

Why did nobody normal want to fight with me? I'd had some six and a half foot ex-paratrooper-type tap dancing on my head and now a total gimp having a second shot at trying to wallop me. I came clean and told Emily about his wife.

"Jesus," she exclaimed. "What does she look like?"

Bearing in mind that her husband was indeed the utter runt of the litter, it was a valid question that needed addressing. Not at least from a self-preservation and integrity angle, as I couldn't have her thinking that I'd been banging some circus act with a high forehead and sunken-in eyes.

"She's really quite pretty," I said, trying to convince myself.

"As pretty as me?" she replied.

"No one's as pretty as you," I said, which I knew was a really brilliant answer.

"What about Nicole?"

Mmm. I wasn't expecting that.

I tossed and turned all night after I had woken in a cold sweat after a nightmare in which the Tall Dwarf was wearing a wedding veil and bridal gown and was about to give me a blow job – I think? I tried to offset this in thinking that could have easily been his sister, but he or she was doing a lot of fumbling with her hands. I had to stop logging into the porno sites before I went to bed. The last thing I had watched was a long clip of this woman wearing a wedding dress getting knocked all over the shop by a bloke that was a dead ringer for Kanu. I had then wondered what Kanu was doing nowadays. I remembered Arsenal first buying him and how unorthodox he was in his play, and how powerful and agile he was. No defender ever knew what to expect. The back heeled goal versus Middlesbrough, the hat-trick versus Chelsea, the way he had led from the front and helped win the game, which gave us the title at Old Trafford. Was I going mad?

I finally nodded off, and got woken by voices downstairs as Emily was directing some traffic from Appliance City into the kitchen.

"Wow, what's all that?" I asked as I copped her checking the contents of each box as they were wheeled in.

"You wanted the holes filling?" she smiled after giving me the double entendre.

"Two glass-fronted ovens, a ceramic hob, a washing machine, an extractor fan and a fridge and a freezer," said the man before he left. "Sign here."

I liked getting new things but hated all the unboxing and installation and made myself scarce by copping a shower and going in to work. As it happened, and what I didn't know, was that Emily was a brilliant organiser and had got some local electrician out of the book to do the deed, and I hadn't really needed to get to the office for 8:00am. I looked at the dozen CDs that had been cut of Eddie yacking into the camera, and at some point I knew I had to watch them and take notes about points of interest and at which and what time and sort of build up the programme.

It all sounded immensely interesting, but in reality it was immensely boring. I was more a butcher than a surgeon. I had the great idea and could certainly stick all the bits in to make it look like it worked, but Sooty was the more level-headed one that sought perfection. Well, he wasn't really – he just made sure I did it.

The stuff on World Cup 1970 still reverberated on our lack of an attack-minded midfield and the fact that Francis Lee was continually huffing and puffing but couldn't blow the house down. Malcolm Allison had told Eddie as well as everyone else in the UK that Alan Mullery was a one-paced carthorse, who didn't deserve to be in the same team as Colin Bell and Alan Ball. He never mentioned his Ealing Studios gangster-haircut and Bob Hoskins accent as everyone could see and hear them anyway. I am certain he thought about it. If he thought that of Mullery, then what of Stiles?

Eddie was laughing on the camera. "Mal told me not to even get him on that subject, and as for Charlton," he said, shaking his head.

Charlton had been the golden boy of English football. A survivor of Munich, World Cup Winner in 1966 and European Cup Winner in 1968. He had appeared both undroppable and irreplaceable, which is exactly what Frank McLintock must have thought until he was told by Bertie Mee to 'fuck off' and never darken his doors again.

I watched the England games of 1970 he played in. He wasn't that bad, but he certainly wasn't that good either. Eddie had candidly stated that the heat and thin air of Mexico would have been ideal for a player of Sammy's calibre, adding that it was Allison that had first mentioned it.

Ruud Gullit mentioned something similar in later years – that there was far too much running in the British game, and in the conditions of Mexico a more thoughtful game should have been played. Eddie's hero and mate at that time had been Jimmy Bloomfield, who had been raving about Sammy not being there when England were trying to unpick the lock of the two lines of four from Rumania and Czechoslovakia.

"Arsenal had a similar problem with a French side in the cup," Eddie had explained. Rouen were a moderate but well-drilled French side who had no intention of playing Arsenal at their own game, and their ambition solely relied on seeing out both games as 0-0 and taking them on penalties.

"Bob Wilson may as well not have been there in the game at Highbury," Eddie had said. "It was sheer torture – and ten times as boring a game as both the games against Rumania and Czechoslovakia."

I had watched both games and could have thought this as being impossible, however I'd watched Denilson notch up over 150 appearances for Arsenal and I knew exactly what being underwhelmed and bored was all about.

Sammy had told reporters after the Rouen game that it shouldn't be a case of supporters knocking the team effort for not sticking five past them, there should be more praise given to the organisation of the opposition. It wasn't word for word, but Sammy wasn't bothered. He had broken the deadlock in the eighty-eighth minute and Arsenal were in the hat for the next round.

Me and Sooty did a bunk and went out for an early lunch to the Greek coffee shop down a side street off Grays Inn Road. Fosis was remarkably clean shaven and in good spirits and offered me an ouzo.

"No – the last time you got me on that stuff I woke up eighty-quid lighter and had a hangover for three days," I replied. "I'll stick with an espresso and Perrier."

We sat down at the bar and talked about our twin project, which Abigail had been trying to hard sell over at the Emirates. Trying to get your product on general sale at The

Armoury (the club shop) was about as easy as trying to get Wenger to admit he was wrong. It certainly wasn't going to happen overnight.

"You want sandweech?" Fosis asked.

I nodded a 'yes' and he fired up the hotplate. There was nothing like a house brick of a sandwich to kick up a severe bout of indigestion. I loved Fridays. We stayed in the coffee shop until around three before I skived off home and copped Emily pulling up in her Mini at the same time with a load of shopping in the back.

"You're home early," she said.

I was – it was an astute observation.

I treated her with ten minutes of unbridled passion on the new sofa, and another ten minutes on the toilet of trying to get out what I had put in her. She told me how brilliant I was and I agreed, and were it not for the wife of the Tall Dwarf glaring at us through the window it would have been near perfection.

"Who's that?" she asked.

"Nobody – draw the blinds," I replied.

She was beginning to be a pest and was as hard to get rid of as a dose of clap. I had to draw the blinds to every lousy window. In the end I called the police and I ended up giving them a statement which bordered on the 'DH Lawrence' but was in reality very 'Fatal Attraction'. I don't know who was more impressed, the two coppers from the Met jotting down the details or the pair of electricians that were now fitting the oven. Emily appeared unbothered and went about her business of putting the shopping away.

"Doesn't all this bother your wife?" asked one of the policemen.

"I doubt it," I said. "She lives in Clerkenwell."

"Sorry, I mean your fiancée," he corrected himself.

"Again, I doubt it," I said. "She lives in Walthamstow."

"So forgive me for asking," said the policeman. "Who's the lady that's here at the moment?"

"She's my girlfriend," I replied, totally glad that I had got that out of the way. "She's moved in as her husband has kicked her out."

"Why don't you tell them that I'm pregnant?" said Emily, both smiling and shaking her head.

"Oh yeah, and she's pregnant," I said.

"What – and your husband has kicked you out?" said the other policeman, trying to catch up on the gossip.

"Yes," she replied.

"That's unfortunate," came the copper's reply.

"For him," I said.

Emily glanced me another smile. She liked that until I mentioned to the copper that she was fourteen weeks on and that it had been me doing all the 'ploughing the fields and scattering' and not the hapless ex-paratrooper with the size thirteens and fist of iron.

"You're a right little busybody," one of them commented.

If things couldn't seem to be getting any worse, then I would be wrong. Jeanette turned up with the kids.

"What's going on?" she said on seeing north London's equivalent to Cagney and Lacey being part of the King's Cross tea set.

"It's nothing to worry about," I reassured her. "Take a seat – I'm getting stalked again by the Tall Dwarf's wife."

"I thought you said it was the woman from the debt collectors," Jeanette replied.

I was getting a bit sick of everyone knowing my business, so I put her straight and stated that Ms. frigging Lyndsey Bracken had only just started stalking me and at the moment it was only via phone and text.

By now both electricians were apparently in awe of me and were sat on the bar stools listening, as the big ham and triple cheese panini sandwich that Fosis had lobbed together and squashed down to literally nothing with his hydraulic sheet metal press, which he doubled as a sandwich maker, began to unravel and started giving me a bit of gyp.

When everyone had gone home I managed to cop a bit of quality time with the kids, and Emily must have thought it fascinating that they actually liked me.

In all the haze that was the statement taking, which turned into a very one-sided interrogation, some new beds had been delivered and my suggestion that we drag the old bed out into the garden, douse it with petrol and burn it seemed extremely appealing to the kids. It was better than bonfire night, and within twenty minutes I had the same two coppers at my door along with a couple of units from the fire station who managed to quell the inferno just long enough to rescue the eight families of Kosovan squatters that doubled as my near neighbours.

"Dad, that was brilliant," said my son.

I had to admit, that was one hell of a fire. They were talking about it for ages afterwards.

Emily must have thought it as exciting as hell living with me as both kids were nagging me to take them to the Emirates for the next Arsenal match – as she asked if she could come too.

That was a strange one. Never, ever did any of my women ever ask to go to the football. They certainly furnished me with the excuses not to go and moaned like hell when they did. However, no one had ever asked to come.

"'You sure?" I asked.

"Of course I'm sure," she replied.

Chapter 9
Eddie's Tales – Take 3

Abigail had waved me off on the six o'clock train from King's Cross and I had mixed feelings about leaving what Abigail and Faranha duly labelled 'The Madhouse'.

The few days I'd had in north London were brilliant and, if I'm being honest, were a million miles away from the indignity of semi-retirement and a crappy part time job on the town council.

As the train pulled away I phoned Pauline to let her know I was on time and then browsed through the notes and the few photos that I had accumulated whilst being part of the said 'Madhouse'.

Sooty had claimed that at times his 'other half's' life was in the toilet, whilst he had been there continually yanking at the chain. At first it appeared callous, but the more I got told of the goings on the more it made me smile.

"Don't get involved," Abigail had smiled when Sooty had come into the office sort of really upset. Someone had parked a battered sky-blue caravan with two smashed windows and flat tyres outside his house, which was followed by about twenty-odd people phoning him up as an advert had appeared in the *London Evening Standard* stating 'Luxury Tourer For Sale – first to see will buy – £1000'.

"Whatever you do, just don't get involved," Abi added.

Both lads loved each other, but that never stopped them try to usurp or 'one-up' the other and if you didn't know them, you would think they were absolute gits. However, trying to piss each other off never really got in the way of the healthy respect they had for each other.

The 'other half' had told me that Sooty had been one of the best right-backs around, and that being the case, both Leeds United and Blackpool were looking at him prior to him being involved in what was apparently a horrific motor-cycle accident at a notorious four-way junction in a village near Rotherham.

"He was brilliant," his other half had added. "He had all the power and pace and if truth be known, he was a right dirty bastard – every time I had played against him he kicked me up in the air."

Sooty had played this down when I'd asked him, however he wasn't backward in coming forward when he explained that his other half once clocked him doing the 100m in just over ten and a half seconds.

"It was a one-off," he said. "I could get under eleven seconds all the time, but that was the best – the thing that pissed me off about it that there was no-one there watching."

"He was like fucking lightning," stated his other half. "Nobody could get near him."

·"It was a BMW that hit me," stated Sooty. "I tried beating the lights as they hit amber and the bloke in the car jumped them and that was that – my knee, cartilage and cruciate ligaments were all bollocksed."

We had spoken in length as regards injuries. Leeds's Paul Reaney had missed the World Cup in 1970 due to a broken leg, which sort of upset the balance of the side, as like Sooty, both he and Terry Cooper were extremely quick and marauding wing backs. Keith Newton and Tommy Wright did an amiable job at filling the void, but the set-up – if I was being brutally honest – looked a bit lop-sided, and the fact that – along with both Charlton brothers and Stiles – these two never pulled on an England shirt again told its own tale. In fact, nine of the 22 never played for England again; however it is worth noting that centre-back Brian Labone was always going to take early retirement from football, but it was his love for his club and country that made him stay on a couple of years longer than he had wished.

As for our 'main interest' – Sammy – he must have been sitting on the top of the world during the 1970 World Cup and looking towards the oncoming season with a fevered anticipation. Well, why not? He had just recently married the gamine looking sixties model that was Angelé Morley-Clarke, he was one of the top schemers in European football and tied to the club with one of the best contracts in British football, and he and young Charlie George were the cogs within the machine that was currently one of the champions of Europe, and between them played exactly the same sort of football the Brazilians had just graced the world's stage with.

He had hit a goal in Arsenal's easy victory against Watford before the team started out on its tour of Scandinavia and in the second game of the tour, hitting two well-taken goals in the 5-0 rout of Kungsbacka IF of Sweden.

With Sammy and George in the side Arsenal had both creativity and power, which had been seen first-hand in the 3-0 demolitions of both Ajax and Anderlecht – however within eleven days everything that was planned post-Anderlecht had gone up in smoke.

Sammy limped off after ten minutes of the next match in Denmark with a broken ankle, and was followed by not only central defender Peter Simpson who suffered a cartilage injury, but also Charlie George, who sustained a broken ankle whilst equalising on the opening day of the season in a match up at Goodison Park against the reigning League Champions, Everton.

Injuries, however, can work to the team's advantage and the reshuffling that followed formed the catalyst of a side that would go on to make history. The initial sticking-plaster solution meant right-back Peter Storey moved into midfield with 21-year old Pat Rice taking his place, and the no-nonsense Welsh centre-half John Roberts covering for Peter Simpson, whilst the extremely raw 19-year old Ray Kennedy came in for Charlie George.

Mee and Don Howe certainly hadn't planned the system – they'd just had their hand forced. For a time it worked as they played to their strengths, hitting the opposition with their industrious and dominant aerial football, something which was picked up on post-1970 World Cup and which was the only thing which actually rattled the South Americans. However, being reliant on the diagonal long balls from the back to Radford and Kennedy, Arsenal were occasionally found out – in one instance away at the Victoria Ground where they had been annihilated if not totally humiliated 0-5 by Stoke City. Another match springs to mind, that tends to be forgotten about in the history books, was that in a League Cup replay and in front of a crowd of 45,000 plus at Highbury, they went down 0-2 against a mediocre Crystal Palace side. Palace's Scottish striker Gerry Queen gave Arsenal's defence a torrid time, slotting a coolly taken goal past Wilson on 16 minutes – and on 56 minutes he had gone through for a one-on-one and bundled into Wilson, with the no-nonsense John Roberts taking recourse and slinging him to the ground in quite dramatic circumstances and giving the referee no alternative but to award a penalty, which Bobby Tambling duly hammered home.

The cracks were starting to appear and two weeks later both Sammy and Simpson were fit to play and back in the team.

I got picked up from Doncaster train station by my wife and I was initially told that the council had moved on their proposals regarding funding for new Christmas lights and that there was to be another meeting about dog fouling and an erroneous planning application for an extension. This was a million miles from the place I had just come from, where two young men had been living life to the full. Well, at least one of them was.

"So what were they like?" asked Pauline.

I shook my head and just smiled and I thought back to just the other day when Sooty had taken me to this coffee shop.

"Whatever you do – you can't tell him we've been here," he smiled before he summoned the owner to fetch us a pair of ouzos and some feta cheese and olives. "This is like his hangout."

"How is main man?" asked its owner, who I was soon to know as Fosis. "Is he still with woman with short skirt?"

"Which one is that?" Sooty asked. "He's got half a dozen on the go."

"I have seen him with small one with blonde hair," he replied.

"They're all small with blonde hair," Sooty explained before divulging in great detail about the fact that his wife had thrown him out after his twenty-third affair and he had been living with another woman but who had thrown him out as he had been having an affair with a married women who was now carrying his child. This was coupled with the emergence of an old flame, who had been the twenty-third affair and the nail in the coffin to his marriage, and who had the greatest chest ever along, with a woman from a debt collection firm of Grays Inn Road that he had recently been sending into.

"That is the one," stated Fosis. "She have office on Grays Inn Road – she came in here with skirt up arse and briefcase."

"When?" Sooty had asked.

"Yesterday, maybe."

He then looked over at a bald fellow wearing a green suit with a white shirt and tie who was reading a newspaper through his steel-rimmed spectacles, and words at volume were exchanged in Greek before others on the table opposite, who were playing cards, got brought into the conversation.

"Definitely yesterday," stated Fosis. "The girl was called Lid-nes-day."

"Where did they go after that?" Sooty had asked.

Fosis mentioned something at volume with the bald fellow and then for a few minutes with a couple of people at the card table, none of who seemed to speak English.

"She live in flat in Putney with big fat bastard woman," Fosis had said. "I think he not see her any more."

I had to hand it to Sooty – it was amazing watching how he went about the business of surveillance on his best mate.

"I knew he had some domestic issues," I had said.

"Domestic issues?" Sooty had stated whilst shaking his head. "Ever since I've known him he's had domestic issues – the ironic thing about it is the girlfriend who has just thrown him out looks exactly like the one that's just moved in with him – it's as weird as hell."

"How do you mean exactly like?" I had asked.

"The same," he had replied. "I can't describe it any plainer."

"And this is the girl from Putney?" I had asked.

"No, that's a different one," he had replied.

On getting in the house, I realised that the remainder of my days would be taken up by sitting on the Town Council and weeding the garden. I wondered if this is how

Sammy felt now. Nearly seventy years old and the thought of feeling useless.

Pauline ordered a Chinese and I ate my cardboard concoction whilst apparently being part of a one-sided conversation, which I neither heard nor reciprocated.

"Sorry Pauline, I was drifting," I said.

"This thing has really got to you, hasn't it?" she said.

She was absolutely right. I'd been made to feel needed again and by two lads who had the world at their feet.

"You have to meet them," I said. "I've never met anyone like them before."

I hadn't. They seemed to always be doing nothing, yet whilst they were apparently doing nothing, they were on with doing a hundred other things. I couldn't wait to see how all this would turn out.

"Are you going back down?" she asked.

I certainly hoped so, however it hadn't been confirmed as such. Then again I hadn't looked at the messages on my phone, one of which was from Sooty's other half who had thanked me for coming down, but had also mentioned that he would be calling up to see me shortly. And a lot sooner than I thought. That certainly brought a smile to my face.

Chapter 10
Hull

I'd managed to get in touch with Geoff over Twitter and got four tickets dropped off late Friday night. Geoff always had a few spare.

We'd had a great night and Emily made pizzas whilst the kids monopolised the 60-odd inch flat screen TV I'd scammed off Paypal. Nicole had never really bothered with the kids and if I'm honest, she had felt threatened by their presence. I've no idea why, as they quite liked her – I think it must have been an 'age thing'. That being the case, I had never really had them stop over at hers much and whilst my house had been commandeered by the Russian fraudsters I had reverted to being a 'day tripper' rather than a weekend type of dad.

Emily was slightly older and a lot more laid back, and although her life must have been in turmoil she never ever let it show, and the kids felt immediately at ease with her – and at her request they called her 'M'.

Our relationship had been founded on deceit. My deceit with Nicole and hers with her husband. To me, and I can never emphasise it enough, Emily and Nicole were perfect in every way and they both loved me. Without sounding a right sad bastard – if I could draw you my fantasy woman it would be their face looking back up at me from that piece of paper. Looking in from the outside, one could say Nicole fought back and lost what she had, and in return had gained her life – whilst Emily did exactly the opposite and let it play out and got what she deserved – i.e. me.

"Your children are lovely," she said as we laid in bed.

I knew that. Jeanette had done a great job, and I assumed she was angling for a cot and pram type of conversation, which she wasn't.

I was awoken just as it was getting light with both kids in bed with us, and that being the case I got up and went downstairs, had a jog around a couple of blocks, came back in, kicked the percolator up and I switched on BBC Radio 5 and my laptop.

I watched a bit of Eddie talking about the press's love affair with Brazil. And talking of journalists asking questions such as, "Why haven't we got players like Jairzinho and Rivelino?" to which Malcolm Allison replied, "We do – But 'you' (the people and the press) don't appreciate them."

He then pointed at Arsenal, who had just won a major European competition, easily beating the soon-to-be best team in world football – Ajax Amsterdam, and adding the fact that his and Mercer's dynamic side – Manchester City, had always struggled against them.

"Look at their schemer – the man in the middle – the man who makes them tick – top scorer in Europe and the one who scored their winning goal – then look at Rivelino and Jairzinho taking their goals – when I say someone is ten years ahead of his time I don't mean fucking Martin Peters."

Eddie had added, "This journo," tried to mock his reply and Mal just cut him dead.

"Watch 'your' Jairzinho and Rivelino both play the ball and hit the ball, and then look at the goal Sammy hit in the European final and draw your judgement," Allison had said.

The thing about Mal is that he was like Jimmy Bloomfield in that he could see the bigger picture and the bigger picture was the future – not quite his own – but he mentioned a young surly Alan Hudson, a young Tony Currie, a young Trevor Brooking, a young Charlie George and a young Rodney Marsh.

"These are the types of player that you'll see in the future," Mal had said.

I sat back and watched Eddie tell the tale on my laptop. He was brilliant.

"Jimmy Bloomfield mentioned Paul Madeley being a victim of his own versatility and that he was ten times the player of Stiles and Mullery, and could easily have provided the back up to Labone, Moore and Hunter – which negated the need to have Jack Charlton hanging around like Lurch out of the Addams Family," Eddie had stated.

I looked up and saw Emily at the door wearing only my Arsenal 1971 shirt.

"Are they still asleep?" I asked.

I got a nod and a smile in reply and, "Is there any coffee going?" for good measure.

"Help yourself," I replied.

I continued taking down some notes and timings and writing on two different jotters as she watched on, sipping at her coffee.

The kids awoke about 8:00am and came downstairs, and it wasn't so much me that they craved the attention of but that of their new mate 'M'.

"Dad, what are Brentford like?" asked my son. "They aren't better than Arsenal are they?"

That was a strange question coming from a five-year old so I asked, "Why did you ask that?"

"They are Paul's favourite team."

Paul? Who is Paul? I thought.

"My mum's friend, Paul," he added.

"They used to be really good in the old days," I said.

I may be a lot of things, but I never liked knocking another man's football team and the fact that my wife's boy-friend-if-you-like followed Brentford not only intrigued me, but sort of impressed me.

"Arsenal have only ever beat them about three times ever," I said. "They play at somewhere called Griffin Park, but I think they're on about building a new stadium."

"Is it like the Emirates?" he asked.

I smiled. I could talk about football all day.

"The new one probably will be," I said.

For a guy to follow a team like Brentford when there are bigger and more successful teams within a few miles takes a lot of guts – a lot of guts. I've always said that Arsenal fans are fickle and if ever the time comes when the club are facing mid-table mediocrity and third round cup exits as in the barren years in the sixties when Billy Wright had the reins, or when Mee rescinded power and let his 1971 luxury signing boss things on the pitch, attendances would suddenly plummet.

During the run up to country hosting the 1966 World Cup, the attendances for Arsenal's final home matches were nothing short of abysmal: Newcastle United 13,979 (1-3) - West Bromwich Albion 8,738 (1-1) – Sunderland 25,699 (1-0 Sammy) – Leicester 16,441 (1-0) and Leeds 4,554 (0-3), the latter of which was the lowest first class gate ever.

Even in the away games at the back end of the season both the attendances and results were crap – Sheffield United 15,045 (0-3) – Aston Villa 19,039 (0-3) – West Bromwich Albion 16,044 (4-4).

The supporters Arsenal have now are possibly even worse than they had back then and certainly aren't up for any dogfight.

"If Joey Barton signs I'll never support them again" sort of sums up the new breed of Arsenal supporter and if I thought that was a strange statement, nothing could compare with the idiotic response from some of our supporters turning their noses up at possibly signing one of the greatest strikers on the planet.

It is thought that when he was with Newcastle United, Joey Barton could possibly sign for us. Granted he had baggage – but he also had a lot of history playing against us, which is partly to do with who he actually is and his fantastic ability to get inside weaker-minded players' heads – the majority of whom are either African or French-African.

Barton is an extremely intelligent lad who was brought up in the suburbs of Merseyside and who was taught to look after himself from an early age. When he was the main man at Manchester City there had been an incident with Osmane Dabo, another mediocre import and rather underwhelming journeyman from Serie A who just happened to be a French-African. This guy's only claim to fame was that there was a training ground bust-up whereby Joey Barton gave him a bit of a slap. Training ground bust-ups happen all the time, and more recently there have been certain incidents at our club with Adebayor and Nicklas Bendtner and Adebayor and Robin Van Persie, which culminated in the common denominator being shipped out to Manchester City and Wenger being given another £20 million-plus to waste on shite.

This training ground slap, however, was a bit more vicious, and Dabo took a beating in which he received a detached retina when the two squared up after a couple of feisty tackles and a bit of jostling took place. Barton did no more than put him on the deck and beat him up. Dabo labelled him a coward, whereas Barton referred to him as a bully.

"Next time he should think twice about throwing his weight around – I was taught to look after myself and he deserved what he got," stated Barton.

There is nothing cowardly about sticking up for yourself against someone who is much bigger. However the fact that Barton did a number on a French-African seems to be made the point rather than the fact that he just refused to be bullied. The fact that in the same year he was picked up on CCTV giving another Scouser in the street a pasting shows that he is not one to discriminate, but it also showed the masses how he apt he was at dishing it out.

There must have been something said in the Arsenal dressing room before a match with Newcastle United at The Emirates, as one of our newly arrived French-Africans – Samir Nasri in this instance – immediately went into the referee's book for a petulant challenge on Barton. I've obviously no idea what was said, but it most certainly would have been related to the fact of the 'Dabo incident'.

In a later game up at St. James's Park we were absolutely on fire and leathering Newcastle, and were four goals up within half an hour. Then Barton turned the game on its head. He bossed his team back from 0-4 down to 4-4. Why? Because he knew Abou Diaby was the weak link, and the Achilles heel of the Arsenal side – and more to the point he knew that he could get into his head.

He immediately set about getting under his skin and Diaby was sent off after 50 minutes. In a bare knuckle fight on the street Barton would have easily battered Diaby, yet when Diaby made a grab for Barton, Barton lifted up his arms to tell the referee, Phil Dowd – 'Hand him a red when you're ready, pal.'

The general scheme of things 'all things Arsenal' was that it was Barton's heavy tackling on Diaby that led Diaby to react. The fact that Diaby suffered a horrific career-threatening ankle injury in the past gave cause to his reaction, but the real point was not only our two lost ones but that Joey Barton had earned his club one. You cannot take it away from Barton – he was immense that afternoon.

In a following fixture the season after he did same with another new arrival – this time he got two Africans for the price of one and he did exactly the same with Gervinho – who eventually left the field on 76 minutes following two yellow cards from referee Peter Walton. As for Alex Song, he nipped in to get a bit of recourse on behalf of his mate, and he ended up taking a three-game ban for stamping which, with the loss of them both, more than helped Manchester United hammer us 8-2 in a following fixture.

I don't know whether the problem is a French-African and African thing, or a Wenger thing. I think it is a combination of both, and in my mind both parties are better without each other, yet Wenger continually strives to try and recreate his second Thierry Henry and Patrick Viera whilst French-Africans and African players with far less talent and with far lesser clubs continually try and whore themselves out to him.

Sometimes it drives me mad with frustration thinking about it – that and the fact that the most boring and meaningless competition on the planet in the ACON (African Cup of Nations) robs a team of its African players for around ten weeks of the season.

"Have you been watching any players at the ACON?" one hack asked Wenger.

"No, we have the best player in Africa in Gervinho," he replied.

That says it all – to be a Brentford supporter, eh?

The kids were always excited to go to The Emirates, not so much for the football, more the general two hundred quid it costs me to get them out of The Armoury and the eating of the overpriced crap we get served inside the ground, however the tickets that I'd had dropped off culminated in a trip up to Hull City the next day.

"Does that mean we can't go to The Emirates?" asked my daughter.

"No, we can go today and then go do something else," I replied

I was rolled over in The Armoury for a lot more than two hundred dump as I had to buy Emily a home shirt, which sort of looked out of context with her short cream two-piece that she was wearing. "Who are you having put on the back, M?" was the kids' main question, and as Emily knew absolutely nothing about either football or the team it was a case of looking down the faces of the players; therefore she obviously picked out the one she thought was the best looking, which was Thomas Vermaelen, a player which looked uncannily like her nutter husband.

"Is he any good?" she asked.

"He never plays," said my lad.

"He might be on his way in the summer," I reaffirmed whilst getting a bit twitchy about the fact that Vermaelen was indeed a nailed-on ringer for him.

"What about him?" she asked, pointing at Podolski.

He looked more like Thomas Vermaelen than Thomas Vermaelen did, and that being the case was just as haunting as her husband. In the end she had a No. 5 put on the rear of the shirt and I was asked by my lad if we could go and have some dinner.

"You've had three hot dogs and a Mars bar already," I replied, however unbeknown to me Emily had sold the kids the concept of 'The Garden'.

"Covent Garden?" I said, shrugging my shoulders.

"They've never been," she replied, shrugging hers.

"It's rubbish," I said.

"But we want to go to 'The Garden'," said my daughter.

I drove as near as I could get to the lousy, stinking place whilst Emily told them about how 'The Garden' used to look, with all the vegetable wholesalers and market traders and explained that when he was alive, her father's father used to work there at the time Alfred Hitchcock made one of those 'wrong man' kind of films. Both kids were in complete awe of her. She didn't look like someone who had a granddad who flogged cabbages and carrots, however both kids hung on to her every word.

I knew a place off The Strand I could park and did so by the skin of my teeth, and we walked up Southampton Street into what Emily had termed 'The Garden'. There were still as many supporters of Manchester United kicking around this day as there were the last, but the way Emily had described it made me appreciate it that little bit more. I still thought it was crap and a place which was used to fleece tourists, but watching the kids mingle with the crowd and watching the outdoor performers was quite nice.

"Dad, can I?" was always the question with, "Yes," always the answer, however I regretted letting my son go inside the spinning chrome ball after he had parted with the three hot dogs he'd had been served up on the way over to The Emirates. It didn't deter him though.

"Dad, can I have another go?" he asked after Emily had wiped his chops.

The man sweeping the vomit up looked less than impressed.

We did the London Transport museum, which to me was about as interesting as watching both Balzac and Beckham being interviewed by Garth Crookes, yet my kids thought it to be exactly the opposite, and when I was fleeced by some market trader for two great spiders in two glass cases my kids were on the verge of ecstatic – something which was totally surpassed and blown out of space by Emily's words of, "The London Dungeon."

"Is it good M?" asked my lad.

"Awesome," she replied. "The most scariest place in the world."

She got a pair of 'Wow's and on getting in the place, only the Tall Dwarf with a circular saw in his hands could surpass it for fear factor; the bloke jumping out at us pretending to be 'Jack The Ripper', I had to say, was pretty unnerving.

It had been a great day which had turned into a great evening and after they watched Shrek for the nineteenth time I tucked them in bed.

"What's Hull like, dad?" my lad asked.

"It's nearly the seaside," I replied.

"Can we have fish and chips then?" was his next question.

"Yeah, sure," I told him.

I caught Emily at the door, and she smiled at me as I gave him a peck on the forehead.

I sat downstairs on the couch and watched on as she made us a sandwich and I had time to dwell on what had been. My lover turned lodger had not only turned my week and my house around, but me also, a fact that was emphasised next day when a goal from Aaron Ramsey and two from an uncanny look-a-like of her husband blew our cup final opponents out of the water. However that would be tomorrow and this was now.

"Are you sure you fancy going up to Hull?" I asked.

"Of course I'm sure," she smiled. "It'll be nice."

"I have to call in on the way up to drop off something if that's okay," I said.

Chapter 11
Eddie's Tales – Take 4

I got a call early Sunday morning from Sooty's other half to say he would be passing through on the way up to Hull.

"It's eight o'clock," I said, looking at the clock.

"Yeah I know – I'll be up at yours about half nine," he replied.

At exactly 9:30am a big black Italian sports car pulled outside my home and on looking out of the window I could see him inside the car, possibly checking to see that he'd got the right house.

"I think there's someone in the car with him," I said looking at Pauline, who opened the front door to greet two children running down the garden path followed by a pretty petite young woman possessing blonde hair in a long bob style, with her hair pushed back behind her ears – and which was more than complimented by her blue eyes and adorable smile.

"I hope you didn't mind us calling in?" she said. "I did ask *him* to check first."

Him – Sooty's other half – was on his mobile phone and decked out in some light beige Armani suit and a white shirt. They both had a vibrant look of elegance and youth – and one thing that was for sure was that you certainly knew at first glance that they weren't from around here.

"I'm Emily or 'M'," the girl said, firstly pecking my wife on the cheek and following suit with me.

"You must be Eddie – I've heard so much about you."

That I liked. I liked that a lot.

Although Sooty had mentioned her quite regularly, I had never seen her before. Now here she was stood in front of me, smiling and possessing a look very similar to someone both Pauline and I once knew, but I'll get to that later. I certainly wouldn't have taken her for someone who'd had an extramarital affair, was carrying another man's child and had been 'sort of' living out of a suitcase for the past week. I could certainly see it the other way around – say if a besotted admirer had left his partner and had been living out of a carrier bag in anticipation of her.

We invited them in and rather than use the sofa, Emily knelt on the floor, whilst Pauline asked the children if they had eaten breakfast – and if not did they want some toast and marmalade? That question was duly answered and they eagerly followed her into the kitchen.

"This is for you," stated the Armani-suited *other half*, as he passed me over an envelope smiling. "It sort of works out at over ten grand."

I opened the envelope to see two cheques bearing my name.

"This is far too much," I exclaimed, looking at them both.

"No it isn't," he replied. "You've done great – however there's a bit of a catch."

I shrugged my shoulders.

"Me and Sooty may want you to come back down and do some more on both programmes," he said.

"He's always talking about you," explained Emily.

"I don't know what to say," I replied, knowing that I had a bit of a lump in my throat.

"Say you'll do it," he said.

It went without saying that I would definitely do it.

"Do you want a tea or coffee?" asked Pauline.

"We'd both love one," Emily replied, smiling.

"I can always do a coffee," he nodded.

"I'm glad you liked it," I said in reference to the pieces I'd done for them.

"It's a pity there's so little footage readily available," he said whilst sitting back on the sofa and looking around. "I'm hitting loads of brick walls."

He was right; back then there was no mass media coverage of football on TV. The coverage back then consisted of finals, England's international matches and two sets of highlights on both a Saturday night and Sunday lunchtime – therefore apart from the Jimmy Hill or Brian Moore-type punditry and the odd boring fifty second interview with a player or coach, football supporters were reliant on feedback from the terraces or newspaper reports, some of which were poor to say the least.

"It's criminal that some of the best goals were lost," he explained. "To my knowledge he must have had over twenty goals disallowed."

He was right, however I'd never thought of this before – I knew I'd seen him have a couple ruled out, with 'goals' against both Rouen and Sporting Lisbon immediately springing to mind.

"I'm assuming one of them was some kind of 'thunderbolt job' that nearly took the back of the net out as the camera certainly never caught it," he said.

"Where did he have that goal disallowed?" I asked.

"Queens Park Rangers," he replied. "From what I can gather it was a twenty-five yard strike and Bobby Gould had strayed offside."

"And there's no footage?" I asked.

He shook his head. "Not yet," he said, smiling.

I'd been to Loftus Road before, although that particular game wasn't one of them.

"I'm not kidding when I say it," he replied. "This guy must have been brilliant to watch – in just about every game he played he's shooting from distance and cracking the woodwork – he hit the woodwork twice in one match against Coventry City."

"Just think what he would have been like in the right side," I replied.

I knew that was the thing that got to him. Sammy was a continental type player – astute, thoughtful and powerful but Arsenal only ever played that type of game the two seasons prior to the Double – in the English first division back then you couldn't really play that way, and all Mexico 1970 had taught us was that the best way to beat the Brazilians was to resort to ferocious tackling and aerial bombardment, something which Arsenal took heed of, therefore abandoning their pragmatic short ball style and resorting to type.

I told him that I had seen Arsenal play a very good Rangers team in the summer preceding the 1967-68 season – the season when they got to their first League Cup final.

Sammy had been described by the *Daily Record* and other Scottish media as being Arsenal's danger man – one of their so called 'Big Three' – and a 'scheming forward with great talent and a ferocious shot who had been on the verge of full England honours'.

They weren't wrong and amidst major crowd violence on the North Bank, Sammy firstly brought out a first class save from Rangers' Scandinavian goalkeeper Sorenson before he put his team 1-0 up by hammering a 20-yard drive into the net.

This was followed by an even better second goal to put Arsenal 3-0 up, and which could only be described as a blistering 30-yard strike of Brazilian proportions that swerved away from the goalkeeper smashing against the woodwork on its way in.

"That was possibly one of the best goals I had ever seen, and if it had happened now, we would have been talking about it well into next season – that is, after he'd been signed by Barcelona for fifty million."

Sammy could have easily had a hat-trick but was denied it when his volleyed shot beat the goalkeeper, only to see Scotland international Ronnie McKinnon who played in the team that beat England 3-2 at Wembley in the same year – the team that were dubbed 'The real world champions' – clear the ball off the line.

"This project is all I've been thinking about," he stated.

"He was up until half-past one this morning downloading newspaper articles," Emily smiled.

And that is when he explained an angle of how the documentary would possibly go. He explained that at the moment there was only so much footage of Sammy, however there was one match in particular which had been captured by TV cameras, and here he had continually shone.

"I watched the 1969 League Cup Final the other day," he said. "It's a strange as I'd never really watched it before."

All the 1969 League Cup Final told anyone is that in history, people only remember the result and not the real story or stories behind the result. Arsenal had beaten both Liverpool and Tottenham to get to this particular final, the latter by a bruising two-legged semi-final, which nowadays would have culminated in several red cards, only to be pitched up in the Final against third division opposition that was Swindon Town. Back then the gulf in class between the first and third division was certainly not what it is now, and that Swindon side contained several players that went on to play for very capable first division sides, such as Rod Thomas and Peter Noble. Newspapers from that time reported an influenza epidemic at Highbury, citing that it was certainly a possibility that the match wouldn't be going ahead. The club had eight players down with the flu and looking at the state of the Wembley pitch, the match certainly shouldn't have gone ahead. Nowadays there would be hell on if clubs had been forced to play their major assets on a pitch that was no better than a waterlogged turnip field. It was so bad that there were heaters spaced around the pitch to help dry out the playing surface, and the subsequent saturation of water within the soil over-topped the players' boots.

Sooty's *other half* made me smile when he stated, "There must have been hell on when Princess Margaret had to trudge through it without a pair of Wellington's."

Swindon however ought to have been unceremoniously spanked into next week by Arsenal, however a defensive mix-up early on in the first half gave Arsenal a mountain to climb and Bertie Mee justification in the fact that Ian Ure's Arsenal career was just about coming to a close, and that the young, highly-rated albeit highly-problematic Peter Shilton could be next in through Highbury's revolving doors. Bob Wilson survived the bullet, but Ure didn't and Wilson would go on to play his part in other high profile mix-ups, such as the blunders in the televised top of the table clash versus Leeds United in 1969, which was the game where Wilson's opposite number – Gary Sprake – put Bobby Gould on his back with a tasty left hook, the 1971 FA Cup semi-final versus Stoke and the 1973 FA Cup semi-final versus Sunderland; however Arsenal's continental-style defensive football, the man that he is, and his consistency during the 1970-71 Double season gave him credibility.

The 1969 League Cup Final will be remembered by Swindon Town supporters, not just for the result, but for the performances put in by their goalkeeper Peter Downsborough and their enigmatic winger Don Rogers. Nothing will be mentioned as regards any Arsenal players playing well as the result was a humiliation of the worst kind, and a humiliation which was part-manufactured by Arsenal's coach Don Howe, who certainly should have known better.

Arsenal didn't play badly – it was just one of those games where you know that all you are going to get at most is a draw. Games such as this that spring to mind are the then-mighty Leeds versus non-league Wimbledon and their wonder-keeper Dickie Guy in the FA Cup in 1975 (0-0) or against second division Sunderland and their wonder-keeper and the highly rated and uncapped Jimmy Montgomery in the FA Cup Final 1973 (0-1).

Sammy had cracked two shots from distance into the corner, which had been both very well saved by Downsborough and the *Daily Express*'s Desmond Hackett would even have you believe that he had even headed against the post, however in this instance it had been Bobby Gould. Sammy had continually picked up the ball in midfield and drove through the mud and at the packed Swindon defence whilst meticulously spraying it around the park. In one instance he picked up the ball from a throw on the left hand side of the eighteen-yard box, nutmegged a defender before cutting it back from the byline for the onrushing Radford, Graham and Bobby Gould, only to bollocks it up. Make no bones about it: Sammy deserved to be on the winning side that day and at full-time, with the scores at 1-1 courtesy of an opportunistic equaliser from the ever-enthusiastic Gould, Don Howe made his worst mistake and instead of closing the game down in extra time and going for the replay, he negated common-sense and went all out for the win. The Arsenal players, however, were literally knackered and all Howe's gung-ho tactics were offset by the quick counter-attacking of Swindon's fleet-footed winger, whom Bertie Mee had previously slighted in the press deeming him not good enough for The Arsenal, and who consequently rammed those words back down Mee's throat.

Although no one would think it – the 1969 final was a blueprint for Arsenal's future success and it wasn't just Ian Ure and Bob Wilson that were looking at the exit door; so was former captain Terry Neill, new signing Bobby Gould and winger George Armstrong, the latter of whom had delighted Highbury's fickle fans with his hard graft and trickery on either flank, which was something reminiscent of Stanley Matthews – something else that I myself had got rammed down my throat by Sooty's *other half.*

Most Arsenal supporters are blinkered and would state that this was 'never so', but it was. After flirting with Willie Morgan, who again Mee was in the press slighting as 'not being up to scratch' for The Arsenal, he opted for Hibernian's £100,000 long-haired winger Peter Marinello, who was duly ripping it up north of the border. Marinello was in, Armstrong was out. It was ironic that on Marinello's first appearance at Old Trafford – the home of George Best – that he scored a solo goal, which was very reminiscent of the man, however what was more ironic, and what the Arsenal history books never tell you, is the man that scored the winning goal for United to win 2-1 was none other than ex-Burnley winger Willie Morgan, who like Don Rogers had rammed Mee's words well and truly down his throat.

Maybe Bertie Mee should have kept his opinions to himself?

Like Sammy, Marinello was a feature of Arsenal's following European success. He was an outlet, but as Sooty's *other half* had continually said, so were the toilet doors in the khazis down at The Emirates, something that Arsenal's more recent fleet-footed winger Gervinho ought to have had his head put through after missing an open goal away against third division Bradford City (1-1).

History repeating itself? One of those games against lesser opposition where you know that all you are going to get at most is a draw?

Sammy, new purchase Marinello and Charlie George – who had 'risen from the ranks' and was newly-promoted from the reserves – were players that oozed class had had a touch of European if not South American flair and flavour about them. These should have been the future of Arsenal, although as successful as Arsenal's future was, Mee had a somewhat kamikaze approach and had eventually lost all three, each one of them certainly being capable of playing at the top of their profession for many years. As for George Armstrong and Bob Wilson, these were both nice men and 'club men' and certainly not ones to 'rock the boat'.

In life, it is strange how things work out.

The pinnacle of Arsenal's following success was, as already stated, the 3-0 win at home to Ajax in their successful European campaign. Charlie George had hit the first goal with a 25-yard strike that put Ajax on the back foot and Sammy orchestrated the game through the midfield, with Ajax's humiliation further compounded when he had made it 2-0 with a shot which was firstly saved by their outstanding keeper Gert Bals, before rifling a second attempt past him. George had made it 3-0 at the death with a penalty. The irony was that Peter Marinello, who was brilliant throughout the European campaign, was replaced at 1-0 due to injury, and failed to feature again the rest of the season, even though the following two results in Europe were a 0-1 reverse in Amsterdam and a 1-3 defeat over in the first leg of the final in Belgium.

Mee was a hard man to figure out.

Sipping at his coffee the *other half* explained that Sammy in the 1969 final had reminded him a bit of Glen Hoddle. It was a fair comparison, especially if you watch the first leg of the 1987 League Cup semi-final where Arsenal went down 0-1 to Tottenham; however, in my mind Sammy had been not only a better player, but over one thousand times the man Hoddle ever was.

"I can't give you a like-for-like example," I explained as there was only ever one of him. "But if you could imagine a cross between say David Beckham and Brian Talbot, it wouldn't be that far out."

"Beckham?" he replied with a grimace on his face whilst at the same time I noted a grin emanating from Emily's as she got up off the floor and went into the kitchen.

I explained that I meant the David Beckham circa 1998/99 and not the 'celebrity' that he became post-celebrity marriage to Victoria 'Spice'.

He may not have liked what I had said but it certainly got him thinking. Take all the glitter and razzmatazz that surrounded David Beckham and there was a lot of Sammy about him. Brian Talbot, on the other hand, was an extremely hard working football player with an exceptional demeanour who had by strange coincidence been born in the same town as Sammy, had played for the same club and in the same position, and who – like the focal point of our project – had lost two finals with Arsenal and scoring in the one they had actually won. History repeating itself?

The only difference was that Sammy could strike the ball as good as Beckham and Talbot could not, however Talbot's faultless endeavour had brought him something which Sammy had craved – four England caps. A point worth noting was that Sammy's goals per game ratio was around one in five (around 3.5 if you added the goals which had been disallowed or 1.5 if you added the times he had hit the woodwork), which was not only a lot better than Brian Talbot, it was also better than both Alan Ball and Liam Brady, both of who collected a fair percentage of their goals from the penalty spot. Beckham's was around one in 4.5, however you had to take note that his Manchester United side were a damn sight more cavalier in their approach than the Arsenal side of the mid to late '60s.

I had heard often the *other half* bollocking young Ginge when he used statistics to back up claims to his love affair with African players, which always brought a smile to my face – Alex Song and his so-called assists in particular.

Emily, decked out in a brilliant white dress, brought the two children into the room and explained the time. Her *other half* gave her a wink, and within a minute or so they were gone as Pauline and myself waved them off.

"Weren't they lovely?" she said.

She was right, they were.

"And that's the lad you were on about with all the woman trouble?"

I nodded a 'Yes'.

"He doesn't seem to be having any trouble there – she's gorgeous."

"She's also married to another man but having *his* child," I replied.

"Really?" she exclaimed.

"According to his business partner he has another girl-friend who looks exactly like her, maybe an inch taller than her – but exactly like her."

Pauline knew it was complex, as I had given her a brief summary of *his* situation, but she was totally unaware of the depth of the complexity, especially when I told her about his wife, the woman from the debt collection agency and a wife of an ITV executive who had to have a restraining order put on her.

"He seemed really nice," she said, shaking her head.

"He is really nice – that's why he's juggling around with half a dozen women – half of whom don't belong to him."

"They seem very well suited to one another," she explained.

I looked in earnest at the cheques I'd been given by him and I nodded my head. "He's a good lad – soft as a brush, but a good lad."

"I hope it works out for her," stated Pauline.

"Don't you think she looks a bit like our Dawn?" I asked.

Pauline smiled and nodded. "She does a bit."

Chapter 12
The Greek Tragedy and the Ferrets

Hull had been brilliant – a goal from Aaron Ramsey and two from a look-a-like for her husband blew our cup final opponents out of the water.

"You like it?" I'd asked, smiling over at Emily after Podolski had wrapped it all up.

I got a lovely nod and a wink back as my daughter who had been obviously bored to tears had fell asleep on her lap.

"It's so nice to see you happy," she had said.

It was so nice to be happy, and the drive back from Hull was nice as both kids slept and Emily told me more about her father's parents, who for a time had lived in Tilbury after the war, and then about her husband. It was the first time ever that I had taken notice of who she actually was.

I pulled up outside Jeanette's at around 7:30pm where I was greeted at the door by her boyfriend, who I knew hated me just as much as everyone else I'd ever pissed off.

"Do you get down to Griffin Park much?" I asked as the kids raced past me and inside with their bags to tell their mum how brilliant it had been.

He was quite literally taken aback. "Er, now and then," he replied.

"Nice one," I nodded. "I reckon they'll get a result in Milton Keynes tomorrow."

I've no idea why I said that, but I think it was something to do with having 'common ground' with someone. As I said, I never hold with the 'them and us' theory when it comes to proper football supporters. Football's a game that should bring people together and it's both simple and enjoyable, and it's only when agendas and politics are brought into it that it gets dirty.

That night I half-watched as Emily made us some food whilst half doing some things on her laptop, which I assumed was work-related, and every now and then she smiled over to me as I sat on the couch whilst taking down some more notes of things that Eddie had told me, and which needed backing up by hard facts. I had lived with Nicole and Jeanette, but I had never had a feeling that I'd felt like the way I was feeling now. I had also lived with a woman called Yasmin, which lasted about six days and which I'd prefer not to talk about; it was one of the main reasons why I tended not to want to get tied down.

Monday morning came around quickly and the World Cup 1970 editing was taking precedence, and although what we were doing was good, we were always getting sidetracked by our 'Sammy' project, which we both thought was a fantastic story and in short – a brilliant bit of journalism. However, the former of the two was going to pay us the big bucks so we had to do what we could do and I had toiled on writing the narrative, however a voice that was known was needed to relay its content, and that meant possibly biting into our budget.

Ginge was always full of bright ideas and immediately gave me a list of dozen coloured players including the list's stand-out performer – Garth Crooks, which made me smile. At the other end of his dirty dozen was Ian 'Wright, Wright, Wright'. As much as I loved Wrighty as a player – and I did

– as a pundit I despised him equally as much, as his form of punditry ruins the grace of the game.

We had loads of food for thought by the time I nipped out for a coffee to my favourite Greek coffee shop, where I was again unknowingly met by one Ms. Bracken wearing some high stilettos, a pair of two hundred quid shades and the self-same short, short skirt.

"Hiya you," she said, smiling.

I nodded and ordered my espresso and Perrier water at the counter.

"You want sandweech?" asked Fosis, who today was wearing a short sleeved and checked number, which was again unbuttoned to the navel revealing his black chest hair and crucifix.

"No – a bit heavy going for me if I'm honest," I replied. "In fact I'm still feeling the after effects of Friday's sandwich."

Now for Ms. Bracken. I walked over to the table at which she was sat and pulled out a chair.

"So," I asked. "What brings you here – again?"

"You," was her blunt and sincere answer.

Oh yeah? I thought.

"All I've thought about all weekend is you," she added.

I certainly had that effect on people and I knew Emily's husband would be thinking exactly the same, however she wanted me to have a little tootle around in the Vauxhall whilst Emily's husband just wanted to rip off my head.

It was one of those conversations where she gave the suggestions and I gave the excuses and then she offered me various permeations to overcome those excuses, and after ten minutes my head was ready for exploding. However my imminent destruction was postponed when Nicole came through the door and walked swiftly towards us. I introduced them and Nicole reminded me that they had indeed already met before.

"We've met," stated Nicole whilst she looked Ms. Bracken up and down, "I threw her out of your house, remember?"

"Do you want a drink?" I asked.

I copped a nod and asked Fosis for another espresso and within seconds I had a great Greek with a dead dog end in his mouth and shirt nearly off his back mulling around the table both collecting crockery and jockeying for any leftovers of conversation I may offer to offer him.

"I had my mother telling me that I was in Covent Garden with you on Saturday," stated Nicole. "One of her friends had told her."

This 'mistaken identity thing' is a total bitch, I thought.

"It took me nearly half an hour to convince her that it wasn't me," she added.

"How is she?" I asked.

"Like you give a shit," was Nicole's reply.

Ms. Bracken was feeling decidedly left out of the conversation so just to get her back in Nicole invited dialogue by asking, "So what's the story with you?" which was followed by, "Just watch you don't get caught on – he has a knack of getting women pregnant."

Ms. Bracken smiled. "What's to say he's not already got me pregnant?"

That was a really, really nasty barbed comment, and one which rattled my cage a bit especially as the dialogue was now in full flow – the subject matter of which was very much of me.

Nicole was brilliant in the way she had answers to every question. She had been the same with me – not that it ever did anything, because I just did what I wanted anyway. The only way Nicole could ever get to me was by restricting 'great sex', which was a bit like taking the keys to my Maserati. Unfortunately she had found out that I had another one

(Maserati) on standby, and now had enough evidence to suggest that Ms. Bracken was trying to give the keys away to her Vauxhall, which was totally in breach of the Trades Description Act as she was wrongly describing it to Nicole as it being something of a Maserati – if you understand all that?

There was no doubt about it, Nicole knew what she had, and she hit Ms. Bracken with a one-liner which hit home like a crow-bar across the teeth and which nearly had them squaring up to each other.

I had only come out for a coffee and when I relayed details of the lunch break to Sooty he literally pissed himself laughing. And then Libby phoned me, which was followed by Jeanette and then Nicole, the latter of whom apologised and started the process of angling for me to go around before she realised that I was the bastard who should do the apologising and go crawling to her.

I missed Nicole nearly as much as I didn't miss Ms. Bracken, but just to keep me on my toes I got a visit from Old Bill to tell me that they had had a word with both the Tall Dwarf and his idiot wife and that they 'weren't pressing charges'. I blew a fuse, and subsequently told them of the escapade in Charing Cross Road and about the stalking. In fact I was sick of talking about it and I showed them the door. Fucking policemen – who needs them?

The day had been a disaster and I got into an empty house around 8:30pm, which seemed strange as there had been loads of people in and out from decorators to ex-girlfriends through to policemen and stalkers. I ordered a Chinese take-away and kicked up Sky Sports and immediately got Steve McManaman spitting into the mike, therefore I trawled through the full range of the Sky package which I had been fleeced for just to find that there was nothing worth watching and ended up reverting back to McManaman talking about Liverpool being in contention for the title. Well, I assumed that was what he was on about, as between him and Phil Thompson, that was all they ever talked about. However, he couldn't talk forever.

I walked over to the breakfast bar where I was greeted by a yellow post it note which was stuck to a DVD.

'Love U. M xx' it read. It was a DVD titled 'Frenzy' by Hitchcock.

Sound, I thought.

I stuck it in the player and spent an hour and half biting my nails and worrying like hell that the murderer of those women had gone unpunished while the innocent dick head with the bad manners was going to swing. I never liked Barry Foster when he was that boring Dutch detective when I was a kid, never mind a perverted murderer who had "Loverly" as his Bruce Forsyth 'Nice to See You' catch phrase when he was ripping off their tights and pants.

Speaking of the latter, it was getting late and Emily hadn't really said were she was going, and the last thing I wanted her doing was hanging around Covent Garden with some ginger-haired psycho on the loose. Therefore I did something completely against the grain and I sent her a text.

'You OK?' I asked.

'No can U cum get me? x' she immediately replied.

'Where are U?' I asked.

'Home.'

I left Frederick Street and shot down the A201 and across Blackfriars Bridge and went through every nook and cranny I could to get to their place in Greenwich, where I came face to face with her husband who immediately bust mine with one of those Joey Barton style punches, which stated that he was anything but a coward. Again he followed through with a head stamp, but this I was a bit too quick for him and he only managed to crush my right hand, however he did follow that with a couple of decent kicks in the head. I was down but not out and as soon as I pulled my phone out and threatened to call the police he backed off.

"I want Emily outside now," I said, "Or I'm phoning the fucking police."

Emily ran outside and I immediately noticed swelling down one side of her face. I got her in the car and drove back towards North London. It had turned out that she had gone back for more personal possessions and he had called in at the same time and as a matter of course she had been thrown down a few stairs. The fact that she had started bleeding from downstairs had me worried and I pulled off down Ludgate Hill and into the nearest A&E which was at St. Batholomew's and got someone to see her, however the doctor seemed initially more concerned about me. I had some nurse looking at my head as they wheeled Emily into a room. I needed eight stitches and had a couple of bruised fingers, which I will admit were really starting to throb a bit. I got patched up within a couple of minutes and went to see Emily, who had a load of people in white coats around her, which to me appeared highly disturbing.

At that point in time I didn't know what to do so I phoned Libby, who calmed me down a bit and who also thought in her wisdom to phone Jeanette and within twenty minutes I had both of them at my side followed by Sooty, and Jeanette's bloke Paul.

"I don't know what's happening," I said. "They'll not tell me anything."

I have to say that for as much as I had pissed both women off, they showed a lot of concern for the overall situation.

"I just didn't know what to do," I said, shaking my head.

Libby, being Libby, immediately took control of the situation and found out via a nurse that Emily hadn't miscarried but just needed rest, and when the doctor eventually made his presence known she went about asking him every question imaginable about every potential outcome, was very forthright in her dialogue and was truly immense under pressure.

"So will she be alright to go home?" she snapped.

"She will be fine so long as she rests," he said before he waved his wand at me. "You – do not go to sleep, you have had a heavy blow to your head."

I didn't need a doctor to tell me that. I was there on the floor watching it happen.

All of us ended up back at Frederick Street and there to greet us was a bag of Chinese takeout, which Libby and Jeanette reheated and which was duly handed out on some plates, although neither I nor Emily really felt like eating.

I took her upstairs and put her to bed.

"Are you okay?" she asked, smiling.

That was Emily to a tee and which was something that stuck with me about her - just remember that line. 'Was I okay?' She had been thrown down a flight of stairs, but 'Was I okay?'

"Sure," I lied. However I can tell you now that I had never ever been as badly beaten as this since the last time her husband beat me up. There was something quite sinister and professional about the way he distributed pain.

"I love you so much," she said.

"I watched that DVD," I replied.

"Did you enjoy it?"

"It put me dead on edge," I replied.

She smiled.

I walked downstairs and I looked at all four of them stood around the breakfast bar eating my Chinese.

"Is she alright?" asked Jeanette.

That hit me like something you wouldn't know, and looking over at Libby the feeling multiplied.

I had been hurt that Emily had been hurt, and the fact

that they all cared made it hurt far more than a few cuts and bruises.

"Thanks," was about as much as I could say, before Libby gave me a pat on the shoulder and a smile, which in its self was worth framing.

I then reached into my bag that I had brought home from work and passed Jeanette's bloke a DVD; he looked at me and shrugged his shoulders.

"I got one of the lads from the office to upload some footage we had in our database," I said. "I was going to drop it in next Sunday."

"What is it?" he asked.

"Some footage of Brentford," I replied. "It's not much, but it's a good couple of hours."

That got me another pat on the shoulder from Libby and a kiss on the cheek from Jeanette.

The next morning I awoke a bit later than normal and I got Emily rigged up with a cup of tea, some orange juice and some bran flakes.

"Take it easy," were my words of wisdom before I left.

By the time I had got to the office I had received a nice text off Libby, an 'I love you' from Emily and a 'Cheers for the DVD' from an unknown number which I assumed was Jeanette's bloke.

All the office bar Sooty appeared concerned about the kick-in I had taken, and Ginge was hoping that my bad hand wouldn't lead to him having to do a shed load more extra work. Both the World Cup 1970 and the 'Sammy' programmes were going great and some of the footage we had found was first class.

I knocked off early and firstly went for my weekly haircut and shave from Tony the Barber then I called into the coffee shop down the side street for an espresso and Perrier, where

I was greeted by Fosis.

"Tony say about your face – what happened?" he asked, gesticulating.

I gave him a pigeon Greek explanation and he appeared concerned.

"He hurt my girlfriend," I stated. "He hurt her in the stomach."

"And this girl is wife of man, but have your baby?" he asked.

To say he reckoned not to understand much English, he wasn't half bad at understanding English when it was handed to him in the form of gossip, as I was certain that I had never told him that.

He shouted over to a man sat at the card table who I often referred to as Andreas. He was a suited man in his 60s, with a bald head and both a diamond sharp trimmed dome and a prominent nose. He regularly sat cross legged at the card table and in between playing cards and sipping coffee he read the paper and watched Sky News on TV. He was something of a character in that Fosis's other customers referred to him as *'To Eidos Illikomenos Kyrios sto Prasino Kostoumi'*, which apart from being a right mouthful had a rather minacious and threatening ring to it, especially as he possessed the look of some villain out of James Bond. Words were exchanged, and there was a bit of shouting and Andreas put his hand out for me to go over and talk to him.

"And the man did this," he said shouting, and expressing that some great horror had occurred. Fosis kicked in his two penn'orth and suddenly there was loads of shouting and all hell broke loose. I have to say that the Greeks were a rather dramatic bunch. Andreas kicked over the card table and immediately demanded satisfaction, and two old men sat on the opposite table did the same with their table. Another table in the coffee shop was upturned and chairs were being kicked all over the place as more shouting ensued. I'd only gone in for a coffee.

"You tell me the bastard who did this to you and your woman and I will slice his face open like a piece of lamb," snarled Andreas. And he wouldn't let me near either a chair or the exit door until I had scrawled his address on piece of paper.

"That is better," exclaimed Andreas. "Now sit and drink your coffee."

Andreas did a couple of clicks on his fingers and within seconds all the furniture was restored to normal and the table cloths put back on. From total aggression to the first stage of coma in less than sixty seconds.

The afternoon went unhindered at work and when I got home around 7:00pm I found Jeanette in the house with Emily.

"Is everything okay?" I asked.

Jeanette smiled and left, but before doing so I got a peck on the cheek. "She's lovely – look after her," she said.

She had soon changed her tune. She had initially advised me to give her a divorce and marry Nicole. Now she didn't want the divorce and liked Emily. Women can drive a man around the frigging twist. Emily was moving around okay but some midwife on a bike had been round and told her to take it easy.

"The police have been around," she said.

"Yeah, what did they want?" I asked.

"That woman who was hanging around on Friday – she is having a nervous breakdown – They told me to let you know."

I'd have a nervous breakdown if I'd been getting humped by the Tall Dwarf, I thought.

"Really?" I replied.

I had a bit of tea and kicked up the laptop and got Emily

at the side of me watching. I showed her a bit of what was to be part of the World Cup 1970 programme and told her that there was an angle to it, in that the manager negated the need for more younger, fitter and on form players, to stay loyal to a few of those who had won the competition in 1966.

"Loyal?" she asked.

Mmm. I didn't like that word when it was thrust at me like that.

"There's loyalty, M, and there's misguided loyalty," I replied. "And I don't think Alf Ramsey was actually misguided, just a bit deluded."

Delusion plays a big part in football nowadays. Managers like Ramsey in the past and Wenger in the present, can or have become deluded, and have in some cases picked up a touch of Hans Christian Andersen's 'The Emperor's New Clothes' syndrome, especially bearing in mind some of the stupid comments he's come out with. But so can the players, none more so than Nicklas Bendtner, who has slung out some right howlers in his self-assessment. If he would just keep his mouth shut, work hard and show a bit of humility he could have done okay, however and unfortunately for him that won't happen.

Just recently it has been football's governing authorities digging themselves into the pit of delusion, first by trying to stamp out racism, which has seen more players slinging verbal bananas at each other than at any time ever, with Manchester United's answer to the Beano's 'Plug' still adamant in his delusion that only white people can be racist.

However this new law which covers the 'Suppression of Free Speech' has meant more delusion from the top – certainly after Tommy Hitzlesperger came out of the closet to make a statement on homophobia within the game. It is strange how he has spoken about it now and not when he was playing. Since his outing however, the good old F.A and F.I.F.A have been beating the drum that it is 'just not on', and just like racism it should be stamped out. Maybe both bodies can explain why we are having the next World Cup in Qatar, a country that is totally homophobic and which considers being gay a crime. Saying that, Qatar is quite a hypocritical country in that it can flog you booze in Doha International Airport yet you cannot drink it, and that half the male population who live there act extremely gay.

I am an all men to all things kind of person and I have no problem with gays as such. On one hand I am the first to admit that good looking lesbians are brilliant, especially those on those porn sites where they wear pantyhose, and where one sort of domineers the other. In fact I pestered Nicole for ages about it before she sort of succumbed and said that she could 'probably do it with a dikey-looking bird' at a push. Libby went ballistic when I mentioned it to her.

Yet on the other hand I once saw Ronnie Kray kissing Sgt. Tony Wilton out of 'Soldier Soldier' and for as much as Gary Kemp was smirking while he did it, I still nearly threw up.

I don't know of any gays that have played for Arsenal in the time I've followed them, although there was a lot of finger pointing at Sol Campbell. I liked Sol – he was one-third of three great centre backs at the club and was as solid as a rock, but gifting two goals against West Ham and then running off to be an actress at half-time didn't up his profile too much.

He certainly didn't look gay or dress gay but some that do I suppose never get twigged. I once saw the ex-Hull City manager Phil Brown on Sky TV looking very dandy in a striped shirt and donning a pink jumper over his shoulders, along with possessing a sun tan on par with David Dickinson. I liked Phil Brown and the Premier League is worse off for not having him. He was a guy who didn't mind looking a pillock.

The delusion is that you can urge people to tolerate gays, but as with racism, you cannot make people do what they don't want, as everyone has their own opinion, be it morally right or morally wrong. Politics – like I said, it's everything that is currently wrong with the game.

I had a couple of detectives at my door at around 6:05am the next day. I was getting more police attention than Oscar Pistorius and beginning to be the talk of the street. There was certainly no need for them to bang on the front door and use a megaphone to get my attention, I was just looking for my trousers. I finally let them in and found to my delight that Emily's husband had been visited by some mad Greek with a bald head, brandishing a cut-throat, who had allegedly booted over his table.

"Do you know anything about it?" one of the coppers asked.

"No," I lied.

They didn't go into great detail and basically left after ten minutes. I just told Emily that her husband had been in some disagreement and had pointed the finger at me, leaving out the tiny details such as 'bald Greeks and cut-throats'. I thought it was absolutely great news and it put me on an upper all day long. I didn't realise that sanctioning violence could be so therapeutic and it was only when Sooty mentioned the words 'potential come back', did the grin drop off my face.

That being the case I nipped around to the coffee shop and was greeted by Andreas like his long lost son and got a hug.

"I sorted the lousy foul bastard for you," he said spitting on the floor.

He then sat back in his chair, crossed his legs and told me that I now owed him a couple of thousand euros. That seemed a strange way of doing business. Strange but effective. After hearing in great detail how they had kicked his table over, there was certainly no way I was not going to pay it. Maybe if we approached the BBC like that we might get more work off them?

I got back home at around 6:30pm and was greeted by Emily who immediately gave me some great sex, which easily made it into my top ten. I noticed two things. One – that small women are dead easy to throw around the bed, and two – that she seemed to be really appreciative that someone had stood up to her husband. Well, in my case, it was more a case of being duped out of eighteen hundred quid by some bald Greek.

We celebrated by going to a wine bar, having a meal and ending up at that place down the side street which played indie music, and where we were becoming regulars. I was really beginning to enjoy life. However, things don't always go to plan.

Next morning was really stressful, which wasn't helped by the fact the kids' schoolteacher had brought some ferrets into class and they now wanted some ferrets.

"What's a ferret?" asked Ginge.

I found it strange that he didn't know what a ferret was, so I got him a photo of one up on Google.

"Jesus, that's massive," he gasped. "It's like a big otter."

"No you prick, it's just a big photo," I replied. "They're only tiny."

"Do they bite?" he asked.

"I'm assuming so," I said.

We managed to run the first draft of the World Cup 1970 programme without narration and it looked pretty good. It had been a lot of hard work and both Ginge and Fred were integral to what we currently had, however the 'Sammy' programme we had sort of stumbled on blew it away.

"You know something," said Sooty. "This is BAFTA tackle."

He was right. It was that good.

Jeanette phoned me and a conversation regarding me getting the kids some ferrets ensued.

"I'll buy them no problem," I said. "But if I have 'em I'll be the one cleaning them out."

Jeanette's excuse was that they couldn't have them at theirs as there was no garden – as for me, I did have the space at the rear.

I knocked off early and called at the nearest pet shop, and its idiot owner tried to flog me the concept of an 'under the counter' deal which involved me giving him five hundred quid and him giving me a cobra.

"You must be joking," I replied.

I must admit, the thing looked impressive, and it did a lot of staring at me. In fact it had a bit of a look of Sooty.

"You want it?" he asked.

"Not really," I replied.

I was open to a lot of things, but I couldn't have one of them in the house. I'd have nightmares if it got out. The order of the day was ferrets and did he have any? I have to hand it to him – he was very deflective in his answers and was indeed a great salesman, and although he never admitted to not having any ferrets, he did his level best to flog me everything else in his shop and appeared heartbroken when I left. He didn't look quite as appealing, but he had a forceful nature on par with the Tall Dwarf's wife. I then wondered how she was getting along. I then thought of the Tall Dwarf, but he was the last thing I wanted to think about.

Nicole rang me as I went into the next pet shop on my list. It was one of those phone calls which kicked off sort of nice and turned really nasty when she realised what she was actually saying. She was getting particularly well-versed in these. I would have complimented her on it but I couldn't get a word in edge ways. She had heard that I had been beaten up and word had spread like wildfire that I had gone back in the middle of the night and kicked over some bloke's table. I hated gossip, especially when it was wrong and most of all when I was its subject matter. She then mentioned sex, which I could have easily done, however when I did it with her last time she was immediately on the phone to Emily.

"I really miss you," she said.

And I really missed her, however I knew once she captured me around at hers it would be dead hard to get away, and she'd end up upsetting Emily, not that Emily ever showed any upset when it came to me and other women. Then Nicole played the role of the submissive and told me the details of 'this and that', and that I could do more 'this and that' and that she'd be wearing 'this and that'. I must admit it sounded great, and a far better than getting saddled with a pair of ferrets for thirteen years.

"Thirteen years?" I replied, sort of aghast after the Indian owner of the pet shop relayed to me their potential longevity.

He then showed me a pair of white ones, which raced around the box like a pair of mongoose and which stunk rank.

"Yeah go on, wrap them up," I said.

Meanwhile Nicole was doing her damned hardest to sell me the concept of nipping over to Walthamstow and giving her one.

"You need something to put them in," said the owner.

"Stick 'em in one of those boxes," I said.

"No, a cage," he replied.

I had still got Nicole on the phone nagging me as I scrawled my address down on a piece of paper for delivery and parted with sixty quid – a fiver apiece for the mongoose and fifty quid for some shed.

The conversation was cut dead when Nicole lost her way and stated yet again, "You can't have us both, you fucking moron."

I knew that I knew that and I knew that she knew that, I just couldn't fathom out why she just wanted to call me up just to tell me that. I knew that I'd hurt her but for some reason she was just hanging on to me. I wasn't stupid enough to think it was just to have me, just more a case of Emily not having me and her making my life a misery for another thirteen years. I couldn't believe that ferrets lived thirteen years. That was as long as a dog. Sooty had a dog. Sooty also had leads and chains and things. Sooty didn't only look like that cobra, he had some weird snakelike vices as well.

I was once telling him about the Tall Dwarf's wife when we first started getting it on. She was a dirty little bitch but she used to always give me running commentary when we did it, and I have to admit, that voice of hers drove me bats. Sooty gave me something the next day which was a bit weird. It was some form of mask with a pool ball that sort of filled the mouth. I had some reservations about it, but I was up for most things so I thought *Yeah, okay, I'll give it a bash.*

'Motor-mouth' comes into the Northumberland Hotel in this really slaggy dress and she's on about a variety of boring subjects in the lift, from her mum's boyfriend to the price of jam, when I sort of broke the monotony and mentioned tying her up and putting this thing on her. She shut up for a minute and then gave me the heads-up.

"Don't you dare touch my boobs though," she had said.

Great stuff, I thought.

It took some getting on as different women have different sized heads. Libby was around six foot tall and the Tall

Dwarf's wife was a good deal shorter than that, and that being the case her head must have been a good couple of pounds lighter, so it needed some major adjustment. As soon as she put it on I felt a bit unnerved, but Sooty was right, all the talking was just garbles and it seemed a bit hard for her to breath.

"It's the lack of oxygen that gives them the buzz," Sooty had said.

She didn't look like she was buzzing and just looked a bit red in the face. I nailed the chains to the headboard and fastened her arms as wide as I could. It was interesting but if I'm honest it was doing absolutely nothing for me, and again if I'm being honest it looked a bit weird. I pulled her dress down from over her boobs, and I had to admit that these were certainly the best ever and dead real. They weren't the biggest but they were really, really good and definitely a 'ten out of ten'. She was garbling around the pool ball a bit and rattling her chains when her words in the lift came back to me – "Don't you dare touch my boobs though."

I couldn't resist and I gave them a right old mauling and then all hell broke loose. She was like some frigging ghoul ripping at the chains and growling – and then she broke the bed head to get loose and started tugging at the mask trying to rip it off. I had never seen anything as scary as that since I saw a picture of Ben Gunn in an old Robinson Crusoe book my grandma used to have. She couldn't get the mask off and ended up passing out on the floor. As for me, I got a bit panicky and I called the concierge.

"I've never been as fucking embarrassed in all my life," she snapped afterwards. "What did you want to call them for?"

It was alright her whining – I had to pay for the damage. The ferrets, including bits and pieces, arrived around

6:00pm and Emily had arrived from work ten minutes later to see me in the garden chasing two mongoose around the garden.

"Aw, aren't they cute?" she said.

"They are like frigging lightning and they bite like hell," I replied.

Emily put a couple of plasters on my fingers as I looked out of the window at the animals in the cage and expressed my reservations, thinking that the dodgy cobra from the first shop might have been a safer bet.

"The children will love them," she said, pecking me on the lips. "It was a really nice thing to do."

I rang them and told them about my new lodgers and they immediately wanted to come around and see them, and they were so insistent about it that their mum dropped them off thirty minutes later with their overnight bags, and asked if I could drop them off at school the next day. Not only had I acquired two ferrets for the next thirteen years, my wife was now dumping the kids on me through the week.

Emily made some tea whilst the kids played in the garden with their new pets and not once did they get bitten by them.

"I'm calling mine Arteta," said my daughter.

It's a damn sight quicker and a damn site nastier than Arteta, I thought.

"Mine looks like Giroud," said my son, holding it up so I could see.

He was right – it did a bit.

It had taken the kids less than an hour to move the ferrets from the garden and have them racing along the floorboards of the lounge. The place stunk of them. Emily cuddled up to me on the sofa and as I watched the kids play I thought *Life doesn't get much better than this.*

Chapter 13
Liverpool

Emily was standing at the breakfast bar in her white dress when she told me that she was carrying my baby boy. She'd had it confirmed earlier but had wanted to tell me when she saw me. I knew that she didn't want to make a big deal about it, as she felt that it put me under pressure as in the past it had been the last thing I wanted to talk about. My life had been 'The Me Show' starring 'Me', with special guest star 'Me' and co-starring 'Me' with all the other characters being general walk on – walk offs – or lay downs and then get lost.

I didn't know that Emily had been living out of a couple of carrier bags for a week after her husband had kicked her out and that her job had suffered immensely. Why? Because I didn't ask. Why? Because I didn't give two shits. I was me and that is how I was.

"Shallow and unreliable," Libby had snapped. "You do really need to grow up."

Jeanette had said more or less the same but there had been a few more nasty superlatives added when she had said it.

Emily had been camped at mine only a few weeks and my life had changed. Arsenal had also started winning again, but I think that was more to do with Aaron Ramsey being back in the side than Emily. She worked long hours and she never moaned, always seemed happy and cheerful and also possessed the most pleasant demeanour I had ever known. It was my initial thought that she would have gone elsewhere if there had been anywhere else to go, and of that I was sure. I went over and gave her a hug and got one back plus a few tears. I didn't do it often, but I put a bit of thought into what I said.

"Everything will be fine – we will all be fine," I assured her.

"Will we?" she asked, still a bit teary.

"Of course," I replied.

I was separated from Jeanette and had been for nearly twelve months, whereas she was more recently separated from her nutter husband. It was an out of the frying pan and into a fire scenario, which was basically getting away from one wanker just to move in with another.

The hospital's confirmation of the gender of the lump she was carrying and the accompanying photograph of the scan had made it very real. You have to understand this was no bullshit Richard Curtis film starring a posh and stuttering Hugh Grant who meets the ever-so-fluttery Bridget Jones and they have a whirlwind relationship and move into a mansion in Kensington and dine with the even more richer D'Arcys along with the two half-baked idiots from the Vicar of Dibley eating nut cutlets and other vegan shite, whilst talking pretentious bollocks and making it all a bit 'with it' by having someone say 'fuck'.

For a start who would want the D'Arcys as mates? My best friend is my business partner and a serial pervert whilst my other best mate has absconded bail and was on the lam over in Thailand.

I would say I sat her down with a hot cup of tea, but that wasn't me either.

"Do you fancy being taken out?" I asked.

"That would be nice," she replied.

I took her down to what she always referred to as 'The Garden' and to the crap restaurant that we had recently been to and which served a wide variety of goat's cheese and that being the case I ordered a blood red fillet steak in some poncy sauce, and as I knew I had been thoughtless before, I kicked up the baby and pram conversation.

"We don't have to talk about it if you don't want," she said.

"Yeah, we do," I replied.

And the night went swimmingly and next day I got in from my jog around 5:40am to see Emily throwing up in the bathroom.

"I'm so sorry," she said. "I thought I was done with this."

"I wouldn't worry about it," I replied, watching her wrench her guts up whilst on her on her hands and knees. "Sooty's missus is always being sick."

"Why – is she bad?"

"No, just married to Sooty," I replied.

I knew Emily had said that she was due at some creditors meeting or something in Stevenage that morning, however from where I was stood, I would have certainly given that a miss.

I nipped back downstairs and kicked up the percolator and nipped outside to let the ferrets have a run and heard the noise of the traffic. North London in spring is something else. It was great living back in a house. Back inside, I fired up the laptop and checked out some more archives on Dropbox that I had been sent by Ginge whilst I poured two coffees. Emily came into the kitchen as white as a sheet and I told her as much.

"I think I've probably been overdoing it a bit," she said.

"That doctor did tell you to rest," I replied, sipping at my coffee.

However that was certainly not what it was and I didn't find out until around 2:50pm as I was leaving for the coffee shop what it really was.

I received a text which read, 'Gone to my parents for a bit – need time to think x.'

A couple of weeks ago I would have thought nothing of it, and would have probably just rang up Nicole and then see how it panned out. I mentioned it to Sooty and he told me to give Libby a shout so I rang her over at her office and told her the scenario, which was met with a 'What had I done?' to which I innocently replied, "Nothing."

"Everything was good as gold this morning," I exclaimed further.

"Are you sure?" she asked.

"Of course I'm sure – I think?"

"Do you want her?" Libby asked.

"Of course I do," I replied.

"Then go and get her."

It was sound advice, but there was a problem. I knew I'd heard her mention a couple of times that she was from up north, but I didn't know where.

"I've just been thinking," I said, shaking my head and looking over at Sooty. "I know absolutely nothing about her."

"What's her surname?" he asked.

I didn't know. I didn't even know her name and I'd been seeing her at least once or twice a week for around five months.

"Do what you generally do," Sooty said.

I gave him a shrug of my shoulders.

"Remember that receptionist you were seeing?"

"Which one?" I asked, as he was being rather vague as I had known quite a few.

"That one who worked on Bayswater Road," he added.

Again, he was being vague.

"She was foreign."

"Ninety-nine percent of receptionists in London are foreign," I said.

"You both came over to ours when Libby had done that dinner – the guy from ESPN," he said sort of deep in thought. "Yeah, and you and her stayed over and Libby had to tell you both to be quiet."

I smiled to myself. "Yeah, I remember that."

"Well look how you got to find out everything about her," Sooty said. "You knew nothing about her at the start."

I had completely forgotten about her.

"It was the same with the Tall Dwarf's wife," he said.

"Don't mention the Tall Dwarf or his wife," I said. "I've been having nightmares about them both."

It was true. He had started to become extremely prominent in my dreams, which was a bit unnerving. The other night I had him doing Emily from behind on one of those four poster beds – and she actually liked it, whilst me and Ginge were checking under the sink to see if we could find some dishwasher tablets.

"You really need to see someone," Sooty had said when I told him.

He was right. I hadn't even got a dishwasher.

"So?" he asked.

"Katrin," I said, nodding.

"That's her," he said. "Do what you did when you wanted to find out about her – you mimicked that bus journey – at least ten times to my knowledge – harangued staff in every office and hotel around the bus stop near to where she got off and left no stone unturned."

If I'm being honest, it sounded a bit creepy when he said it like that.

I set about checking with Zoopla, which is a sort of property guide, and as soon as I got the proper address along with the purchase date and price of purchase I paid the £4 and downloaded the land registry file. The property was mortgaged to a Mark Hubert Smith and an Emily Ann Smith, with a purchase date of June 2006 – the purchase price paid was £357,000 and the mortgage itself had been secured by the Halifax Building Society.

He certainly didn't strike me as someone with a middle name of Hubert and it had to be some relative's name he'd been saddled with. There was no way I'd call my kid Hubert. Everybody would laugh at him. Mind you, names nowadays are both stupid and meaningless. You can't beat Dave or David – a good old bible name. I wanted to call ours Dave, but it reminded Jeanette of the fat plumber we had that took eight weeks to fit our bathroom, five of which he spent talking on his mobile phone, with another two working on other people's bathrooms. I think he actually spent a total of nine hours at our house but billed us for around three thousand. I told the fat bastard go bollocks and we sort of split the difference, albeit heavily in his favour, and Jeanette told him never to darken our doors again.

The surname 'Smith' was always a crap name to find as well as there are millions of them.

Sooty had been doing a bit of 'backgrounding' of his family tree and had just set up an account with the www. genesreunited.co.uk website. He had got as far as his grandparents and stopped. It was hardly a case of him finding out that he was an unwanted offspring in a Tesco's bag dumped outside the Town Hall, just that his granddad wasn't his real granddad. I kidded him on that the guy who looked like Clarke Gable who fiddled around with his genitals when he was a kid wasn't his real granddad and that it was some mean stranger who had killed his real granddad to steal his grandma's jewels – well, that's what I told their kids. Libby went ape shit.

I jumped on the website and logged in Sooty's account details and searched for some Mark Hubert Smith who had married some Emily Ann and narrowed it down to the year 2006 with a -/+10 years difference to see what came back. There were, if I'm honest, quite a few, not so much Mark Hubert but Mark 'H'. Even the website thought the name Hubert too stupid to list, however one stood out – maiden name 'Orr' married in 2002. So I checked it out. Emily Ann Orr, born April 1982 – Wallasey. She was a Scouser? She didn't sound like a Scouser. Mind you, I'm from South Yorkshire and I don't wear a flat cap.

I did a bit more background checking and then downloaded a copy of her marriage certificate from one of these governmental websites. Emily Ann Orr – Spinster – Occupation – Teacher – aged 20 – Mark Hubert Smith – Bachelor – Occupation – Bodyguard – aged 22.

That really, really pissed me off. I knew nobody normal could hit anybody like that, however I had things more pressing. Emily's parents were a Michael and Sylvia Orr. Piece of piss. I hit the electoral roll and found them in Birkenhead.

"Sooty – I'm out of here," I said.

The drive up into the north west was a bit of a non-event, and all it did was give my mind time to wander even more, especially when I was on the M6 either driving at 20mph or stood in traffic. Him being a big brutal bodyguard was a bit unfair. Well, not a bit unfair, very unfair. I drove up outside the address at around 6:45pm. It was a standard semi-detached house in the suburbs. I just hoped Jimmy Tarbuck wasn't in there. I got out of the car and walked down the drive and knocked on the front door to be greeted by some sullen looking chav wearing a beanie hat, which immediately had me thinking that I had gone to the wrong house.

"Yeah?" he said.

"Is Emily in?" I asked.

He looked me up and down a few times before acknowledging my request then yelled, "M, there's somebody at the door for you!"

To make things a bit more interesting, a girl came to the door and I began panicking like hell – mainly due to the fact that she only looked about twelve. This was what I meant by delusion – you think that you are right because everything you are thinking points to the thing to tell you it is right. But it is your thought only, and sometimes in life we can't see the wood for the trees or what is staring you straight in the face, which in this instance, was certainly not Emily – and the fact that the little girl was smiling at me sent a shiver down my spine.

However, the really good news was that she wasn't an Emily at all, according to the older woman who was now stood in the door, but a Lucy. The older woman intrigued me as she certainly seemed to know who I was, and asked me to come in. It was quite a small house for a lot of people to be in and as I entered the lounge I saw Emily stood in a dress that I hadn't seen her in before, first smiling and then looking a bit tearful. I could understand the first bit, but not the second. All the same, she looked great.

"Do you want a cup of tea?" asked the older woman, who was definitely a stone wall Scouser.

"Sure," I replied.

She then looked at the chav and the twelve year old and told them to leave us on our own before asking me how I liked my tea. I didn't – I hated the stuff, but I was just being polite.

"White with sugar," I replied.

"No, he doesn't mam – he hates tea," Emily said. "Make him a coffee – strong – milk and no sugar."

Thank god for that, I thought.

"What are you doing here?" she asked, still with tears in her eyes.

"I was just passing by," I lied. "So I thought I'd drop in."

She smiled.

"It's miles up here," I said looking around. "I never knew you were a Scouser."

"Don't say that to my mam," she replied smiling and wiping her eyes. "She'll go mad."

"Would your mam mind if I brought the ferrets in?" I asked.

"Stop being silly," she smiled, before asking who was looking after them.

"Sooty said he'd call around and sling them a chicken in," I said, looking further around at the surroundings I was now sat in and at the young girl peering around the door at me.

"How did you find me?" she asked.

I gave her a nonchalant shrug of my shoulders, not wanting to give away my trade secrets when it came to stalking women, and deflected her question with one of my own.

"Why did you leave?" I asked.

I wish I hadn't asked that as she started crying, which made me dead edgy as her mum came in and gave me my coffee, which I firstly thought she was going to chuck all over me. I did thank her for it, though.

"I'm so glad you came," she said, wiping her eyes. "Really I am."

"I can see how happy you are," I said.

"No, I really am," she said.

Then her mum came back in and did a bit of pacing about before telling both myself and Emily to sit down, and we did so on the sofa, whilst her mum sat opposite. I would say it was very cosy, but it was quite the opposite and was a bit intimidating if I was being honest. I'd not taken a proper bollocking off someone's mother since I was, like, seventeen, and that's when she had come back from the pub early to find me naked in the kitchen washing baby oil out of my eyes whilst her fifteen year old daughter was sat on the rug in the other room watching 'The Fall Guy' in only a pair of stockings – I'd told her not to squirt the stuff at me.

Anyway to sort of try and offset what was about to come, I sipped at my coffee and mentioned the weather twice and a big ship that I saw on the River Mersey as I came out of the tunnel. Her mum, however, came over as quite a straight talking lady and was very matter-of-fact in her delivery, with her opening dialogue being, "Has she told you?"

"Has she told me what?" I asked, shrugging my shoulders. "What, about the baby?"

Well that was fucking that – Emily had said absolutely nothing whatsoever about the baby, and suddenly I had a room full of Scousers breathing down my neck. I had no idea where they had all come from. It was like the all the cast of 'Bread' had descended on me, and her dad did indeed look very much like Jimmy Tarbuck. Much lighter hair, but like Jimmy Tarbuck all the same.

"'You've not told them?" I asked.

She shook her head, "No, not yet."

"Well I think they've got the gist of it now," I replied, looking at all their faces.

"It's a boy," I said rather proud. "She's got a photo of the scan."

"Is it that bastard's or his," asked the father, not really being clear about who 'that bastard' or the 'his' actually were.

"Hold on a minute," I said. "I'm here, ask me."

That was when Emily threaded her arm through mine and held my hand.

There was loads of talking and absolutely none of it I could understand. They talked really, really fast.

As it transpired I was 'his' and her husband was the 'bastard'.

"My dad hates him," she said.

"Sound – join the club," I said, pointing to the stitches on my head which had everyone peering at them, which was nearly as unnerving as the actual beating I took to get them.

"And she's pregnant as well?" stated the father.

I looked at Emily and she sort of looked at me a bit and then at the floor. I could understand her being pregnant may not be at their top of their 'most wanted' list, but it wasn't as though she was fifteen.

"And she's just been finished from her job," he said.

"So what? She's with me," I innocently replied, which brought a squeeze of my hand from Emily and loads of disconcerted looks from the rest of the family.

From what I could gather – and I'm certainly no professional – it appeared that everything had come on top all at once – the affair – the baby – the separation – being homeless – the uncertainty with me, with her only independence being – her job – a job which had now been taken away from her. This was possibly the 'straw that 'broke the camel's back'. To be honest, it was a damn good guess, because that is exactly what happened – the firm Emily freelanced for had gone into administration.

"You've got kids, haven't you?" asked her father.

"Yeah – what about 'em?" I replied.

"So you have to support them," he said.

"And?" I asked, shrugging my shoulders and not knowing where the hell he was coming from.

"And you've got two houses and a family to keep and that big car my lad says that you've come up here in," he added. "And now you are saying that you've gone and got my daughter pregnant?"

"What are we talking about?" I asked, shrugging my

shoulders. "Money?"

"Yes, lad," said her dad. "Money – that's a lot of outlay when she's not got a job."

This was like some scene out of 'When the Boat Comes In' and I didn't like being assessed – especially from people who obviously knew a lot more about me than I did of them.

"What's he on about, Emily?" I asked.

"He's not meaning to sound offensive, he's just being concerned," she said, looking at me and then giving me another squeeze of my hand.

I wanted to get out of there and get out of there fast, but I looked at all the dozen people looking down or over at me, all of who possessed quite concerned looking faces.

Emily was their daughter, sister or some other relation or family friend and they didn't want to see her hurt any further, and looking at what was essentially a superficial bloke in some ripped-off Savile Row suit and white shirt who was sat beside her, I knew didn't really fill them with much confidence. These were obviously real people. People who held a genuine concern for a loved one.

"Your daughter is perfect – and I love her a lot," I said.

Wow, I thought after I had said it. I didn't know who was more shocked at that comment – me or Emily – nevertheless it broke the ice and the mother started crying, which sort of set Emily off and a couple of her aunties.

Eventually things calmed down and I was left on my own with her at sort of regular ninety second intervals, while we talked. I began to feel like King Kong in my dad's bullshit version of his 'King Kong' story when Tarzan captures him and puts him in a cage and takes him to New York – then this woman who looked like the old biddy in the 'Giles' cartoon starts poking the big monkey with her umbrella and saying, "Look at him, Look at him – throw a lump of muck at him," before he breaks free, rips her head off and eats her. I had more dints in me from umbrellas and had never shaken as many people's hands as this ever. I really did think the mother had been selling tickets.

As for Emily, not once did she move from my side and every now and then I got the lovely smile which I saw in both her mum and her younger sister.

I mentioned leaving around 9:30pm as it was a long drive back, but her and her mother insisted I stay; however there was no way on earth that I was going to get to sleep with Emily as she would be 'top and tailing' with her sister, so it was either a case of getting slung in with the chav or kipping on the sofa. I therefore elected on the latter and I ended up underneath a quilt with Emily, who was wearing my 1971 long-sleeved Arsenal shirt that she had packed.

We talked into the night and she offered me a 'special love' at least three times, but I declined, as it was a small house, and certainly too small to for me to take the Maserati for a spin.

The next morning I had a wash and borrowed Emily's toothbrush to clean my teeth whilst being monitored firstly by Emily's mum and then by her little sister.

We had sort of a big family breakfast which I had not seen for a long time, and I picked up on some conversation, this time regarding the chav – who I knew by now was Emily's younger brother. Apart from him being a "little bleeder," as his both his mum and dad put it, he had got in with the wrong crowd, and had been driving his parents crackers.

"So what do you do?" her father asked me whilst heavily salting his poached eggs on toast. "My lass says you have a job at King's Cross."

She had made me sound like some bloke on a Platform 8 with a whistle, so I had to put that right. "I'm a partner in some media business down the road from the station," I said. "I don't actually work in it."

"Advertising?" asked the mother.

"No, we do mainly football programmes for TV," I replied.

Bang. That got their attention.

"And there's money in this?" asked her father.

"A bit," I replied, not wishing to boast too much.

"So how much?" he asked.

What was this thing about her father and money? Again with the money? It appeared that her dad loved the stuff.

"I'm ticking over at between forty-two and forty-eight this year," I said.

"Forty eight grand a year's alright up this way, but I bet it doesn't go far down there," he replied.

"A year?" I replied. "That's what I earn in a month."

You could have heard a pin drop.

"I'm expecting a dividend this year," I said, nonchalantly chewing at my toast. "I'm hoping it will pay off all my credit cards, so I should be alright if that's what's worrying you."

"So you're rich?" asked Emily's sister.

"Not as rich as Sooty – he's dead rich, mind you he's a right tight git. He puts a brick in the cistern and he only lets his wife and kids have one bath a week so as not to use water," I said. "He sends the wife and kids out stealing while he sits up at night counting his money under a candle."

I knew the little girl would be impressed by this.

"You fibber," said Emily, slithering up to me and taking half my chair and toast. "Don't believe him – Tim and Libby are lovely."

"Who's Sooty?" asked Emily's sister.

"Tim Sutton – he's my business partner," I replied. "I've thought about murdering him and stealing his half of the business, but I'd have nobody to look after the ferrets."

"You have ferrets?" asked the sister.

"Two," I replied. "If things get a bit tight we can skin them and sell their fur."

"Stop it," smiled Emily.

"Have you done anything we've seen?" asked the chav, which were the first words I had actually heard him say since I'd met him on the doorstep.

"Probably," I replied. "We've got a few jobs on at the minute – one's a job for Sky on the World Cup and the other is a bit more journalistic and about a football player from the mid-'60s," I explained.

"Who, Bobby Charlton?" asked her father.

"Definitely not Bobby Charlton," I smiled.

"Who is it then?" he asked. "George Best?"

"Sammy," said Emily. "He played for Arsenal and was overlooked for Mexico in 1970 and helped give Arsenal their first trophy for eighteen years and was then hounded out of the club by a section of supporters who didn't really understand football."

Wow. I was impressed. She had listened and understood everything I had said and was now relaying it to her family.

"He was a bit like David Beckham," she added.

"Does anyone ever tell you that you look like David Beckham?" asked the younger sister.

"No, never," I lied. "I hate David Beckham."

"I've never heard of him," said the chav.

"He was a good player," said her father. "Not as good as Bobby Charlton, but a good player all the same."

"Some players are good in their time," I said. "But some players are that good they get lost in their time – and Sammy was one of those."

"Do you know much about football, then?" asked the chav.

"It's my life," I replied.

"He watches it all the time," said Emily. "He took me to The Emirates and then we watched Arsenal up in Hull."

"You never told me that," said the chav.

"You never told me either," added her father.

"I don't get to every match," I stated. "But I make sure I see them all."

"So you're an Arsenal supporter," the father asked.

"It's a frustrating business," I said. "I've contemplated suicide at least four times in the last ten years, but it's the hope that stops you. It must be a similar feeling if you follow Liverpool or Everton."

"My dad follows Tranmere," stated the chav.

"Your dad's a proper supporter then," I said. "My ex-wife's bloke's the same – he follows Brentford."

We all sat around eating our poached eggs and toast talking. If I am being honest it was quite nice and they were a truly nice set of people.

"Tranmere once beat Arsenal," I said trying talk as Emily wiped egg from my face. "We lost one-nil at home in a League Cup match – Eddie Loyden scored."

The dad nodded and smiled. "So you do know your football," he said.

"We had Mancini playing," I said. "Apart from him we put a decent side out."

"Who's Mancini?" asked the chav.

"A bald bloke we bought from QPR – he looked a bit like Olive's Arthur in 'On the Buses'."

That brought a laugh from the old man.

"The thing is, with Arsenal, they have always struggled to buy good players."

"Suarez is good," added the father.

"Yeah and we didn't get him as well," I replied. "Suarez isn't just good, he's world class – there's a difference, something Arsenal don't seem to realise – he makes a nil–nil become a one-nil."

"He can talk about football all day," said Emily, smiling.

I helped Emily with the pots and we talked and talked. I had never met anyone like her and she had a great family, even though the twelve year old sister was constantly in my glare and tracking me like the Tall Dwarf.

"She says you're fit," Emily smiled.

"Am I?" I asked.

"You know you are," she replied.

That was cool – I got a kiss.

I left Birkenhead around 11:30am and half of the street waved me off in the process.

Sometimes it was great being me.

Chapter 14
Dick Whittington

When your life seems to be going great there is always a few bumps in the road to try and knock you off course; mine came from Emily who phoned me from Birkenhead a few days later. It appeared I had impressed the chav, or her younger brother rather, that much he had come down to have a look and to possibly seek his fortune. I got Ginge to nip out and pick up young Dick Whittington from outside Euston Station and fetch him over to the office. I told Emily to tell her parents not to worry and that I'd look after him, which when I told Emily certainly didn't ease either her or their worry.

When he arrived he appeared a bit sheepish in how he'd come down, which to me was water off a duck's back. He was a bit sullen, but he was sixteen. I remembered me being sixteen and I was the same. Sooty was even worse and wanted to beat everyone up, including me. But then again he was a Leeds United supporter.

"You okay, young 'un?" I asked.

I got a nod back and I introduced him to my teamsters. "You've met Ginge, that's Fred Nerk and Abi and the one the phone is Faranha – I think Sooty's in his office either watching Leeds or having a wank – or both if I know Sooty."

I had to break the ice.

I took him into my office and got him brought a cup of tea and some biscuits.

"So?" I asked. "What are you wanting to do – your mum and dad are a bit worried – and your sister is, especially now she knows that you're with me."

"You made everything sound so good," he replied.

"Life's as good as you want to make it," I said. "Or as bad as you want to."

"What's it like?" he asked.

"What's what like?"

"Being you."

"Crap at times – I've been beat up twice by your extremely big brother-in-law, stalked by a load of women and attacked by an oversized midget and had the police around at my house suggesting that I'm an internet fraudster from Russia – and that's only in the past few weeks."

He smiled, and believe me that was the first time. And I immediately saw his big sister in him.

"Stay down for a few days – we'll have a good time," I said.

That smile ignited into a, "Really?"

"Sure."

I phoned Emily and she passed me onto her parents. "Don't worry, I'll look after him."

On hearing that I had got a sixteen-year old protegeé, I firstly had Libby on the phone followed by Jeanette, both of who gave me the third degree and gave me all the frigging the dos and do nots with a damn sight more of the latter than the former.

He was a good kid – Stuart, they called him. Initially he sat and watched as we did a bit more editing on the 1970 World Cup but as Ginge told him what he was doing he got quite interested. "You follow a team?" asked Ginge.

"Manchester United – sort of," he replied.

They get everywhere.

He took to Ginge as he explained everything that he was doing in triplicate and even the generally bolshy Freddy spoke in detail. I knocked off around 4:30pm and we walked down Euston Road and to the house.

"Is this yours?" he gasped as I put the key in the door.

"You should see Sooty's," I said. "His is massive."

The kid was absolutely gobsmacked and in complete awe of the surroundings he was now in.

"Chuck your bag down get a wash or whatever and I'll take you out for some tea."

He did exactly that and spent half an hour in the bathroom while I relayed the afternoon's events to Emily, who in turn relayed them to her parents.

"I think Lucy and my mum want to come down," she joked.

It was nice to feel wanted.

I put on the TV and watched a bit of Sky Sports on TV in between letting the ferrets out for a run and getting bitten by Giroud, whilst also noticing a pungent aroma emanating from the bathroom window that I knew only too well.

When he came downstairs and into the kitchen I gave him a bit of a glare.

"I aren't your mum or dad," I said. "But I don't want you smoking any of that shit either in my house or in front of me."

He said nothing.

"It's a wanker's game," I said.

He still said nothing.

"I owe it to your parents and your Emily to tell you that," I said. "But as far as I'm concerned it's the end of the subject."

It wasn't a case of getting off on the wrong foot, more getting him to stand on both his. I hated drugs, including the cheap nasty crap he had been smoking. I'd had mates on it in the past. The stuff makes you lazy and paranoid.

I said no more and we jumped on a tube and I took him down to Brick Lane and treat him to a curry – a crap one if I'm honest – before taking him around the corner and into the Blind Beggar pub where I illegally bought him a beer – well, a small bottle of Becks L.A really.

"Don't you drink?" he asked.

"Sure," I replied as I sipped at my pint of soda water. "I'll have a few wines, but as I've got older beer tends to blow me up."

"Is this your regular?" he asked.

I shook my head. "This is where Ronnie Kray shot George Cornell through the head – however nowadays there aren't many original East Londoners in Bethnal Green and Whitechapel, just loads of Manchester United fans."

I received a phone call from Jeanette asking how I was getting on, negating to tell her that I was in the most infamous pub in London and getting my girlfriend's sixteen year-old kid brother intoxicated on stuff that looked like beer, and then from my kids who firstly inquired about their ferrets, secondly about their mate M and then about the kid at their dad's house.

"It's Emily's younger brother," I said. "He's come down to London to have a new leg fitted."

"Dad, you're fibbing," said my daughter.

"I aren't," I replied. "Wayne Rooney stole his."

I always made Rooney the villain.

"How old are they?" asked Stuart, sipping from his bottle.

"The boy's five and the girl's six," I said.

"What are you and our M going to call your baby," he asked.

"I might think about calling him after you if you impress

me enough."

"Sorry," he replied.

"What for?" I asked.

He shrugged his shoulders. "Smoking weed."

"I told you, I aren't your mum and dad," I replied. "Your mum and dad love you – I'm just the guy you met the other day who's been seeing your sister."

"They do my head in," he replied.

"Who, your mum and dad?"

He nodded.

"Do they belt you?" I asked.

"No," he replied looking at me, sort of more in shock than anything else.

"Mine did – well, my mother."

Now that got his interest.

"I couldn't wait to leave home, and every girl that I've ever been with I've treat like shit, including my wife and mother of my kids and if I'm honest your sister," I said. "You want to talk about shit that does your head in – then I'm your man."

"But your wife's just phoned you," he said.

I nodded. "She might still love me, but she certainly doesn't like me," I smiled. "I made her life a misery."

"Did you leave her for our M?" he asked.

"No – she threw me out after about twenty others, including one that I had on the go who looks exactly like your sister," I said.

"Twenty?"

"That's a rough figure," I said. "There may be one or two either side of that number."

"God, that's a lot," he replied.

Mmm. Maybe I shouldn't have told him that? I could be a total gob shite at times – and just as I was about ready to tell about my week in Thailand with Bondy.

"Sex can be meaningless," I said. "But sometimes – when you want someone and love someone, it's everything."

I had really got this kid's attention.

"Is it that good?"

I nodded. "It's definitely that good."

We finished the drink, caught the tube and made our way over to Clerkenwell where I introduced him to my wife, my kids – and Paul the Brentford fan. I had a good forty-five minutes with them and a cup of coffee before we left, and whilst waiting in Farringdon tube station he asked, "Your wife's like a model – why did you leave her?"

"I told you – she threw me out," I replied.

"I wouldn't have messed around if I'd have had a wife like that."

I listened to him and smiled.

"And now you're with our M?" he said, shaking his head.

"What's that supposed to mean?" I asked, smiling.

He just gave a shrug of his shoulders.

"Your Emily's your sister, so I don't suppose you see her like I do," I replied. "But believe me when I tell you – your sister is as pretty a woman as you can get."

"Do all your girlfriends look like that?"

"Look like what?" I asked, smiling.

"Are they all good looking?"

I then educated him about my very strict 'No Dogs Policy' and they all have to fit within a certain blueprint – less than 5'4, have great legs and small feet and weigh nothing above 125lbs.

"I'm a shallow bastard – but those are my general guide-lines," I said. "I have been known let the odd one through the turnstile who doesn't fall within that criteria, although she'd either have to be top rank or me pissed."

He looked at me in awe. "It's okay for you though."

"Me?" I asked as we jumped on the tube.

"Yeah, look at you – you look great."

"Don't be getting gay on me," I laughed.

"I'm not."

"Good," I replied.

I watched him as he pondered deep in thought so I gave him a bit of advice, whether he needed it or not. "Get shut of that daft hat you're wearing, get a proper haircut and a shave, get some clothes that actually fit you – and never ever wear trainers outside of going to a gym."

He looked at me.

"Even the ugly fuckers can get away with being ugly if they dress okay," I said. "You're one up on them in that you aren't ugly."

He liked that.

We got in and I put the TV on and made a few phone calls. As I thought, Sooty wanted Eddie back down in London to do the narration on both programmes. I couldn't fault that as he knew what he was talking about and we had some great footage of him talking already. It was just a case of stringing it all together. I've said it before – it might sound amateurish, but it was anything but.

I rang Emily who was watching TV with her folks and I made sure I spoke whilst her younger brother could hear me, as I hated whispered comments – especially when they were about me.

"I love you, yer know," she said.

"I was sure I heard a Scouse twang there," I said smiling.

"It was not," she replied.

I got up about 5:30am next day and did my morning jog, stuck the percolator on, let out the ferrets and copped a shower.

"Are you out of bed?" I asked.

"What time is it?" he asked.

"Seven."

He dragged his carcass out of bed and came downstairs to see me suited up and eating toast and watching Sky Sports on TV.

"What time did you get up?" he asked.

"Early. Drink your drink, eat your toast, shower and brush your teeth – I've got like a million things to do."

"Can't I just chill here?" he asked.

"You can do that up in Liverpool," I said pointing at him with my toast. "You're in the capital now – act like you're in it."

The first port of call was the office to see how we were and to check my mail. The second port of call was to get the chav parted from the hat and get him a haircut, which wasn't as easy as it sounded. Tony the Barber eventually did a sound job and gave a clean shave with a cut throat razor nearly slitting his throat in the process.

"Sit still you stupid she-et," he said as Stuart kept on wanting to talk to me whilst I was reading the paper.

"Does it look okay?" he kept on asking me.

"Sweet," I replied. "Just sit still or he'll have your ear off."

I took him into one of those trendy teenager shops that flog cheap name-branded clothing along with shoes not too far from King's Cross, which a lot of the football lads use.

"If you want to see other lads your age who dress good, then get to a home game at The Emirates," I told him.

"I like this," he'd say

"It's shit," I'd reply.

He pranced around a bit and eventually picked out some clothes, which if I'm honest looked alright. The downside was the shoes. Why did every youth think it great to wear white trainers?

"Stick to plain colours and never put anything white on your feet," I said. "Put those fuckers on and you'll look like 'cousin Eddie'."

"Who's he?"

"Some cousin of Chevy Chase's wife who has shit taste like you," I smiled.

He ended up picking a couple of pairs of shoes and put them on.

"Fasten the friggin' laces or you'll ruin both the shoes and your ankles," I said.

"What do you reckon?" he said, looking at me rather proud.

"I think if your mum sees you she'll burst out crying, kid," I replied. "You look the dog's bollocks."

He started welling up, and that I couldn't have, so I got him out of there and I introduced him to the Greek coffee shop I used, where today Fosis had the same dead dog end in the corner of his mouth, and was dressed in a slightly fetching blue pinstriped number which was again opened to the naval and which made him look like a Greek butcher.

"The woman with very short skirt been looking here for you – I tell her to 'piece off' because you not here," he said whilst making an espresso.

"Yeah, which one?" I asked, the words of which immediately impressed my stylish young counterpart.

"The one with the big tits," he replied gesticulating an exaggerated larger bosom, which I have to say impressed the kid even more.

"Believe me, Stu," I said shaking my head. "No woman has boobs that big."

It was a fairly brief explanation and if I'm honest was a bit rangy, although I assumed that he meant Ms. Brackley. He didn't.

"Is that our M at the window?" asked Stuart as we sat at the table, me sipping an espresso and him a Coke.

I turned around. "It looks like your sister, kid – but it's not," I said. "Believe me."

Nicole walked in wearing a short dress and backless shoes and immediately had 'my lad' on tenterhooks, and a "Wow!" was all he could say.

"'Wow' how much she looks like your sister or 'Wow' as in how good she looks," I asked.

"Just 'Wow'," he replied.

"I've been texting you," she said as she walked up to the table before asking, "Who's this?"

"He's a new lad we're training up," I lied.

"So?" she asked. "Where have you been?"

"Liverpool mainly," I replied.

"And didn't you have the courtesy to text me back?" she said.

"Stuart, this is Nicole," I said. "Nicole, this is Stuart."

"Oh, hello," she said as she sat down.

In between drooling he managed to nod a, "Hello," before going bright red in the face.

"So what's happening?" she asked. "A couple of girls from the office are on about going to Indonesia and they have asked me to go."

"So?" I replied, not really knowing where she was coming from.

"Should I book it or not – I mean, what's happening?"

"What, with us?" I asked.

She nodded.

"Nicole, I've had this lad's sister living with me for the last two weeks – and she's having my baby," I said, which if I'm honest had every Greek in the establishment looking over at me, including the psychotic Andreas, who was sat cross legged and nonchalantly sipping at his coffee whilst half reading his paper and I dare say contemplating booting over another table.

"So you are with her?" she asked.

"You knew that the other day when I told you," I replied.

"And that's her brother?" she asked.

"Leave him out of it, he's just a kid," I said.

"He doesn't look a kid," she said.

"Believe me, he did half an hour ago."

"I really loved you, you know," she said. "I really loved you."

"I know," I replied.

She sat there in thought as Stuart didn't really know what to do with himself.

"Do you want me to go?" she asked.

This was a conversation which was going nowhere and after clutching at a few straws she left.

"I prefer you not tell your Emily about that," I said.

"Doesn't she know about her?" he asked.

"She knows about her," I replied. "I just don't want her hurt anymore."

"Who is she?" he asked, whispering.

"It's pointless whispering in here," I replied. "Fosis has tape recorders under every table. This lot in here know more about me than I do."

"So who is she?"

"My wife threw me out and I lived with her for a few months. I started seeing your sister and when she found out she threw me out. At a similar time to that your brother-in-law threw your Emily out."

It sounded complicated at first, but the more I mentioned it, the more it made sense. It was weird.

"The bright spot about that is that you've found out a couple of things," I said. "One – that your sister is actually drop dead gorgeous and two – that you don't look like some greasy little oik in a 'Benny hat'."

He smiled. "They're called Beanie hats."

"Believe me kid, they're 'Benny hats'."

We drank up and when I got in the office everyone sort of sat back and looked at the kid.

"See, what did I tell you?" I said. "Clean your teeth and everyone wants to be your mate."

Later that evening I had to pick up a van from a seedy little place off Crinan Street, not too far from the station itself. I hated parking up around this area as drugs and prostitution was, if I'm honest, a bit rife. The idea was to borrow a van to clear out Bondy's flat of all my gear, however the kid I knew was nowhere around.

"What's this place?" asked Stuart.

I never really gave him an answer, and fired up the car and left and made a couple of phone calls, none of which got me the van. The place however was dimly lit and a mixture of leaking car repair garages and dodgy warehouses, some of which were frequented by eastern Europeans. I drove out of the area and back across Euston Road and pulled up behind a van which was parked outside a flat. I opened the driver's side door and the key was under the mat. We had lift off and we went over to Bondy's place; the exact place where I used to take the kid's sister on a Sunday night.

"Come on – Let's get my gear drop it back off and I'll take you to this place where me and your Emily go that have indie music on – it's top drawer."

He seemed extremely pleased with that. I looked in the back of the van and it appeared quite clean, but just to be on the safe side I put a few sheets on the floor. The flat had always been mine and Emily's place, and as I switched on the lights and went inside the first thing I noticed was the empty bottle of wine on the side and the pots on the draining board that had been washed the next morning. It may have been a few weeks ago, but the memory was fresh.

"I've got something bad to tell you," she had said. "I'm twelve weeks pregnant."

"Is it mine?" I had asked.

"Most definitely," she had answered.

How did I know it was mine? Was I certain? Was she lying to me? These were all valid questions that I could have also asked, was it not for the fact that her husband couldn't have kids, something which had been confirmed a few years prior. Would she lie to me? It is possible, but doubtful. She had lied to him though, so why not lie to me? Why would she, what could she gain? That could be construed as a conceited denial by me, and one that if I am being honest had no real ground to stand on.

"I'll see about a termination," had been her final say on the matter, and I was off the hook, however on finding out about the pregnancy the husband hit the roof and she was thrown out. He knew he couldn't have kids, more than she did. It was him who had sat through each and every test, not her. He was sterile and she was not. Now she was having something he could not give her and I remember her telling me how he'd thrown her downstairs in his callous way to make her abort just hours before I got her out of there. Adultery is seedy at best and certainly isn't pleasant for the innocent party. Emily had done what she had done and like me before her, had paid a price.

I started emptying the wardrobe and putting my clothes on the bed where it all happened.

"Whose are all these DVDs?" asked Stuart.

"Mine," I replied.

However before we could start transporting the gear back and forth we had visitors in the guise of the police, two in plain clothes and two in uniform.

"Are you Yusuf Elias?" asked one of the plain clothed policemen.

"Do I look like I'm Yusuf Elias?" I replied.

Then I heard a struggle in the other room and I pushed by the policeman to see what was happening – the police were trying to pin down Stuart.

"Stu, stop panicking, mate," I said. "We haven't done anything wrong."

He was slithering about like an eel as the two policemen restrained him.

"Hey, there's no fucking need for that," I said pulling one of them off him. "He's a sixteen-year old kid."

The next thing I know we were both handcuffed. They had found something on Stuart.

"Tell them your name, and say 'no comment' to any other question," I shouted to him. "Are you listening? Stu – are you listening? Name only and 'no comment'."

We got carted off to some police station in different cars, with my main remit being to call Sooty and get our legal people on this. It's no use arguing with the police or kicking off with them – it's a slow process but the majority of the time things become clear. I may have got a clean record but I had sailed close to the wind a few times. I certainly wasn't a happy bunny when I found out that the police reckoned the gear they had found on Stuart was iffy at best.

"I need to make a phone call," I said.

"You'll be given your phone call, we just need to know what you were doing in that property?"

"This is an arse about face way of going about things," I said. "That's my girlfriend's younger brother you've got. He's sixteen. He was helping me pick up some gear I had left at the flat."

"Was that gear drugs?" he asked.

"Don't be stupid," I replied. "A few suits, some DVDs and

a load of other personal stuff in boxes – you know exactly what it was as you saw us doing it."

I may as well have been pissing in the wind as they began processing me.

"I want either a phone call or a duty brief," I snapped.

It was no good arguing the toss. I got processed, stripped of my wallet and mobile, shoes off and slung in a cell and all that was going through my mind was the lad. Why did he panic and what the hell had they found on him? My mind was working overtime.

Around fifty minutes later my presence was requested in the custody room where I was given a phone call.

"Libby, it's me," I said. "I need you to get a brief over to Muswell Hill nick. I was clearing out my stuff from Bondy's with the lad and we've been pulled by the police. I think they've had the place under observation."

"Are you okay?" she asked.

"I'm fine, but I'm worried about the lad," I replied.

It didn't happen immediately but it happened, and I got some sharp suit from the legal firm that represented us who gave me the 'runners and riders'.

"They're saying that they've found a quantity of a substance on Mr. Orr, which they are led to believe is class A," he said.

"What?"

The brief nodded.

I couldn't believe it.

"I can get you out of here now," stated the brief, "however, they're wanting to question Mr. Orr."

"Get me a senior policeman," I said. "The lad's sixteen."

"Sixteen or not – they have him on possession."

The custody sergeant gave me my phone and wallet back as I put on my shoes, and to be fair he apologised for the mix up, but told me that the two detectives were adamant that Stuart stayed.

"What will happen to him?" I asked.

That was a stupid question as the police never tell you anything.

"Don't worry, I'll get him bailed," said the brief.

"Yeah, that's a morning in the Magistrates Court – that can't happen – I need to see a senior copper."

Fair play to him, he got me an inspector, who didn't want to really converse with me in any way or shape or form, and that being the case he certainly didn't want to negotiate and after two minutes of bullshit patter I asked him if I could be frank, but frank out of the way of other people's earshot and away from the internal CCTV and my brief.

He took me in a room and it was then when I hit with a few lines of patter, which would either work, or get me six months.

"Get the lad out – kick his arse and give him a verbal caution," I said.

"It's too late – he's going up in court tomorrow."

"Bullshit," I said. "Kick his arse and give him a caution and chuck him out."

"I've told you, that's not going to happen."

"He's gone in there and hit the 'no comment' button – get me in front of a tape and you'll have the I.P.C.C crawling all over this as I will tell them that I saw one of your officers plant the fucking stuff. I have a clean record and I'll throw money at my five hundred quid an hour legal firm, and believe me when I say it – he will walk, but you will have a fucking inquiry."

"Do you know what you are saying to me?" he asked.

"I know exactly what I'm saying to you. I care about the lad and you don't – the most he'll cop is a two hundred quid fine and a few hours of whatever it is that they do."

"Well if that's the case, what are you worried about?" he asked, albeit with an air of smugness about his reply.

"Because he's sixteen years old and impressionable," I snapped. "I don't want him going out there thinking he can do it again."

There was hell on after that and even my brief started to panic a bit.

"What have you said to him?" he asked. In fact he asked that three times in one minute.

Whatever it was, he knew I'd rattled them. I phoned Libby and gave her an update. I think she was panicking more than the police.

"You told him what?" she yelled.

"I had to – they weren't listening."

"Jesus Christ – you know if you go down you'll lose everything?" she said.

I was aware of that – I think?

"You bloody idiot," was all she could say.

But I'll tell you what! Within twenty minutes I had a young kid stood in front of me who had just had his arse kicked and thrown out. Nothing was said as the brief dropped me off at Bondy's where I picked up the van and replaced it for my car at the place I'd picked it up. All the way home not one word was spoken, however that was soon to change as soon as I got through the door.

"You stupid fucking idiot," I snapped, giving a bit of finger pointing. "Do you know what could have happened?"

"A fine or bound over probably," he replied.

"Look at me! Look at all this!" I said. "I didn't get all this from being a bum – I got it through effort and hard work."

"Yeah it's all about you, innit?" he said.

"No it's not about me, you fucking idiot, it's about you."

He said nothing.

"You want to be like your dumb Scouse mates, keep on doing what you're doing. A bit a blow, a bit of gear, rob some old lady's house – buy a bit more."

"It was only a bit of stuff," he mumbled

"What?" I asked. "Tell me that again, I didn't hear you."

He said nothing.

"You've been stopping in my kids' bedroom with that in your possession, what if you'd have dropped it and the kids had got it?" I shouted. "I took you into my wife's house, and you knew you had that stuff on you – these are the people I love and you do that to me."

"You can't love her that much," he sniped.

That was it. I grabbed him by the throat and rammed the back of his head against the wall.

"You want to tell me that again?" I snapped.

I was about to punch his lights out when something hit me. I looked at his face and I didn't just see Emily and her little sister in him, but my young lad in ten or eleven years' time. My mother beat me, and it never altered a fucking thing – it just made me despise her. The kid was just a kid. He was immature like all the other kids. I knew that, as I had been the same at that age.

"Go get to bed," I said, releasing my grip on him and shaking my head. "But I tell you now, you've disappointed me."

I texted Libby and with fifteen minutes both her and Sooty were round. If ever you needed someone, they were that someone.

"I don't know what to do," I said shaking my head. "I think the kid's an idiot or something."

"No he's not," said Libby. "He's like just about every other lad his age."

"Drugs?" I said, shrugging my shoulders. "What does he want with drugs?"

Libby nodded. "It's rife out there."

"Someone's got to have a word with him," I said, still shaking my head.

"You've had a word with him," she replied. "Believe me – he'll listen to you a damn sight more than he'd listen to any social worker."

I got to bed and managed a couple of hours sleep and picked the kids up from Jeanette's around 8:00am.

"Is M there, Dad," asked my daughter.

"No, she's still up at her mum's in Liverpool," I replied.

"Has she had the baby yet?" asked my son.

"Not yet," I smiled.

"I can't wait – I'm glad I'll have a brother to play with," he said.

"Can I have a sister after that?" asked my daughter.

After last night's episode, I wouldn't want to bring any kids into the world. Maybe being sterile was god's way of relieving a parent of any stress. I stopped off and got four bacon, egg and mushroom sandwiches from a café and pulled up outside the house. The kids jumped out of the car and went inside and caught a view of Stuart in the back garden cleaning out Arteta and Giroud.

I tapped on the window, "There's a sandwich in here for you," I said.

He came inside looking sheepish and took the sandwich. "Sorry," he mumbled.

"Don't say sorry if you don't mean it," I said. "Otherwise it just becomes another meaningless word."

He nodded.

"Mean what you say," I said. "Always."

I left it at that and flicked on Sky Sports.

I'd had her brother under Fred and Sooty's supervision, and to be honest there was little to report back apart from the fact that he had told me 'sorry' a total of twenty-eight times. I don't know whether that was because he was actually sorry, or he just didn't want the news relaying to his sister and parents. I hoped it was the former, although the jury was out. I know Libby had had a word with him. I've no idea what was said but I knew he had a similar expression on his face to what I always had on mine when she told me off.

Anyway, he was going back home in a couple of days. I'd blackmailed him by buying him some more clothes. That's not to say he didn't earn them. The next day (Sunday) we spent the morning and half of the afternoon in the garden digging trenches to lay a network of 150mm pipes in the ground and attach it to the ferrets' shed. There must have been a good two hundred foot of pipe in the ground. The nosy neighbour across must have thought we were rigging up some underground heating system and kept looking around her curtains at us. When the kids came out of the house they thought it was great.

"What are you doing, dad?" asked my lad.

"Building the ferrets some tunnels to run about in," I replied.

"Won't they get lost?"

I thought it highly unlikely, but it did make me wonder all the same.

I drove the kids back to Jeanette's around 5:00pm and when she saw me in a sweatshirt and muddy jeans she appeared slightly bemused.

"What have you been doing – playing football?" she asked.

"No, digging two hundred feet of tunnels for those stinking ferrets."

"You didn't have to do that," she said.

"Yeah, I did," I replied. "Apart from cleaning the two

pounds of shite out every morning, I'm having to handle, exercise and feed them – I tell you – it's more demanding than having a pack of huskies."

"Do you want to come in and have a coffee?" she asked.

"No, I've got Pablo Escobar at the house – if I'm longer than ten minutes he'll be setting up a grow."

"Come in and have a coffee – he'll be fine."

As it turned out I ended up having two coffees and it was the divorce papers that I'd had served on her a couple of weeks ago that she wanted to talk about. She had wanted shut of me of that there had never been any doubt, however there had been something quite final about having divorce papers served. I had told her that I would do whatever she wanted me to do, and if she didn't want to go through with it, that was fine. However, now she did. Mmm. The reason – she and Paul were thinking about taking it one step further. I had to be honest, in my mind he was nowhere near good enough for her, but then again in my mind, who was? For as much as we had pissed each other off in the past, we still sort of loved each other, and Stuart had been right in his assessment, that she was indeed very beautiful.

"It's entirely up to you," I said. "So long as we stay friends and I can have access to the kids, I'll do whatever you want."

I thought it was a great answer, but I sensed there were feelers being put out in the opposite direction.

"And of course you'll be free to marry as well," she said.

Me nodding like a dog to placate her sort of set a few more questions in motion.

"Do you think you'll marry Emily?" she asked.

I gave a shrug of my shoulders.

"Is dad going to marry M?" asked my daughter.

"I don't know, ask your dad," answered Jeanette.

"Are you, dad?"

I didn't know – I certainly hadn't thought of it beforehand.

"Are you, 'dad'?" asked Jeanette, this time through what I sensed was gritted teeth.

Mmm. There was I sensed, an air of resentment

"Honestly, I've never thought of it."

"She's pregnant, you've been up north to meet her folks, you've got her brother staying at the house and you've not thought of it?" she asked.

"Don't you like her?" I asked.

"Yeah, she's nice – but what's that got to do with it?" she replied.

"I thought this was about you and him and not me and her – you both wanting to take it a step further and that?"

"I didn't know you were on about marrying her," she said.

"I'm not – it's you who's mentioned it."

I left Clerkenwell in a bit of a daze. For as much as knew about women, I certainly couldn't figure any of them out. Marriage had certainly never been on my agenda. If I wanted pain and torture, Arsenal could keep me ticking over quite nicely. To add to the gloom I took a call from Libby. She sort of dropped it on me that they'd had some informal chin-wag about me over some tea and biscuits earlier in the day, the main topic being my sudden maturity along with the recent accountability of myself.

"That's nice," I replied. "'You manage to break it up with a couple of films, did you?"

"It wasn't like that," she snapped.

"Really – I've just had Jeanette playing a game of 'Double Jeopardy' with me. The thing is, she was the only one who knew we were playing."

"We were just saying how mature you've been acting of late," she said.

'Acting' was an apt adjective. She didn't know that for the past week I'd had Sooty on a dating website. It had been a real struggle getting him a date though, not that he actually knew anything about it. My idea was to do a bit of chatting up and get the bird to go around to his house. I'd not actually said it, but I sort of initially referred that he was living with his 'mad sister' and her two kids. I'd cleared the first few hurdles like a good 'un. She was impressed with his job and that he still had his own teeth – that kind of thing. Miscellaneous likes and dislikes, such as was he a vegetarian? Did she smoke a pipe? Then as soon as the sister was mentioned they didn't want to know. David Cameron may call this his 'Modern Britain', but as PC as he'd like to think we all are, there's still a rather unhealthy stigma attached to lunacy.

I had therefore revamped his profile and turned Libby into not quite the compulsive liar, but sort of said that she had a slight disorder whereby she couldn't handle reality and as a consequence, told great stinking fibs. I managed a bit of traffic, but nothing to write home about. I was hoping that I could get him a date in time for her birthday as we were having dinner with the D'Arcys that night and I really wanted to see how he handled it when some old dog turned up at his front door.

After Libby had hung up from pissing in my ears I took a call from Emily, which I took from the car into the house and onto the sofa. The upshot was that she missed me and she loved me and she couldn't wait to see me and would I put Stuart on a train or fetch him back up north as the truant officer from school had been around.

"Truant officer? I thought he'd left school?"

"Not yet, he's still fifteen," she replied.

"I thought you said he was sixteen?"

"No – I didn't say that," she replied.

"Hey – Pablo," I asked looking at Stuart who was playing on the kids' Xbox. "Did you tell me you were sixteen?"

"I may have done," he replied.

I shook my head.

"My mistake," I replied.

After giving him a bollocking for lying to me and making him get a shower and putting his new normal clothes on, we drove up to Birkenhead. Sunday nights were great for driving, as all the Yorkshire Pudding and B&Q set were now sat at home in front of the TV watching 'Songs of Praise', and so as to impress my co-pilot I got the car up to 180mph on the M6 but told him not to tell his sister – or mother – or father.

We arrived on the Wirral about 9:30pm and within two minutes we had half the street inside their house, but this time it wasn't me they were poking and prodding, it was Stuart. As I had anticipated, his mother burst out crying when she saw her baby minus that idiot hat, with a nice haircut and rigged out in his 'spring collection'. It was a bit like the scene in Pinocchio when Geppeto's wooden boy is made into a real boy by that fairy who sang 'When you wish upon a star'.

Emily offset me thinking of me as the fairy by planting one on my lips and taking me in the living room where I was passed around between three or four aunties and her young sister, who certainly wasn't backward at coming forward.

"How old are you?" I asked. "And don't tell me you're sixteen."

"Nearly thirteen."

"Well, behave yourself," I said.

I didn't mind handing out kisses, but I certainly drew the line about having a tongue thrust down my throat by a minor. It was very intimidating, not at least because she had a tongue like a lizard, which drew me to the conclusion that she'd certainly be more popular with boys than her brother ever would be with girls.

It was all very nice, and after the furore had died down

over Stuart, his mother turned her attention to me, firstly by making me a salmon sandwich and secondly by rubbing my thigh, which I have to say didn't go unnoticed by Emily.

"Are you staying over?" she asked – Emily, that is.

Well, I certainly didn't fancy driving back.

It turned out that Emily had spent some quality time with her family, but was really pleased to see me and was glad that I was here.

"Have you thought what you are going to call the little chappy?" asked one of her aunties.

"I'll leave that with Emily," I replied.

"Aw, isn't that nice," was sort of passed around the room between the aunties as Emily again linked my arm and squeezed me.

It was weird that in London everyone thought I was a dick head and treat me like shite, but up here everyone loved me.

"I bet it's going to be a beautiful baby," exclaimed one of the aunties. "I mean look at them – such lovely looking kids."

I wonder if that's what Peter Beardsley's auntie thought when her sister was nearly twenty-weeks on?

The fair-haired Jimmy Tarbuck came into the room and seeing as though I wasn't driving back, he kindly offered me a tin of his beer. I let him know that although I used to happily guzzle the stuff, that I was more tee-total these days, although I'd happily shift a bottle of wine in the right company.

"He doesn't booze or smoke," said Emily's mother rather proudly. "He's the perfect man."

Well I wouldn't go that far, I thought, as I did have certain other vices – one of which had been a message in my phone since Edge Lane.

About 11:45pm we were left to our own devices and were finally alone. As it happened Emily had bought a new set of handcuffs from an Ann Summers in Liverpool and one of the first things she wanted me to do was to tie her down and 'rape' her. She had an unhealthy obsession with this and in no uncertain terms I candidly let my feelings be known. I got a wry smile back and a playful prod in my face with her foot, which was quickly followed by an, "I've really missed you," and her trying to drag me on top of her. As great as it sounded, and it really did, the impending terror of her mum walking in on us, and then sort of wanting to join in, left me with both a level-head and the handcuffs in the box, although Emily partly got what she wanted as I had to keep my hand over her mouth, whilst I was used as some form of Sybian sex device for ten minutes while she did whatever she did before I copped off.

I was the best ever, she had told me. It didn't really cut any ice with me as I had said that to hundreds of women over the years, however Emily and Nicole were by far my favourites and occupied all the places within my fabled top-ten. Even Jeanette couldn't get anywhere near them and she'd spent years of trying. She was the 'Mark Randall' of my sex life. She may look like the part, but no matter how long she hung around, she would never get a place in any of my starting line-ups, and now after all the years of trying, it looked like she was facing a free transfer to Brentford.

I got up around 5:00am, left Emily asleep under the duvet on the couch and drove back to north London where I assessed the contents of my mobile phone.

Nicole had flown out to the far east with a couple of girlfriends, which was one monkey off my back; however, my accountant clarifying an opening and a needing to see me spelled-out another monkey looking for something to climb on.

My finances were all over the place, but it wasn't that I was worried about, it was the accountants' office itself. One of the partners who ran the place was a fat sex pest called Deryck Wicks or 'Big Decker' as he liked to be known, and that being the case he only ever employed 'top totty'. I always thought the criteria I set out for my women was quite invariable, but his was unbelievably strict and how the board of equality and prejudice haven't rumbled him I'll never know. The man sets a very stringent criteria, and that being the case it is a very successful establishment that attracts a massive clientèle. I couldn't believe it when I first walked in – it was like some scene out of Vogue – I had to check twice to see if I'd come into the right place. 'Big Decker' himself was a strange looking character. In one off the wall moment he could like Bob Wilson or Gordon Banks and in the next the sex predator and child murderer Fred West. It was uncanny. I once spent half an afternoon in the office sort of matching up all their faces. 'Big Decker' wouldn't have looked out of place at a dinner part with either of them, as he could have been either of their brothers – a missing link between the two, so to speak. Maybe he was from Chesterfield? He also had a strange Fred West persona about him in that he liked to ask me questions about my sex life, which I'll get to in a minute.

Obviously when you work in an accountants you have access to facts and figures, and the fact that I was at the time trying to write off a Maserati as tax deductible, and that I was paying in tax what some of their staff earned in a year, soon got round the office and I ended up taking one of the secretaries out after I had bumped into her in a wine bar off Euston Road. As it transpired, she had just got married to some kid up off Whitehall Street in Tottenham but the relationship was going slightly pear-shaped. My presence in the grand scheme of things made that said shape look a bit more permanent.

She was a cracking looking twenty-year old with a great

rack and legs, and as in the song she sort of wiggled when she walked, and giggled when she talked.

It took me a full four dates to get her pants off, however Bondy had locked me out of his flat after I'd left the bath running a few days before and flooded out his neighbour, and by the time I'd got to the car park of a hotel with an empty room, it had sort of lost its flavour. I made a final play after another couple of dates and I got a three hundred quid deal at the Savoy and took her there. It had been some hard graft to get it to this stage and it lasted less than two minutes when she bollocksed everything up. Thankfully I'd done the insemination process straight after I'd slung her on the bed.

Her saying, "You don't waste your time," was quickly followed by her kicking off her shoes, which when I saw the state of her feet set me off gipping and I nearly threw up. It was horrible. She had great thick toes with long nails that sort of reminded me of Oddbod's feet in 'Carry On Screaming', but sort of minus the hair. Thank god I'd done her before I saw them.

As for 'Decker', he was always very 'Suits You, Sir' in his mannerisms and all he wanted to know is who I was seeing, but when he found out I'd taken this Clohe from his office out he was very inquisitive in a 'fumbling of hands under the table' kind of way.

"Did she go like a steam train?" he asked. "Oh, I bet she did, I bet she did – whoof."

I delayed the visit to the accountants until I could be accompanied by an appropriate adult – which was generally Libby.

Chapter 15
Baggage

As I pulled on to the street I saw Emily's Mini parked outside the house, which didn't just mean that she was back from her mother's – it meant I had to park at the other end of the street.

On getting through the door Emily immediately showed her appreciation and I received a performance that could have been included in my fabled top ten, if it were not for the restrictions placed by the ever-growing lump.

"That's got big in the last few days," I said.

"That's why I asked you to do it from behind," she replied.

"Yeah, and then I can't see your face," I said. "What's the point of that?"

"What a really nice thing to say," she smiled.

Really? I thought.

I copped a kiss and another great smile.

"If it gets any bigger I'll have to start seeing to myself," I stated.

"You do and I will feel upset," she replied, shaking her head. "New 'rule one' from Emily – anything that comes out of you goes in me."

"I thought 'rule one' was no arguing or bitching."

"No that was about 'rule number five', although I never argue with you so it's a pointless rule," she joked.

"So what was 'rule one'?"

"You know very well what rule one was," she smiled pretending to prod me with her forefinger.

"I never knew you were a teacher," I said, sort of changing the subject.

"Probably because you never asked," she replied.

I didn't. I hadn't. Why did I never ask any questions? Probably because I didn't want any answers. There was loads I could ask, but the last thing I wanted was being pissed off if I didn't like the answer. Outside of the basic line of 'what was I doing', and 'which way do you want me', she never asked me many questions either.

"How's your parents?"

"My mum likes you, that's for sure," she said, grinning.

I certainly didn't like the way that sounded.

"She wouldn't shut up about you to the neighbours," she added. "Dale Fox's mother got the right hump with her."

Who the hell is Dale Fox? I thought.

"I'd not been home for ages," she said. "I've seen everyone this past week."

Including Dale Fox? I thought.

I wondered if Dale Fox resembled her husband? A bigger and more violent man and with a Scouse accent. I wonder if she cleaned his ferrets out and drunk Perrier water with him whilst sat out in the sun in 'The Garden'. I bet she didn't. I bet he kept her in the house whilst him and his Scouse mates had ten pints of bitter and when he came home drunk he breathed stale beer over her whilst mauling her. I had to get this Dale Fox geezer out of my hair.

"Who's Dale Fox?" I asked.

"A guy I used to sort of know," she said.

Damn, I thought. I knew I shouldn't have asked that.

"Little guy, is he?" I asked.

"No," she frowned. "Why?"

I knew I shouldn't have asked that either. Nicole never had no Dale Fox bloke that she could drag out of a cupboard to taunt me and piss me off. I should have let this one ride out. I mean she'd be well upset if I listed my past in an A to Z fashion or even told her about Thailand. Even Fosis at the coffee shop was upset when I told him about Thailand.

"When you go again you should tell me," he said.

For two weeks after that he greeted me in the coffee shop decked out in his trunks and flip flops with a lilo under his arm. "We go Bangkok yet?"

I'd been Bondy's hero. I did twenty-nine of them in one week and by the end of the holiday I was like the pied piper with a pack of rats following me. 'Me love you long time' wasn't in it. I needed another holiday in Thailand after it I was that knackered. One even asked if I would do her mum and she'd give me a hundred baht. This Dale Fox? He had nothing to come.

"So did you go out with him a long time?" I asked.

"A bit," she replied.

'A bit' wasn't an answer. Well, if it was, it was a very vague answer. A bit could be a short time or long time or even a very long time. I knew she had been married at twenty years old, so that gave at least four years before that. Mmm. It also meant that she'd has twelve years with Hubert the ex-bodyguard-cum-commando. What was a matter with me? This was the Tall Dwarf syndrome all over again. I sat on the couch and kicked up Sky Sports. I was glad Ramsey was back in the side. Emily lifted her dress up slightly as she squeezed on the sofa beside me.

"What you did was lovely," she said as she cuddled up and pecked me.

Maybe I was being duped here. Maybe I wasn't the father and it was Dale Fox's baby she was carrying. 'Don't worry Dale, as soon as he's born we'll have his money and his house'. Jesus Christ, could anything like this happen? She was a Scouser as well. Very conniving are Scousers when it comes to crime. I mean, her kid brother was only down here a day or so and he was running some drugs cartel.

"So this Dale guy?" I asked. "Did he... er, yer know."

She looked at me with a strange expression and then smiled. "Yer know? Yer know what?"

"Sort of – do it."

"Mmm. A bit," she replied.

Again with the 'a bit'. This was driving me insane. All I'd got in my head was this great dirty big Scouser humping her senseless on her mum's couch, or even worse in her bed. I wondered why she was so good at it. I'll tell you something, you need loads of practice to get that good. I've had top class call girls who couldn't ever be that good – even now, and even though she was pregnant.

"Emily, this is driving me nuts," I said. "Who is he?"

I had cracked. I was jealous. I loved her.

She just looked at me smiling. "I am thirty-two," she said.

Yeah, and I'm thirty-six, I thought. *So what?*

"I met him when I was sixteen and we saw each other a couple of years, then I met my husband."

Well that was two years down the pan in one sentence. Two years equates to one hundred and four weeks and over seven and a half hundred days and nights. They didn't just 'know each other' that long. They had to have at least watched TV or had a cup of tea, even though they lived in Birkenhead. You can't just 'know each other' and end it there.

The fact that I didn't give a shit that Wenger was considering starting Yaya frigging Sanogo for the next match was a complete irrelevance now, when generally I would have been climbing the walls and putting my foot through the TV. Wenger had 'as good as him' players out on loan in the Championship, so why did that useless git get the head's up over them? He couldn't crack a cow's arse with a banjo, never mind lead a line during a Premiership game. He was about as nimble on his feet as Bambi on ice and had the presence of a stalker on the late shift in Tesco's.

"Is something bothering you?" she asked.

"Yeah," I said. "I just don't want to find out that when the kid comes out that it's got a Scouse accent and the first thing it wants to do is crawl over and rip out my car radio."

Nicole would have gone ballistic if I would have said something like that, although Emily did not.

"Believe me," she said, looking at me. "This little bundle I'm carrying has your name on it and no one else's."

She had sort of called my bluff with a paternity test a couple of times already, but doing one couldn't hurt. It might be a bit embarrassing, but not half as embarrassing as me turning up at school with a kid looking like Bob Carolgees with a perm and moustache and wearing a shell suit and white trainers.

"You fancy doing it again?" she asked.

"Again?"

"Mmm. I haven't seen you since Sunday."

No, but I bet she's seen Dale Fox, I thought. If I could do twenty-nine Thai women in seven days I bet he could do her half as many as that, which meant they could have done it fourteen and a half times. A half? How could you do it 'half a time'? Maybe it was one of those that never got finished. I'd had loads of them, not at least the Tall Dwarf's wife in the hotel. That started but certainly didn't finish. That was a horrible thought. Maybe he did that with her, maybe Dale Fox fastened her to the bed. Why not? She loved handcuffs. She also loved other things that I'll not go into.

Mmm. I hope Dale Fox never did that. I really hope Dale Fox never did that.

"Did Dale Fox do it – yer know?" I asked, without really thinking.

"Did Dale Fox do yer know, what?" she asked.

"Like we sometimes do it – yer know," I replied.

"Me and Dale Fox was a long time ago," she smiled.

"Yeah, exactly sixteen years ago and you had over seven and a half hundred nights together, the majority of which would have probably been spent on your mum's settee."

"You've put a bit of thought into this," she said, looking at me and smiling.

I had. It was all I'd been thinking about for the last half hour, but I'll tell you something, the next drive in the Maserati was frigging awesome. I now had Dale Fox at the wheel and he was some driver. He had it purring around every corner ramming down from fourth, to third and back up into sixth again, screeching and squealing until it was rammed tightly in the garage. As I said, that car was one hell of a ride.

"Wow – that was really, really nice," she said.

Autographs later folks, I thought. *And up yours Dale Fox.*

I nipped back into the office and I caught Eddie talking with Ginge.

"You two okay?" I asked.

Ginge gave me a nod.

"It's looking good," said Eddie. "I can't believe how you've done that Arsenal programme – Sammy looks a world beater."

If you know what you're on with you can get things to look a lot better or a lot worse than they actually are. Statistics are there to be manipulated to suit, whether you are for something or against it. Eddie told me that it was the same with politics. Pinpoint the good and blow it out in your favour. Pinpoint the bad and either hide it or chuck it on to someone or something else. Meanwhile, I had a date with www.genesreunited.co.uk and a certain Dale Fox.

It was dead easy. Dale Fox, born 1975 – Birkenhead.

Mmm. I didn't like the sound of that. He was seven years older than her. That would make him twenty-three and a pervert when he met her.

"Hiya," Sooty said as he popped his head into the office. "This Sammy and Arsenal thing is the dog's bollocks – you want to see?"

"In a bit kiddo – I'm just checking something out."

I typed in 'marriage' and kicked in his age. Mmm. He'd been married twice. Once in 1993 and again in 2002. I was no super-mathematician as such, but I knew that meant that he was married when he was seeing Emily. Or had at least been married. I didn't like the sound of that 'bringing experience to the table' – or couch in their case, kind of thing at all. Then something hit me which I hoped hadn't happened. I wonder if he had married Emily before the Hubert bloke?

No, that couldn't have ever happened, I thought.

However, I did a search all the same.

No, she had just been married the once, but just for good measure I downloaded copies of each of his marriage certificates, not that I was getting obsessed or anything.

Dale Fox – Bachelor – Age 18 – Occupation – Trainee borer married 1993. Jane Turner – Spinster – Age 21 – Occupation – Machinist

and

Dale Fox – Divorced – Age 27 – Occupation – Borer married 2002. Margaret Orr – Aged 17 – Clerical Worker

Arsenal's website it may have been able to butter up his statistics to look as appealing as Alex Song's, however this told me a couple of things – one – he had initially gained experience from an older woman – and two – that he liked young girls. And a couple of other things were bugging me – what the hell was a borer? A bloke who was a professional at boring people? And this Margaret Orr, was she related to Emily?

I went in to the editing suite to see what the final version of the 1970 World Cup programme was looking like, however it was the 'Sammy' project that was making the headlines within the office. "It's a truly brilliant piece," exclaimed Abigail. "ESPN already want it and BSkyB definitely want to see it."

We needed the World Cup 1970 completing so we could get them billed and no-one better than Sooty knew this, however he was keeping his cards quite close to his chest and when he suggested – no, he actually told me – to go home an hour or so early, alarm bells rang. One – why was he not pushing for completion on this – and two – why did he want me out of the way?

I was soon to find out. The studio needed vacating at 6:00pm as some 'indie' company were using it for a scene for some shitty film they were doing about some coloured guy who had come over in the 1960s and had struggled with both his autism and racial prejudice to rise to be the boss of some big company or something, but was now dying of AIDS. It sounded right up Channel 4's street – a right old pile of shite. No wonder the nation would prefer to sit and slit its wrists to Simon Cowell's 'Britain's Got Talent' or 'He's a Dick Head Get Me Out of Here'.

Interestingly I met the director as I was about to leave the building, along with some minor league actress who, by the look of it, was trying to impress him by tap dancing down the corridor alongside of him. Either that or she had a bad leg.

Mmm. I have to check in on this, I thought – and Freddy and I looked on as they set up their lighting and some props, which comprised some plastic flowers, a pair of matching jardinières and a wicker settee.

"There's not much scenery," I said, looking on.

"They do one of these every week," said Fred. "Same main characters."

"I thought it was some film?"

"Sooty's been pulling your leg – the billings for this alone pays the rent for the building."

"Really – he told you that?" I asked.

Fred nodded.

"So what is it – like a series?"

"You could say that," exclaimed Fred, smiling. "I caught the first one two weeks ago – not bad."

I asked Fred to give me a shout when they were ready and nipped back into my office to see what more information I could kick up on this Fox dude, but instead I got a couple of nasty emails from some other joker from Nigeria who had emailed me the other day offering me loads of money he had been given from the World Investment Bank. He was another one who needed somewhere to store it. I only told the guy to leave the cash in a locker at King's Cross station and post me the key and he gave me loads of abuse and called me a racist prick. You just can't help some people.

Now for the fabulous Mr. Fox.

Doing something like this is a bit like waiting for a diagnosis for cancer. You want to know the outcome, but you're shit scared that the man in the white coat isn't going to come back and tell you to starting sorting out your favourite songs and organising a buffet.

I had a fake Facebook account I'd set up in Sooty's name so I ran a search and ended up getting a few of them back. I never thought there would be so many, although the big fat fucker with the bald head from Liverpool looked a likely candidate so I nipped in to see who he was and I hated him straight away.

Likes: Bodybuilding, cage fighting, boxing.

Dislikes: Southerners.

He had to have just put that there last week, surely?

Favourite Films: Saw, Law Abiding Citizen, Texas Chainsaw Massacre, Children of the Corn, Grease.

This was definitely the profile of a pyscho. Grease? Where did that spring from?

Fave music: S Club 7, OMD, Abba

He was either listing these for a laugh or he was a right prat.

Hoping that I wouldn't be coming out to the clanging chimes of doom, I nipped into the selection of photographs that he'd posted and nearly threw up. Every one of them had him in a pair of Speedos, and in a wide selection of colours posing on a beach somewhere. What professes people to think that wearing Speedos is actually cool? I could be ripped like Peter Andre and hung like Jordan and I still wouldn't wear them.

I then did an electoral search and he came up on The Speke, but not living with any Margaret Orr but with someone called Tracey Hump. I bet she's hoping he gets a divorce. I then hit Google Maps just to see the locality he resided in, not being nosy as such, but just wondering if there was any nice wine bars and eateries nearby. The street having the dustbins out made it dead handy for me as generally you have to zoom in on the number, which causes problems as they tend to get a bit pixelated. That fact that there was a great whacking No. 25 scrawled in white gloss on the bin made finding his house a piece of piss. He lived in a similar type of shithole to what Fred lived in, but whereas Fred's was worth around a million quid – I could have bought his on my Visa. I had to get this lot printed off.

"They're starting," said Fred as he poked his head into the office.

"Two minutes," I said as I put the Mac on print.

I went in the studio and to be honest it all looked dead tacky. A big tall coloured bloke in a sailor suit reading his lines with that idiot actress that I'd seen earlier.

"There doesn't look much of a plot," I said. "Where's the rest of 'em?"

"Shhhh," said the director.

"He looks dead like Eboue," I whispered.

"I think this one's set in the early nineteen-twenties," Fred whispered back.

"Is that why they've got one of them wicker settees?" I asked.

"Maybe," he replied.

"I had one of them in my first house," I said. "Dead uncomfortable – my grandma gave it me – that and a TV."

"Shush – can you be quiet?" asked the director.

"It's like watching paint dry, this," I quipped. "Anyway where's his ship?"

"There isn't a ship," whispered Fred.

The director then hit the 'camera, lights, action' and it started.

"When are you leaving, Emmanuel?" asked the actress.

"I told you it was Eboue," I said.

"Stop!" shouted the director before he turned on me. "Are you some bloody moron?"

"Who, me?" I asked.

"Yes, you."

Jeanette had called me it me a moron a few times but there was no way I was telling that pompous twit that, so I gave him an innocent shrug of my shoulders.

"Button it," he said and he hit the 'camera, lights, action' for a 'take two'.

"When are you leaving, Emmanuel?" asked the actress, albeit this time rather more dramatically.

I had to admit that I couldn't hear the sailor's reply as it was a bit mumbled – in fact, he was a bit of a crap actor if I'm honest.

"Is that when your ship sails?" she asked.

"I told you there was a ship," I whispered.

Again I couldn't hear Eboue's reply.

"If I was the director I'd be having second thoughts about casting him," I whispered. "He's shite."

"You know Algernon wants to wave you goodbye," said the actress.

"Who the hell's Algernon?" I asked Fred under my breath.

Then this skinny bloke walked on to the set dressed in some Laurel & Hardy garb.

"That must be Algernon," I whispered.

"I think it is," whispered Fred.

"Are you going, lad?" asked the gadgy in the bowler hat, trying to throw some piss-poor Lancastrian accent.

Again the sailor mumbled something inaudible.

"Well, you can kiss the missus goodbye," he said.

And they kissed for a bit and I have to admit, I sort of lost track of time after a couple of minutes.

"Friggin' hell Fred, this is a bit strong isn't it?" I whispered. "This has to go out after nine o'clock."

To make more interesting the man in the bowler hat got in on the act and took over kissing the sailor.

"Jesus Christ," I shouted.

"Cut!" shouted the director and then turned on me.

"Don't look at me, pal," I said, pointing. "This is frigging disgusting."

"Leave," he said.

"Leave?" I replied. "I part-own the studio."

"Leave now," he stated, but this time a bit more dramatically. "Or I'll take it up with Mr. Sutton."

"It's a right load of rubbish anyway," I said.

I walked out of the studio and into my office and rang Sooty. He was engaged, so I rang Libby.

"You want to get down to the office," I said. "There's a great big coloured sailor kissing this old bloke in a bowler hat."

"Are you drunk?" she asked.

Thinking back at what I had just said, I knew that it didn't sound at all right.

"No."

"Then what are you on about?"

"Sooty's rented the studio out for this Channel Four crap and there's some sailor hooked up with some bloke in a bowler hat and to be honest, Libby," I said adding a bit of drama to my summary, "It's pretty disgusting."

"Yeah, Tim said it was a bit arty," she replied.

I sort of had a morbid curiosity to go back in there, but I thought better of it and passed on it. I had enough baggage to see out the week without having some bloke in a bowler hat wanting to dress me up as some sailor and chase me around in my dreams. I went home hoping that I still had the 'Grease' DVD, not that I ever remember watching it after I got it. I just had a splurge on John Travolta films after I'd seen 'Get Shorty' and it was one of those I bought. It had to be better than that garbage I'd just seen.

I got in to see Emily knelt on the floor of the lounge sorting some things out.

"What's that?" I asked.

"Just some things from home," she replied, smiling. "You want some food?"

"Sure," I replied.

I ferreted around in the DVDs for a good half an hour hoping to come up trumps. Sometimes you can look that hard that you can't see what you're actually looking for, and the film 'Grease' was hardly awe-inspiring. I needed a room where I could put them all in alphabetical order. It was okay for Sooty – his collection I could stick in my back pocket. Well, that's a lie – I could definitely stick it in is younger sister's back pocket. In fact if she had that horrible thing on she was wearing at her dad's funeral the other year, I could have stuck my entire DVD and CD collection in it – or under it. What possesses women to want to get themselves that fat? Okay a couple of pounds, but when we start to talk tonnage, you've got to question the husbands. As a rule I don't do fatties, but I've met some really nice looking ones. Their heads may be a bit wider and their arms quite chunky, but some have still been quite pretty. I got talking to one a few years ago who sort of had the hots for me and she mentioned it was some kind of glandular problem. It's worth noting that a lot of them say this – mainly those who are too lazy to lose weight. I thought I was helping her, but she went berserk when I mentioned having her jaws wired.

"Just a couple of months and you'll be sort of back to normal," I had said. "You need to find a surgeon to whip off all the overhang though, because that's ten times worse than being fat."

I must admit, the left hook she led with was quite alarming and were it not for the fact her husband caught me stepping backwards, it could have been untidy.

However, and there's a moral to this story – she now texts me quite regularly and is now down to her fighting weight of 145lbs. I'm dreading the day when she loses another twenty pounds, and it may be a case of me having to leave the country. In fact, I've had to start sending her chocolates hoping that she'll flip out of this obsession and kick back into eat dripping sandwiches, however Sooty gave me the outlook of a turkey by saying that this won't happen and that she's adamant that she'll be ready for me by Christmas.

I eventually found the 'Grease' DVD and took it downstairs, where Emily was still doing her bookkeeping or whatever it was she was doing in between cooking me something.

"You're not watching anything, are you?" I asked.

"I've been sort of watching 'House in the Country' on and off," she said.

"You don't mind if I put a film on, do you?"

She shook her head. "Not at all."

However as soon as Frankie Avalon started singing the intro she sort of stated, "What have you put this thing on for?"

"I fancy a bit of American Graffiti," I lied.

I was bored after five minutes but I put up with it, however something occurred which made me sit up and think. The character 'Sandy' was a very similar looking version of both Emily and Nicole.

"Wow, you look like her," I said.

"No, I don't," she replied.

"Yeah, you do," I said. "String her up in a pair of handcuffs and put some stockings on her and you're dead ringers."

"Don't be daft," she said.

I wasn't. Emily was a slightly smaller and prettier version of the character.

"You've got to buy a yellow dress," I said, smiling.

"You want me to buy them flat shoes as well?" she asked.

"Nope, just the dress," I said.

She got up off the floor, shaking her head, and opened up the cooker to put out some food for me.

"That smells nice," I said. "What is it?"

"Beef Wellington."

I'll be honest – it totally looked like a pie to me.

"You like it?" she asked.

I nodded my approval.

I bet she made loads of pies for Dale Fox. It certainly looked like he'd eaten plenty.

Chapter 16
Eddie's Tales - Take 5

I had been met off the train by both Abigail and Faranha, who made sure that the room in the St. Pancras hotel was up to scratch. They had brought me up to speed on all the gossip and had explained that the *other half* had gone up to Liverpool at short notice but was currently on his way back down.

"Liverpool?" I asked.

"Yeah, his girlfriend's from up there," stated Abigail.

"Emily?"

"Her brother has been staying with him," she replied.

It was all news to me and as I had told Pauline, I couldn't wait to get back amongst it. On me getting into the offices I was greeted by Sooty who immediately kicked up the World Cup 1970 documentary, which I thought was awesome – however, nothing could prepare me for the guts of the 'Sammy' documentary. It was nothing short of fantastic. These boys were at the top of their profession and what they had done so far, I thought was a work of bloody genius.

"Where did you get all this footage from?" I asked on seeing Sammy hit at least half a dozen twenty-five yard shots into the back of the net.

"The majority of football matches at Highbury were videoed for tactical use," explained Sooty. "They're not the greatest films, but we've cleaned them up and added noise and commentary."

This was amazing, and what was more amazing was that they had included the footage of the first Arsenal match I had ever seen – versus Brazil, which according to Faranha cost just under £400 to acquire. As did the footage from the Arsenal versus Ajax and the Arsenal versus Sporting Lisbon game, the latter of which Sammy had a fine goal ruled out with no one actually knowing why.

As it transpired the other half had worked doggedly to get as much footage as he could from the club, however Arsenal – as ever – had called the shots.

I watched replays of Arsenal take on Manchester City in August 1968 and watched on as Sammy destroyed them with his range of energy and passing, scoring the second goal in what was a 4-1 win against one of the teams of the moment. I had to admit, I had been at the match as one of the 40,766 and seen it as possibly the best Arsenal performance outside of them beating of Ajax. That Arsenal side that had got the League Cup final against Swindon had a continental look about them. One of the things about that side was that throughout the entire league campaign that season they only conceded 27 goals – which was only one more than champions Leeds United who had taken the title with a record 67 points; however, something which was even stranger that season was that second placed Liverpool, who Arsenal had drawn 1-1 twice with and knocked out of the League Cup 2-1, conceded only 24 goals. Back then defensive football ruled.

On a Monday night in late March the same season Arsenal had pitted their wits against their more stylish north London rivals who they had already beaten 2-1 over two legs (1-1 and 1-0) to get to Wembley, and 2-1 over at White Hart Lane in the opening game of the season, however nothing was to come close to this. After 40 minutes Sammy unleashed a 25-yard shot which swerved away from Pat Jennings and into the top corner. It would have been a nailed-on contender for Match of the Day's goal of the season, however for 45 years and with the exception of the 43,942 who witnessed it, it had never been seen – which was a total travesty, in that it was as good a strike as you would ever see.

I sat shaking my head and looked up at both Ginge and Sooty.

"He was good, wasn't he?" Sooty stated, smiling.

He was. He was without doubt one of the finest players of his era, yet to say he was under-appreciated would have been an understatement.

"We thought we'd use a few front and back page stories at the time," said Sooty.

"Marvellous!' and Suki gives Jones a kiss' was the headline on the front page of the *Daily Express* after Brian Jones of the Rolling Stones had been convicted of drugs in 1969, whilst on the back page Arsenal were up at the Old Show Ground, banging Scunthorpe United 6-1, with Sammy the star of the show and turning in with a goal as a part of the rout.

The Christmas Eve edition of the *Daily Mirror* in 1968 ran with the headline 'Earth a World Away' with a massive photo of the earth being taken from Apollo 8, whilst the big headline that ran on the sports page was 'Arsenal Two Games From Glory? The Next Two Games will Tell' with a Monte Fresco photograph and caption covering the engagement of Sammy to his 21-year old model girlfriend from Northampton – and who said that he wasn't like David Beckham!

I sat back in the chair with a lump in my throat.

What a great time to be alive, I thought. And to have been a part of it was nothing short of fantastic.

As I sat there watching the video, the *other half* came in with a smile on his face as contagious as his work I was watching.

"Good, isn't it," he said whilst summoning a cup of coffee from Faranha.

"I can't believe some of the stuff you have on here," I exclaimed.

"Nor can I," he replied. "But we've got it."

There was even a clip from Boxing Day 1969, of Sammy knocking over the Nottingham Forest goalkeeper Alan Hill with a ferocious shot that cannoned back off him. The strange thing was that shortly after that Hill broke his arm in four places, something which sadly ended his career.

That was the thing with the two lads, they didn't continually droll on about the subject in question, which in this instance was Sammy, they liked to refer to the other teams in question and players, dates and times and what was happening with the clubs themselves.

Sammy didn't just hit a 25-yard strike against Pat Jennings, he hit a ferocious 25-yard strike that swerved and outwitted one of the most outstanding goalkeepers of his era and who was part of a very capable Tottenham Hotspur team that had recently won the FA Cup and who would go on to win both the League Cup and UEFA Cup.

And as for the commentary surrounding the 1969 League Cup Final which not only highlighted the individual play of Sammy in detail – which in itself was unbelievable – they had offered explanation, rather than just blame it on the Horse of the Year Show the week before, bad rain and the fact that Arsenal's match the week before had been postponed due to the said influenza epidemic, which included Sammy who was sent home a few days earlier with a throat infection.

What was never stated was that England had also

churned up the pitch during their 5-0 demolition of France on it three days prior, and newspaper reports had emanated whereby the England players themselves had complained about the pitch. Not only that, but Wembley officials had told Nigel Clarke of the *Daily Mirror* that at the time there was close to 55,000 litres of water currently on the pitch.

"The trouble is that water has not been getting away," stated the Wembley official. "Over the years it has been soaking through and collecting. Several drains have collapsed and must be renewed. Plans have been worked out for the installation of a new drainage system, which will mean digging up all the pitch in summer."

The two lads loved their history, and they weren't done yet.

"We'd like you to do the narrative," stated the *other half.*

"What's the matter with the narrative that's already on?" I asked.

"The content is sound enough," he replied, "However my dialect is shit for TV – yours, on the other hand, will be sound."

I wasn't so sure about that and I gave them my thoughts.

I was invited out to a meal that evening with Sooty and his wife at some fancy tapas bar near London Bridge. It was the first time I had met Libby. She explained that she worked for a financiers in the city, was extremely switched-on and eloquently spoken and without any doubt, loved her husband – and as strange as it may seem and in light of what I had been told – his *other half* as well.

"I have to keep him in check but he can be such a lovable rogue," she said, smiling.

She then went on to explain how they had to shackle him into not squandering his money, and having to keep certain things from him.

"It's a case of being one step ahead of him," explained

Sooty. "Which is dead hard if you know him, as he's generally always ten steps of you already so all you're essentially doing is trying to play catch up."

"He seems really happy with this girl," said Libby, whilst sipping at her wine.

"They are a lovely couple," I confirmed.

"Jeanette said she must be rubbing off on him," she replied.

"Jeanette?" I asked.

"His wife – Jeanette. She's lovely."

Libby then went on to tell me about how his wife Jeanette had struggled to cope with his numerous affairs which culminated in the straw that broke the camel's back, the said straw being one Stacey Tirford – the wife of an executive down at ITV.

"Is this the Tall Dwarf?" I asked.

Libby shrugged her shoulders, which along with a grin emanating from Sooty sort of stated that she didn't know of any moniker that had been given to the husband.

"The woman is a bloody idiot – she caused Jeanette a load of grief," said Libby, shaking her head before looking daggers at her husband. "He doesn't help things either,"

"I don't just think it's Emily that's rubbing off on him," stated Sooty. "It could be the Sammy guy in this documentary we are doing – he's well into it."

Libby then went on to tell me that unbeknown to the *other half*, her husband had signed off on a deal for a six-month lease for some adult entertainment group to use the studio two nights a week and that the said company were two months into their tenure.

"I have to admit," said Sooty. "It's been a right bitch arranging it so he doesn't twig."

"I'm just glad Emily is keeping him occupied," added Libby.

"I told him it was some serial for Channel Four," grinned Sooty. "He was as good as gold until he copped part of what was essentially a 'gay flick' and the director ended up throwing him out."

"He was going ballistic with me down the phone," smiled Libby.

I'd had what was a great day and rang Pauline to tell her so. Libby had also suggested that I bring Pauline down, as they were having some party for her thirty-fifth birthday in a couple of weeks' time.

"Will Emily be there?" Pauline had asked.

"I'm assuming so," I had replied.

I got in the office next day to see Sooty's *other half* in his office signing for a load of parcels.

"Edward," he smiled on seeing me. "I may have some more footage to add."

He had Arsenal versus Cologne 1971 (2-1), Sunderland versus Arsenal 1969 (1-1), Leeds United versus Arsenal 1966 (1-3) and that Arsenal versus Rangers friendly in 1967 (3-0).

"Jesus, where did you get that lot?" I asked.

"If you know where to look and who to ask, my good man – it's a piece of piss."

"I'll take your word for it," I replied.

"Saying that," he said. "I'm not sure what the quality will be like."

The thing about these two lads was that they didn't go off half-cocked. I'd seen the Arsenal 1970-71 Double Year video quite a few times, and all you actually see is footage from a few games that were shown on the BBC, even though there was quite a few others shown on ITV. That, for me, is just lazy journalism aimed at making a quick buck. On the flip side, here was a young lad in awe of his subject and trying to construct a true to life documentary of a player who was the complete midfielder and several years ahead of his time, who – partly due to injury and partly due to Arsenal's successful long ball and battering ram approach to the game – ended up being targeted by a minority and ended up leaving the club he loved to be the focus of a massive transfer scramble in the summer of 1971, and created the 'horrible history' that was to come. Sammy was the first part of the dismantling of the successful European Fairs Cup and Double team – however it is also worth noting that coach Don Howe had left the club to take over the reins of West Bromwich Albion a couple of weeks earlier.

Sammy went to Leicester City for less than half his real worth after Ipswich looked his most likely destination, although it was well-documented at the time that Leeds United, Chelsea, Newcastle United, West Ham United and Nottingham Forest all sought his signature.

In fact, none of the successful Arsenal side of that era raised much money as Mee continued to break up the side, the most surprising being Charlie George, who was sold off for what was literally peanuts.

Bertie Mee's delusion of outstanding man-management was his greatest mistake and in the following 1971-72 season both Arsenal's form and once successful long ball and battering ram approach had been found out and Sammy's replacement – the player who broke the British Transfer Record – the £220,000 valued and 1966 World Cup Winner Alan Ball, was struggling to adapt within a side that played this type of football. It was true they made the FA Cup Final, however as Double 'chasing' Leeds United were their opponents, they were hardly likely to win it.

Chapter 17
Turn of the Decade

I had suddenly got my own personal fan club up on the Wirral, however there had been a tussle for its chairmanship between the mother, youngest daughter and young 'Pablo'. Emily had sort of told me that her husband had never had much to do with her family, however I would get to know more about that sooner than I thought. She had also told me that Lucy was wanting to come down for the weekend.

"What, this weekend?" I asked.

"Why, is it a problem?" she asked, flashing those big blue eyes and giving me a smile.

"No – I think your family are great," I replied.

I got a big hug and a kiss and an, "I love you so much."

Why was I so brilliant at answering questions? I had to admit – it was still pretty great being me. The thing is, I wasn't lying either. It was. However I suddenly had a new text pest in my midst in the guise of her younger sister. 'Thank UUUUUU so much xxxxxxxx'. This was followed by 'U are soooooo brilliant xxxx'.

Mmm. I then remembered the fact that she was under the disillusion that I was her David Beckham fantasy, and reminded Emily of that.

"Don't worry, she's been told," said Emily, still smiling.

I'd brought home some extremely rare footage of Arsenal's failed Fairs Cup campaign of 1971 where they had been knocked out by Cologne. According to Eddie who had been at the match, this was a tie they should have won comfortably. He had said that it had been a cagey affair and that after going 1-0 up through McLintock, the Germans had replied with a series of close calls with Bob Wilson having to defy several attacks, before being stupidly beaten by the towering 6'2" Karl-Heinz Thielen before half-time – and more embarrassingly, direct from a corner kick.

Don Howe had panicked and dragged Sammy off and replaced him with George Graham to go more 'route one'. Arsenal ended up winning 2-1, however, the principles of the previous campaign, whereby they had dismantled what the *Daily Express*'s Norman Gillier claimed was 'one of the most feared attacking sides in Europe' with ease, had been forgotten. Arsenal's European flair had been replaced by first division football and pumping long diagonal balls into the area for Kennedy and Radford. However Cologne didn't have a weak defence like, say, Manchester United or West Bromwich Albion at the time, and with 53-cap international Wolfgang Weber back in the side, they capably contained Arsenal in the second leg and beat them, albeit with a controversial penalty, 1-0 to go through.

"Is this for your Sammy project?" Emily asked.

I nodded. "There's a huge difference between playing English football and continental football now, but back then the difference was massive."

"How so?" she asked, stealing half my chair as she huddled up to me and looked at the monochrome footage on screen.

"Continental football has always been a safer, more probing game," I said. "It's something that you don't rush. Arsenal reverted to it in the first leg of the Fairs Cup Final of 1970 when they went one-nil down and ended up being three-nil down, without really knowing it. They thought that battering the defence with high balls was key, when it was not. When they lost possession they had players committed and got caught on the counter attack."

She smiled at me as though she understood, but I knew she didn't.

"In European football, and against the better teams you try and pick the lock to the safe – you don't use a rubber mallet to try and open it – in 1971, because it was working in the league, they tried doing the same in Europe."

We'd had a big debate about this earlier on this morning in that Arsenal could have won the treble in 1971 if they had have rotated a few players and used Sammy and Marinello in Europe; however back then rotation was quite unheard of, and they didn't. Rotation – or lack of it – was the main reason why Leeds United's 1970 season imploded, when in reality they should have won the lot.

I was going ga-ga by about 9:00pm and I knocked off the laptop.

"You fancy take-out?" I asked.

"I can make something if you like?" she replied.

I think she was trying to justify living here rent free, but the last thing I wanted was a slave watching over me. I might have been a git in most people's eyes, but if I was, I was a fairly laid back one. She had mentioned earlier about feeling a bit uneasy that she was now out of a job.

"Why?" was all I could muster at the time. I was never the best conversationalist when I was either busy with work or the subject was boring. And this, although it wasn't her fault, was a bit of both.

I looked at her stood waiting for my reply as regarding her possibly cooking me a meal. A slave was something I certainly didn't want.

"Come and sit down," I said.

"I feel awful about not doing anything," she replied again, flashing those blue eyes.

It must have been hard for her – she'd had her independence and now she had none. Having the baby would take out another sixteen weeks and then it's growing up until probably six months. On the face of it, it was a year's 'time out'.

"I really need to get rid of the car," she added.

"Yeah and then you won't be able to see you folks or go shopping or whatever," I said.

"I feel a right leech."

"Do I complain?" I asked, knowing that the answer would be a 'no'.

"No, you're great," she said. "You never complain."

I'm glad we got that one cleared up, and just to initially test the water I put it to her – "Why don't you serve your husband divorce papers – I'm sure that'd pass a bit of time."

I really, really enjoyed saying that.

"That's unless you're on about going back to him," I added.

"Don't be daft – that definitely won't happen."

"I'll get you an appointment with one of the legal people we use if you want?" I said.

To be honest she looked in two minds about it all, so I hit the 'all systems go' button. "I was talking with Jeanette the other day about ours going through."

"You are getting a divorce?" she asked.

"Yeah – she's wanting for her and that Paul to sort of take it one step further – but I think she's more concerned that it will free me up to marry you."

"She said that?"

I nodded a 'yes' as I watched her face light up.

That put the cat amongst the pigeons.

"What else did she say?" she asked.

"That Dale Fox is big, fat and bald," I replied.

That put a smile on her face. "She certainly didn't say that, you pig."

"She did, I showed her a photo of him."

She laughed. "He married a cousin of my cousin on my dad's side," she replied.

"Well she isn't with him now," I said.

"Really?"

"Really," I replied.

"So come on, what did Jeanette say?" she asked, still smiling.

"Just what I told you – she wants the divorce, but she sees it as opening the door for me to marry you."

There was a silence but I could tell she was happy – I think?

"Why, would you want to marry me?" she asked.

"You must be joking – you're a right leech," I said.

"I do love you, you know."

"I know – so stop moping about and do something constructive."

I got another cuddle and it was confirmed over a quick chicken salad that she would set divorce proceedings in motion. I would have loved to see the big bastard's face when those papers dropped through his door.

Next morning kicked off with a jog around the block at 5:30am and a shower. We had a meeting with BSkyB and they would be getting billed. They also wanted to see a bit of the 'Sammy' project before ESPN could take it away, however ITV had got wind of it through connections with the Tall Dwarf's boss down at ITV and they wanted first dibs, so a meeting was also set up with them.

I rang Jeanette on the way to work, basically to sound her out further about our divorce. That was a mistake, and straight away she smelled a rat.

"You *are* on about marrying her," she said.

"No I am not," I said. "I just told her what you said to me."

"Yes, and what was that?" she asked.

"That you want the divorce, but you see it as opening the door for me to marry her."

"I never, ever said that," she replied.

"I beg to differ – I was there when you said it."

"I can't remember saying that," she replied.

I got into the meeting and surprise, surprise they wanted to move the goalposts on our World Cup 1970 programme.

"You've portrayed Ramsey as a bungling idiot," the first suit said.

"No we haven't, we've portrayed Ramsey as Ramsey, and how top managers of the time portrayed him," I replied.

"And Bobby Charlton – That's terrible how he's come out," added the second suit.

"It's a true portrayal of the failings of 1970 – It is well documented," stated Sooty.

"Bobby Charlton was a great player," stated the second suit.

"He was during his time," I replied. "As was Jimmy Greaves, however 1970 wasn't their time."

"It's wrong," stated the second suit.

"Manchester United supporter, are you?" I asked.

"Yes, so what of it?" he replied.

"I could do you a documentary on Munich '58 by the end of next week, and pull down the glory of Manchester fucking United in one foul swoop – stating how they treat the players who survived the crash but who couldn't play anymore," I snarled.

"That would be interesting," said the first suit.

"Well get this signed off," I replied, "And I'll do you a draft on Munich."

That put them on the spot, but I'll tell you something – it got signed off.

Next up ESPN, however I had something else pressing, which was getting the accountant to shift my money around a bit more, as I knew I should certainly be getting better access to it – Jeanette had had me tie a load of my money in ISAs or whatever, which was part of the reason I never felt that I had the amount of money around me that my endeavour deserved; however, the last place I needed to be was in those offices of 'Vogue', so I got Libby to set up a meeting at twelve bells with 'Big Decker' at the coffee shop and who didn't disappoint.

"What's this I hear?" he immediately said giving me a nudge, nudge, wink, wink.

"What?" I asked.

"That you're slipping it to two look-a-likes, a girl from the Clarion Debt Agency on Grays Inn Road and you've had a restraining order put on lovely girl with a huge chest?"

"You shouldn't believe gossip," I replied.

"It was your wife who told me."

"My wife?" I asked.

"The tall woman with the big thighs," he said.

"That's not my wife, that's Sooty's."

"Are you sure?"

"I think so," I replied. "All my women are similar sizes – and I don't do big ones with big feet."

"What about Yiannis'?"

"Who's he?" I asked.

"The Greek restaurant owner from Camden Town?"

"'Does he come in here?" I asked.

"He does – fat mat man with a stern face."

This was something I didn't know about.

"She said you look like David Beckham."

"Who did?" I asked.

"She did."

I didn't know any Yiannis's wife. Why didn't I know of any Yiannis's wife?

"She's a little woman with a rather large chest and one big foot," he explained. "She's allegedly got the hots for you."

"One big foot or two?" I asked.

"One," he replied.

"I'm fairly selective, Decker," I replied. "I think I'd notice some bird with a big foot."

"Well she told your wife that you got thrown out of the studio because you couldn't stand to see her being kissed."

"Who the hell made this shit up?" I asked.

"It was your wife that told me."

"I told you – I don't have any wife with big thighs."

An eavesdropping Fosis, dropping me off an espresso and a Perrier water, sort of backed me up on this one.

"It is true – he big pervert and have thing for small women with small leg," he said.

"Cheers," I said.

"No problem," he replied. "Does man know that new bitch likes to be chained to bed with big bar?"

"Fosis, go dust your counter," I said.

"He total pervert," Fosis candidly added. "He go Bangkok without me and shag twenty-nine beautiful women and get paid for it."

The accountant was hooked.

"There's a big translation issue here, Decker," I stated.

"He see dwarf with big titties and he have husband arrested."

The accountant was hooked even further.

"Fosis – go lurk somewhere else," I urged.

I tried to explain that was a load of bullshit sort of lost in translation, however by now my accountant wanted to move in with me and have my babies.

"Oh do tell me about the dwarf, boy," he said. "Tell me that you hit her like an express train and did she have to pull the emergency chord – whoof – did you, son? Did you? Whoof?"

This guy was on a different planet.

I managed to shake him off but he was adamant that I had to tell him about it next time we met, which in my mind was never. I had to get Libby to switch accountants. Meanwhile and unbeknown to me, Jeanette had asked Emily around for a coffee and a chat, the subject matter being me. If Emily wanted me last night, she certainly wouldn't be that keen today. Well, that's what I thought as soon as she rang me to tell me.

"What?" I asked.

"She's lovely," Emily replied.

When it came to verbal opposition, Jeanette was Christian Ronaldo and Emily was George Cohen. I had Alan Finney, the ex-Sheffield Wednesday winger tell me one night how he used to run rings around Cohen every time they played Fulham, and how he had no idea how Cohen ever got in the England set-up. It's weird how fellow professionals come over to each other.

"Yes, she's lovely," I said. "But so are you, and I don't want some viperous ex getting her fangs into you and poisoning your mind."

I got back into work and had to debrief Sooty about the accountant.

"He's a frigging basket case, he is," I said. "He has this thing about trains."

"Yeah?" shrugged Sooty. "What about 'em?"

A shiver went up my spine thinking about it.

"Anyway who's this Yiannis's wife with the foot that Libby's been on about?"

"She's the actress in that thing they've been shooting here," he replied.

If a shiver went up my spine before, you could times this one by ten.

"Her?" I exclaimed. "She's a right fucking idiot – ten times worse than 'Big Decker' – you ought to have seen her with that sailor – she didn't give a shit."

Then I debriefed him about Jeanette versus Emily.

"Bloody hell," said Sooty. "Jeanette will run rings round her."

See, what did I tell you?

Next up ESPN. Three suits and a female PA came into the office. They were extremely nice people, and wanted to know about the 'Sammy' project in more detail before they signed off on it. I let them know that we'd just had BSkyB in and their suits had been edgy about the World Cup 1970 content, and that they thought we'd made Ramsey look bad.

"Football moves on," I said. "Brazil set the benchmark for 1970 and Holland took it one step further in 1974 – a competition that we couldn't even qualify for – and look at the players we had back then."

Sooty nodded at my appraisal.

"Ramsey said after the 1970 World Cup – 'We have nothing to learn from Brazil'," I added. "He was referring to the lack of players – but compare Sammy of Arsenal to, say Stiles. It's like comparing a fillet of steak with Pedigree Chum – they were worlds apart. Ramsey had the players at his disposal – but he refused to take them – he stayed loyal to a certain crop of players from 1966."

"Stiles was a holding player, wasn't he?" asked one of the suits.

I nodded. "Sammy was the complete midfield player, with the vision of Giles and a shot as deadly as that of Peter

Lorimer – wrong place at the wrong time."

By the end of the meeting I think ESPN wanted our 1970 programme, however they went away with signing off on the 'Sammy' project after watching the guts of it.

Sooty was dead happy. It wasn't often that you could do a million quid's worth of work in one afternoon – however ITV were a minor problem, in that it was possible that they wanted it too. Sooty explained that this could not happen, and we could get around it by combining both programmes – a sort of pull on the 'Turn of the Decade'.

"It's doable," he said. "We've got some excellent footage."

I knew we'd got some excellent footage – it was me who had got it.

I knocked off happy around 6:00pm and then remembered Emily, along with the lump you could now see with my name on it, had had a coffee with Jeanette. Mmm. This could be a bit strange.

"Hello," she said, smiling as I came through the door.

That I wasn't expecting.

I knew they had spoken before but it was polite dialogue – 'Hello', 'How are you?', 'Has he pissed you off yet?' and that kind of thing – just general politeness. However my 'ace' card was always the kids. The kids loved their 'M' and I was nothing short of God in their eyes. It was me who had chased their ferrets down the street when they had got out, me who nearly set the opposite house on fire. I was a fairly exciting dad, if I'm honest. A lot more exciting than Sooty – he made his kids learn French and do sums. Mine had an Xbox and a thousand inch screen TV with surround sound.

"I've just got in," she said. "We picked up the children from school."

We? I thought.

"I bet they were pleased to see you?" I said.

"Very," she replied. "You're such a great dad."

And then she started crying – I wasn't expecting that either.

"Jeanette said no matter what rubbish has been going on in your life at the time – you've never neglected your children – and believe me, she said, you've had a lot."

Mmm. I didn't like the sound of that.

"What, children or rubbish?"

"Stop it – she just kept on saying what a brilliant father you are and that there is no-one that could compare with you and that you'll be a great father to the baby," she said wiping her eyes. "She really, really loves you, yer know."

"She might love me, but she certainly doesn't like me – she's dead bossy, and nearly as bossy as Libby," I said. "And was that a Scouse twang I just heard?"

She laughed as she wiped her eyes. "Sorry, my hormones are all over the place."

"What? You think I'm kidding?" I asked. "She gives me lists of things to do, and not to do with the kids, and then interrogates them afterwards to see if I've disobeyed any of her orders – Batman is the most versatile tool in my armoury when it comes to managing her expectations – however he's starting to wear a bit thin with my daughter."

"Batman?" she asked, smiling.

"Batman eats his carrots – Batman says 'please' and 'thank-you' – Batman wipes his arse when he's been to the toilet," I said. "Unfortunately there are no female superheroes and me telling my daughter that Mercedes Fisher of Hollyoaks flushes the chain after she's been to the bog resulted in a lot of questions, one of which was, was I seeing her – even Jeanette was convinced I was knocking her off."

Emily laughed. "See," she said. "Everyone loves you."

I smiled at my ever-burgeoning popularity.

"I really want this to work, you know," she said. "I just feel sort of useless when I see how everyone perceives you."

"Go 'round to Libby's – I'm sure she'll give you a reality check – she hates my guts – saying that, she's not that fond of Sooty – and even her own kids do her head in."

I got a cuddle, a kiss and a smile.

"I had a word with my accountant this dinnertime," I said.

"The slimy one with the fat head?" she replied.

"I didn't know I'd mentioned him," I replied.

"Yeah, you have – loads of times."

"He has this strange fascination about trains," I said, before going on to explain, over a coffee and a king prawn and cous cous salad that she'd made me, that I was to open a few bank accounts – two of which she needed to go sign for.

"Me?" she asked.

"A joint one, and a savings account for the baby," I said.

"What, really?" was her reply.

"Yeah, but the baby won't be able to get a Mastercard or Visa until he's five – and then he'll not be able to gamble online."

She laughed. "That's so sweet."

"Is it?" I replied. "Dead restrictive when a parent can't use his own child for internet fraud – this country's going to the dogs."

"You don't half cheer me up," she said.

I had to let her know that if she was running the house and having my child, then she needed some form of independence to do so, as one thing I did know was that she had been buying the food I was eating with the money she had. I'd thought about this quite a bit – not as much as Arshavin not being used as the false nine, when it was his perfect position, but I had thought about it.

"Four grand a week will go in there," I said rather proudly, and left it at that.

"You are so lovely," she stated.

"So when I need to use a call girl, you can just do a straightforward BACS payment."

She knew I was kidding. Well, I hope she did, as I tended to use Sooty's Amex for most of the call girls I'd done. In fact, Libby was adamant that he was investing in some chocolate factory when she found out that he'd been putting around a grand a month into 'Pink Candy'. I must admit he went berserk when he found out, however when I told him they all thought he was fantastic, he sort of forgot about it. I couldn't use the card again though.

That night was lovely and we curled up on the sofa and watched Arsenal wallop Newcastle 3-0. I was intending to knock one out to Gabrielle on 'Fetish Fun Wives' but Emily insisted on rule one, which amounted to a good hour's graft instead of a six or seven minute 'lamb shank' in front of the laptop.

I'd been out for my morning jog when I got picked up by the police at the bottom of Frederick Street. It was the same two clowns that had been around to the house a few times before.

"Is this yours?" he asked.

It was Giroud the ferret.

"Where did you pick him up?" I asked.

"About three streets back," he replied. "It had been upsetting someone's cat."

I gave an innocent shrug of my shoulders.

"What was it doing out?" asked the policeman.

"I generally take him jogging, but he's only got short legs so I sort of lose him on Packenham Street."

Starsky & Hutch slung me the ferret and I bollocked him for getting out – again. I got back to the house where Emily was already up and was half-watching Sky Sports, which was playing on a 36" TV which I'd recently had mounted on the wall – and where the other one had been before it was shipped off to the Ukraine by my ex-tenants, along with all my other appliances. I had to hand it to her, 6:00am in the morning and she was up pandering around me – that must be love.

"I was sick again," she said.

Uh, I was wrong.

"That doesn't mean you're leaving me again and going back up to Birkenhead to see Dale Fox, does it?" I asked.

"Don't be silly," she smiled, before copping sight of the ferret in the pocket of my hoodie.

"What are you doing with Giroud?"

"He's a damn sight quicker at getting out of the garden than he is on the field," I said. "Those two policemen had him in the car and picked him up three streets away."

"What was he doing down there?" she asked.

"Flashing some old lady and then trying to smuggle her into a hotel room, the copper said – that's why they arrested him."

Emily shook her head and laughed as I picked him up and looked at him, and then let him run around on the kitchen tops before he fell in the sink. "I told you, his close-control is crap."

Emily fished him out of the sink and took him out into the garden. I really needed to back-fill all that piping as it looked a bit sinister – sort of like a ventilation system for some meth lab – and the old woman from across kept on peering down at us from around the curtains.

"She watches me all the time," Emily said as she put the escapee back in his cell.

I sipped at my coffee as I watched Giroud try to do his Houdini act again and then over at the twitching curtains.

"The children said that you told them that she's a witch," said Emily. "And that you said that if she caught them that she'd boil them up in a big pan."

"They told you that?" I asked.

"Yeah, and that she'd put a straw in their ears and suck out their brains."

"I had to say that – my little lad was chucking stones at her window," I replied.

I got in work to see Sooty giving Ginge a bollocking through the glass window of his office – I had no idea what about, as that was his department, but I was sure that Ginge would tell me afterwards. It could have been about mistakenly wiping a load of data before it got archived or starring as the 'third man' in that 'indie' garbage that was being shot here for Channel Four. Either that or it was a strong, albeit pointless, debate about Ginge wanting more coloured managers in the Premiership.

"What's up?" I asked as he came out of Sooty's office.

"He's a prick," exclaimed Ginge.

"I know – but what's up?"

"I'm after a bit of a pay rise – my girlfriend's pregnant," he said.

"How much are you on?" I asked.

"Not enough," he replied.

I nipped into see Sooty, and Ginge was right – what he was earning in comparison to what he actually did sort of correlated very badly.

"His girlfriend's pregnant," I said.

"I didn't do that," Sooty replied.

"I'm not saying you did – 'Happy in thy work' and all that," I said before asking the million dollar question.

"He's wanting an extra five grand a year," stated Sooty.

"What – a hundred quid a week? – I spend that getting insulted at the coffee shop."

"It's his attitude as well," stated Sooty.

"What, because he doesn't agree with you?" I smiled. "He doesn't agree with me either – or Fred – or Abi."

"He was a bit on the aggressive side," snapped Sooty.

"Why?" I replied.

"How the hell do I know," he replied.

I shouted Ginge back into Sooty's office, and the surly little turd shuffled over and came in.

"What?" he asked.

"What are you after? A pay rise or pissing your boss off? Or both?" I asked.

"A pay rise," he replied.

"And who can give you a pay rise?" I asked

"What?" he asked.

"And who can give you a pay rise?" I asked again, this time with added gesticulations.

"Sooty," he replied.

"In other offices Sooty would be called Mr. Sutton," I said. "But here we try to run the place without that kind of thing. In here we are all on first name terms – it works well – however at the end of the day – that guy – Mr. Sutton – he makes the decisions, that either keep you in a job, or help you lose that job – there is no need to spit and snarl at any of us."

"I'm helping you dig a gold mine here," he said.

That took me aback. "Really? Then perhaps you should go take your fucking shovel and go dig one of your own – sort of see how easy it is."

He said nothing.

"It's been a struggle for us," I said. "Really."

"We put everything into this," exclaimed Sooty. "We expected nothing and certainly had nothing given."

It was true, we were knocking out cheap quality DVDs at the start. Totally plagiarised and totally illegal, but totally good fun. We had literally kicked off from nothing.

"You work hard and you earn your place," I said. "Nothing comes free."

He still said nothing.

"Look at Emmanuel Frimpong," I said.

"Di Natalie said he was the hardest player he'd ever played against," quipped Ginge.

"And that makes him good?" I asked. "Any shit player can put the boot in and pick up red cards."

"He isn't shit," said Ginge. "He just didn't get his chance."

"He got it with Barnsley – got sent off in the first half hour of his debut and he's just helped them get relegated to the old Third Division," I replied. "At Arsenal he thought he was a celebrity, chucked his weight around a bit and expected everything given. His attitude stunk the place out – he was more interested in the person he thought he was than the player he could become."

Ginge said nothing.

"Look at Bacary Sagna – he gets on with his job and never shoots his mouth off in public – he overcame two broken legs in twelve months, which bollocksed around with his form and he took a bit of flak for it – the model professional – I'd much rather have a Sagna than a Frimpong."

"You're still learning," said Sooty. "Get your head down and think about what we are giving you and not the other way around – if you are good, it will come."

"So, now that's out of the way," I said. "Who's the unlucky girl you've got up the duff?"

"Rachel – The sister of the guy that did your decorating," he replied.

"I hope she's better fucking looking than him," I said.

Ginge smiled.

"Go on – piss off and get on with your work – I'll sort this," I said.

Ginge left the office.

"So?" said Sooty, shrugging his shoulders.

"So give it him – it's not like we can't afford it."

We had ITV come in around 11:00am and Abigail did

some impressive presentation about some programme that was a cross-reference of the two that we had just done – both of which they watched – the Sammy one was looking as impressive as you could get, and their alleged Head of Sport was continually shaking his head all the way through.

"I hate buttering up failure, as I like the truth when it comes to football," I said. "As for Sammy, his career could have been a thousand times better if he had been more extrovert – and sort of nastier – but he was how he was and nothing can change that now."

"And Abigail mentioned one on Munich?" said the Head of Sport.

If you want honest sport progamming," I said. "You'll always get it from us."

They were very impressed and we left the room whilst they talked. I grabbed a coffee with Ginge and told him of his impending pay rise and asked him if he could get his future brother-in-law, Adebayor, to do a bit of a back fill and landscaping job on the garden.

"Thanks," he said. "I appreciate it."

We went back into the room with the suits from ITV and we got a shock. It turned out that they were after upping their profile as regards football, and wanted around four hours a week filling, and could we do it? A six-month trial, which if successful would be renegotiated.

It was a dream for a small company like ours and after they had left, to say Sooty was cock-a-hoop was the understatement of the year.

"I haven't felt like this since Leeds won the League," he said.

"You want to get a life, you sad bastard," I replied.

I went home around 5:30pm and had a surprise waiting for me as Emily had picked up both kids from school and they were in the kitchen playing with the ferrets.

"Jeanette had to work," she said.

"Wash your hands after you've done with them," I told the kids. "I'm even starting to stink like a ferret."

"M says we can go to McDonalds when you come in," said my daughter.

"Sure," I said. "If you don't tell your mum."

"They've been great," said Emily. "They don't half cheer me up."

"Who, the kids or the ferrets?" I asked.

I slumped on the couch and Emily followed suit, as did the kids and both ferrets, one of which was running around my head and scratching my ear.

"Dad, it likes you," said my daughter.

"I know – it likes me that much it keeps trying to escape."

I blackmailed both kids into putting them back and washing their hands by telling them that I had a brilliant idea, that I would let them in on if they did, and in the meantime I asked Emily if she had a passport.

"Yeah, why?" she asked.

"I fancy a week in the sun," I said.

My idea was an all-inclusive bash in Sri Lanka or India, but I knew that a long haul flight and a load of injections for Emily was a no-go. She could handle the ten-hour flight but I didn't want the kid coming out looking like Peter Docherty – I would have said Peter Beardsley, but I can't keep on using him as some deformed yardstick.

"Us go abroad?" she asked.

"Yeah, sure," I said.

I don't know who was happier, her or the kids. We went to a McDonald's, came back and I had them bathed and rigged out in their pyjamas before I drove them back over to their mum's in Clerkenwell.

"Thanks for that," said Jeanette. "It was a big help."

I got a nod from Paul the Brentford fan, and sort of

reciprocated it before I drove back over to north London. It didn't take long for Jeanette's interrogation of the kids to have them inform her that I had mentioned a holiday.

"A holiday?" she asked. "Where are you on about taking them? You've never taken them on holiday before – why are you on about a holiday now?"

I had. I had taken them to Brighton but it chucked it down and it was crap, so that didn't count. We had also had an aborted sortie out into Cornwall, but I had to come back after a day as we got a rush job in from BSkyB – although the fact that my lad had a bit of sickness and diarrhoea and shat himself in the car sort of sped up the coming back home process.

"I've no idea, Jeanette," I replied whilst getting out of the car. "It's only just been mentioned."

The upshot was that she thought that I must have a reason. One of those secret reasons that only she knew I had, and which was that secret even I didn't know about it.

"When are you on about taking them?" she asked.

"I've no idea, Jeanette," I replied, and just to play her at her own game I slipped in a four-letter googly. "When it's convenient – I'll work around you and Paul."

"Paul?" she replied. "What's he got to do with it?"

"I don't know, maybe you have something planned."

It may have shut her up, but I could hear her mind ticking away in the background, waiting for any opportune moment for her mouth to explode. However it didn't.

Inside the house Emily was both talking to her mum and trawling through holidays on the internet.

"My mum says hi," she said.

"Tell her hello back," I said.

"I'm just telling mum that we're going off on holiday," she smiled.

I wouldn't get too excited just yet, I thought.

I switched on Sky Sports and trawled through a few of the sports channels, one of which was Arsenal TV, which if I am honest is extremely poor. The club like to come across as a club who are in the top tier of their profession, but there is so much more that they could do.

I received a text message on my phone. 'May 11 – 18 is ok. Jeanette x'.

I text back. 'Thanks Jeanette. I do appreciate it. I do love u and the kids x'.

I got an instant reply. 'x'.

"We're okay for the May the eleventh to May the eighteenth," I said.

Emily screamed sort of excitedly down the phone to her mum, "Did you hear that, mum – yessss!"

However there was one thing I had forgotten, that Jeanette had not. Arsenal were due to play the FA Cup Final on the 17th. That was a bit naughty of her. I had left myself open to some major manipulation.

"My mum says can she come," Emily smiled.

I gave her a smile back, but at the back of my mind I knew Jeanette had worked her 'flanker' – it was a test to see how much I would adhere to what she said, and for her to see how much I did love my kids.

Chapter 18
The Dividend

ITV were extremely interested how we were going to set this all up. BT Sport, BSkyB and the BBC had the monopoly on the Premiership, so this made it an awkward one for football's 'current affairs' or even results; however, working with one arm behind your back was something Sooty and I were never averse to doing.

"Do a forty-five minutes results service," I stated. "Just make it better than Sky's and the BBC's."

There was a bit of umming and erring from the suits.

"Come on," I said. "It's a piece of piss – Sky Sports are the benchmark and what you're looking to emulate, as what the BBC are running with is basically crap and is shoved down the aerial on prime time Saturday afternoon – be better than Sky and you'll take the lot."

There was less umming and erring the second time around as they knew what I was saying, and for as eloquently spoken as Garth Crookes might think he is, nobody actually wants to listen to him.

"We could hook up with the main bookmakers, and I could get some great statisticians that would blow your mind," I added. "Believe me when I say it – no one knows football like us – we'll blow the others away."

"Okay, so that's a forty-five minute results service," said the ITV's Head of Sport.

"No it's not," I replied. "You make it the start of something big – there is a huge amount of potential talent out there – and more in tune with what's happening than ninety-nine percent of any ex-pros that are hanging on to their pensions – this will help get your stars of tomorrow, and this will form the foundations of the other programmes we do, whether it's something current or something in the past tense – I'm telling you again – no one knows football like us."

There was quite a deal of discussion and one of the suits was interested in our 'Sammy' project and how it affected, or in his case, didn't affect the 1970 World Cup.

"Do you actually know him?" asked the suit as regards Sammy.

"Nope," I replied.

"Then how can you be so frank in giving an appraisal?" he asked.

"I'm a 'reading between the lines' sort of person," I replied. "You get close to someone then you lose the truth – that edge – for fear of upsetting the equilibrium that's been formed. Sammy as a person was like that – an absolutely fantastic footballer and a true gentleman, however he would have very little on the negative side to tell you about any of his fellow pros, not just for fear of upsetting the said equilibrium but because he was just a really nice guy – I don't know David Beckham, but what I do know is I wouldn't like to be stuck on a desert island with him – he's nearly as boring as Garth Crookes – however, if Sammy knew either of them, I'm sure he would never tell you that."

That raised a few sniggers.

"With Sammy it was a confidence thing," I added. "Not that he didn't have confidence in his own ability, as he did, but when you've got 40,000 supporters and you've just hit a goal with two minutes to go to put your side into the next round of a major competition you don't just stick an arm in the air and shake your mate's hand. You run up to the crowd and swing your dick and get them involved and make it known that you actually care – that was his biggest downfall. It's always the small things that affect the way you are perceived."

"There's been a lot of talk of goal celebrations of late and the need to calm them," said the Head of Sport.

"Why?" I asked. "Football's a passionate sport – it always has been and always will be."

"The Nicolas Anelka thing with the Quenelle salute," he replied.

"What a load of bollocks – Anelka got his hands rattled because he's Anelka and no one likes him. When Gervinho hits a goal and he gives it the dozen or so Zieg Heil salutes nobody bats an eye lid – if Podolski had have done that he'd have copped eighteen months – fortunately, Gervinho never scored much, so it kind of got overlooked – maybe if he'd put his boots on the right feet he may have done a bit better."

"He was a strange player," said one of the suits.

"Who, Sammy?" I asked.

"No, Gervinho," he replied.

"He's quick," I said. "I once saw him running down Tottenham High Street with five lads chasing him."

We came out of ITV studios with Sooty in awe of me. Well, sort of.

"You were sailing close to the fucking wind in there," he said.

"What are you on about, they loved us," I said. "It looks like I'm out of the country for the Cup Final, though," I said.

"You're joking," he replied. "Nine years since the last one

and you're away? There's no way I'd be going away if it was Leeds in the final."

"Sooty, you can book the next twenty years' holidays in May," I said. "And I guarantee that Leeds being in a final certainly wouldn't affect your plans."

The rise and fall of Leeds United was always a sore subject. We had done a documentary on the Don Revie years for Irish Television a couple of years ago and I have to admit, it was an exceptional subject as at the time they were a truly exceptional team – powerful, ruthless and like a machine. Nowadays however, they are nothing short of a shambles. Revie was wrongly painted black in my opinion. You ask anyone from within Arsenal at that time and the majority will tell you that Leeds were a remarkable team who set the benchmark for every other club in England. Bertie Mee said after the 1968 League Cup Final, "We are still a couple of years behind Leeds at the moment, but we're getting there."

Obviously he meant that partly as praise for Arsenal, but more so for Leeds. As I said, it's the 'little things' in football, and *that* final itself was billed as a final to forget, with there being more violence on the pitch than there was in the stands. It was a match me and Sooty have watched hundreds of times – that and the 1972 FA Cup Final, that is.

Jack Charlton rammed his elbow into the head of 'Fumbling Jim' Furnell on the corner, the ball got half cleared and Cooper lashed it into the back of the net before running the length of the field on an imaginary pogo stick. Sammy had a twenty-five yard effort turned around the post by Sprake and Graham had a goal disallowed, but apart from that Leeds were never in any real danger. Don Revie was to Bertie Mee what Mourinho is to Wenger, and could read him like a book. Back then, nobody could beat Arsenal like Leeds.

When I got back in I slumped into the chair opposite

the couch and Emily joined me by sitting on my knee, with loads of cuddles and a kiss. I sort of make it sound very 'Hugh Grant' with some other posh bit of 'umph' but it was nothing of the sort. This was a bit heavy if I was being honest, and I got offered dirty sex with basically anything I wanted, but I pushed the 'hang fire' button on all the naughty stuff as soon as I found out that Libby had been on the phone to her, and that one of my worst nightmares was about to occur.

"I said we'd go around for around half past seven," she said, before seeing my expression drop from 'happy to be home' to that of impending doom. "If that's okay with you."

Emily had never been to Sooty's before, and it was one of those once in a lifetime experience that you'd prefer to forget, but are hardly likely to. Not quite as exciting as a bad motorbike crash, but more on par with near suffocation or drowning.

"She says you've both had a great week," she added.

"We have," I replied. "So, why spoil it?"

"Did I do wrong?" she asked.

I shook my head. I wish she would stop being so nice.

"I told Libby about our going away on holiday," she added. "And she mentioned Hawaii."

The anticipation of being subjected to the torture of their Hawaiian vacation including holiday snaps plus three and a half hours of video footage again hung around my neck like a noose.

"Don't you like them?" she asked.

"Course I do – I love them both," I replied. "They are great people."

She shrugged her shoulders and gave me that smile.

"Okay then," she said as she de-clung herself from around me and went to upstairs get changed.

I sat back and flicked on Sky Sports and took down some notes to quell the anticipation of five hours of boredom.

Fifteen minutes later Emily sort of stole my concentration a bit as she paced up and down the room floor in her stockinged feet.

"You lost something?" I asked.

"Libby wanted to borrow your Grease DVD – me and the children watched it the other day – I can't seem to find it."

"That's had a bit of air time this week," I said knowing that Dale Fox saw her as the 'one that he wanted' or his 'Sandy, bay- aby' – git.

I got an ummed reply as I sort of peered around her at an Arsenal press conference on TV and listened to what Arsené Wenger had to say, or didn't as it turned out. He was getting to be as illuminating as a ten watt light bulb.

"Will Sagna sign a new contract?" He couldn't even answer that properly.

I walked over to get a coffee and noticed a load of holiday brochures on the breakfast bar. Jeanette had given me parameters which I had passed on to Emily, who had wasted no time in serving me up the potential delights of Marrakesh, Dubai and Jordan, however I now had to explain that although each one of them sounded great, Saturday the 17th was a large part of my make-up and none of these were guaranteed to have a huge flat screen in a bar with Arsenal playing on it.

"Found it," she said, before clocking me looking at the brochures. "'You fancy Marrakesh, then?"

"I think Marrakesh sounds brilliant," I replied. "However, I think I'm part of a test."

She gave me a look of bemusement.

"Jeanette has specified a date which includes the date of the FA Cup Final – I think she thought I'd back down from taking the kids – I really need somewhere where there's a TV so I can watch it – I'm not so sure some hotel Marrakesh even has electricity, never mind being able to pick up the game."

"What, like Benidorm?" she asked.

"You must be joking," I replied, smiling.

It was just another obstacle that had been placed in front of me – a television at 5:00pm UK time that could pick up ITV wasn't a big ask.

We drove down to Sooty's, which took about ten minutes to get there and around half an hour to park up – and to immediately be met by his two brats at the door, who wasted no time in tap dancing in my face by doing their fifteen-times tables backwards and reciting the first chapter of Nabokov's 'Pnin' in French.

"They're very clever," said Emily.

"They're also very boring," I said.

"Aw, they think the world of you," she said.

It was true – I may have thought I had the appeal of Robert Helpmann's 'Child Catcher' out of Chitty Chitty Bang Bang, but their kids did not, and were highly insistent on my being entertained by them, or vice versa as it turned out.

"Dad says you jumped on a car roof singing Greased Lightning," stated one of the brats.

Mmm. I wondered what the Grease DVD was really for?

"Did you do that?" asked Emily grinning.

"Not recently," I replied.

"Dad says you dinted its roof," added the brat.

"No that was your Auntie Catherine – we threw her off a bridge."

"You did not," disputed the brat.

"We did – she completely squashed the car – there was a man in it as well – when they pulled him out he was dead."

"You're lying," argued the brat.

"It was your wicked Uncle Ernie," I said.

"We haven't got no wicked Uncle Ernie," it said.

"I know – he's dead – I told you – your Auntie Catherine killed him."

"We've got an Uncle Mark, though?" stated the brat.

Which Uncle Mark – the thin one or the one with fifty-eight front teeth?"

There was a bit of thought and discussion, however they were both adamant it was the thin one.

"Uncle Mark ate his own wife's brains," I said. "It was in the news."

"Uncle Mark's married to Auntie Catherine," stated the brat.

"I know, that's why she's stupid and has to wear that ginger wig to cover the hole."

"You're lying," they said as Libby came into the lounge brandishing two cheques that I had to countersign.

"Ask your mum?" I stated.

"It's for yours and Tim's dividend," said Libby, handing me the cheques.

I was impressed. I wouldn't have kicked up half as much fuss about going over if I'd have known I was getting a dividend. I'd not had a dividend for – well, ever.

"You have to pay off your credit cards," stated Libby.

I knew that. She didn't have to tell me.

"He's got around eighty-thousand pounds of debt on them," she blabbed.

Well, eighty-seven really; I had Emily re-fit the kitchen and I'd bought a bed or two.

"He's bloody rubbish with money," she blabbed further.

When Emily copped the accumulation of noughts on the cheque for the dividend she nearly dropped the baby there and then and if I wasn't a 'catch' then, then I certainly was now.

"Make him pay those cards off M," stated Libby. "I

wouldn't mind but he doesn't even need them."

I did. I loved my credit cards. I thought they were great. There's no feeling like going into a shop and wasting money that you don't see on something pointless that you don't need. The power of plastic.

"This is for a quarter of a million pounds," said Emily.

Libby nodded. "Just watch he doesn't squander it."

"Does that mean we have to watch that rubbish holiday video?" I asked.

"Don't be cheeky," said Libby. "We'll eat first."

I got through Libby's asparagus soup like a good 'un, but I struggled like hell with the belly pork.

"What the hell have you bought this for?" I asked. "It must be the worst meat ever."

"I told Tim exactly the same," Libby agreed.

"I'll put a stone on if I eat this," I added as I poked it with my fork. "It's like gnawing through blubber."

"It only cost me six quid," he said.

"I can see why," I replied before getting nudged by Emily.

We made it home around midnight and the really dirty sex I got offered earlier was re-offered and executed with precision by the man with the healthy dividend – the lump not really hindering me, even though I had chronic indigestion. I had to hand it to Emily: she was great at implementing both the new rule number one and the old rule number one, and both at the same time. It's just a pity they made such a mess. That was twice this week already I'd seen the bedsheets go around the washing machine.

I got in from my morning's jog about 5:50am to see the percolator on and Emily sat at the breakfast bar sipping at her coffee with a line of cheques, statements and envelopes in front of her. That was quick.

"Are you my accountant now?" I smiled.

"I bloody hope not," she laughed. "Get these signed and I'll post them for you."

She was making a great ally for Libby, that's for sure, and I did as I was told.

"Have you thought about which bedroom we can have for the baby?" she asked.

Nope – I've never given it one thought, I thought.

"Why, what are you thinking?" I asked.

"It'd be easier if he was on the same landing," she said, which from reading her face she seemed a bit hesitant in letting me know – the fact of the matter being that my kids shared the two other rooms on the same landing.

The house itself was basically a white washed inner shell with floorboards. I'd had the place fumigated and jet washed after the Russians had left and given it a bit of fill and a paint job, but if I'm being brutally honest, apart from the downstairs, it was a bit sparse. I knew Emily had something on her mind and rather than let it stay there, I asked for her opinion.

"I don't want the children to feel that they are getting pushed out," she said.

"We've got two fairly big rooms on the top floor," I said. "Get them done out and do one of theirs for the kid – your sister's down later, isn't she? It'll give you something to do."

Wow. I nearly got rule number one and rule number one again, and to say she was happy was an understatement and I literally had to beat her off me with a whip.

Later that evening I came in from work to find her sister Lucy sat on the couch watching Hollyoaks on TV and two coloured guys in the back garden both scratching their heads and talking to Emily. It could have been worse – it could have been the other way around.

"Hiya," Lucy had said on me entering the house.

"'Your brother okay?" I asked.

I didn't get much of a response, just an 'mmm' and the feeling of being undressed and groped along with knowing that all her family were obsessed by sex.

This Adebayor dude could turn his hand to anything and he was currently trying to con Emily into giving him the heads-up for a ten grand landscaping project, when I only wanted the piped ferret run back-filling, a bit of turf chucking on top and the burnt out mattress slinging.

"Ten grand?" I exclaimed. "What are you on about sticking in – a swimming pool?"

The garden wasn't that big you could actually do anything with it – which was one of the main reasons I bought the house in the first place.

"Your girl wants a fence to stop the old woman looking over at her children," said Adebayor.

My girl – her children? I thought – I quite liked the sound of that.

"Yeah so that's about a hundred quid for a bit of wood – so enlighten me how you're going to mug me of the other nine point nine grand," I asked.

I must admit, he had a great sales patter and made it sound quite good when he mentioned back-filling it enough to get it raised for a swing and slide for the kids, and promised me that he would construct it so that both Giroud and Arteta would never escape again – that in itself was worth around five grand. I was sick of fetching them. Their recent sortie had taken them down to the Mini Stores shop on King's Cross Road before being picked up by a traffic warden and brought back, and whilst he'd been on with that, he'd asked to see my parking permit, had a coffee and watched a bit of the highlights from our 'Sammy' project.

These ferrets were hardly the most loyal of animals. They were costing me around thirty-five quid a week in cooked chickens and tuna – we were cleaning them out every day – and the kids were even bathing them twice on a weekend – not as though it ever got shut of their smell – and the first thing they did when they got put in back in the hutch was to try and 'jimmy-up' the floorboards and get out again.

I wanted a take-out for supper, but that wasn't happening, and I got another concoction served to me which had yet more green in it.

"Salad again?" I said.

"Chicken Caesar salad with parmesan," Emily replied, smiling. "It's good for you."

I looked at Lucy whose meal looked ten times better than mine. "What have you got?"

"Spaghetti carbonara," she replied. "You want to try it?"

Before I had time to answer I had a fork full of the stuff rammed in my mouth, the fork of which made its swift return into her mouth to be licked clean. I would have asked Emily if she'd seen it but it happened that quick. These Scousers had a right sleight of hand. It was like sharing the breakfast bar with a sex starved pickpocket.

"Is it alright?" asked Lucy.

"Yeah," I said, albeit rather cautiously. "I'm glad I never moved while you were doing it, or I would have had an eye out."

"Good job you didn't then, eh?" she replied, winking.

Emily joined me in having a Caesar salad, which if I'm honest was a bit heavy going and once she and her sister started a discussion as regards the amount of parmesan that was overly present in mine and which was nowhere to be seen in hers, I sort of got the gist of why it felt like I was chewing sawdust.

"That was a full packet," said Emily to her sister.

Mmm. It sort of felt like it was about that much.

"Sorry," apologised Lucy. "All the plates look the same."

Was I missing something? What was that supposed to mean?

I eventually shifted the salad and sat over on the couch and jotted down some notes and read a few emails whilst the two girls talked and rinsed the dishes.

Lucy eventually slumped down at the side of me and looked at what I was writing.

"How many kids have you got?" Lucy asked me.

"Two," I replied. "Why – how many have you got?"

She just looked at me, grinned and said, "None."

Emily dried her hands, came over and clicking her fingers said, "Oi you – sit in that chair," whilst at the same time winking at me.

Lucy partly adhered to her sister's request and sat on the room floor to make room for Emily, who sat on to the sofa next to me and lifted up her legs to get comfortable.

"So what are you both planning tomorrow?" I asked.

"I thought we'd go see about those rooms," Emily explained.

"What do they look like?" asked Lucy.

"What, the rooms or my kids?" I asked.

"Your kids," she smiled.

"Like my wife," I replied.

"Our Stuart says your wife's right pretty," she said.

"He's right – she is."

"Why did you leave her?" came her next question before Emily tried nipping the minor interrogation in the bud with a, "Lucy, you can't ask questions like that."

"Yes she can," I said. "There's nothing wrong with asking a forthright question, just as long as you're prepared for an answer that's just as forthright."

"Forthright?" inquired Lucy.

"It's like when a fat woman asks her husband 'Am I fat?'"

and he says 'Yeah, massive' and then she kicks off and smacks him in the mouth," I explained. "She's asked a forthright question but she didn't want the forthright answer."

She just looked at me.

"It means honest," I smiled.

I got a smile back.

"Jeanette threw me out because I wasn't very nice to her," I said.

"How not nice?"

"Just not nice," I replied.

There was a slight pause for thought.

"Do you still love her?"

"Yeah, I still love her," I said. "She's the mother of my two kids."

"Does she love you?" she asked.

"Yeah, she loves me," I said. "I'm not so sure if she likes me though."

"It's the same, isn't it?" asked Lucy.

I shook my head. "No – love is a bit more special."

"Do you love our M?" she asked.

"I do, I love her a lot."

That got her big sister immediately wiping her eyes as she shifted around a bit on the settee.

"And you like her as well?"

"Yeah, I like her a lot."

"What do you like about her?"

"Lots of things."

"Like what?"

"She's very pretty and she never ever complains or moans," I said, "But what is more important is that she is very good with the other people in my life that I love, which is a really, really big thing for me."

"You mean your kids."

"I do, Lucy – I mean my kids."

"Do you like me?" she asked.

I couldn't help but smile. "Yeah, you're as cute as hell."

I wasn't lying – knelt on the floor she just looked like a younger inquisitive version of Emily, with all the similar mannerisms, and after telling her that she had a smile from ear to ear.

"Will you marry our M?"

"We've sort of talked about it," I replied.

If nothing got Emily's interest before, then this is the one thing that did.

"Stop asking him questions," said her big sister, wiping her eyes.

"That's being forthright," I said, winking at Lucy.

She nodded and smiled.

It was a bit strange as I'd not spoken that candidly to anyone, yet I felt at ease by talking to my girlfriend's twelve-year-old kid sister.

"I want five kids," she said. "All girls."

I laughed.

"Five is far too many," said Emily.

She looked for my approval.

"Kids are the best," I said, winking.

"How often do you see yours?" she asked.

"I have them every weekend and sometimes through the week – now your sister's living here it makes me happy as I can see them a bit more often."

"Does your wife like our M?"

"There's nothing 'not to like' about your sister, and yeah, your Emily and Jeanette talk to each other," I replied.

"Dale Fox's first and second wife hated each other's guts."

I smiled and shook my head as I got my arm linked by Emily.

"What you have to understand is that there are two little people involved that have done nothing wrong," I said.

"Jeanette is really nice," said Emily. "You'll probably see her tomorrow."

"Does she have a boyfriend?" asked Lucy.

"She does," I replied.

"Does it bother you?" came her quick-fire reply.

"If I am being honest – yes, it did," I answered. "However, since your sister has been here my feelings have – well, sort of changed."

That was as straight an answer as I had ever given on the subject. I hated his guts at the start, however as I had begun to see a bit more of Jeanette and the kids, there was very little resentment on my part, if any. In fact I quite admired the fact that he was his own person – that and the fact that he was good with my kids.

When we eventually went to bed I felt really happy and content. What I had initially seen as some sex-mad adolescent was just a young girl with loads of questions to ask, but no one to ask them to, and more importantly no one to answer them. Her sister was twenty years older than her and had left home when Lucy was just a baby.

I got back in from my morning jog around 7:00am to see Adebayor and his mate in the back garden prodding and poking at the piped ferret run, whilst inside the house both Emily and her sister were up and the percolator was on. The house was beginning to have a feeling of being a home.

"'You sleep alright?" I asked the younger sister.

She smiled an appraisal.

"I think your Emily's on about moving my kids' bedrooms up on the top floor, and doing that room out that you slept in for the baby," I said whilst grabbing a bottle of water out of the fridge.

"What are you going to call it?" asked Lucy.

"That's up to your Emily," I said.

"Yeah, but it's your baby as well," she replied.

"She's right," stated her elder sister.

"Well, if it was a girl I'd name it after you," I told Lucy, whilst giving her a wink.

"Yeah, but it's a boy," she replied.

"I know," I smiled.

I said nothing more on the subject, however I was soon to receive my second bout of questioning.

"Did you get this house after you and your wife split up?"

I shook my head. "I bought it as an investment just before we split up and I rented it out to some Russian people."

"So if you didn't live here, where did you live?" she asked.

I looked over at Emily who gave me a shrug of her shoulders.

"You want me to be forthright?" I asked Lucy.

She smiled.

"I had a girlfriend – that is why Jeanette threw me out. I really hurt her and hurt even more when I moved in with her," I said.

"What was she called?" asked Lucy.

"Nicole," I replied.

"Is she pretty?" came her next question.

"She is," I said. "She looks a lot like your sister."

"But I am a bit older," added Emily.

"How old was she?" asked Lucy.

"Twenty-four."

"Did you love her?"

"I thought I did for a time, but looking back at it I would honestly say no."

This got Emily's total undivided interest as she pulled up a bar stool and sat next to her sister.

"Although I got on with Nicole – and I did – there was a big thing that made it not possible for me to take it any further," I said.

"You and our M?" asked Lucy.

"Not just that," I replied. "She didn't want any involvement with my kids."

"You never told me that," said Emily.

I nodded as Lucy and Emily listened on.

"It is true. I was a Saturday or Sunday dad, but had nowhere to go – it upset me a lot."

Emily's eyes began welling up again.

"Remember what I said last night when I told you what was more important is that your Emily is very good with the other people in my life that I love, which is a really big thing for me? Well it is – and that's why at the moment everything in my life is good."

Emily started crying. "That is so, so nice," she said.

Lucy looked at her elder sister but couldn't really get the gist of her sudden rush of emotion.

"When you get to fifteen or sixteen, you'll understand it a lot better," I said, smiling.

I left Heartbreak Hotel and went out into the garden to see what 'Hansel and Gretel' were on with before I took a shower and drove over for the kids, who were more than happy to see me.

"Dad, can we go to London Dungeon with you and M again?" my lad asked.

Jeanette smiled at his request and I gave her a peck on the cheek.

"Emily's younger sister's over," I said. "I think she'd like to meet you."

"Really?"

I nodded.

"Bring Paul," I said.

I took them into north London via Toys R Us and explained that their friend M was going to have all the top floor of the house done out for them, and that Adebayor and his mate were going to put them a swing and slide in the garden.

"I thought Adebayor played for Tottenham?" asked my little girl.

"He does, but they don't pay him that much," I replied.

"You said he was a filthy millionaire," she said.

"He was but he blew all his money on loose women and ferrets."

"Dad, has Adebayor got ferrets?" asked my lad.

"Thousands," I lied.

On getting back to the house they had their first meeting with Lucy, whom my daughter took to straight away. "You look like Britney Spears," she immediately stated, which had Lucy beaming.

"See," I nodded. "How can you not love kids?"

"Where are we going on holiday M?" asked my lad. "My dad wouldn't tell me."

I wouldn't tell him because I didn't even know myself and within five minutes we had a pair of ferrets running up and down the floorboards and the Xbox playing on the TV.

"We're thinking about going to Marrakesh," said Emily and she picked up my son to show him some photographs in a brochure. "I'm just waiting for the hotel to call me."

This was news to me.

"We need to make sure we can watch Arsenal in the FA Cup Final," she smiled.

Later that evening whilst Emily and Lucy along with my kids were doing some baking – well, getting flour everywhere, anyway – there was a knock at the door. It was Jeanette and Paul.

"Come in," I said. "Just watch you don't let the ferrets out."

"What, you keep the ferrets in the house?" asked Jeanette.

"Only on a weekend," I replied. "It's murder – I can never get in the bathroom."

I nodded a nod to Paul, and Emily, full of flour, went over and kissed Jeanette on both cheeks.

"How are you feeling?" asked Jeanette.

"Big," she replied before shouting over her sister. "Come and meet Jeanette, Luce."

Lucy came over and gave an immediate and forthright appraisal. "Our M and Stuart are right – you are dead pretty."

There's nothing like a compliment to break the ice, but I knew it must have been one hell of a bind for her boyfriend to come over; however, we had more than one thing in common.

"I see you've got fourth place sewn up," he said.

"We dropped some silly points," I replied. "We should have been pushing Manchester City all the way."

The house being full of people talking and smiling was quite nice if I'm honest, and Jeanette and Paul stayed long enough to have a couple of coffees and a baked bun and on them leaving we thanked them both and waved them off. It's the little things in life.

Chapter 19
From Paris with Love

I had been tear-arsing around trying to get more 8mm and 16mm film transferred onto digital and to be honest I'd been running in circles when I came home early that Tuesday tea time. My phone had been red hot as well, mainly with some foreign bloke getting the wrong number and talking bollocks – so much so I ended up being a bit off with him. I half thought it was Sooty pulling my leg, but it couldn't have been because one of the times that this guy had phoned I had seen him bollocking Ginge. And then Ginge bollocking him back.

I got in the house and kicked up my laptop and found out that this foreign bloke had also got my email and it appeared that he was also demanding a few hundred euro – but for what I didn't really know.

"Hiya," Emily said as she followed me in through the door, getting on tippy-toes firstly to give me a peck on the lips before booting her shoes off across the floor and pulling out loads of pans and then putting them all back again, and then sort of scratching her head.

I put the message from my email through Google Translate and found the gobbledygook it contained to be Dutch. Meanwhile my mad girlfriend was looking in and out of the cupboards before reverting to doing a bit of chin scratching and drawer opening.

I put on the percolator and tried to send some form of translated reply to the guy who was, as it turned out, offering me some footage of a friendly match in front of 60,000 between Arsenal and Feyenoord in November 1967. Meanwhile the mad girlfriend now had her dress up around her waist and was on her hands and knees sort of checking under the sofa and chair, and in between sort of doing a bit of deliberating.

"As much as the view is good, M – and believe it is, can I ask what's up?" I said whilst sending my emailed reply.

"I was in a bit of a rush earlier and I've mislaid my iPhone," she said.

I rang it and she found it to be in the fridge and wrapped up with some mortadella.

"You're not going mad, are you?" I asked.

She smiled at me and told me of her hectic day in which she had to rush back from a hospital appointment to the solicitors and back to the hospital and over to a bathroom shop and then to B&Q to pick up some white paint for the kids' bedroom. I've no idea where her wrapping it up with the ham came into it, and to be honest I never inquired – but I had to admit, she had been rushing about a bit.

I had an instant reply on my email. Good televised footage by Dutch TV station KRO, albeit highly illegal pirate, of Feyenoord 3, Arsenal 2, with two goals by Sammy – one a 20 yard strike – and on video and not lousy Super 8. Two hundred and fifty euros.

"Do you fancy doing anything tonight?" I said as I watched her peel her phone from the pink spotted meat.

I got a big smile back from her, thinking that a nice meal out could be on the agenda.

"Where are you thinking?" she asked.

"Paris," I replied.

"What – *the* Paris?"

I nodded and told her that there was a guy over there claiming to have the full ninety minutes of a match between Feyenoord and Arsenal, where Feyenoord scored the winner in the last sixty seconds of the game.

"We can go tonight, book into a hotel and have a meal – I'll pick up the thing in the morning and we can have a day and a half over there and back in time for tea the next day," I said, sort of shrugging my shoulders.

"Paris?" she asked.

"That's unless you're not bothered."

"I've never been to Paris," she smiled.

"I've never seen anyone wrap a phone up in ham and put it in the fridge before," I replied.

I could tell she was happy the way she screamed, gave me a hug and then rang her mum.

"Where are we flying from?" she asked.

We weren't. We were driving down.

"What, you're driving to Paris?" she asked.

"Dead right," I said. "We'll be there by ten o'clock – we'll have dinner overlooking the River Seine."

I must admit, I did make it sound loads better than it actually was, and at 5:00pm Emily was still packing whilst on the phone to her mum and debating which of seventeen dresses, which were scattered on the bed, she'd wear to go over in. Maybe 10:00pm was being a bit generous?

I emailed the Dutch guy who was offering me the illegal copy and said that I'd meet him in a restaurant close to the Eiffel Tower around midday tomorrow, and after doing that I swiped the card over the internet for some city centre hotel on Rue Cler.

I heard her dragging what I assumed was a dead body down the stairs.

"I'm ready," she smiled.

"You sure you've got enough clothes there?" I asked.

She nodded to tell me that she had.

"And you know I've only booked us in for two nights and not twenty-two," I asked.

She was adamant in her confirmation and I managed to squeeze all her worldly possessions into the car along with a pair of my socks.

I could tell she really liked the ferry ride over there by how green she was, whilst watching through the window at how the boat crashed against the waves.

"I don't think I'd fancy going on a cruise," she said.

"Me neither," I replied. "It looks a bit choppy out there."

After she had thrown up, I saw that a bit of colour had come back to her face.

I had to hand it to her, I loved watching her on her hands and knees.

We shot down the motorway and by the time we'd checked into the hotel, got trapped in the lift on the way up, dropped off our clothes, watched Emily brush her teeth, got stuck in the lift on the way back down and then managed to get back outside, Paris was shut.

"I thought it'd be a bit livelier than this," I said.

"Me too," she replied.

"At least you look nice," I said.

"I feel a bit over dressed," she said whilst giving herself a once over, looking down at her diamanté mules and then straightening her tiara. "Look at everybody else."

She was right. Everybody else was wearing jeans and hiking boots, apart from the dog on the corner and the man in the mac it was with – who was definitely pretending not to see it having a shit in the street.

We managed to find a restaurant that was actually on the River Seine – and which was actually open – and which would actually serve us – and which really did a great job of relieving me of a lot of money, whilst offering us both an underwhelming meal and even more underwhelming service. But the company was good. It was always good. And I listened to her rattle on about her mum and her auntie and then her auntie's husband's sister who'd had a burst appendix and her cousin over in Wallasey who was moving back to Birkenhead. She did a truly great job of making all these Scousers sound dead interesting.

After a walk along the river, her barefoot as her shoes had been rubbing, we got back to the hotel room, which was really good fun as the room itself was smaller than our bathroom at home, and which itself also included a bathroom – a really, really small bathroom of postage stamp proportions.

I was treat to the new rule number one, and then had the privilege of listening to her fumble about in the bathroom, which sort of had the toilet and the pillar my head was currently laid on both located at the same angle, and separated by less than an inch of hardboard and a sheet of wallpaper. I did, however, compliment her on the way she tried whistling and running the taps to sort of disguise what she was really doing. And that being the case, we slept with the French doors open all night and awoke to an even worse smell outside than that had been in the bedroom.

"You been to the toilet again?" I asked.

"No," she said trying to convince herself that she hadn't been sleep walking.

I had a look over the balcony, and as bad as it smelt – and it did, I was met by a truly lovely sight, and we had a bustling street-length market with a fish mongers opposite and a lousy smelling cheese shop straight beneath us. Paris had opened, and we loved it.

"I've just got to buy some cheese," she said as she put on her make up after showering.

"Have you?" I asked.

"Shurrup," she twanged.

We walked a few streets and enjoyed every minute of it and around 1:15pm I met my dodgy contact with the dodgy video cassette and I gave him the money.

I had initially put an advert on Ebay and this was one of the responses I'd had back, and for as cagey as the both the deal and the guy looked, it would turn out to be a rather fantastic bit of footage which, amid the commentator moaning about the smoke flares and the noise, saw Arsenal contain the Dutch club and take a 2-1 lead, with Sammy in magnificent form stringing passes right, left and centre and hitting a wonderful goal past 47-cap Dutch international goalkeeper Eddy Pieters Graafland with the outside of his right foot from 20 yards. I couldn't make out if he had scored both goals or just one as the amount of smoke was unbelievable. I was coughing just sat watching it on TV. In fact, at one point it was that bad I thought the telly was on fire. Even the papers had been confused. The *Daily Express* had reported two goals by Sammy and the *Daily Mirror* one by Sammy – the 20-yard strike – and the other by John Radford.

The brilliant 43-cap Swedish international striker Bengt Ove Kindvall hit two including the winner, whilst the 26-cap Yugoslavian international winger Spasoje Samardžić scored the other for Feyenoord. It was a truly fantastic piece of footage.

Kindvall would go on to score the winning goal in the 1970 European Cup Final where Feyenoord beat the same Celtic side 2-1 that had helped knock out Leeds United in the semi-final and thus robbing them of the Treble, and who would also go on to be the Eredivisie top scorer in 1968, 1969 and 1971.

We acted like fully fledged Parisians drinking wine and coffee and I even managed a Ricard in a back street bar, after having being treated to a rather heated conversation which concluded that France were shit and that they certainly wouldn't win the World Cup. The French were nearly as emotional as the Greeks down at the coffee shop, and they certainly didn't like it when I stated that Ligue One was as getting as bad as the Scottish Premier League, and that Clement Grenier would be much better off in the Premiership at Arsenal.

Emily totally backed me up and told everyone how brilliant I was when it came to football. She also told them how brilliant I was at just about everything else and that being the case I had to prize the glass of Ricard out of her mitts before she divulged any more of my trade secrets.

As nice as it was, I wouldn't like this Parisian social life. I'd be dead within a year – either that or destitute. You couldn't be in their gang unless you drank 40 coffees, guzzled two litres of red wine and a case of Ricard, whilst smoking a packet of Gitanes every hour. No wonder there were smashed up cars everywhere.

"I really, really love you," she said on walking back to the hotel.

And I really loved her, however when I woke up from my late afternoon slumber and found three kilos of cheese in the really, really small bedroom, I had to call her on it. Especially as she had secretly opened one to try it.

Everyone on the landing must have thought we had B.O. It was dead embarrassing, so much so I blamed Emily when she wasn't there.

"She might look little and cute," I told this American

couple as she fumbled about in her handbag looking for the key, "But she stinks like hell."

We could have brought the ferrets with us and no one would have noticed – that's how bad the smell was.

Later on we had a nice meal at a really posh restaurant that charged really posh prices and I reverted back to soda water, however just to purposely annoy me Emily stayed on the vino and ordered cheese and crackers afterwards.

It was a great couple of days, and on driving back she did ask if we could do it again.

Paris – dead cramped, dead expensive and dead smelly – but dead good fun. We most definitely had to do it again.

When I got back I gave Sooty a kilo of cheese.

"Emily brought that back for you," I said.

He was chuffed to bits. That was, until he opened it and left it brewing it in the fridge for a couple of days. He was actually contemplating buying a new fridge it had done that much damage.

That was Paris. It stays with you.

Chapter 20
The Fabulous Mr. Fox

I got back in from work around 6:20pm to a rather gloomy looking girlfriend in the kitchen.

"You not feeling well?" I asked.

"Not really," she said.

"I'll put 'Grease' on for you if you want," I said, trying to bring a bit of levity to the situation.

She smiled.

Her husband had refused point blank to give her a divorce, not that him refusing it would alter the outcome, it would just prolong it.

"I knew he would," she said.

"It's an obstacle," I said. "Nothing more – we'll sort it."

Or I would, I thought.

There had been numerous phone calls and text messages that had preceded this latest development, one of which was a strange one in that he'd have her back tomorrow. God knows how that would work? He had even had both her parents on the phone telling them what a whore they had for a daughter, which I felt on one hand was a bit wrong but on the other I had to admire their stance on their assumption that I was a million times better than him. Lucy had got over the heartbreak and tears of leaving us Sunday night to include what her mum had actually said to him within the hundred or so text messages that she had recently sent me to tell me 'thanks' and 'how great I was'.

"I wouldn't let him get you down," I said.

We ate some form of tuna pasta salad and talked through a range of subjects from our respective divorces through to how great I was at bringing her off, to the five-man defence and its three central defenders Arsenal had sometimes used during the 1988-89 season and through to the fact that the hotel had emailed back to give us the heads up that they did indeed have electricity, and then through to the highly sensitive subject of that she was feeling very fat.

"You're pregnant," I said.

"I feel really fat."

"Yeah, because there's a baby in there."

"I'm scared that you'll go off me," she added.

"Not while ever you keep making me implement all them new rules I won't."

That brought a smile to her face.

"Paris was great, wasn't it?" she said.

"Paris was fantastic," I replied.

Paris had been great and there was one Kodak moment where I watched her, both radiant and in a cream dress, feeding the ducks in the park opposite the Louvre – she was beautiful and I told her so.

That made her happy, so I thought I would try and keep it up.

"So have you booked the holiday?" I asked.

"No – I was waiting for you."

"Why?" I asked. "Go book it."

There was nothing like typing in your card details for a purchase to cheer you up – and I had noticed the five new pairs of shoes from Modatoi that had arrived this morning, which did sort of tell me that she was trying her best to wave away her gloom.

"Look at it this way," I said. "You'll be able to wear all those nice shoes you've just bought."

"My feet will probably not fit in them," she said, shaking her head.

"Well, I'll definitely dump you if you stop having nice feet," I replied.

The prospect of me dumping her cheered her up further – well that and the 'highly therapeutic' five grand that went sailing out of my current account and into British Airways' to cover the cost of the holiday, which was upped by another couple of grand when I insisted on flying at least Club Class. And when I had another idea of cheering her up further, it may have cost me another grand and a bit, but I got the new rule number one – and while I was sat at the breakfast bar. I'm only glad the ferrets weren't in to see it.

My idea was that as we were taking the kids – why not take Lucy? It would be company for them and a bit of help for her pregnant sister. There was a further part of the idea, that made the idea a bit more special, not so much the fact that she'd only ever been abroad once before, but in that we'd not tell her just yet, which was fairly big ask as since Emily had moved in with me, she was now speaking with her family every day. In my mind a few thousand quid was nothing if we were all happy and I let Emily phone Jeanette to let her know that the holiday was like the baby in the womb, and both live and kicking.

"You're in for an experience," Jeanette had told her.

"I wonder what she meant by that," Emily said.

Now that was out of the way I had to sort some other stuff out, one of which was the draft for the Munich '58 programme we had promised BSkyB and the other was that ITV had given us our four hours per week. This was a big earner, and would take our profile through the roof. Sooty got the staff into his office and let them know – and no one was happier than Ginge.

"This is why you get your head down and keep on listening and learning," I said. "Because you'll soon have some other kid who was once like you, working under you. And he or she has to learn in exactly the same way you have."

I nipped into the Greek coffee shop around 12:30am to see Fosis wearing a plain black shirt with his customary crucifix gleaming through the unopened seven top buttons.

"You want snails?" he asked.

"No thanks – just an espresso and a water."

I looked over at Andreas, who was sat back in his chair watching over a card game and dressed in a leather jacket with his customary collar and tie.

"I could do with a favour," I asked him.

"You tell me who he is and I will slit his throat," he replied.

"It's not that extreme," I replied.

I then told him that I wanted a visit paid to Greenwich as I needed confirmation that the divorce papers would be signed off.

"And this is the same big bastard I see for you the other week?"

I nodded.

"His wife have your baby and he acts like this?" he said, shaking his fist before revealing the highly personal details of our conversation and talking, both at volume and in Greek, to not only all of the coffee shop but more importantly to a quietly spoken man with a square jaw and moustache who I knew as 'Turkish George'.

"I sort it," said George and he gave me a nod.

I got in earlier than normal, at around 4:50pm, to firstly tell her that I had sent one of my legal representatives down to Greenwich and who would help hurry up the process of divorce, and secondly to make a call to her brother to see if he still looked like the kid I had dropped off the other week.

"You okay?" I asked him on the phone.

"I'm great," he replied. "It was a nice win Monday for us, wasn't it?"

"Us?" I asked.

"Arsenal."

"Just because you look like an Arsenal supporter doesn't mean you have to be one – you can't go changing clubs like that."

"I weren't that bothered about United anyway," he said.

"You keeping away from those stinky fags?" I asked.

"Yeah, I'm sorry."

"Yeah you told me that about a thousand times already," I exaggerated.

"And you told me to only say 'sorry' if I meant it."

"Well, at least you learned something," I said.

"I did – it was daft – they all do it up here."

"What about down here?" I asked.

"It's great down there," he replied.

"Do you reckon you'll do okay with your exams?" I asked.

"Not bad."

"Well, have a word with your mum and dad – we've just been given the heads up from ITV for what is a massive contract for us and there's a job down here for you if you want it," I said. "However there's one major ask – I need you to get passes in your English and Maths."

The kid was ecstatic, and so much so it put a bit of lump in my throat. I may have hung up, but Emily's phone was red hot exactly two minutes later with both her mum and dad on the phone.

"I know nothing about it," she said, looking over at me as I watched through the window at both Adebayor and his mate doing what looked like a half-decent job.

She was still on the phone after I'd had a shower.

"My mum wants to talk to you," she said, handing me her phone.

"Hello," I said.

I couldn't really make out what she was saying as she was crying but I sort of got the gist that she was really happy. "You've only been – a few weeks – everything around," was all I could really make out.

Emily smiled as she took the phone back off me and told her mum, "Ta ra."

Every time after she spoke with any of her family I could sense part of her softly spoken posh voice revert back slightly to the Scouse dialect that I knew she'd once had.

"You didn't have to do that," she said. "It was really, really nice – but you didn't have to do that." And then she started crying and telling me that she loved me so much.

It was great being me, and nobody was better at doing it, than me.

We went out that night and had some sushi – well, I did, as she was now under some notion that fish was bad for the baby, so she had some other stuff called tofu, which I wouldn't recommend as it tasted like shit.

The next day I arrived home from work I had a house full of decorators, loads of boxes and a really massive bath.

"You're not feeling depressed, are you?" I asked.

"No – why?" she smiled.

"Every time you feel down you have a tendency empty half the bank account."

"I do not, you fibber," she replied.

Emily informed me that she had made a start on the kids' new upstairs bedrooms and the baby's bedroom.

"What – you're sticking that great bath in for the baby?" I asked, looking at the big white thing which filled the hall-way and which you could have sailed across the Channel in.

"Don't be daft," she said. "I thought while the decorators were in we could have a new bathroom – it was only three hundred and fifty pounds."

"Oh right," I replied.

"I thought they may as well do our bedroom while they were here as well," she added.

I was well impressed with the two 32" flat screen TVs which she'd bought and told her as much. "A TV for the bedroom – nice one," I said, nodding.

"Those are for the children's bedrooms," she replied. "Our bedroom's for sleeping… and that."

"And that?" I asked, which brought a great big smile on her face

I had to hand it to her, she shopped a lot better than I did, and she knew what she wanted and how to get it – and she was frigging awesome at giving out instructions.

The house began to revert back to a house around 8:00pm, but stunk of paint so I brought the ferrets in to try and get shut of some of the new, nice clean smell.

"I think they miss the children," she said as I had them running around the breakfast bar whilst finger-feeding them Mortadella ham.

"So how was work?" she asked.

"Great," I replied. "Apart from the fact that ESPN have been trying to flog our Sammy documentary to ITV for twice what they paid us for it."

"I didn't think that was finished," she said.

"It isn't," I replied. "But it's getting there."

She slung some garlic into the frying pan and took some king prawns out of the fridge and within minutes I was eating a meal that I'd easily pay thirty quid for off Euston Road, and which was interrupted with a knock on the front door.

I opened it only to be confronted by my nemesis – her

husband – the Hubert bloke, who had already kicked shite out of me twice as well as slinging Emily down a flight of stairs.

"Yeah, what do you want?" I asked.

"Is M in?" he asked.

She was, but there was no way I was letting that psycho anywhere near her.

"I just wanted to let her know that I've signed off on those papers for the divorce," he said.

"Is that it?" I asked.

He nodded a confirmation and I closed the door on him and turned to see her looking at me.

"Are you okay?" I asked.

She said she was, but she wasn't, and him coming to the door of the house where she lived sort of panicked her.

"How does he know where we live?" she asked.

"Probably the same way I know where he lives," I replied.

She went to sit down but passed out before she did only to come around with Jeanette and Libby in the room with her. She had been pushing herself too much, or so the doctor had said, and he gave me a right bollocking for making her turf the back garden, decorate the spare rooms and carry two flat screen TVs upstairs.

"I didn't make her do any of that," I innocently claimed.

He still didn't believe me and called me from a pig to a dog to the amusement of both Jeanette and Libby. She had been spaced out when he had arrived and sort of mentioned that she had to finish the bedrooms and the garden, and him only speaking pigeon English translated that into 'his version of events' – and that I was a lazy selfish pig.

She hadn't been eating properly either. The trip to Marrakesh with a bundle stuck up her jumper wasn't sitting well with her, and she came clean with Jeanette and Libby who let me know. She did however tell them how brilliant I was, not that it washed with Libby who still gave me a bollocking for supposedly not looking after her properly.

"I hope you bollock Sooty like this when he's done nothing wrong," I said.

"Just look after her," Jeanette had said, smiling. "She'll be fine."

She was and even though she was feeling crappy, she had still overseen the two idiot plumbers putting the new bath in properly after they had initially installed it the wrong way around.

The next morning I came back in from my jog around 5:30am to the smell of the percolator and Sky Sports playing with Emily watching a piece on Arsenal.

"What are you doing up?" I asked. "That doctor said that you needed to rest."

"What did Libby say to you?"

"She bollocked me for calling you a fatty and saying that you had to lose weight."

She laughed at my poor attempt of humour.

"I think you look great," I said. "Just eat the right stuff, rest and get 'laddo' out of there in one piece at chucking out time."

She looked down at the ever growing bun in the oven. "I just seem to have got big really fast," she said.

"It's called being pregnant," I replied.

I got a smile back, which was nice.

While she was in the shower I called her mum and expressed my concerns and reserved her and her husband a couple of first class train tickets up at Lime Street Station – and when I was in work later in the day and bollocking Fred for some crap editing on some footage I had scrounged from the store room up at the Stadium of Light, a 1-1 draw in

October 1969, where Sammy had equalised on 74 minutes, catching a Radford cross on the toss and volleying home from 20 yards – I received a teary phone call to let me know they'd arrived.

"My dad wants to know where your tins of beer are?"

"Give me fifteen minutes," I said.

I walked down to the house to be greeted with a hug and a kiss off the mother and a hearty slap on the back from Jimmy Tarbuck's better looking brother.

"You didn't let her know we were coming," he said.

"I know – I thought I'd leave it as a surprise."

I was in two minds to offer to take her father out, but as I knew he was as concerned about his daughter as his wife was, I hung fire on that idea. However when he appeared bored post tour of the house, watched Adebayor flashing his gnashers at some bloke who had scraped his bike up against his van and listened to half an hour of pushchair and pram talk, I offered him a change of scenery and he nearly ripped my arm out of its socket. We got in the car and I shot down the City Road towards Whitechapel, ringing Sooty as I was on my way.

"I've got Emily's dad in the car and I'm just taking him for a few drinks in the Blind Beggar," I said.

I managed to get a parking spot off Brick Lane and we made our way to the pub, where just the other week I had taken his son.

"We appreciate what you're doing," he said.

"That's okay," I said. "You've got a fantastic family."

"The kids all think the world of you, and it's great to have our M back talking to us again."

Mmm. That last bit was interesting and I felt the need for a 'probe in the bushes'.

"What, you fell out?"

"No – she fell out."

And that was the limitation of his 'falling out' story, so I kicked it back up.

"So why did she fall out?" I asked.

"She was going to marry another lad," he said.

"Dale Fox?" I asked.

He nodded. "You know him?"

"Not personally, but I've seen some photos of him in a pair of trunks."

Mmm. That sounded a bit weird, I thought.

"And I know he married a cousin of a cousin on your side," I added. "And he's now living with a Tracey Hump."

The old man looked at me with a rather strange expression on his face.

"I've got an inquisitive nature," I said sipping at my pint of soda water which had been watered down even further with about seven lumps of ice.

"She just took off and married the bloke that she's now trying to divorce," he said.

"Didn't you like him?" I asked, sort of leaning towards a forthright 'No I hated him' kind of answer.

"I never really knew him," he replied.

I was stunned - *How did that one work out?* I thought.

"What about Emily's mum?" I asked.

"What about her?" he replied.

I have to be frank – this guy told a lousy tale.

"Did she meet this Mark Smith?" I asked.

"Four or five times," he replied.

"Then how did they meet and get married and that?" I asked after being blindly guided into more dark.

"He worked for a security firm that was policing some freight yard on the docks, we got up one day and she'd gone."

I certainly didn't like the sound of this.

"He left his missus and two kids," he added further.

"He had kids?" I asked, knowing that I had been told on several occasions that it was physically impossible for him to have any children.

"Two boys," he replied.

"So where did they move to?" I asked.

"Bermondsey," he replied. "We never really saw anything of her for three years."

I really felt the need to get back and do some interrogation of my own. This was turning out to be a truly crappy story; that turned the gorgeous piece of ass I was in love with and who was having my kid into some right conniving, vicious old slag.

A message was text through to my phone. 'Thanx. Love U so much – Rule one and rule one later x'.

Mmm. I wonder if Dale Fox and that idiot Hubert fought over who was having rule one and rule one?

I left the Blind Beggar in a daze and dropped her old man off at the house and went into the office, only to find out that Sooty's Genes Reunited account had been suspended, which meant I had to set up my own account. It took ages and I was that frustrated with all the details they wanted that I nearly slung the Mac through the window.

'Mark Hubert Smith' born '1980' I typed.

Every Mark H Smith came up – there were millions of them.

Beep. Beep. 'When U coming home?? x' the text message read.

'Never', I was going to reply, although I didn't.

I specified the word 'Hubert' and there was one – born in Bermondsey.

I then hit his details, however I only got one hit on a marriage, and that was to an Emily Ann Orr born 1982 – my Emily.

I trawled around a couple of similar sites and basically

they had said the same. I had hit a brick wall.

I then had the notion of downloading his birth certificate, which if I'm honest took ages.

Mark Hubert Smith born 1980 – Bermondsey:
Parents – Linton Fox – occupation – Borer,
and Marie Ann Tate – occupation – Sewing Machinist.

A boring fox? I thought. That was too much of a coincidence, and that being the case I went searching through my desk for that downloaded copy of Emily's marriage certificate and the details of her husband's parents – Eric Smith and Marie Ann Smith.

Eric had to be his step father? I thought.

I then looked at Dale Fox's two marriage certificates:

Parents – Linton Fox – occupation – Borer,
and Alice Fox – occupation – Housewife.

Mark Smith was Dale Fox's illegitimate younger brother and the cuckoo in the nest.

This new monkey on my back was bothering the hell out of me and I got in around 8:30pm to see Emily sat on the floor cross legged and talking with her parents, whilst looking at some old photographs. It turned out her parents were stopping over until tomorrow, however I really felt the need to get this out of the way as it was gnawing away at me.

"The husband came around last night," I said.

"They know," Emily said smiling. "I told them."

I certainly wasn't leaving it there.

"It's strange that you never told me he had been married before and had two kids," I said.

"He wasn't married and he certainly didn't have any children," she replied.

Her father shrugged her shoulders.

"What have you been saying, dad?" she asked.

"That he left his wife and kids," he replied.

That wasn't his wife and they weren't his children," she stated. "He lived in West Kirby with a woman who had two children."

"Who was she?" I asked.

"Helena something or other," Emily replied.

"Not Fox, was it?" I inquired.

"I don't think so," she replied.

I must admit, if Emily had been lying then she was a thousand times better than me, as it really did look like she was telling the truth. Mind you, saying that, I often looked to Sooty as if I was telling the truth when his Amex Gold Card had gone missing, and I had said that I hadn't seen it or used it.

"What about his brother?" I asked.

"Whose brother?" asked Emily, shrugging her shoulders.

"Your husband's brother," I replied.

"Mark didn't have a brother," she replied.

"You wanna bet?" I stated.

"I'm telling you now, that Mark didn't have any brothers or sisters," she said again, shrugging her shoulders.

Again, I had to admit she was brilliant at disguising a blatant lie and her mum and dad were extremely impressive at sort of backing this up as well.

"Who's your husband's dad?" I asked.

"Eric?" she replied.

"No, it's not – I'm on about his real dad."

"Eric was his real dad," she replied.

"No he wasn't."

She shrugged her shoulders and looked at both her parents both of who gave a respective shrug of theirs.

"Where did you actually meet your husband?" I asked.

"He was a friend of the Foxes," she replied.

"He wasn't, Emily – he was visiting his dad."

I will tell you something, if her mum and dad were impressed with me before, they were absolutely fucking cock-a-hoop after I told them that and the smiles on both their faces – especially her mum's – were lit up like the sea front at Blackpool.

"Linton's his father?" Emily asked.

"One hundred percent," I said.

And just to prove it I handed over downloaded copies of both her husband and Dale Fox's birth certificates.

"So Dale and Mark were brothers?" Emily said.

I nodded a confirmation.

"The stuck up bitch," snapped Emily's mum. "The shit she has thrown at our family over the years is un-bloody-believable."

That is why Emily had fallen out with her parents – Dale Fox's mother had called Emily a lot of spiteful names after it looked as though she had dumped the boyfriend and taken off with some friend of the family who would be both her husband and ex-boyfriend's brother, and had made Emily's family's life hell.

"I can't believe this," said a dumbfounded Emily.

I wanted to ask loads of probing and intimate questions, but the opportunity didn't really present itself as her mum was busy on my phone telling all her neighbours.

"I'll tell you what, lad, you're like a dog with a bone," her father said.

However, if I'm honest, all this appeared a bit disturbing for Emily and I received one or two glances that suggested I was perhaps out of order bringing up her past.

The next morning I had my jog around the block and got indoors around 5:50am to the smell of coffee in the percolator, Sky Sports on TV and Emily sat at the breakfast bar in my 1971 Arsenal shirt she had since claimed as hers whilst sipping from her cup.

"Morning," she said.

Mmm. That certainly wasn't the regular tone I got from her, so as in cricket I sidestepped the ball so to speak, and went for a single.

"I'm sorry about all that last night – that thing your dad said got my mind racing and a bit of insecurity came out in me."

"You made me look a bit of a 'nana," she twanged.

"Again, I'm sorry," I said, certainly not knowing what the hell a 'nana was.

"My dad hates him," she said.

I wanted to say, "Join the fucking club," but I didn't which was a good thing as she began to talk.

"I always knew there was something similar about them," she stated.

I take that back – the last thing I wanted her to do was talk, however talk was what she did.

"They were both very violent people – not with me as such – and they were both very jealous – I suppose you could say Linton was the same."

"I suppose I'm a naturally inquisitive person," I replied. "I'm sorry."

"It's not your fault – it was just a bit of a shock, that's all."

I liked the bit about it not being my fault.

"When I think about it, his father – well, Eric - used to always mention that useless, lazy Scouse - yer know."

"Yer know? I love it when you talk Scouse for me," I smiled.

However I didn't really get a smile back.

"At first I thought he meant me," she said.

One of the things with Emily is that she never swore. Well, if she did, I certainly never heard her.

"Why would somebody ever say that to you?" I said.

Then I got a smile.

"Come on – you're with me now – life is good."

"Your right, life is very good," she smiled.

I heard footsteps coming down the hallway to be greeted by the smiling face of her mum.

"Did you sleep well?" I asked.

"Champion," she said looking me up and down before passing comment. "You're all wet."

"Yeah I've been for a jog and it's raining outside," I replied.

"Do you always get up this early?" she asked.

"Always," I nodded. "There's plenty to get up for when life's great."

Emily winked at me and smiled.

"D'you want a cup of tea, mam?" she asked, her Scouse twang becoming evident.

"I'll do it, love," her mum said before passing further comment. "I bloody love this house."

I got in work to find Sooty biting his nails. "What's up with you?" I asked.

"Libby's dad," he replied.

"Frank? What's up with him?"

"He got took into hospital last night and she's on at me for us to go up there."

"Then what are you hanging about for?" I asked.

"We are snowed under here – Libby's overworked at their place – the kids are in school."

Libby's parents were from Derbyshire and Frank had been the manager at some cotton mill before he retired. From what I could gather he was suffering with some form of emphysema. I liked Frank, he was a nice man.

"We're okay here – I'll pick the brats up, just get Libby to sort it at her end," I said.

"Are you sure?" he asked.

"Sure I'm sure," I replied.

Chapter 21
Moving Forward

I had been hard at it all day, the ever growing 'Sammy' project was being chopped and changed to perfection with footage turning up here on a daily basis. It may have been hard work, but it was great work. Getting Eddie to speak to autocue wasn't so straightforward as he'd never done it before, and that being the case, he initially sounded like one of those tin-looking Martians on the old 'For Mash Get Smash' adverts, and when Freddy hit him with the, "They peel them with their metal knives – boil them for twenty of their minutes – and then they smash them all to bits," line, it sort of made him a thousand times worse.

As I was about to call Emily to let her know that I had to drive up to Edgware to pick up Sooty's brats from their dead posh Colliegate School – my phone rang.

"It's me," it said.

"Oh, hello," I replied. "How are you?"

"Missing you – I think."

It was Nicole.

Rather than egg her on, I tried to immediately nip it in the bud, however she was fairly insistent that she wanted to see me.

"We've been through this a million times, Nicole," I

said. "You threw me out and I'm now trying to get on with my life."

"Yeah, with that Emily," she said.

"Yeah, with that Emily," I replied.

"I really loved you," she said.

"I know," I replied. However the last thing I either needed or wanted was to go back to the complexity that was my life of a few weeks back. Even the thought of it left me feeling shattered.

The phone call ended after twelve minutes or so, but I knew then that it wouldn't end there.

The drive up Edgware Road was a pain in the arse and trying to get parked amongst all the other parents' Range Rovers and Mercedeses jockeying for a parking berth was a nightmare. As it was short notice I had to go inside school to see some tutor or other before they'd sort of release the kids to a non-parent, as this place being an all-girls school was, in short, a heaven for the sexual predator.

"I've come for Mia and Zooey Sutton," I said.

The female tutor looked me up and down.

"I'm an 'uncle' if you like," I said feeling a bit unnerved. "Their parents – Tim and Libby – have had to go to Derby as Libby's father has been taken ill."

She didn't say a deal and just gave me a nod and a bit of a grunt.

A definite, stonewall carpet muncher here, I thought.

The kids got brought into the room where they identified me.

"Hello brats," I said.

"My mum says you have to make us do some maths and French," one stated.

"And you can't take us to McDonalds," stated the other. "Mum was quite adamant about that."

The tutor glared at me as I escorted them out of the door.

"Are we stopping with you?" one asked.

"Until your parents get back," I said.

"How long will they be?" asked the other.

"No idea," I replied.

Being seven-year old girls, the Maserati impressed them, but not quite as much as the kids' ferrets when I got them to the house.

"You should go bring the children over," smiled Emily.

"Yeah, then we'll have a house full of kids," I said.

Emily shook her head and rang Jeanette and within ten minutes I had four kids and two ferrets running around the room, with my ex-wife sat at the breakfast bar in dialogue with my girlfriend – the conversation being that Jeanette would have had Sooty and Lib's kids but she was on early each morning and the drive from Clerkenwell to Edgware is really out of her way, et cetera, et cetera, blah, blah. I was so glad her job at Sainsbury's was more important than mine.

"Mum says we have to do some maths," stated one of the brats as the other one confirmed the parental request with a quite sincere nod of her head.

"Can you do ratios?" I asked, the question of which did not go unnoticed by both Emily and Jeanette.

"How do you mean?" asked the brat.

"If George Armstrong played five hundred games for Arsenal and scored sixty-eight goals, how often did he score?"

"What, exactly?" asked the other brat.

I nodded.

"One goal in seven point three five (1:7.35) games," she stated.

Wow, I was impressed – especially as my two had only just learned to read and write – and both badly.

"Do you want a job?" I asked.

"Are you going to give us some more?" asked the other brat.

"Sure," I said, and they immediately sat down in front of me and got their pads out.

"What? You want me to give you like a test?" I asked.

"Yes," they said in unison.

"Okay then. Question one – if Sammy of Arsenal hit a thirty-five yard shot into the goal against Manchester United, how many inches did it travel?"

They scrawled down an answer within seconds.

"Question two. If Arsenal and Leeds United had both played forty-two games, a win was two points and a draw was one point, and Arsenal lost six games and won twenty-nine and Leeds lost five games and won twenty-seven, how many games did they draw?"

"If that's the question why did you mention the points?" asked one of the brats. "And it's three points for a win, not two."

"Because, smart arse," I replied. "There's another question as part of the question and back in the olden days it used to be two points for a win."

As Emily and Jeanette sniggered from over the breakfast bar, the twins immediately scrawled down their answers.

"Question three. So, how many points did they both have and who would be the superior team?" I smiled.

I always loved to hear that Arsenal were better than Leeds!

This went on for half an hour and even Emily and Jeanette struggled with the answers, however the two arithmetic kids were answering the question more or less by the time I had ended my sentence.

"Would you like to be as clever and boring as Uncle Sooty's kids?" I asked my two.

"We are not boring," stated one of the brats.

"Wanna bet?" I replied.

"Anyway, we've got to do some French," stated the other.

"That's easily sorted," I replied and went into one of the twice-newly decorated bedrooms and brought down a handful of DVDs.

"These are all French," I said. "Which one do you want on?"

After both Emily and Jeanette had reprimanded me for offering them 'Betty Blue' as part of the DVD selection, Emily put 'Le Diner De Cons' on the big screen for them, which kept them quiet bar their laughing for a good hour and half, and by this time the ferrets were back in their hutch and my two kids and their mum were back in Clerkenwell. I'd never had much time on my own with Sooty's kids before and to be honest, it was quite an experience – especially when they told their mum over the phone how great I'd been with them.

Things weren't going totally to plan, neither up in Derby nor down here. Sooty and Libby ended up staying the night as her father wasn't looking too clever, whilst down here I'd eventually managed to free one of their kids from the bathroom after she'd locked the door with no handle on it.

"What did you want to lock the door for?" I had asked on her rescue.

"Just in case anyone comes in," she had replied.

"Like who?" I had asked. "There's only me, Emily and your sister here."

"Yeah, as I said – just in case anyone came in."

"Well next time just whistle and we'll know you're in there," I replied. "It'll save me borrowing the neighbours' ladders – that's twice in three weeks I've had to get them – I'm sure he thinks I'm some peeping Tom."

"What's a peeping Tom?" she had asked.

"Never you mind," I had replied.

"They are so cute," smiled Emily.

"Really?" I replied.

"It's a big bath," she said, on getting out.

"Yeah, it's for when Emily balloons out like a whale after I've married her," I said. I didn't know where that came from, but it semi-impressed Emily – not so much 'ballooning out like a whale' part of the sentence – more the 'after I've married her' part.

"You keep threatening me with that," she smiled.

"Anyway," I said, changing the subject, "Did your mum and dad get off okay this morning?"

She just looked at me with those big blue eyes and kissed me on the cheek.

"Are we going to be bridesmaids at yours and Auntie M's wedding?" asked the brat at the right side of the door.

"Why, would you like that?" asked Emily.

"Yeah, weddings are great," she replied.

I put them to bed but refused point blank to tell them a story, as whenever I did tell them one they had continually pulled me up on each and every event within it. Therefore I ended up telling them a story – however, this one was sort of real and started off about me and their dad breaking all the windows in one of the greenhouses in one of our teachers' gardens – and which went on to a school trip to Hornsea Potteries where security had to be called as a few of us had gone into the bike sheds and we had been seen dismantling toddle chains, pumps, bells and horns and such from the workers bikes – and then on to a story of us robbing a caravan while we were wagging school – and which culminated into me setting the Old Hall on fire. It's strange how pointless jabbering about shite from an adult has some kids in suspense. I'm sure when they were eventually interrogated by their mum, that she would be impressed with mine and her husband's stories.

I eventually got downstairs just short of ten bells, after story time had concluded, to an effervescent and smiling girlfriend.

"You want some tea?" she asked. "I bet you're famished."

She was right – I had been on the go all day, my only respite being twenty minutes in the toilet and ten minutes listening to Arsené Wenger on the telly in the kitchen talking about the up and coming West Brom game. To be honest, I'm not sure which interested me the most.

"So, if I asked you," I sort of inquired, "Would you marry me?"

I got a sort of exaggerated, "Yeah" as an answer and a look off her that I'd never seen before – whether or not it was the hope and anticipation of the proposed deed, or the horror of being let down, I'll never know, but all the same I gave it my best shot.

"Okay then, will you marry me?"

"Yeah, I will," she replied, which was followed by a scream and her jumping up and wrapping herself around me along with a few kisses, and which was quickly followed by a really, really nice version of the new rule number one on the sofa.

"We'd have to get our divorces through first," she said.

"Yeah, it's a bit of a bummer that, us both being already married."

"Can I tell my mam?" she asked, smiling.

I couldn't see why not and therefore she did, and within two minutes I had a crying mum on the other end of the phone, again telling me how brilliant I was, which was quickly followed by a text from Lucy demanding to be a bridesmaid and another from young Stuart saying how brilliant things were. I had to admit – it was still great being me.

Still on the phone and half covering the mouthpiece, Emily asked, "My mam and dad want us to go up at the weekend."

That was all well and good, I thought, however barring the odd emergency I had my kids at the weekend, therefore I gave her a sort of shrug of my shoulders.

"We'll have to bring the children up with us though, mam," smiled Emily, who knew exactly what I was thinking.

After thirty minutes she got off the phone all smiling and happy.

"I can't believe all this is happening," she said. "Really I can't."

There was still that big black dog in the room as I knew the major stumbling block would be Jeanette. I really needed to tell her of our plans before anyone else did, and after I had dropped off Sooty's kids at school the next day I sent a text message over to Jeanette and asked if I could see her, preferably on neutral ground. This was going to be hard.

'I'll meet you at your coffee shop at 1pm x' came her texted reply.

The last place I needed this to be was at the coffee shop, as if Fosis had known of the potential content of the dialogue he would be having it beamed over to Athens via satellite for prime time viewing.

'K x' I texted back.

We had been flat out at work when I left the office, with Eddie's once-wooden narrative now totally gone.

"Just be yourself," I said.

"It's hard to be yourself when you're reading lines and talking into a mike and he's on my back when I bollocks it up," Eddie had said, with slight reference via way of a finger at a grinning Freddy.

He had a point but I wasn't telling him that.

I made tracks to the coffee shop where I not only saw Jeanette, but a rather tanned Nicole, both of whom were inside talking to each other. This was a nightmare scenario of epic proportions and as I walked through the door I was greeted by the lurid smile of its Greek proprietor, decked out with a dead dog-end in his mouth and a grey silk shirt, which had been subsequently ripped open to the navel.

"You have two women wait for you," he grinned in pigeon English whilst knocking me up an espresso. "You need hand – you let me know."

I walked the plank towards the shark infested waters and sat at the table.

"I didn't set this up, Jeanette – I swear," I said with reference to the gatecrasher.

"I believe you," she replied, sipping at her cappuccino.

"I knew you would be in here," stated Nicole.

"The tan suits you," I said, trying to be honest whilst at the same time making myself look even more shallow. "However, I do need to talk with Jeanette."

This immediately grabbed Jeanette's attention.

"There's nothing more I can say to you, Nicole, that I've not already said – I'm sorry. I'm sorry for being an arse, I'm sorry for hurting you – I'm sorry – and I really mean that."

Nicole breaking down crying only made matters worse as Fosis came over with my espresso and water, along with that idiotic and lurid smile on his chops, whilst nudging all his regulars to watch out as there could be some decent viewing to come. He wasn't wrong, Nicole called me from a pig to a twat before she left, telling me that I 'still didn't get it'.

Get what? I wasn't really sure.

Cue: Jeanette.

I thought I'd handle this one from a different angle, but Jeanette was really clever in that she knew how I worked. Re: tactics she was José Mourinho and I was Wenger. In fact no – she was Don Revie and I was Bertie Mee, and any tactics I used, I knew would be obliterated ten seconds after kick off.

"Is there any chance that we will get back together?" I asked.

"You want to marry Emily," she replied, shaking her head.

I had to hand it to her – she was brilliant at deduction.

"I love you a lot," I said, still in denial. "And I have no need to tell you how much I love the kids. Things are great at the minute and I wouldn't change them for the world."

"... And you want to marry Emily?"

"I don't want things to change," I said.

"... But you want to marry Emily," she said, looking straight at me.

"And I want to marry Emily," I confirmed.

There was a tense quietness about it all for a few moments.

"You know I still love you?" she said.

"And I do you," I replied. "And Emily knows this."

"You were horrible with me," she said.

"I know and I am truly sorry," I replied. "And I am not lying when not a day goes by when I don't think about you, and how I hurt you."

"And now you want to marry Emily?"

I nodded.

"Are you sure that's what you want?" she asked.

I think so, I thought.

"Emily's really nice," she said. "And I can see how much she loves you and you her."

"But?" I said

"There is no 'but'," she replied. "Only that whilst I'm still married to you – on paper that is – I know I'll always have a bit of you."

"You'll always have me," I replied. "You're not only the mother of my kids, you're one of my best friends."

I expected applause from the captive audience, however I got none – although they were well up on the conversation as Fosis was duly translating it, so much so that Tony the Barber and Turkish George were now sat on bar stools at the counter listening to him, as every now and again he took down notes.

"I'm wanting to take the kids up to Liverpool at the weekend," I said.

"To see her parents?" she asked.

I nodded.

She knew that there was never any chance of us getting back together, and if I am being honest, I knew that better than she did. How things stood at the moment, everything was good and everyone was happy, and not only that, we were still very much part of each other's life. However it is obvious that most things in life move on, and that being the case, neither of us were ever going to hang around for long.

As I left the coffee shop I got a big manly pat on the shoulder from Fosis, and I knew that I now had some form of closure from Jeanette. However, I have to say that after I had given it some thought, it broke me in two and I phoned Sooty, as upset as hell. Sooty being Sooty put Libby on the phone, who after she'd thanked me for having the kids, answered my question about her father's health and bollocked me for telling stories of mine and her husband's criminal past, then duly listened what I had to say, which was duly relayed to Jeanette who sent a text over to me a hour or so later – 'I'll always love u x' – which did absolutely nothing to help the way I felt, so I went home to be greeted by Adebayor and his mate, who were erecting a swing and a slide in the back yard.

"You seen Emily?" I asked.

"She went out about fifteen minutes ago – I think," stated the filthy millionaire.

"Okay pal," I replied.

"I think she went to see your wife," he added.

I didn't really like the sound of that, however in life you can't stop people doing what they want to do – you just have to let them get on with it and deal with the consequences later.

I checked my mail and walked back up to the Euston Road to see how we were getting on, and on getting in there I saw some suit from ITV sat with Eddie, Fred and Abigail watching some footage from the 'Sammy' documentary.

"I've got to hand it to you," he said. "This is the best piece of sports journalism that I've ever seen and the footage is unbelievable," he said.

"We keep on tweaking it," I replied, "but every time I think we've got it finished another football club or some foreign TV station forwards us some more footage – this morning we had a ropey piece of footage on super 8 from November 1964, which one of Bill Shankly's brothers – Bob – who was a manager at the time, sanctioned – Arsenal beating Dundee up at Dens Park 7-2, with Sammy netting a couple."

"Dundee?" he asked.

I nodded. "A friendly in front of around 12,000 – sort of part of the deal that took Ian Ure down to Arsenal."

Dundee may not sound compelling opposition nowadays but back then Scottish football was as good if not better than English football, and with Alan Gilzean, who would later play for Tottenham, leading the line, Dundee were a dominant force in Scottish football. They won the Scottish Football League championship of 1961–62, three points ahead of Rangers and the following season they got to the semi-finals of the European Cup, beating quality opposition along the way – Cologne 8-1, Sporting Lisbon 4-1 – Gilzean getting hat-tricks in both matches, and Anderlecht 4-1, where Gilzean grabbed a couple of goals and then beating AC Milan 1-0 at Dens Park in the Semi-Final with Gilzean scoring the only goal of the game. Unfortunately Milan had beaten them the previous week at the San Siro, and in front of a crowd of just short of 74,000, 5-1. A year later, and seven months before Arsenal spanked them, they had reached the Scottish Cup final, losing to Rangers 3-1.

The suit from ITV was seemingly impressed with what we were all about, however I wasn't really in the mood for conversation and I was really glad when Sooty walked in and took over.

I went into the studio to see both Ginge and Fred do a great cleaning job on the film before slotting it in its correct frame in the timeline, and before the Leeds game up at Elland Road where Sammy had hit a 25-yard screamer to put Arsenal 1-0 up after 18 minutes – and then hobbled off injured after he'd had Norman Hunter go through him.

He also scored the winning goal after 56 minutes in a rather bruising 3-2 win away versus Birmingham City – a match which was sandwiched between both the Dundee and Leeds games.

I knocked off around 6:15pm and walked home where I was greeted by Emily, who was cleaning up outside after Ade and his buddy had done.

"Never ever vill ze ferrets escape again," she said, giving me a crash course in German.

"Nice one," I said.

"You hungry?" she asked.

"I'm cream crackered," I replied.

"You fancy going upstairs for a couple of hours?"

"Going upstairs with you won't be resting," I replied, sort of shaking my head and smiling.

"Too true," she replied, before adding that she had bought a dozen big prawns which she could cook up for us in five minutes.

"That sounds nice," I said.

"Chilli, garlic?"

"I'm sure however you do them will be fine," I said.

"Jeanette told me that you'd spoken with her," she said.

I nodded a confirmation as I watched her cook.

"It's really good that you still get on," she said. "I really, really mean that."

"I know you do," I said.

"And you do know I love you?" she said.

"I've never ever been in any doubt of that," I replied.

She gave me a smile, but she never ever let on what had actually been said between the two. We ate together and spoke at length about a variety of subjects – the holiday and getting married mainly – but not Jeanette. It was a strange one, that.

"I'll get our legal people to push it if you like?" I said. "We might be able to get you and laddo up the aisle with a nice tan."

She liked that.

Emily was a great organiser and was very matter of fact in her delivery when it came to getting what she wanted, and I don't mean that in any nasty kind of way – she was just very efficient. I mean all my credit cards were now clear, I had plenty of money in the bank and all my maintenance and utility bills were being paid. There was organisation in my life that I hadn't had before; however, from a nasty bitter prior experience, a wedding was the 'bitch of bitches' when it came to organisation, and that being the case, there was no way I wanted any involvement bar parting with the cash for the thing and turning up on the day.

"Don't worry," she said. "I guarantee there will be no hassle."

As I said, she was truly great under pressure.

Chapter 22
Eddie's Tales – Take 6

They were both workaholics, the *other half* especially. Sooty had told us one morning that his *other half* had gone over to Paris to collect a VHS that he had paid just over two hundred quid for. It was a videotaped recording of a match which must have been re-aired sometime in the 1980s, of a 1967 friendly between Feyenoord and Arsenal.

"Why is he so interested in a friendly?" I had asked.

"It's just his attention to detail," Sooty said. "And he loves the player."

He was right. If it was up to him this Sammy documentary would be neverending as he was continually sourcing footage, every piece of which he had watched, taking timings of which bits he wanted and archiving the bits he did not. He drove Freddy and Ginge round the twist with some of his requests, however they both knew that what he had requested was essential. Both lads thought the world of him, and although he was the boss and the man that everything within the business ran around, he never ever acted conceited.

They had got me doing the narrative, when the narrative had already been done. I thought his narrative was fine, but he didn't. He wanted me. I liked that. Any person reaching the twilight years of their life will tell you that it was nice to feel wanted and more so to feel useful. Both lads always made me feel like that.

I came in one morning and there he was doing a draft on Munich '58 for ITV whilst jotting down notes about the 1970-71 FA Cup Semi Final with Stoke City, where Arsenal came from 0-2 down to draw 2-2.

What history will tell you about that game was that Peter Storey scored a last minute penalty against Gordon Banks after John Mahoney had handled on the line.

What history doesn't tell you is that Sammy was brought on as a second-half substitute when Charlie George had gone off injured and provided a more cohesive and balanced approach to the side, something which if you look back at the newspaper archives, as the *other half* continually did, was quite well-documented. Sammy was a genuine part of the reason that they did the double.

The Guardian stated at the time: 'Even if George is fit he may be omitted in favour of Sammy, a more experienced player whose ability to make long passes made a huge difference when he came on as substitute for George at Hillsborough.'

"I don't get it," stated the *other half.* "Charlie George had played shit, and between him and Bob Wilson had gifted them their second goal. He goes off – Sammy comes on and they get back into the game to take it to a replay, then Sammy doesn't get the nod to play even though most journalists assumed he would."

He was right and I remember hearing Desmond Hackett state something similar that Sammy 'would most definitely be playing', and he even wrote something similar in the *Daily Express.*

I must admit, some of the decisions Bertie Mee made drove him to despair.

"Yeah but they did do the Double," I had said.

And he knew I was right, however doing just enough was never his way, as he continually sought perfection in everything he did.

"The Double? They should have won the lot."

He was right. They should have. That squad was capable of winning the lot, however the hero of the previous European campaign was overlooked as Charlie George had been brought back into midfield and Peter Storey moved up into midfield.

To make matters worse, Peter Storey shouldn't have even played in the FA Cup Final as he had an injured ankle which was being treated with injections; however he did, and ended up being withdrawn after twenty or so minutes. Storey blamed Bertie Mee for its re-inflammation, but there could be a case that Storey himself knew that it was no good, and just wanted to play in the final at any cost. Football players will do anything to play in a final. Even lie.

Eddie Kelly came on as substitute and the rest was history, you could say. However what is not said is that Peter Storey could have cost them the game. In the end it didn't, but it could have.

If you think it was bad how Sammy was treated, then it was nothing compared to that of Marinello. He came off injured in the semi-final against Ajax when Arsenal were 1-0 up and rarely played again, yet he along with Sammy were one of the reasons why they were there in the European final in the first place.

Like I said, Bertie Mee was a strange man and drove him - Sooty's *other half* – absolutely crackers.

"He was a disciplinarian," I had said.

Mee didn't like a lot of what Marinello was about. Marinello was a young lad who'd had his head turned by the London life and the media.

"He wasn't that much of a disciplinarian," he had replied.

"Alan Ball had Mee's number and ran rings around him."

He was right, he did.

History tells you a lot, but it certainly doesn't tell you everything.

I came in a couple of days later and he was on his laptop taking in two excellent games as part of the 1970-71 season – some poor colour footage of a 3-0 away win at Wolves and the 2-1 away win against Manchester City in the FA Cup, both games in which Sammy had a huge impact.

"He should have gone to Leeds," he had said, shaking his head.

Leeds wanted Asa Hartford in May 1971, got initially knocked back, and then they inquired about Sammy. He would have been a perfect fit, however in Johnny Giles and Billy Bremner they had their two cogs in midfield, so how would he have fitted in?

"The same way as Hartford would have, probably," stated Sooty.

Sammy was transfer listed at his own request at the end of the 1970-71 season at less than half his real worth and Leeds knew that, but what they didn't know was that Leicester's new manager, Jimmy Bloomfield, was Sammy's football idol from when he was a teenager – and also that the man who would become one of the most respected managers in world football – Bobby Robson at Ipswich Town, both would both immediately kick up the said asking price.

Leeds United's umming and aahing meant they faced an early season injury crisis, which forced them into the transfer market and to make a both a firm and substantial bid of £177,000 for West Bromwich Albion's diminutive midfield dynamo Asa Hartford, which history tells us fell through due to a failed medical that diagnosed that he had a hole in his heart.

Hartford was five years younger than Sammy, and

although he was a less powerful player bearing in mind his size and stature, he would have been an ideal fit for Leeds. Sammy, however, was in his prime and would have been a much better fit as Leeds were a regular feature in Europe and played a continental type of possession football, something which Malcolm Allison had picked up on and had mentioned several times on TV.

As for Don Revie – he told the media: "After seeing Asa Hartford to his car, I stood outside Leeds City station and cried like a child. Hartford had begun his journey back to Birmingham and it was then that the agony of telling him his transfer to Leeds was off really hit me. It was the worst experience I have encountered, because I also had to tell this brilliant young footballer that his career was threatened according to the specialists who had examined him."

And there are people out there that continually knock Don Revie.

Both lads never did. They loved their football, and Don Revie was all about football and was always part of some conversation or other.

However there is something else here that the history books never ever speak about, and that is that Asa Hartford wanted to go to Leeds United more than anything in the world. Leeds United was his dream move and he was absolutely heartbroken that the move fell through.

Now that has been stated, maybe someone could explain why some sections of the Leeds United crowd used to chant, "You've got a hole in your heart, Dear Asa, Dear Asa" every time the player visited to Elland Road with either West Bromwich Albion, Manchester City or Everton. I can understand that football is a really passionate sport, however there are always some parts of the game that helps take things to a new low and it is a fact that some football supporters are just downright stupid. Why hurt a player, when all he ever wanted to do was play for the club you support?

It has been well-documented that Sammy had also taken some barracking from sections of the crowd, but strange as this may seem it certainly wasn't from the away support, but from sections of the Highbury crowd – his own supporters. Again, it is well noted that the Arsenal support throughout the years has been as being extremely fickle at best, and to some extent it still is. The most simple and easiest explanation could be that some of the non-football or non-technical minded supporters just didn't understand the player himself or what he was trying to achieve. It is a valid point, and there was a lot of that.

Another explanation could be that he didn't exude an outgoing persona in his relationship with the home support, some of which is duly noted from the surviving film footage. Whereas the likes of John Radford or Charlie George would run into the crowd and punch the air to share their joy on scoring, Sammy did not. His celebrations – bar his goal up at the old Leeds Road stadium versus Huddersfield Town in the 1968 League Cup semi-final where he ran onto a pass, chested down the ball before lashing it home and then turning a cartwheel – were fairly reserved. Again this is a valid point.

There is also another explanation, which is a far, far more valid point however. Goal celebrations are all to do with body language and the crowd react to that, but so is the way you act on the pitch.

Frank McLintock initially touched on something in his original biography 'True Grit' and stated that he thought that Sammy suffered from either breathing or fitness problems, citing very possible – and certainly unknown – asthma. That was as much as he said on the subject, however it is well-documented that a 'lack of fitness' certainly wasn't an issue with Sammy. However if you look at this in more detail, the so called 'breathing problem' – it could give people the impression that after a 40 yard burst of energy that Sammy's jogging back into position whilst puffing and wheezing was part of a player physically not being up to scratch – and that being the case it is something that could very easily alienate some of the supporters.

Both lads noticed this in his second game back after injury during the 1970/71 Double season versus Liverpool at home, and after he had let rip with a 20 yard shot which was an inch over the bar. Sammy may have looked like he was out of shape as he casually jogged back into position trying to catch his breath, but that was never the case, and his catching his breath or getting his breath back could have made it look like that – but as stated, it was certainly not that. Sammy was an athlete in every sense of the word and was more concerned with managing his body than putting himself under any unnecessary stress, and even in this game he was man of the match, with commentator Barry Davies stating with a dramatic air of exuberance early on in the match, "He's really in the mood for it today."

However this 'body language' – the casual manner to get back into position – could be easily misconstrued, as could his lack of vigour in his goal celebrations or his lack of screaming and shouting on the pitch, putting the boot in or racing around like an headless chicken. Lots of little things make a big thing, but there was a reason for this – a real and valid reason. It was never a lack of fitness nor a lack of commitment, it was just a case of the player continually pacing himself and managing his body.

Sections of the home support cottoned onto any one of these three points and barracking became a regular occurrence. It was hardly as shameful or hateful as 'You've got a hole in your heart, Dear Asa, Dear Asa', just the odd grumble and moan, with some of it being counter-productive bordering on moronic.

An old Arsenal supporter Andrew Nicoll recently told us, "I remember Sammy well and of some of the pointless flack he took. There was this bloke in a red and white woolly beanie, about six foot two and in his forties, who used to stand with his mates in the paddock in front of the West Stand – who was continually on his back and in one game in particular was yelling 'Get yer fuckin' hair cut Sammy' every two fucking minutes."

Sammy was a sincere, articulate and thoughtful person and he would admit himself in later years that he put far too much emphasis on the rumblings from the crowd and as with Aaron Ramsey a season ago, Bertie Mee started using him in matches away from Highbury as he thought it could affect his performances – not that it ever did, however.

Sammy loved Arsenal – they were his club. He perhaps ruined a future England career by opting to play for Arsenal rather than his home town club, and the one- or two-season wonder that was Alf Ramsey's Ipswich Town. Who knows? What is true was that he was hounded out of his club in the prime of his career by a moronic minority. The most elegant midfielder of his generation with the most powerful shot in British football – a player who had scored the goal that had won them their first trophy in 18 years had been 'forced' out of the club he loved.

Asa Hartford was diagnosed with having a hole in the heart when he was 21 years old. True, it botched his big move to Leeds, but at least he knew, and that being the case he ably managed his body and went on to play for his country and had a successful career. Not quite as successful as Sammy's career, but successful all the same.

For Sammy, however, he assumed there was a problem,

but it was never diagnosed until much later – 36 years later when he was 62 years old.

Sammy had the exact same medical anomaly as Asa Hartford and although he managed it – it came at a price. His Arsenal career.

As for Sammy's goals, we were at a loss on which of the forty or so we had were his best. We all appreciated his most famous goal, which was a 35-yard strike which never lifted more than two foot off the ground and which bent away from Alex Stepney; however, he had scored better goals, but the quality of footage certainly wasn't as great as that of the BBC or ITV. He had scored a very nice goal against Charlton Athletic in the 1969 FA Cup fourth round in front of 55,760 where in the seventh minute he had dispossessed Charlton and Scottish U23 central defender Alan Campbell on the right before unleashing a thunderbolt of a shot from an extremely acute angle.

Sammy had told Norman Gillier of the *Daily Express* afterwards that he should shoot more, and Gillier went on to explain, "Sammy proved that he is as deadly a marksman as anybody in the Arsenal team but so often this season he has created openings, and then passed to colleagues when he has been better positioned to score – it is all so typical of his sporting and unselfish character that he is."

That wasn't the whole story. The story was more about confidence.

What happens if I shoot and miss? Sammy could have thought after being jeered by the moronic minority. *It's better to pass and keep them off my back.*

This was a truly valid point. A lack of confidence puts a dint in the players overall play.

"I'm sorry mate," said Ginge after seeing it. "I didn't see it."

Neither of us did – Sammy's strike hit the back of the net that quick, but Norman Gillier had a point.

"If he just hadn't been such a nice a guy," stated the *other half*.

He said that quite a lot, and he had a point. Having an edge such as aggression gives you that bit extra in your game, and as stated, the supporters appreciate it.

There was the 'lost goal' from the Queens Park Rangers first division match a couple of months later on 22nd March 1969, where he unleashed a 30-yard drive after 43 minutes that hit the back of the net and shocked everybody, including Bobby Gould who couldn't get back onside quick enough.

The goal would have stood now, but it didn't back then and Referee Gordon Hill disallowed it with *Daily Mirror* journalist Steve Curry stating afterwards, "How Gould was supposedly interfering with play is beyond me."

That was as good as a goal we had seen him score and we were all a bit upset that the footage wasn't better.

"How many is that?" asked Ginge.

"How many is what?" asked the *other half*.

"How many goals do we have him scoring that have been disallowed?"

"About ten, I think," stated the *other half*.

They didn't. They had fourteen, and all on film, including a fourth minute mix up where he banged it in the net against Shrewsbury Town.

"He scored in that one," stated the *other half*.

"Yeah, he also had one disallowed as well," stated Sooty.

This was a FA Cup third round replay in January 1968 in front of a crowd of 41,958, which according to both Desmond Hackett of the *Daily Express* and Albert Barham of *The Guardian*, was a game that they had made hard work of and at times had resorted to spoiling tactics – and this against a third division team. Sammy's actual goal had been a bit of gift by goalkeeper – the rather spiky Alan Boswell, who went on to get his big move and play for Wolves and whose daughter Faye Turney was one of the Royal Navy personnel from HMS Cornwall, who were held by the Navy of the Iranian Revolutionary Guards for 13 days in 2007. Boswell was also sent off for fighting in a game against Swansea. As I said – spiky.

It was around this time that Sammy was being tipped to get his first full England cap and as both lads knew that the *other half* went in search of footage from the England under-23 game versus Austria from 10th May 1967, from firstly the FA then Hull of all places, but drew a blank.

"There has to be some frigging footage," he said.

I had been at Boothferry Park that day and saw Sammy hit a fine goal that Johann Cruyff in his prime would have been proud to claim – and Sooty's *other half* knew that – and because he knew that, he wanted it. He had Faranha continually hound Lancaster Gate who to his dismay sourced us a British Pathé video of the full England team beating Austria in Vienna 1-0 from the same year.

"It's readily available on YouTube," stated the girl on the desk.

"Tell me about it again, Eddie," he said sitting back in his chair. "Tell me about his England goal."

And I did. The goal itself came after 36 minutes and was a fierce half-volley on the turn, which the way he had positioned himself made look like he had taken it at shoulder height. It was a truly great goal. This drove him nuts and he even told us that he had his girlfriend phone up Lancaster House and put on a Scouse accent – not that any of us believed him of course!

"Tell them you're Tommy Smith's daughter," he had supposedly said. "And tell them that your dad's going to go down there and smash the place up."

"I can't say that," she had told him. "They wouldn't believe it."

In fact the *other half* had quite an affection for Tommy Smith, as Tommy had allegedly told him a tale about Burnley's Welsh International winger Leighton James.

"A right coward, and blind as hell," Tommy had stated. "He took the mickey out of me early on in a game so I clattered him. I never saw him after that – ever – and we played against Burnley loads of times."

Both lads truly loved their football.

Chapter 23
Preparation

For some reason Paul hadn't been at Jeanette's when I picked the kids up Friday night, but as I always did, I got invited in.

"Are we going up to Liverpool, dad?" asked my son as he showed me some drawings that he had done at school.

"Near there," I said.

"Is it as far as Hull?" inquired my daughter.

"Sort of – I think."

"Is there a river there like in Hull?" asked my lad.

"Yeah, but the river at Liverpool is the River Mersey," I replied before asking, "can you remember what the river at Hull was called?"

"River Humber," proudly stated my daughter.

Then suddenly and completely out of the blue Jeanette burst out crying and that was something that I hadn't seen for … well, like, ever.

"What's up?" I asked.

She shook her head. "Nothing, just go."

I stood there like some lemon, not really knowing what to do, before I took heed of her second request to 'get the hell out of there', which was followed by some major verbal.

The drive over to King's Cross was a strange one. I'd not been bollocked like that by Jeanette in quite a while, as I was sort of towing the line with just about her every request, and believe me when I say it, her requests were always fairly demanding.

When I got back to the house the kids gave a swift 'how do you do' to Emily before racing past her at full pelt and up two flights of stairs.

"Wow," I said.

"I think they're eager to see their new bedrooms," smiled Emily.

I sort of mentioned the 'thing with Jeanette' as I sent her a text message over – 'Is everything ok? X'.

I immediately got one back. 'Like u care'.

The thing is – I did care, and I told as much with the next text and I got another one back. 'Just go enjoy L-pool'.

Mmm. I picked up the Batphone and rang Libby, who candidly informed me that Jeanette had been a bit down as regards me and Emily, but Libby had been sworn to secrecy and had been told by her that **under no circumstance whatsoever** was she to say anything to me – therefore she immediately spilled the beans.

"That's not to say she doesn't like M," she had said. "She really does – I think that's the problem – I think she'd feel better if M was horrible and hated her guts."

Now here's where the story turns.

As it transpired, Emily had gone to over to Jeanette's – in fact they were both in each other's company quite a lot, and a damn sight more than I actually knew, and that being the case they had become quite friendly. Without sounding a right sad bastard – again – you could not 'not' get on with Emily, she was just really nice. And believe me when I say it – if she had been some conniving bitch, she would have been slung out of the 'Big Brother house' on 'Day 2'.

The upshot was that Emily obviously wanted my daughter to be a bridesmaid, along with their Lucy and Sooty and Lib's two brainy brats, and rather than be aloof in her own self-importance she had asked Jeanette, as a friend if you like, if she wanted some involvement, but stating and I quote: "I can fully understand if you don't."

Me personally, I would have given even thinking about that request a huge wide berth, however Emily is Emily and being the person she is, did not. You could say that 'Yeah, but she flaunting it in front of her', which in itself is an apt observation, but I have to stress again – Emily just isn't like that.

Libby had also informed me that Brentford-fan Paul had got the hump about it all.

"Where does he actually live?" I'd asked.

"With his mum," she'd replied.

How old was he – ten? Me and Sooty had left home at eighteen and the last place on earth I'd want to live is back with my mum.

Sooty had also told me of a conversation between the pair over at theirs, which I also wasn't supposed to know about and which Jeanette had stated, "Just look at her – she's got no lines, perfect white teeth, her hair's always immaculate and look at her figure? She can never be bloody thirty-two."

"You're not turning, are you Jinny?" Libby had asked – which was obviously the part which had grabbed Sooty's attention.

"And what's with her smiling all the time? I lived with him ages and I never smiled like that."

"She seems just a nice woman," Libby had stated.

"Bollocks – nobody's that perfect," had been Jeanette's concluding summary.

"What's the matter?" asked Emily, who by now had got all the baking equipment out for the kids and had all begun a series of 'mixing', as she had told them that they had to do some chocolate buns for a special party they were going to up in Liverpool.

"I think Jeanette's really got the hump with me," I replied.

"Why, what have yer done?" she asked looking a bit concerned, and giving me another one of her Scouse twangs.

"If I'm being honest – I don't know."

"It will be me," she said. "I shouldn't have really asked if she wanted to help with the wedding and that – I just thought that it would be nice to have her and Paul there."

"You could still have Jeanette and Paul there without asking her to help run the buffet," I replied, which to the amusement of the kids resulted in me copping a lump of baking mixture in my face.

"I never asked her to do that," she smiled. "I asked if she wanted to pick the bridesmaid dresses for the children."

"Do you know Paul still lives with his mum?" I asked.

She nodded. "Yeah, Jeanette hates her."

"I think asking her to get involved in the wedding of her husband is a bit close to the knuckle, M," I said reverting back to the subject of Jeanette being pissed off with me.

"I like her, she's really nice," she replied.

I sort of left it like that until I saw how many loads of buns were going in the oven.

"What's happening up there?" I asked. "I mean – will we actually get that lot in the car?"

Emily then told the kids about the bouncy castle her dad had arranged for them and that they would be 'camping' in Lucy's bedroom and seeing all her young cousins.

"They are all sort of your age," she smiled. "Everybody's been asking about you."

"Really?" asked my daughter.

Emily nodded confirmation and gave them both a smile. "They are all really excited."

The kitchen looked like a bomb site, which was compounded further by the fact that the ferrets were racing up and down the work surfaces.

"Dad, Giroud likes cake mix," stated my son.

"Yeah, I can see," I replied, looking over at the rodent who looked like he'd been dipped in it. "Just make sure he doesn't go near the oven or he'll have a bun growing out of his ear."

"Can they get bathed with us in that new bath?" asked my daughter.

"Then you'll end up going up to Liverpool stinking of ferrets," I said.

The next morning I had a jog and came into the house around 7:00am to the smell of coffee, Sky Sports playing and to see Emily scratching her head. "I think we went a bit overboard with the buns," she said.

"I thought that when you asked if I'd got a wheelbarrow," I replied.

"Giroud's just been on TV," she said, sort of changing the subject.

"What the ferret or the French man?" I asked.

She just shook her head and gave me a smile.

The kids surfaced around 10:00am, which I duly noted was because of the big TVs in their new bedrooms, and came downstairs and shifted a couple of buns with their toast and marmalade.

I got a text from Jeanette a few minutes later, who had obviously realised what an uncompromising sod she had been, and as a matter of recourse told me that my daughter had forgot to take her violin when she left.

Thank god, I thought.

I didn't know which was worse, having Jeanette pissing in my ears or my daughter scraping down that horrible thing.

"Your mum says that you forgot to bring your violin," I stated.

"You said you hated me playing the violin," my daughter replied.

"No, I said I hated you playing the violin here – I absolutely adore you playing the violin anywhere else."

"Can I have a violin?" asked my son.

"Certainly not," I replied.

We set off on our trip up north around 1:00pm, but not before the kids had called over at the shop on the corner to get some reading material. I have to say reading the Beano nowadays was shocking in comparison to what it was when I was a kid and mentioned it sort of nipping back into my past, which more than caught Emily's attention.

"You never talk about your parents," she said. "Like, ever."

She was right. I didn't. However, I spoke at length about my grandma which the kids both loved to hear, and about her 'lobby-hole' full of annuals of the Beano, Beezer, Topper and Dandy and the fact that she had loads of comics delivered each week, yet there were only grown-ups who lived in the house.

"Your grandma sounds lovely," said Emily.

She was right. She was.

"She used to get up every morning at half past four to see your great granddad off to work," I told the kids, who were now sat in the back of the car.

"Did she know me?" asked my daughter.

I shook my head. "She died before she could see you."

"Did she die before she could see me?" asked my lad.

"Seeing as you are a year younger – yeah," I replied, knowing full-well that Sooty's brats would never ask anything so daft.

"Is it that the grandma that knew Batman?" asked my lad.

"Not that I know of," I replied.

"It is," he candidly stated. "You said he used to go every week to pick up money."

"That's the rent man not Batman, you numpty," I said.

As stated, Sooty's brats were on a different planet when it came to intelligence, however his statement did make everyone laugh.

"Did your mam get on with Jeanette?" asked Emily.

"My family aren't like yours," I said. "Yours are really nice."

I felt a hand on my knee and had a cute smile aimed in my direction.

We pulled up outside Emily's parents' house a few hours later and literally had all the street out – again – and I have to say, Emily hadn't overplayed her hand in regards to how they would react to my kids, and the affection was heaped upon them was – in short – out of this world. They were an extremely affectionate family, and I copped hugs from Lucy and young Stuart as soon as my car door opened, which was followed by a kiss from her mum – but as stated, nothing could be compared to the fuss they made over the kids.

"Aw, aren't they beautiful?" said Emily's mum, cuddling them both.

"Are we having a party?" asked my lad.

"We are, love," she replied with tears in her eyes. "Go look and see what we've got inside."

Never had I seen this much affection, and it made me realise, I suppose, just how lucky I was.

I walked inside with both Lucy linking my arm and Stuart with his arm around me whilst being asked a thousand questions.

"They've missed you," said her mum, still wiping her eyes.

"I've missed them," I replied. And you know what? I wasn't lying.

The family had gone to a lot of trouble to lay on what was a wonderful spread, and never had I been received like this – ever. Me, Emily and the kids must have had our photo taken a thousand times in the first hour.

"The baby, the holiday to Marrakesh and getting married," said Emily's mum rather proudly to the family. "And you want to see their house."

Emily loved it all and as she smiled I gave her the heads-up to let her sister in on what had been a closely-guarded secret.

"What is it?" asked Lucy, still stuck around my arm.

"You're coming to Morocco with us," said her big sister.

Well, that was it. She literally screamed the place down.

"That's if you really want," I said.

"Yes, I really, really want," she said, with a smile beaming from ear to ear.

"And that's a forthright yes," I asked.

"It's a very, very forthright, yes," she replied, giving me a hug.

I looked over at her brother, who appeared a bit left out.

"She's still a kid," I said. "You've got all your life in front of you – get them exam results and it will be you coming back up to Liverpool on a weekend showing off your flash car to all your mates."

That cheered him up.

That night was a blur and the kids were both zonked out by ten bells. I tucked them into a makeshift bed of sleeping bags and pillars whilst Emily watched on from the door.

"You're a great dad," she said.

I had heard that said quite a few times of late.

"I'm always telling my mam."

I looked at both kids, then thought of Jeanette. And then of Jeanette's parents and my own. How could people have such contrasting natures?

"You need a ring," I said to her. "I forgot to get you a ring."

"I don't need a ring," she replied, smiling. "I have everything I want."

I gave her a wink.

"But I'll certainly not turn my nose up at one if there's one going," she said.

We went downstairs and sat on 'our sofa' and talked, whilst watching all the happy faces around us.

"Those buns went down a treat," I said.

"I know – I told you they would."

I wish I was as assured as she had been about the buns as I was about Arsenal clinching fourth place, something which young Stuart had just reminded me about.

"If you go in my bag there's something for you," I said, pointing over to a black lump with the Adidas logo and a yellow dress in a cellophane protector laid over it.

"And watch that dress," Emily added as he rushed over to it and pulled out a bag from within the bag.

"Is this it?" he asked.

I nodded as he opened it and pulled out an Arsenal shirt.

"Wow, that's awesome," he said.

"It's not half as awesome as us getting married at The Emirates," I said. "Tell that one to your mates."

"Really?" he asked, looking at his sister.

She nodded a confirmation.

"When you come down you can come with me and Sooty and I'll get you cut for a suit."

The house emptied at just after midnight and as I drank a glass of white wine – which I was proudly told by her father was £8.99 from Tesco's – all the family came to sit with us in the room, and that is when her mum asked me with regards to Jeanette.

"How's she taking it, love?"

"Badly," I replied.

"She still loves him," said Lucy, smiling. "But she doesn't like him."

"Shush you," said her big sister.

"It's the closure thing," I said. "That's all."

"She's dead good looking," said Stuart, which brought a wry smile to my face.

"And so is your sister," I said.

"Will she be going to the wedding?" asked her mum.

"It's a tricky one," I replied. "She's certainly welcome – but if I'm being honest, I think she'll pass."

"What about your mother?" asked her mum.

I shook my head. "As I told your Emily, my family aren't like yours."

"Sorry about that, lad," said her dad.

"There's nothing to be sorry about," I replied. "I have plenty of love in here."

That was a cue for both Emily and her mum to start crying.

"He says such wonderful things," said her mum, shaking her head and wiping her eyes.

Again – it was strange how everyone up in Birkenhead perceived me as being great, yet down on my own turf I was nothing short of a wanker, and something that struck me was of the main character in our documentary – it was the exact same with him. Sammy was appreciated far more outside of London.

"I really, really love you," said Emily, wiping her eyes.

"Me too," said Lucy. "I think you're great."

"And me," said Stuart.

I was just glad her dad didn't join in the appraisal otherwise I might have started crying.

We got to bed around three and I was up a couple of hours later, and after checking on the kids up in Lucy's bedroom, all of who were under the sleeping bags, I had a jog and ended up stood at some quays on the River Mersey and looking over at the Liver Building. People knock Liverpool, but if I'm being honest – it is a truly beautiful-looking city. I got back in to Emily and her mum cleaning up all the debris from the night before, and her dad sat in a chair reading the Sunday paper.

"I thought you'd run off," he quipped.

"And why would I do that?" I asked.

Emily's mum made me a coffee and told me that the kids had gone down the street with Lucy to see Emily's grandma and granddad, which was sort of strange as they were certainly people that I'd neither seen nor met.

"Grandparents?" I said. "I can't recall being introduced to any grandparents."

Emily's mum explained that they were her mum and dad and that her dad – Emily's granddad – was very 'old school' in his thinking, and there had been some family disagreement, which I sort of understood was linked to Emily marrying Linton Fox's secret love child, who was that secret not even Mrs Fox nor Emily knew about it.

"He's a stubborn old bugger," said Emily's dad. "I put up with him, but that's about as far as it goes."

"Have some breakfast," Emily said.

"I wouldn't mind a shower," I sort of inquired.

"The water's hot," said Emily. "I'll go run you a bath."

I had a bath and nipped into Stuart's room to put on a suit and a shirt.

"What's the story with your grandma and granddad?" I asked whilst looking at all the newly acquired Arsenal stuff in his room.

"They're nice," he said. "Well, my gran is."

"Do you see them?" I asked.

"Yeah, all the time – they only live at the end of the street."

He then went on to ask me about Ginge and Fred and then he told me that his last exam would be in June and that he had 'really, really' been swatting up.

"I know," I replied. "Your Emily said you've been getting outside help."

Emily had explained to her mum and dad exactly what he had needed in the way of results, and although Stuart was confident enough in his own ability, his parents wanted to belt and brace the overall situation. Therefore a friend of a friend of the family – an ex-teacher who had been struck off – had been brought in, the upshot of which was that Stuart had been getting an extra three lessons a week.

"Is he any good?" I asked in regards to the teacher.

"It's a 'she' – she's called Caroline."

"A woman teacher who was struck off?" I inquired.

"Yeah, it was in all the papers," he gladly told me. "She was knocking off three or four lads from college and some photographs were found."

"Nice one," I said smiling. "You want to get in there."

"You what – she's like fifty years old!" exclaimed Stuart.

"Look at my car and then go on the internet and kick up a picture of a Maserati Bora and tell me which one you wouldn't want," I said. "A car can be like a person – if it's looked after – it will still look good after fifty years."

That got his attention and as I went downstairs I heard him scurrying for his laptop; however on getting down there I got another well looked after fifty-year old – this time, Emily's mum – checking my hairline, patting a bit of hair down and brushing some dust from the deodorant tin from my shirt and giving me a peck.

"There's a coffee for you, love," she said.

"Where's your Emily?" I inquired.

"Gone to my mam's," she replied, looking straight at me.

I drank my coffee and gave her a wink for tipping me one and after being told their house was number twelve, I took a steady walk outside on what was an extremely nice day. A nice day for three points against an out-of-sorts West Brom anyway. It was a strange one this, and as I approached the house, a woman from the house next door to the one I was going to was standing with her arms folded, and was continually monitoring my footsteps.

"Morning," I said as I checked it was the right house and opened a gate. "It's a nice day."

"So you are him," she said.

"I suppose so, I suppose," I replied.

She was certainly a weird one.

I rattled the front door and Emily opened it sort of smiling. "'Mam said you were on your way down."

I walked inside the house and you know what – it reminded me of my grandma's and I said so as I was greeted by one of its owners, an old lady with a smile you could have framed and who had the name of Edie.

"Hello," I said.

"So you must be Lee," she exclaimed. "It's so nice to meet you."

"And you," I said, giving her a peck on the cheek whilst looking around and being slightly concerned of the whereabouts of my two offspring. "The kids are being no bother, are they?"

"They are in the garden," she replied.

I looked over at Emily who also had as similar smile to her gran and who looked as radiant as ever in her yellow dress, and then through to the back of the house and out of the window and at Lucy laughing whilst talking to my daughter who was being pushed on a swing.

"Go through, love," she said, however what was strange was the fact that Emily was just about to follow me, when her grandmother put her arm on her shoulder and shook her head to sort of tell her 'no'.

On getting outside I was greeted by Lucy, who came over

and gave me a hug which was further added to by another one from my daughter.

"Where's 'Master Fred'?" I asked, with regards to my son.

"He's with Granddad Bill," said my daughter.

Granddad Bill? I thought. *Who's Granddad Bill?*

"He's in the greenhouse down the garden," stated Lucy.

I looked around at the lovely garden and walked down to the greenhouse where I saw an old guy pointing to some plants and my lad with a watering can in his mitts, spraying water over everything in sight. This could have quite easily been my granddad with me thirty years ago, however my granddad wasn't here.

"Hello Dad – I'm helping Granddad Bill water his plants," proudly stated my son. "There'll be toms on them soon, won't there, Granddad?"

"Toms?" I asked, smiling.

"Tomatoes," he replied whilst still watering. "Granddad Bill calls tomatoes toms."

How could anyone not love kids?

I put my hand out to the old man, who I now knew as Bill, and hoped he'd reciprocate the gesture and shake it. "Hello," I said. "It's nice to meet you."

He looked me up and down and cleaned his hand with a towel before handing it me. "You've got two lovely children," he said.

"Thank you," I replied.

And for the next twenty minutes I was in conversation with him, which ranged from the contents of his greenhouse to his garden, his house, his wife, his kids and of course his football team, who were of course Liverpool. That old common ground again.

"Our Stuart says you know your football?" he asked.

"A bit," I said, sort of underplaying it.

"Arsenal supporter, aren't you?"

"For my sins," I said.

"I can't believe how they've thrown it away this year," he said. "That Arsené Wenger ought to have bought a striker in January."

How come some seventy-year-old guy in a greenhouse in Birkenhead knew what Arsenal had needed, yet the man who actually ran the club didn't? We walked down the garden and into the house where both Emily and her gran were sat talking.

"Put the kettle on, woman," he stated whilst washing his hands – and I'll tell you what – the 'woman' did.

"So," he said, looking at me and referring to Emily. "You're going to make an honest woman of her."

For me this was a throwback in time to the 1950s, and I had to admire the fact that this guy held the total respect of his family – well, apart from Emily's dad that is.

"Yes – we're getting married in late June – hopefully," I said – obviously keeping my fingers crossed that we both wouldn't be charged with bigamy if our respective divorces hadn't gone through by then.

"So are we getting an invite to this wedding?" he asked whilst drying his hands.

"I certainly hope so," I replied.

And that was that. Or so I thought.

Amidst Emily and her gran's contrasting emotions – Emily crying and her gran consoling her – I got taken into a room where he showed me an Arsenal programme from August 1967 for a match versus Liverpool at Highbury.

"I went down on the train that day," he said. "There were hundreds of us. Tony Hateley headed an own goal and we were trying to get back into it when Sammy picked up a loose ball and hit a twenty-yard drive past Tommy Lawrence with about a minute left. It was as good a goal as you'd ever see – I thought it was going to rip the net – he was a brilliant player."

"I didn't know you knew what I did," I said.

"This is Birkenhead, lad – up here, everybody knows everybody's business – I don't know if it's a good thing or a bad thing."

"I don't suppose you'd fancy telling me that tale in front of a camera?" I asked.

I walked back up to Emily's mum's house with Emily as she linked my arm and told me who was who and which relation lived in which house. My kids? They were having dinner at their 'new' great grandparents' house with their soon-to-be twelve-year old auntie.

"I see you met Dale Fox's mother," she said.

I gave a shrug of my shoulders.

"The woman next door to gran," she said.

"Oh, her," I replied.

The drive back down to London was postponed until after I had seen Arsenal beat West Brom 1-0 on Emily's dad's Sky TV, by a well-taken goal from the French ferret, which made it a happy drive back down.

I dropped the kids off home and Jeanette was as distant as she had been on the Friday when I had picked them up, and that being the case I didn't get an invite inside. I was losing her, and that hurt.

Chapter 24
Hidden Truths

Work had been manic, and I didn't get back to the house until 6:50pm where I was met by four empty violin cases on the breakfast bar. I either envisaged my worst nightmare or James Cagney and part of the cast from 'Public Enemy' were holding Emily and the ferrets hostage at machine gunpoint. It turned out to be my worst nightmare times three – or four if you like. It appeared my daughter plus Sooty's two were being schooled in the art of 'violinry' in the conservatory – and by Emily.

"I didn't know you could play one of those lousy things?" I stated.

"I can play most instruments," she replied.

That was certainly news to me.

"I *was* a music teacher," she said.

I had always thought she had been some nursery teacher – I didn't know she had been a real teacher.

As it turned out, she had been secretly teaching my tone deaf daughter over the past couple of weeks, but over at Jeanette's – which was another thing I knew I was going to have held against me – and which would be part of the contents of Jeanette's little black book of all things related to me which pissed her off.

Underneath the horrid screeching I could identify some form of music, but it wouldn't have been something that I'd recommend.

I kicked up the percolator and switched on Sky TV before having a rummage around in the fridge. Emily had this penchant for 'nil wastage' and loads of stuff in the fridge was either wrapped in cling film or bagged up with stickers on.

"If you can wait fifteen minutes I'll do you some food," she shouted. "I've got some nice sole."

I'm glad she told me that as I was thinking about copping a bath as I'd wondered what *that* smell was.

I had my sole, and yet another cous cous salad with sun dried tomatoes and feta, whilst I drooled over at the three kids tucking into their quid-fifty-a-piece chicken Kievs, new potatoes, sweetcorn and peas and wondered why she never ever served me nice tasting shite like that?

"So why have we got 'Bill and Ben' over?" I asked as regards to Emily 'sitting Sooty's two overly-erudite sprogs.

"Tim's at work with that, yer know – and Libby's doing some organising for her birthday party."

I understood the latter but not the former, so I pulled her up on the 'yer know' bit.

"It's that thing with the Greek lady that the film company are doing at your studio," she explained.

"Again?" I replied. "I wondered why he had wanted shut of me – we are snowed under at work and he's letting the studio for some idiot to film that load of rubbish."

"Have you seen it?" she asked.

"I caught a bit of it a couple of weeks back," I informed her whilst prodding around with the flat fish.

"What's up, don't you like it?" she asked.

"What, the fish or the series they are doing?" I asked.

"The fish," she smiled.

"Yeah, great," I lied.

"It's good for you and you're always complaining about your calorie intake," she reminded me.

"Was I?" I reminded myself. In that case the calorie complaining would definitely have to stop.

"Look how fit and healthier you are now," she stated.

I think that was more to do with the three of four thousand push ups a week I was having to do as part of a series of techniques to bring her off ten times a week than any fish or salad I was having rammed down my throat. Not that I minded, however.

I dropped Sooty's kids off before I drove over to Clerkenwell and wondered what mood I would find Jeanette in. Paul was there, which was a bit of a plus as she never really kicked off when he was there, however the fact that she wanted to see me and that she made Paul go sit in another room made me a bit edgy to say the least. I was only surprised she didn't make me sit in a smaller chair than hers before the bollocking I was obviously going to receive commenced.

"I can't think of anything that I've really done wrong, Jeanette," I said, sort of shrugging my shoulders. "I may have taken the kids for a KFC the other week against your really strict orders, but that was more to do with the fact that half the week I'm starving."

"Why, doesn't she feed you?" she asked.

"Yeah she's a great cook, but there's a lot of green in it," I said. "And lots of fish and chicken."

"That's good for you," explained Jeanette.

"So is spinach and look at the state of Popeye," I replied.

I was sure I picked up a bit of a smile with that one.

"Anyway," she said, crossing her legs and moving swiftly on to the bollocking. "You know that Emily wants me to have some involvement with this wedding?"

Bollocks, I thought. That was definitely a subject I didn't wish to partake in, so I did what I did best and acted dumb.

"Stop acting dumb," she said. "You know she does – she told me that she told you."

"Did she?" I replied. "I must have forgotten to listen."

"I thought she was being smart and sort of rubbing it in my face," she said. "I was out of order – I now know that she wasn't doing that."

Okay, can I go now? I thought.

"I was being insecure and childish," she added. "And although you continually piss me off, I do still love you."

I shrugged my shoulders, trying my level best not to look dumb.

"All I see is you with this lovely woman and see how happy you both are and then I look at myself and just see a failure. It's really, really hard for me."

Mmm. This was a loaded conversation and only one person had the gun. And that being the case, I knew it was never the best idea to start a return of dialogue.

"The kids told me about the great time they had up at Emily's parents," she explained. "And I know how much her family likes you."

It was still the best option to stay silent, however the fact that she had now shut up and wanted me to talk did, I have to say, put me under a bit pressure.

"I didn't know she was teaching the kids the violin," I innocently stated.

"What the hell's that got to do with what I've just been saying?" she snapped. "I'm on about the fact that she's given you a family – a family who thinks the sun shines out of your backside and who have taken you in as one of their own, you bloody moron."

That was definitely a cue for me to shut up.

"I can certainly see what they love about you – it was the one thing we both had in common – we were both in love with you," she candidly grizzled. "Why weren't you like this with me? That's what I can't bloody understand."

Two points immediately sprung to mind. One – half the time you were a total bitch with me and nagged me like hell – and two – as for your family, your mum was also a total bitch with me and your dad hated my guts – I never said that, but certainly felt like it.

"I feel like I am losing you, and I feel so inadequate," she said before she kicked off crying again – twice in a week – I was well impressed.

I'd pissed her off thousands of times while we were married, and she never cried. She had slung a few things at me, both heavy and verbal, cut up half my suits, put Immac hair remover in my shampoo and burned some great film footage of Arsenal, but she'd never cried.

The fact that I was still paying her mortgage, along with an obscene amount of child maintenance, surely must have made her feel she had some vice-like grip on me. Again, I thought it, but I certainly didn't say it.

"I'm sorry I hurt you," I said. "The one thing I can't alter is 'things past'. I wish I could but I can't. The thing I can alter however, is the future. Those are mistakes that helped me lose you and for a time lost me access to the kids. I never ever want that to happen again."

She was listening, but I was sure I heard her grinding her teeth in reference to the said mistakes – all twenty-three of them, two of which included the wife of the Tall Dwarf and Nicole.

"I love you and the kids, and nothing in my life will ever change that – that I can promise you – I will always want to be a part of your lives. I certainly prefer you in my life than out of it."

She broke down crying again.

"I still really love you," she said.

I bet Paul is dead glad he isn't in here, I thought.

"I want to be part of your life and you mine, but at the moment it's really, really hard for me," she said. "Yours is moving forward and I feel I'm losing you."

I got back to King's Cross a complete bag of nerves and relayed the interrogation I'd had to Emily, but not before I had called in at the office and caught Yiannis's wife tied to a some red settee and being whipped by some dick head who was stark bollock naked bar a bowler hat whilst 'Rod, Jane and Freddy' were sat there watching it. Sooty I could understand as he's a pervert, but as for Eddie and Fred? I had to admit, I was a bit surprised.

"And that isn't a Channel Four series that's being screened," I candidly told Emily. "I just caught Captain Mainwaring the bank manager with a bull whip knocking seven bells out of that Greek bird with the club foot."

There were no gasps of horror from Emily, just her discreet inquiring of how she had been actually tied up. I really had to wean her off this bondage shit. I'd mislaid the keys to the handcuffs twice last week, which one of the times had me having to saw them off the bed head before the decorators arrived. If I'm being honest it was a right ball ache and it would have been easier sawing Emily's arm off.

I eventually got off to sleep about 1:00am but was awoken by a message text sent over to my phone around half past three. 'Thanx for coming round. Sorry 4 being a bitch. Tell M will help sort dresses. Love u x'.

"Everything okay?" asked Emily.

"Jeanette will help sort those dresses," I replied.

"That's good," she said as she cuddled up to me and sort of informed me that the lump with my name on it was a bit restless.

I overlaid and didn't surface until 7:00am, which was certainly not like me, and on getting into the kitchen I copped Emily with a cup of coffee in her hand talking into one laptop whilst browsing through a bridal site on another, which I thought was a bit weird.

"You should have woken me," I said.

"I'm just on webcam with Jeanette sorting through some bridesmaid dresses," she smiled.

"Morning," said Jeanette.

"Yeah, right, morning," I replied, feeling a bit uneasy.

What next? A webcam in the bedroom or worse still, the bathroom.

"There's coffee in the pot and I grilled some bacon earlier," said Emily.

Bacon? Nice one, I thought. It was worth laying in if I was going to get bacon.

I got in work to see Sooty looking over the 'Sammy' programme and arguing with Abigail about the mixing of the sound. The main focus of the documentary – Sammy we knew liked The Hollies, who were a five piece band from Manchester who were fairly prominent throughout the 1960s, and it was therefore assumed, by Sooty that is and not by me, that we run with a few tracks as background or foreground music.

"It's the wrong type of music," explained Abigail. "Even if he liked it, it's still depressing."

"'On a Carousel' or 'Carrie-Anne' aren't depressing," stated Sooty. "I've been listening to them on the tube coming over."

"Sooty – she's right – it's the wrong type of music, mate. You've got some bloke with buck teeth in a Mancunian accent singing about a fairground ride in respect to his love for a girl and in the other some crappy love affair from the infants."

"'Look Through Any Window' is an okay song as well," stated Sooty.

"It depicts the 1960s in northern England – kitchen sink dramas and that – a bit like Herman's Hermit's 'No Milk Today' or the Hollies' 'Listen to Me'," I said. "Sammy wasn't in the north west – he was in the centre of swinging London when it was all happening, we need some 'sunshine pop' rather than some flat-capped Herberts singing about some bike shed romance in Burnley – something bright that we can rip apart."

"He's right, Sooty," exclaimed Abi.

I was always right when it came to ideas. I was a great 'ideas man' and I knew my brilliance in that department always pissed him off.

"So what's your interpretation of 'sunshine pop'?" he asked.

"Something bright and breezy – probably American," I said.

"What, like Buffalo Springfield or Jefferson Airplane," he said.

"Don't be a pillock, Sooty – Sammy was an English foot-baller, not some frigging marine over in Vietnam," I said whilst at the same time thinking that in her prime, Grace Slick of Jefferson Airplane looked a bit like Sooty's Libby.

"Don't you think your Lib looks a bit like Grace Slick?" I asked.

This was something that had us both trawling through YouTube and watching half an hour of the Smothers Brothers show, which both confirmed the Libby/Grace Slick thing and opened a door into a bit of the sort music I was wanting – The Turtles, The Association, The Beach Boys – that kind of stuff.

"We need a sound man to rip off some of this lot," I said.

341

That was Abigail's department. It was all systems go.

Meanwhile at 'Stately Wayne Manor', Libby had received around twenty-odd birthday cards, one of which was from Emily and myself, which was a cue for me nipping into my office and having some amiable chat with Sooty's 'new girl-friend' and telling her how much I couldn't wait to see her. I'd whittled the five possibles down to two, and then this one. All five of them were all a bit deranged if I'm being honest, one of whom was that thick she'd even had the name 'Tim' tattooed on her.

You can always tell the pedigree of a woman by her tat-toos – and this one having the words 'love' and 'hate' on her knuckles told its own story.

I'd ended up opting for this Cherie bird as she appeared the most house-trained out of the lot of them. At first she had seemed a bit boring until I managed to get her knocking one out over some of the stuff 'Sooty' had supposedly said to her on Facebook.

"I think I'm falling for you," she had told him – him, of course, being me.

'Sooty' had delved into the depths of her miscellaneous likes, one of which believe it or not was 'ice cream men' and that being the case he had delved further – and further. Or I did, rather. The story was a bit sad if I'm honest and had culminated in her being run over by one on Streatham High Street. That was after she had had a restraining order put on her by the ice cream man's wife after loads of abusive phone calls and a brick through their window. This was after the said ice cream man had used her then dumped her. She had told 'Sooty' that they – ice cream men – drove her insane, hence why 'Sooty' had told her that he used to be one when he was a student at university and why he had told her he had been wearing a white jacket and unravelling a Cornetto when she was getting it on with herself.

I looked up at my office window and saw that the under-cover ice cream man was lurking about on its other side so I logged off. I couldn't have him seeing that I was 'being him' and playing verbal footsie on 'his' Facebook with this 'Lyons Maid' twit.

"What's up with you?" I asked on his entry into my shallow and surreal world – AKA my office.

"Libby's going fucking hairless," he said. "The neighbours have said that some black dude has just parked an ice cream van outside our house and chocked it up on bricks."

"Yeah right," I replied.

"It's getting worse – it's supposed to be 'permit holders only' and the traffic wardens never do bugger all about it," he stated with an air of eloquence in his voice.

"I'm surprised he could get parked," I said. "We always have to park about three streets away and risk getting mugged when we go to yours."

"We don't have muggers down Holland Park," he stated.

"Yeah you do," I argued. "Ginge got mugged when he was dropping that parcel off at yours the other year."

"That was a tall story at best," exclaimed Sooty. "I'm sure the idiot left it on the tube – who would want to nick my diary?"

Well, me actually. Ginge shit himself when he saw 'the bloke in the balaclava' down Sooty's path and just slung it at me and ran off towards Camden Hill.

I'd arranged to meet Emily over at the coffee shop around 1:00pm, which had everyone in there sort of nudging each other and whispering as they all assumed it was 'back on' with Nicole – the mistaken identity thing. I would have tried explaining, but what would have been the point? Fosis only made up his own tales anyway.

"It is nice to see you back with beautiful girlfriend," explained Fosis. "It is good that you dump married old hag with baby."

"This is the married hag with the baby," I said, pointing to the lump with my name on it.

"Why do you ever come in here?" Emily asked with a bit of disdain in her voice.

"I enjoy being insulted," I said whilst looking over at the three shopping bags she had in her possession. "What's in them?"

"A dress for tonight," she replied.

I nodded.

"And some shoes," she added further.

"I don't know why you buy so many pairs," I replied. "You never seem to have any on your feet."

That was an astute observation by me. Not only did she do a lot of sitting on the floor with her legs crossed, she was always walking around with no shoes on. Me? I only took mine off when I went to bed.

"Libby liked her present," she said, smiling.

"Why, what did you buy her – a rifle?"

"Don't be daft," she said, giving me a twang of Cilla. "Two box tickets for La Traviata."

"Sooty will love you," I said.

"Doesn't he like opera?" she asked.

"About as much as I like listening to my daughter scratching that horrible fiddle she keeps smuggling into the house."

"She's getting really good at it," she said.

"I'll take your word for it," I replied, sipping at my espresso.

"I think I might go back to it after I've had the baby," she said.

"Go back to what?" I asked.

"Teaching."

"What, at school?"

"No, private tuition," she said.

"What, you mean at the house?" I asked.

She gave me a smile in reply.

"Well, that'll be something to look forward to," I said with a hint of sarcasm in my voice.

"Don't be mean," she said, sipping at her coffee. "Anyway, how are you getting on at work?"

I then told her about the music side of the documentary which really interested her. I knew she knew about music, but I didn't know that she knew so much about music, music and its history.

Football is the same – just because Ian Wright, Wright, Wright was a great player doesn't mean he actually knows anything about football history and that it was Denis Compton who picked up an evening paper at Doncaster train station in spring 1953 to tell the lads that all they needed was a win versus Burnley to clinch the title. I did – although for the life of me I can't recall where I'd actually read it.

"Have you seen the Turtles?" she asked.

"What, in here?" I replied.

"Don't be daft," she twanged.

"Yeah, on YouTube," I said.

"Then look at them again and then take a look at the Brian Jonestown Massacre and tell me what you see?" she smiled.

What was this – a test?

"My dad loved that era," she said. "He was Pink Floyd-mad. That's where my name came from."

I gave her a slight look of bemusement.

"Emily – 'See Emily Play'," she said.

"It's a good job you weren't a boy then, otherwise he might have named you after a washing-line raider."

Then she gave me a slight look of bemusement.

"Arnold Layne."

"Shurrup," she twanged.

I loved being with her. She was a bright as a button and had an energy and smile that always made me feel happy. She finished her coffee and gave me a kiss and then left, and as I was about to do the same, some big Asian guy came into the coffee shop and grabbed my attention. I was therefore forced to have another coffee. It was a mate of Bondy's. Bondy needed me to take a hundred grand over to Morocco.

"I'm going on holiday with my future wife and kids," I said. "Anyway, it was only a couple of months ago since I took him the last lot – he spends money quicker than I do."

I then got told a rather tall tale that was littered with all the pink petals of innocence.

"That's a right load of old bollocks," I said. "I've known Bondy for fifteen years. If he wants me to do it – yeah, I'll do it – but don't be telling me it's for some orphanage or whatever. I aren't that much of an idiot. Even he knows that."

I got a big smile in return.

"Anyway, what's the story with you?" I inquired.

The next part of the tale sounded much taller than the first bit, so much so I found myself looking around a lot, and whispering as he messed with my little finger.

"So how much are you wanting to pay?" he asked me.

"Four grand tops," I said.

He gave me a nod and then left.

I got back to the office and all my plans had gone up in smoke.

"We've just had to call security," explained Faranha. "This woman came in and marched straight into Sooty's office jumped on him – and like demanded him to 'cream her'."

Yikes, I don't like the sound of that, I thought.

"Yeah right," I said, trying to play it down.

"It's dead true," she exclaimed. "She was some sort of nutter."

Acting on the information I received I had to immediately wipe my computer as a red-faced Sooty got back into the office.

"You okay mate?" I asked.

"I don't suppose you know anything about this, do you?" he snarled.

Well, I did, but I certainly wasn't going to admit it.

It was a long, long afternoon, which was only made interesting when Libby had told him how the tow truck had bollocksed up with the removal of the ice cream van outside their posh house and that it was now laid on its side with broken glass everywhere.

"She's going berserk," he said.

"How did it fall on its side?" I inquired.

"Because some git had taken its wheels off and as soon as they dragged it off the bricks it flipped over."

I had to hand it to him, he was always fairly calm under pressure. I couldn't wait to see how he'd respond to the three acts of opera he was going to have to be subjected to at the weekend.

I got back in the house around 6:30pm after I'd done some under the counter deal with the big Asian I'd met earlier, in some shithole of a flat in some high-rise just off the A4 flyover. I had to hand it to Bondy – he knew some pretty colourful people.

"Emily!" I shouted on getting in.

I heard her footsteps as she came running downstairs. "Hurry up - I've just run you a bath," she said, before adding further, "we don't want to be late," which was followed by, "did Tim tell you about that ice cream van?"

I looked at her looking back at me.

"What's up?" she smiled.

Then I handed her the thing that had been in my pocket since Hammersmith. You just had to be there – it was dead cool.

She took it off me and smiled, and then sat on the floor as she always did, and opened it.

"It's lovely," she said looking up at me. "You really know how to make me cry."

And then she roared her eyes out.

You want to see emotion? Buy a girl a big ring full of diamonds.

She then told me about a thousand times how much she loved me, before phoning up half of Liverpool and making us late.

We got to Sooty's about 8:00pm and I apologised to Libby for our late arrival and as ever I blamed the parking situation, and as we sort of said 'hello' to Eddie and his wife Pauline, Jeanette caught immediate sight of the expensive lump of rock which was now stuck on Emily's third digit.

"Eddie and Pauline – this is Jeanette," I said in a poor attempt at sort of trying to deflect her gaze.

"Oh, hello," she said as she shook both their hands.

"Where's Paul?" I asked.

"Why?" she asked.

I shrugged my shoulders. "Just asking," I said.

I sensed the grinding of teeth as Emily showed Jeanette the ring.

"Very nice," she growled.

I'll give Jeanette that – she would have made a great ventriloquist. I then knew from that moment onwards that Paul's evening would be a total pisser.

Chapter 25
M

The week had flown by and we were nearly ready for the final showing of 'Sammy'. As we thought it would be, it was nothing short of brilliant. Five weeks of effort had resulted in what was looking to be a fantastic documentary.

"We should have put the bit in about him turning Alf Ramsey down to sign for Arsenal when he was a kid," said Sooty. "That would have made it great."

"We never had that confirmed," I replied.

"Don't let the facts get in the way of a good story," stated Sooty, winking.

"You've been listening to Eddie too much," I said, smiling.

I knocked off around 6:00pm and met Emily at Euston Station as the train from Lime Street pulled in. There were smiles all around as she greeted her mother and sister off the train, which was always lovely to see, and the first thing Emily did after giving them both a love and a hug was to give them a 'once over' of her new ring.

I picked up their bags and flagged down a taxi and within next to no time at all they were at the house, which within another forty minutes became bedlam, as they were joined by Libby and her two kids and Jeanette and mine.

"It's so nice to meet you," said Emily's mum to Jeanette,

before she turned her attention to my two kids. "Come here and give your Granny Sil' a love, you little rogues."

Some seamstress or something or other was the next to arrive and there were loads of measurements taken amidst kids running around the house, and me getting nagged by one of Sooty's to set her some sums. It was a couple of hours of noise and excitement, which culminated in everyone bar Emily's mum and Lucy leaving around 9:15pm, even though my daughter did her utmost to want to stay.

"She's lovely, isn't she mam?" Lucy asked in regard to Jeanette.

Emily's mum just smiled over at me.

I didn't know what she was thinking as she never said it, although I had a fair idea.

"We all make mistakes," said Emily, looking at her mum before smiling over at me.

"We do, love," stated her mum.

I sat and watched a bit of TV with Lucy whilst Emily and her mum went into the conservatory in the other room and sat and talked – at length.

"They'll be talking about your wife," said Lucy.

Of that I had no doubt.

"My granddad likes you," she added.

"He's a nice old gent," I replied. "The old ones are dead interesting, and if you listen, they've got loads to tell us."

"You never tell us about your parents," she said.

"I don't, do I?" I replied.

She shook her head. Lucy was a mini version of her sister, and as I've already said was as inquisitive as hell.

"When was the last time you saw them?" she asked.

My father had died when I was six years old, and I had been brought up by my mother and a string of Vics and Ernies as stepfathers, I sort of informed her.

"My mum was never bothered about me," I said. "Just herself. I was always in the way."

"Our Stuart said that she used to hit you."

I nodded. "She did a bit – I suppose that's why I'm so daft with my two."

"Our M says you're a great dad."

"I try," I replied. "I wasn't always great, as if I was I wouldn't have let myself get thrown out by my wife."

"That's what my mam's worried about," said Lucy.

"Really?" I asked.

Lucy nodded.

"And why would I want to lose you all?" I said, winking at her. "You especially."

"Mam just hopes that you won't get bored," she said.

"Then your mum doesn't know your Emily like I know her," I replied. "You don't get bored with someone like your sister – and you know something – you will be exactly the same."

She smiled up at me and fiddled with the TV channels on the remote before reverting back to the one we had just been watching.

"There's loads of DVDs up in your room," I said

"My room?" she asked.

"Yeah, the one right at the top," I said.

With that she was gone and being as inquisitive as my future sister-in-law; I put my head into the room and asked if anyone wanted a drink.

"My mam is just talking about Jeanette," said Emily.

"I'm sure she is," I smiled as I sat on the chair opposite them both. "If you have something on your mind, I'm sure it's best to say what it is."

Emily's mum looked at her daughter and then over at me.

"If you'd leave someone like Jeanette, love, then what

chance as our M got with you?" asked her mother.

"Every chance," I said. "Your Emily is Emily and not Jeanette."

Her mum smiled at my blunt appraisal.

"Do you not think she'll make it awkward for you both?" asked her mum.

I shrugged my shoulders. "In respect of what?"

"It is a bit close for comfort," stated her mum.

"I haven't said that," said Emily. "Honest."

"I wouldn't have thought you had, M," I said before adding, "I stay close to my wife, or soon to be ex-wife rather, because I love my kids."

By now Lucy had come into the room and was now sat at the side of my chair with a DVD in her hand.

"Go in the other room while we talk, love," asked her mum.

"She's fine," I said, looking at the DVD she had passed me – and patting it on her head I sort of stated, "there's nothing I have to say that I have to hide from this one."

For saying that, I got a beaming smile from Lucy as she pressed her head against my arm.

"Regardless of whatever happens with either me or Jeanette," I continued. "I'll always be there for them."

"He is mam, he's a fantastic dad," stated Emily.

"I know love, I've seen it with my own eyes," she said. "All it is, is that so much as happened so fast, and now I've seen your wife – I don't know, love – I'm just frightened to bloody death that you'll get either get bored or go back to her and we'll all lose you."

"If I wanted nagging twenty four hours a day I've got a lot better alternatives out there than my ex-wife – honestly."

"Yes love, but you still love her," said her mum. "And her you."

"It's a different type of love," I said. "And believe me –

when I see five and a half grand go sailing out my bank account each month I don't particularly love her that much then."

"You pay that much?" asked her mum, sort of aghast.

"I pay her exactly that much."

"That's a lot of money, love," she said.

I knew it was, but that was my penance for being the person who I had been.

I looked down at the DVD and smiled. "Come on Luce, let's go watch your 'Grease'."

That night I laid in bed for a good half hour before Emily hit the mattress.

"I'm sorry about that," she said. "She's been on at me all week and after seeing Jeanette – it completely blew her mind and she just hit the 'panic button'."

"That's okay," I replied.

"No, it's not okay," she replied. "We were out of order talking about things with you and Jeanette."

"She's right on some parts," I said. "Jeanette does do certain things to get at me."

"I'm not completely daft," she said whilst sitting cross-legged on the bed and looking at her ring.

"You'd never leave me, would you?" she asked.

"No – why, would you leave me?" I asked.

"No – would I heck," she replied.

"There you go then – it's sorted. We'll both grow old and senile together and laddo in there will put us in a home to swindle his inheritance."

She smiled. "I love my ring."

"I know you do," I said.

"I love you loads as well."

"I know you do," I said.

"I'll be glad when we're married," she said.

"Why, will you get fat and start nagging me?" I asked.

"No," she smiled.

"You'll not get your hair permed and wear black leather trousers will you?"

"Do you think I look like Olivia Newton-John?" she asked, smiling.

"Did Dale Fox think you looked like Olivia Newton-John?"

"You know he did, you pig."

"Well, just make sure you stick to being the first Olivia and not the other," I said.

I really loved her – the Emily she was now. The cute Emily in the yellow dress.

I dropped her mum and sister off at Euston Station on my way into work and her mum said to me on giving me a kiss before boarding the train, "Please don't get all our hopes up just to let us all down, love – there's a lot of nice people banking on you."

I knew there was, and letting any of them down was not something I was ever intending to do.

"How did it go?" Sooty asked on me getting in the office.

"Her mum panicked after she'd seen Jeanette," I replied.

"Both me and Libby thought that would happen," he said.

Eddie had gone back up north and we were now working hard on a detailed draft of Munich '58 and setting some guidelines for expansion, with one of the first names to be bandied around being a weathergirl from Yorkshire TV who Abigail sort of had the hots for – Keeley Donovan.

"She'd make a great presenter for us," she said.

Neither me nor Sooty had ever heard of her, so we indulged ourselves in a bit of backgrounding, however there would be no way we could have got her to dump the cushy number she had talking about incoming northerlies and light showers for fifteen minutes a day for the rest of her working life, when all we had to offer was some air time on a sports programme that could easily have the plug pulled on it at any time. All the same, I liked where Abigail was coming from – it was a really bold observation and I told her so.

I got back in later that evening to see Emily in the back garden sat barefoot on the kids' swing, whilst talking on her mobile phone. I rattled the window and she waved back and smiled. Looking around the kitchen I saw a lot of writing on a pad with lots of figures and more figures on another sheet of paper. I was hoping it wasn't her totting up the cost of the wedding because if it was there was hell of a lot of noughts on there. I checked in the fridge and thanked god that there was no smell of either parmigiano reggiano or fish. I was getting as though I enjoyed the smell of the ferrets better – not that I fancied eating either of them that is. I took out a couple of slices of mortadella and kicked up Sky Sports. And whilst I snaffled the ham and poured myself a Perrier water it was confirmed that Carl Jenkinson would be a starter in the last game of the season away against Norwich.

"Hiya," said Emily, pecking me on the cheek as she walked through the back door. "I've had a great day."

"That lot isn't the billings for those posh bridesmaid frocks, is it?" I asked.

"You must be joking," she smiled. "That's my cut of the money when my divorce comes through."

I was well impressed. A woman of means.

"Does that mean you'll bugger off after leeching off me the last month?" I asked.

"I told you last night – you aren't getting rid of me, ever."

"So what are we eating – I'm starving?" I asked.

"I really fancied going out tonight," she said.

"Okay then, where do you fancy?" I asked. "And don't say sushi. I can't be watching you eat that tofu stuff again."

"Let's go Chinatown," she said.

Brilliant. A place more stinker than the fridge and the ferret hutch, I thought.

"Brilliant," I lied.

It might not have been my favourite spot, but the night I had with her was great. We had a great Chinese meal on Gerrard Street and caught the tube back into King's Cross and went to that bar where they played the indie music that was nearly as infectious as her smile.

"Isn't life great?" she beamed as she looked down at her ring.

"Yeah, it's not bad," I replied.

I woke the next morning with an indescribable taste in my mouth and checked the clock, however the bed was minus the girlfriend plus the lump, and as I went downstairs pulling on my sweatshirt, I saw Emily at the breakfast bar back re-totting up her sums.

"Morning," she said. "The coffee's on."

I checked the clock again – it was only 5:30am.

"You're up early," I exclaimed.

"He's been moving around a lot," she smiled. "I don't think he likes Chinese food."

I nipped out for a jog around the block and had a natter with the postman who told me that he'd had a £500 bet on Arsenal to beat Hull in the FA Cup Final 3-2.

"That's a lot of money," I said.

"They're great odds," he replied.

"There's a reason they're great odds," I stated. "You've got little chance of a result."

He then asked me my thoughts.

"I certainly think Arsenal will score three goals," I said. "Ramsey will score as well. Stick a few quid on that and at least you'll get your money back."

I was always getting asked on my thoughts when it came to football, so much so it could be like one of those insider trader scenes – say like in Eddie Murphy's 'Trading Places' where the nouveau riche Billy Valentine is asked his thoughts on certain stocks and shares and the room goes quiet. It's weird really, as I rarely ever bet money on football.

I got back in the house to find Emily still counting figures like some old miserly miser and smiled to myself whilst shaking my head. Not only had she had a great result as regards an okay for a settlement once her divorce was sorted, the liquidators acting for the company she had worked for had finally paid her what she was owed. To say she was pleased – well, she was very, very pleased.

"What are you going to do with all your wealth?" I asked. "I hope you're not going to blow it all on hats?"

"I want to put some of it into paying off this house," she said.

"Why?" I asked.

"Because I want to feel like it's mine as well," she said.

I couldn't fault her for that, but in my mind the house was being paid off okay and we were alright. However, it turned out that she was adamant that exactly £100,000 would go into getting the mortgage payment down.

"It's a bad investment," I said.

She shrugged her shoulders. "It's property."

"Chucking a hundred grand at this thing wouldn't do much to the monthly payments," I said. "If you want to put something into the house, have a deep basement put in or something."

She smiled. "That's a nice idea."

"But you don't need to," I said.

"Why are you just so nice all the time?" she asked.

I had no answer to that.

The rest of the week panned out better than okay, and the fact that Emily now had her own financial independence made her feel a thousand percent better. That's not to say I ever minded her spending the money in the joint account however she saw fit – the thing was that she never squandered it, and everything she had bought for her – say clothes, shoes, had come out of what she had already earned from her job. The only time the account was breached was for what went into the house or what we ate. She was like no woman I had ever known. She was a woman who never took the piss.

However, for me there was something else on the horizon and a couple of days later I got home from work and to a girlfriend wearing one of my old shirts and a pair of bright red flowery leggings, with her hair in a ponytail and her hands full of paint.

"Hello," I said on getting in and flopping on the couch.

She seemed excited. Well, more excited than normal and the way she screamed and the way I got jumped on made that quite a giveaway.

"I've got a surprise for you," she said, whilst kneeling over me and smiling and getting paint on my face.

"You're not pregnant, are you?" I asked.

"I am bit," she said, "But that's not it."

"You're full of paint then," I said.

"Yeah, that's because I've been painting," she said.

"Alright then, I give in."

You just had to love her. She could dress in rags and she'd always look great.

"A man called me from Austria," she said.

"What did he say?" I asked, not knowing where she was coming from.

"I don't know," she said, "I don't speak much Austrian."

I shrugged my shoulders.

"He uploaded a file on his Dropbox for me to download," she said.

"What?" I asked.

"A massive AVI file – his bossy secretary made me send four hundred euros by Paypal though."

I immediately knew what it was.

"She was bossy?" I inquired.

"Not half," she said before giving me a rundown of the demand. "You vill send ze four hundred euros viz immediate effect to zis email address and on confirmation I vill give you access to ze files."

I gave her smile.

"In fact, it's got me a bit horny thinking about it," she said whilst in thought.

"Behave," I said.

We went over to her laptop and I copied the file and put it on to mine and we shared a bar stool whilst I watched John Hollins float a ball into the box which Allan Clarke got his head to but failed to direct anywhere and an agile looking Sammy, replicating a goal of Cruyff-esque quality with a fierce if not fantastic volley which did indeed look like it was hit from shoulder height – and for his country. All the chasing and nagging had paid off. We had found the missing goal, or Emily had rather.

"There's two more goals on it," she said smiling. "Did I do good?"

"You did fantastic," I said.

She had. I knew there had to be some footage somewhere, however it was the Austrian FA who had it and it had been Emily who had sent them over a letter. Not many girlfriends would have done or even thought of that, however she did. That was the difference – she cared.

"I've got paint on your face," she said, smiling.

"I know," I replied.

Did I mind? Nope. She was brilliant.

As the weekend drew near I knew that I had to sort the short trip to Gatwick Airport and that we had to get Lucy down from Liverpool as well as getting the kids over, for our early start on Tuesday, which was another thing Jeanette had called me on as I was two days out on her 'strict demands' date-wise.

"My mam will put her on the train," Emily said.

I couldn't have that as she was only twelve and I told her so. "There's too many weirdos knocking about M – I'd feel uneasy about that."

"It's a lot of messing around," she said.

"I don't mind fetching her," I said, "But what might be easier is if your mum and dad come down with her and stay the week here while we are away. At least I wouldn't have to post the ferrets through Sooty's letterbox and leave him a note."

"What? You'd have my mam and dad stay here?" she said, sort of semi-aghast.

"Yeah, why ever not?"

"Because it's your house," she said.

"No, Emily, it's our house," I replied. "Just shift your handcuffs."

She deliberated with the thought of her mum and dad coming down from Friday to the next day and into the afternoon. We were down in South Kensington at the Natural History museum with the kids when she eventually broke her silence.

"If it's okay with you," she had said. "Then it's okay with me."

"I've told you it's okay with me," I replied. "About a hundred times."

To be honest I couldn't understand her reluctance.

"None of them will have a clue with the tube," she said. "And dad won't cough up for a cab."

"Chuck them in at the deep end and let them find out for themselves – they'll love it," I said.

Back at the house Emily rang them and sounded them out, however her dad didn't fancy it. That was until her mum stated quite bluntly that she would go down on her own. Her dad didn't like the sound of that either, but I'll tell you something – he did a 'Nellie the Elephant' and immediately sought out his trunk.

The more Emily thought of it the more it made sense, and the more it made us look like a family. The big TV was on full blast whilst the kids played on the Xbox when we got a knock on the door around seven o'clock that Saturday night. It was Jeanette and Paul – with a bottle of wine and some flowers.

"It's just in case I don't get to see you, M," said Jeanette. "I think the flowers were a bit of a silly idea though."

"No they're not – they're lovely," Emily replied, giving her a kiss. "Anyway my mam and dad are staying here while we're away, so they won't be wasted."

Mmm. I wasn't sure how she would react to that.

"Really?" Jeanette said through gritted teeth.

"Come in anyway – don't be standing at the door," she said.

I'll give Emily her due, no matter what the situation, she kept on smiling – even in the face of adversity, and someone being nice all the time has to eventually rub off – I think.

"You fancy a drink, Paul?" I asked.

I got a nod, but then again he didn't really say a lot to me.

I poured him a red wine as I knew that's what he liked and I asked him a few questions on Brentford – especially as regards the young lad Arsenal sold them – Nico Yennaris.

"He's a nice player," Paul said. "He doesn't play a lot though."

"I think Mark Warburton's doing a great job," I said. "I

reckon with the new stadium being given the heads-up you might see them in the Premiership within the next couple of years."

My golden rule in football – always keep pushing your common ground, and never knock another man's team.

What I thought was going to be a five minute chat turned out to be a full night as Emily cooked some food whilst both kids gave their mum a guided tour of their bedrooms, but knowing how I knew Jeanette, the tour would have taken in hell of a lot more.

"You've got it really nice, M," said Jeanette.

"Thanks Jin," she said. "I do appreciate that."

"So when are you doing the baby's room?" Jeanette asked.

"Let's get him chucked out first," I said.

Jeanette smiled. "You said the same with our two."

Mmm. That was a slight reference to us actually being married and once having a life together.

"It makes sense," said Emily. "Best not to jinx these things, eh?"

The fact that Emily could cook and talk, and sort of talk and cook didn't go unnoticed, and although I wasn't that fussed about salads on an every day basis, I more than put up with this one as I certainly didn't want to piss on her effort. We were working as a team.

"So have you heard any more from those Russians who were living here?" asked Paul.

"I keep on getting threatening letters through the post," I replied. "I just let them know that the police are dealing with it and to contact the DC handling the case."

"What about that woman debt collector?" asked Jeanette.

That was a bit naughty, I thought, so I gave her it back in spades, just so she knew that Emily was very much aware of her.

"Lindsey Bracken? Nicole slung her out when she came to assess the property the other month, and now I just refer her to the same DC," I explained. "I thought I'd told you that?"

Every now and then I kept on noticing those gritted teeth, but after an hour or so I sort of got immune to them.

We waved them off shortly after 12:15am and I knew that Paul's life would have been hell all the way back over to Clerkenwell. As for Emily, I got a peck on the cheek from her and a, "Good boy," for keeping a civil tongue in my head, and of course for 'trying' with Paul.

"You were great," I said. "I don't know how you do it."

"I've got everything that Jeanette could want," she replied.

"I wouldn't go as far as that," I said. "Jeanette doesn't want me – Jeanette just doesn't want anyone else to have me."

"You'd be surprised," she said, smiling as she cleaned up the debris.

Sunday morning was a bit weird as I awoke at 5:30am to find the two kids in bed with us. I didn't mind as such, however as Emily was getting that bit farther on, she wasn't sleeping as well, and two extra bodies moving about under the quilt certainly didn't help. According to the woman with the lump, they had both been a bit scared upstairs, so they had got in with us about 2:00am. However there was something niggling me in that they had quite happily stayed in their respective new bedrooms with no problems, until their mum had actually gone up there as part of the unsanctioned guided tour.

"She asked us if we had seen that woman over in the garden," explained my daughter.

Mmm. That pissed me off a bit, I had to say, however I was as much at fault with this one as I had pulled their legs about her being some witch. Therefore the first thing I did after they had got up and got washed was to take them around to the house on the street behind where this old woman lived, and just for good measure I bought a box of chocolates and some flowers from the corner shop.

I knocked on the door and got an immediate reply.

"Yes?" she asked.

"We are from across the back garden," I said as I introduced both kids. "I'm sorry about the noise that's been going on over the past week or so, and to just say thanks for putting up with the kids having their swing and slide erected, we've brought you these."

I made the kids hand over the Dairy Box and the three quid bunch of flowers.

"Oh, that's absolutely lovely," she said. "Do come in."

I gave her an open invite to come around whenever she wished, and believe me when I say it, that must have been a breath of fresh air to her.

"It was so nice to meet you all," she said on us leaving.

"Please call around," I said, giving her my business card. "And if ever you need anything, please call me on that number."

"She wasn't scary dad, was she?" asked my lad.

"No," I said. "She was lovely, however you need to keep an eye out, as she is really old, and that she doesn't fall, so I think I might have to get a telescope for your bedroom and some walkie talkies so you both can keep in touch with each other."

I was a pretty cool dad – Dad 1, Mum 0.

That afternoon we went down the River Thames and to a pub we liked and saw Carl Jenkinson and the brilliant 'Sammy' of our generation – Aaron Ramsey – score the goals that beat Norwich 2-0 before we drove over to Clerkenwell to take the kids home. However what was to come was a bit strange as it resulted in us being invited in and having to be subjected to a quid pro quo meal of Michelin four star status, served up by a heavily made-up Jeanette in a posh frock and high heels.

"I feel a right scruff, now," whispered Emily, sort of giving herself a quick once-over and a slightly damning self-assessment.

"It serves you right for taking the kids paddling in the river with no shoes on," I whispered back.

"I didn't know we would be invited in," she whispered.

"Nor did I," I whispered back.

"We're a bit like kids whispering, aren't we?" she whispered.

"Yes," I whispered back.

"I won't see you all for a week," stated Jeanette.

Good, I thought. I could do with a rest from all this pretending to be nice.

It was great watching how she bossed Paul around, though. She had him thoroughly at her beck and call, so much so I thought she was going to start clicking her fingers and whistling him. I was dead glad I was with Emily.

"So what time's your flight?" Jeanette asked.

"Twenty past seven in the morning," smiled Emily.

"Are you picking the kids up from here or do you want them staying over?" asked my ex-wife.

That was a tricky one. Having them staying over Monday night would mean a house full of people, three excited kids and nil sleep. However, having us pick my two up from here would mean a possible, albeit definitely manufactured, overlay.

"Whatever is best for you," smiled Emily.

"Probably best if they stay at yours," said Jeanette.

Oh well, nil sleep it was.

We finally got out of dodge around 10:00pm and my scruffy 'girl next door' profusely thanked my ex for all her effort.

"It was really, really nice Jeanette," she said kissing her at the door. "We'll definitely have to do it again."

I wouldn't have gone that far and said as much in the car on the drive back into north London.

"She's pretty, isn't she?" stated Emily.

"Yeah, but don't be getting butch on me," I replied. "I can't have you running off with her and having to pay out another five and half grand a month."

She smiled over at me and then looked at the lump with my name on it.

"I'll be glad when he's out," she said.

"You won't be saying that when he is," I said.

She looked at her ring and smiled.

"We're not doing bad, are we?" I said, winking over at her.

Monday was a big blur. I got up for a jog at 5:30am and got back into Radio Two playing and the smell of coffee and toast and Emily on the phone to Lime Street station talking to some Indian lady in pigeon English, whilst at the same time trying to reserve three tickets.

"Why don't you do it online?" I said. "It must be a million times easier than talking like a Dalek."

"I tried that about ten times – their server must be down," she explained.

Just then there was a knock on the door.

"Who the heck is that at this time?" asked Emily.

I gave her a wink and opened the door to be greeted by Bondy's big Asian mate.

"Come in," I said, and offered him a coffee, which he politely declined before handing me a holdall.

"Hello," said Emily, still on the phone.

He gave her a nod back.

"Did she like her ring?" he asked me.

"Chuffed to bits with it," I replied.

We chatted for a couple of minutes then he left.

"Who was that?" asked Emily.

"No idea," I lied.

"What's in the bag?" she asked.

"Money," I replied.

That certainly caught her attention.

"Remember that flat we used see to see each other at?" I reminded her.

I got a nod as she sipped at her coffee.

"Well, its owner will be passing through Marrakesh next week and he wants some money taking over."

"Can't you just BACS it him?" she asked. "It's got to be a lot safer than carrying cash."

I smiled at her. "Not really."

"How much is he wanting?" came her next question.

"A hundred grand."

"What?"

I repeated myself which resulted in her looking in the bag at loads of £50 notes.

"I've never seen this much money before," she said.

"Sure you have," I said. "Well, half that amount anyway."

She looked slightly bemused.

"What's that thing on your finger?"

She sat back on a bar stool at the breakfast bar and admired her ring and then looked over at the money. "Fifty thousand pounds?" she said, shrugging her shoulders.

Well, not really, I ended up paying £6500, but I got the receipt for a penny short of fifty grand, and that is what it was certainly insured for, and so as there wasn't any uncertainty on her part I passed her both the receipt and the genuine insurance certificate out of the inner pocket of my jacket, which for some reason had been slung on the chair.

"You need to keep these in a safe place," I said.

If she liked the ring before, she liked it fifty thousand times better now.

"You must really love me," she said, shaking her head.

"Well remember how much you love me when that money's in my suitcase being wheeled through customs," I said. "Just don't go secretly declaring it."

"Don't be daft," she said, still looking at her ring.

Monday's blur continued with both me and Sooty playing hard ball with an executive from Chelsea as regards them sounding us out about possibly giving them some content for their TV station. For as rich as Roman Abramovich is, and for as much money has he wasted on crap players, he certainly wanted to know that every penny he spent with us had to be scrupulously accounted for. The thing that swung it was the fact that we offered them a 'play' on their successful late 1960s early 1970s period, something which we could do a documentary on to fill part of our four hour weekly slot on ITV.

In between that I managed a shave and haircut at Tony the Barber's and an espresso and Perrier over at the coffee shop and had Jeanette on the phone explaining that she'd packed some factor 9000 sun cream for the kids, and under no circumstances should they come back brown.

It was hard to fathom her out, as the first thing she did when she hit poolside was douse herself down with chip oil and stick her head in the oven on gas mark ten and lay there until daft o'clock in order to get a sun tan that Phil Brown would have been proud of.

I got home around 6:30pm to find Emily's parents and Lucy at the house, with her father sat at the breakfast bar looking at the ring receipt and insurance certificate whilst sipping at his cup of tea.

"Evening all," I said on getting through the door. "Have we got our inflatable Speedos packed?"

"You wear Speedos and I'll divorce you," smiled Emily.

I got a hug from an excited Lucy along with a kiss from her mum, which was followed by one from Emily.

I was a man in demand, and would have been one further was it not for mechanic in the cloth cap sat at the breakfast bar still doing his sums.

"Dad?" stated his eldest daughter, sort of nudging him.

"Oh, hello lad," he said.

I felt a bit sorry for her dad. He definitely didn't want to be down here and I knew that he'd had to get time off work to do so. From what Emily had told me he was an electrician by trade, but had ended coming off the tools and worked at one of the quays for the past few years. He never said a lot, but he seemed a decent hard working family guy, and that being the case, at times I know I must have come over as a bit of a flash git.

"If you get bored and you fancy a bit of work Sooty's been having some right bollocks with some Polish electrician who he's just kicked off site," I said.

I wasn't lying. Libby had been going ballistic. They'd had some basement extension and half the lights had been shorting. When it had been her birthday party Libby had literally blown a fuse more than a few times.

"I told him that you were coming down and he sort of asked that if it wouldn't be any bother would you mind taking a look at it – he'll pay you for it."

I handed him a piece of paper with his and a load of other phone numbers on.

"What are these?" he asked.

"That's Jeanette's number – she wants a couple of extra sockets running into the kids bedroom and some new lights fitting, and that's Fosis's number from the coffee shop off Grays Inn Road where I go – he wants a load of sockets installing as he's got some gaming machines coming in."

He looked up at me.

"I'm sorry – it's really hard getting tradesmen you can trust," I said. "Everything down here is word of mouth."

"How would I get there?" he asked.

"There's mine and your Emily's cars," I said, shrugging my shoulders. "And there's a load of tools down at Sooty's – just treat the place as you would your own."

I knew that if he was the workaholic that I assumed him to be that he would have been happy as a pig in shit with all that lot, and as I raided the fridge for a few pieces of mortadella ham, some of which I shared with Lucy, I noticed him looking at the numbers and putting them into his phone.

Emily and her mum went to pick up the kids around eight o'clock whilst her dad and I watched a DVD of John Wayne in 'The Quiet Man', which if I'm being honest, ranked as one of my favourite films.

"I still don't get you, lad," stated her father, sort of out of the blue.

"What's there not to get?" I asked.

He never answered me and just shook his head and looked around.

Chapter 26
Summer Holiday

There had been little point in any of us going to bed. The kids were all that excited that they had been talking well into the night, and Emily had been downstairs talking to her mum until around 1:00am and when she'd finally done, she had come upstairs, woke me up and sat crossed legs on the bed for twenty minutes to relay the contents of their conversation, part of which included the fact that they all thought I was great.

I awoke before the alarm clock and went downstairs and put the coffee on and three cereal bowls out, whilst Emily ran the bath.

"How's the lump?" I asked on its owner coming into the kitchen.

"Restless," she replied. "I think my mam's really looking forward to being a granny."

Two minutes later three kids were sat at the breakfast bar eating cereal and reading the back of the respective boxes that it had come out of.

"Are there sharks at Marrakesh?" asked my son.

"No," I replied. "It's in the desert."

"What about whales?"

"No, it's in the desert – there's no sea," I added.

"So, can't we go jet skiing?" he asked.

"Well we could, but it might upset the other people using the swimming pool," I stated.

Emily's mum came into the kitchen in her dressing gown.

"Are you all excited?" she asked the kids, before asking Emily if she had got everything.

"Passports – check, tickets – check, money – check, three kids – check, future husband – check," she reeled off. "I think we're good to go."

The taxi turned up about ten minutes early and we were waved off, but not before my daughter halted the cab and went back inside for a bag she'd forgotten.

"It's a good job your head's screwed on," I said. "Anyway what have you got in it, you're dragging it around like an anvil."

"My DVD, games and my iPod," she explained.

"Dad, are we sitting with the peasants?" asked my son, albeit rather crudely and to the amusement of Emily.

"No, we're going in those big seats at the front," I stated. "I aren't having you fidget around for three and a half hours in economy."

We arrived at Gatwick airport and got immediately checked in, which more than impressed the future wife, who had facetiously informed me that she'd always had to fly 'peasant-class' before.

My lad kept on beeping going through the metal detector and although I informed the security guard of his gold teeth, bionic leg and metal plate in his brain, he wasn't having it – and on checking the pockets of his jacket we found out to our horror that he had a set of handcuffs.

"What are you doing with those?" I asked.

"I found them in your bedroom," he candidly told every-one, including the security guard with the mobile strobe like metal detector, and three people who were putting their shoes back on and a woman whose handbag was being searched.

I would have said that it shocked Emily, but it didn't, and all that she said was that she sort of wondered where they had gone.

We went to a bar where I ordered us a couple of cups of coffee and three lots of pop and that's when I saw Lucy going into her purse.

"What are you doing?" I asked.

"Paying for my pop," she said.

"You don't have to do that," I said. "We've come as a family."

"My mam gave me a hundred pounds," she said.

"Well, I'm sure there's loads of stuff you can spend it on in Morocco," I said before nipping into my pocket and pulling out some twenty pound notes and handing them to her. "Put them in your purse as well and you'll be able to buy your mum and dad something nice."

"Can I have some money?" asked my lad.

"No, you'll just blow it on booze and fags," I said.

"I won't," he replied.

"Yeah you will," I argued. "You were only three when we went to Goa and between you and your sister, you both ran me up a two hundred quid mini bar bill."

That got a few giggles from my daughter.

"I had to put 'em both in rehab when we got back," I lied.

Emily linked my arm. "I reckon we'll have a really great time," she told my kids.

She was right. We would have a really great time.

The flight was on time and apart from the seventeen times my lad wanted to check out the toilet, it was quite stress free. Lucy and my daughter swapped iPods and played games on a pair of seats opposite whilst I eventually threatened my lad that I'd bog wash him if he got out of his seat again.

"What's your mum been feeding you – beans?" I asked.

There was no other alternative – on the return flight back

to the UK he would definitely be travelling with the luggage.

I expected it to be hot, but I didn't envisage the amount of flies I had swarming around my head when we got there.

"You're going to have to get a bath, M – you're attracting loads of flies," I stated, which sort of amused the kids.

We were whisked away to the hotel, which I must say was brilliant.

"Hey, you've done okay here," I told Emily as the bellboy wheeled our cases to the rooms. "Not bad for a fiver a night."

"Dad, can I go in the pool?" asked my lad, which his request was duly met by me slinging both him and his sister in the pool head first and fully-clothed.

"I've been wanting to do that for ages," I told a shocked future wife and an even more shocked future sister-in-law, before I complimented it with a huge lie. "I hate kids really."

That had Emily sort of panicking and trying to fish them out.

"Don't worry," I smiled. "They are great swimmers."

"Come in, Luce," shouted my daughter. "It's great."

"Can I?" Lucy asked me.

"Yeah, do what you want," I replied.

And that was it.

I had three kids swimming around in their underwear with me and Emily looking and waving at them from the balcony. It's those little things in life.

"Glad you came?" I asked the future wife around ten minutes later, after we'd sort of christened the bed whilst at the same time checking out the air-con.

"Dead glad I came," she replied.

"Me too," I stated.

I then went out to the balcony to shout the kids to come check out their room – and get some proper bathing stuff on – oh yeah, and introduce my kids to what looked like some lime-based tile grout, or Jeanette's really strong sun cream, rather.

"Jesus, what strength is that?" asked Emily as she watched me as I tried to shake it off my hands.

"I've no idea, but I know if I don't get it off me soon I'll have my hand in a cast," I replied.

In the end I couldn't do the deed and chucked it, and stuck some good old Ambre Solaire Factor 30 on them.

"They'll be okay if you keep lathering them down," stated Emily.

I looked at her stood in a pink striped bikini along with the lump with my name on it.

"Do I look really horrible?" she asked.

"Do you want a forthright answer?" I asked, winking over at Lucy.

"Not particularly," she replied stood with her hands on her hips.

"You look shit-hot, then," I said.

We got down to the poolside and I introduced the kids to a Mr. Mohammed, and he to them.

"So, if you want a drink, just ask Mohammed and he'll get you whatever you want."

"What, are they free?" asked my lad.

"Yeah, they are to you," I said.

We sat around the sun loungers as the kids played well into the evening before we went up and dressed for dinner. That was when all the posh clothes came out.

"You're catching a nice tan already," Emily told her little sister as she did her hair.

"Am I catching a tan, dad?" asked my son.

"Yeah, you're black bright," I lied.

The food was brought to us in three courses, and the kids lapped up the being posh bit, especially Lucy who was sipping at her cocktail type soft drink and ogling a lad a couple of years older than her a couple of tables down.

"He's dead fit," she said.

"Well, don't keep ogling him," her sister said. "You'll scare him off."

"Dad, do I ogle?" asked my son.

"Yeah, you're always ogling," I lied.

We finished dinner and I took a couple of white wines out into the terrace whilst my two kids opted for more swimming and duly stripped off and commandeered the pool, however Lucy did not.

"Are you okay?" I asked.

She nodded, but I knew she wasn't.

She was at a strange age. Although she was still a child, she wasn't a young child and that being the case she didn't want to go dive-bombing in the pool after she'd dressed up for dinner. She wanted to play at acting like a grown up, and therefore she opted to sit with us. However, what would happen she certainly didn't expect.

"Your little boy says that you've met Arsène Wenger," said the young lad who had been sat a few tables away, to which, when Lucy saw him, went the colour of scarlet.

I nodded. "And who are you?"

"Mark Roper," he replied. "I'm from Drighlington."

"Yeah, I've met him," I said.

"What's he like?" he asked.

"He stinks of garlic and keeps on saying 'mental strength' all the time."

"What, really?"

"No," I replied. "He's quite a nice guy."

"Are you a footballer?" he asked.

"No, mate," I replied. "I make television documentaries about football."

"Which team do you support?" he asked.

"Arsenal," I replied. "Why, who's your team?"

"Leeds," he said.

"They were a brilliant team," I said.

However before I executed my 'golden rule', I felt some introductions were needed, and I therefore did the deed. "This is my fiancée and soon-to-be wife Emily, or M as she prefers to be called, and the little lady with the lovely smile when her face is not looking at the floor is my future sister-in-law, Lucy."

"Hello," he said.

"Why don't you tell your parents where you are and go fetch a drink and we can have a chat about Leeds," I said.

And there it was.

Young Mark from Drighlington came over to sit with us and I told him about the days of Billy Bremner and Allan Clarke and what a brilliant side they had been and about the darker days of them being relegated to the second division under the management of the latter, and struggling several years to return whilst under the management of the former, before getting promotion under Howard Wilkinson – something which was aided by both the brilliant Gordon Strachan, and the enigma that was Vinnie Jones.

"I could talk about football all day," I said.

"Will you be watching the final on Saturday?" he asked.

"I will," I smiled.

Emily and I watched on as the young Mark spoke with a strangely shy Lucy as they walked over to the pool to talk with my children.

"You will make a great dad," she said.

"Hold on – I thought I was a great dad already," I inquired.

"You are," she confirmed giving me a cuddle.

The next couple of days went by fairly relaxed and not

only had Mark from Drighlington attached himself to us, I was being followed by a pack of rats poolside who were sort of aged between ten to fifteen years old who wanted to know everything I knew, and not just about about football either. And if that wasn't bad enough I had a few of their parents to contend with as well.

"My lad says you're getting married," stated young Mark's dad.

"Yeah, we thought we'd have the honeymoon first," I said.

"How far on are you?" asked his wife, looking over at Emily.

"Twenty two weeks and a bit," she said.

"Is it kicking yet?" she asked.

"All the time," Emily replied.

It was only a certain amount of time before we got to know everyone in the hotel, mainly through my kids, who kept on telling lies that I was David Beckham, rumours of which had surfaced outside the hotel walls. And if I thought being hassled in the hotel grounds was bad enough it was a thousand times worse outside. One of the mornings on our way out to Jemaa el-Fnaa – as part of a request from my lad, who had nagged like hell to see the market square dentist with the great piles of teeth – I was greeted by around thirty young lads outside wanting my autograph and any spare money I had going. Emily being with me sort of threw them, so to appease their inquisitive nature I just told them that Posh Spice had slung me out and I'd moved in with M. If David Beckham had half the hassle that I had in being him when he went out, then I felt truly sorry for him.

Emily loved the attention and she had all the kids running about after her opening doors and pulling out chairs for her to sit down. She was treat like royalty, if I'm honest.

"The people are being ever so nice," she had said.

She wasn't the only one either. Lucy loved it as well, and her and young Mark from Drighlington were becoming a bit of an item, so much so Emily had to have one or two words with her.

The interesting part was to come around 2:00pm Thursday when three huge suited-up Asians came into the hotel grounds inquiring after me and got pointed over to Emily who was sat reading.

"Hiya," said one of them. "Is your future husband knocking about?"

That rattled her.

"Why, who are you?" she asked.

"Yusuf," he replied.

"Uncle Bondy!" shouted my kids as they clambered out of the pool.

"Hiya kids, how are you?" he said, kneeling down as they ran up to him and consequently wet him through.

"When did you get here?" I said after being alerted to their presence by Mohammed.

"Just," he said smiling. "Do a bit of business, then I'm back."

"Have you met M?" I said before I formally introduced him. "This is Yusuf – or Bondy as he likes to be known."

"Oh, hello," she replied.

"He always does things arse about face," he said shaking his head. "Generally it's marriage, honeymoon, baby – not with him."

We sat and spoke for an hour or so, before I gave him what he'd come for and then he left; if people weren't talking about us before, they certainly were now.

"How do you know him?" Emily asked.

"When me and Sooty started out he used to flog DVDs for us, but we were always going to go legitimate – Bondy never was, and got hooked up with whatever he does."

On Friday morning the girls went out into the city itself which gave me a chance for some quality time, and time to swot up on some football, and in particularly Munich '58 – if you want any other nice guys in football, read up on Harry Gregg, the goalkeeper who Nat Lofthouse famously barged into the net at Wembley in 1958. What a top bloke!

This lasted about an hour before my lad had got bored in the pool.

"Dad, will you chuck me in again?" he asked.

"I've chucked you in about five hundred times already this morning," I stated.

He stood in front of me wet through as I dried his head and squirted some sun tan lotion on him.

"When you and M get married, will she be my mum?" he asked.

"No, you already have your mum – Emily will always be M."

"What about my baby brother?" he asked.

"What about him?" I asked.

"Will I be its uncle?"

"No you'll be its brother, you twerp," I replied

"Well, Lucy says she'll be my auntie when you and M are married – But Lucy's M's sister."

He was confusing me now.

I sat him on my knee and tried explaining it all, which led to a thousand more questions, mainly about Emily's family. As it happened, her grandparents had made a major impression on him, especially the guy he'd termed as 'Granddad Bill', who had shot from someone I never even knew existed to this green-fingered super hero, and who it transpired had promised him next time they saw each other that they would plant some strawberries together. It's weird how some grown-ups are perceived by kids.

"Tell me about you and Uncle Sooty when you were kids, dad," he said.

So I did.

"We used to have this pretend football league that we did – and only us two knew about it," I said. "I had the first division and he had the second division and we used to have the teams play matches and buy players off each other."

"What, with real money?" he asked.

"No. If it would have been with real money I would have been destitute. I might have had all the best teams and players but Uncle Sooty always had the piles of money."

"Is Uncle Sooty rich?" he asked.

"Filthy rich," I smiled.

"Do you love Uncle Sooty?" he asked.

"I do," I said. "Him and Auntie Lib are really good friends to me and your mum."

"Auntie Libby told my mum that you seem really happy," said my lad.

"Why wouldn't I be?" I replied, cuddling him. "I've got everything I want."

"You've not got mum," he said.

"Watch this," I said before squirting some more lotion over him and taking his photograph on my mobile phone. "Two minutes."

Beep, beep. My phone received a message.

'Aw x,' it said.

"That was your mum," I said. "She's always two minutes away from me, no matter wherever I am – and while ever I have you and your sister, I'll always have your mum."

Beep, beep. My phone received a message.

'Is that the sun cream I sent?' she asked.

'Yes x,' I lied.

This was followed by another text message which contained a photograph of me sat on a sun bed with the two kids on either knee, from what I'd worked out was the other day. It was a great photograph, but it was a bit weird her sending me photos of me whilst 'me' was actually on 'me's' holiday.

'You're not here are U?' I texted back, chucking in a smiley face so as not to look as though I was pissing her off.

'M sent me it x,' she replied.

I would have to have a word with M about sending secret and shirtless photographs of me to my soon to be ex-wife.

The girls got back around 1:30pm and carrier bags upon carrier bags were unloaded in front of me poolside.

"I bought these for my dad," stated Lucy proudly holding up some Moroccan slippers.

"I can really see your dad down at the pub in them," I smiled.

"Has my dad rang you?" Emily asked.

I shook my head as in all honesty, bar Ginge whining on about Arsenal, and the couple of texts I had just had off Jeanette, my phone had been relatively quiet.

"He loves your car," she said.

I didn't doubt that at all. I loved my car and I told her so.

"I hope he's not putting any of his oily tools on the leather seats," I said.

Now here was a thing. Emily's mum and dad – or Granny Sil' or Granddad Mike, if you were talking to my kids – had been thrust into city life at the drop of a hat and were babysitting two ferrets. Her dad, as stated, had been the really reluctant one of the two, but according to his daughter, he had been out of the house 'early doors' and not returning until late.

"You want to see him – he's been a different person since he's been down here," her mum had said.

London does that to you. If you embrace the city, you get it back. When things are good there's no place in the world like London.

"Him and Eddie have been over at Libby's sorting that extension," she had added.

Eddie? I thought. What was Eddie doing back down? Not that I had to ask Sooty – I may have had the ideas but he knew exactly the right way to run a business.

I then got informed that both her dad and Eddie had also been over at the coffee shop and over at Jeanette's. In fact they had been literally everywhere.

"My mam says dad really likes Eddie," smiled Emily.

There was nothing not to like about Eddie. Eddie was a lovely guy.

"I thought tomorrow morning we'd go and get pampered," Emily said, smiling over at my daughter and Lucy and referring to a three-hour indulgence in the beauty salon and massage parlour.

"Can I go get pampered?" asked my lad.

"No, only girls get pampered," I stated.

"Can I have my water gun back then?" he asked.

"Yeah, if you promise not to go squirting them cats with it again," I said, which sort of had everyone laughing as the other day he'd been some 'Die Hard' commando and had over half a dozen terrified and very wet moggies running onto the terrace, and which to the amusement of everyone had one of the waiters and a cat having to be fished out of the pool.

"You have to be responsible with it if I give you it back," I said.

"What can I squirt with it then?" he asked.

"Lizards," I said. "Or that posh family from Rochester with the dad that wears that daft hat."

Emily had tipped me the wink that there had been some 'nudge-nudging' from the guy in the daft hat and his wife after they had learned sort of second or third hand that we were both still married to other partners, along with fact M was dragging around the lump with my name on it. Chuck in the fact that my two delinquent and 'out of control' kids were also with us made it quite an interesting topic of conversation, although as yet they hadn't yet sussed out who the twelve year old girl with the Scouse accent was.

Friday night was a really nice night and we sat until the early hours with the young Mark's family from Drighlington and another family from Longbenton up in the north-east.

Emily got on like a house on fire with both sets of families; her sincere honesty I'm sure fuelled the fire further and not only intrigued both women – but both men. Especially when she let the wet cat out of the bag that I had been stalked by the wife of a senior executive from ITV, and that I'd recently been having an affair with a woman that I'd been having an affair on my wife with, but who I had recently dumped for Emily. If they weren't in awe of me because of my astute knowledge of football, they certainly were when it came to my private life and just so they weren't all left in hope and wonder, an exchange of photographs on mobile phones ensued whereby we showed them ours and they showed us theirs.

Mmm. It sounded a bit creepy when I said it like that.

"So you sort of get on with his wife okay?" Mrs Drighlington asked Emily.

"She's lovely," said Emily bandying around some photographs of Jeanette. "It's nice for everyone to try and get along, especially for the children."

"She is beautiful," added Mrs Longbenton. "Doesn't she bother you?"

Emily shook her head and looked over at me and smiled. "Nope."

Later that night and just after midnight she sat on the bed looking at her ring whilst stroking the lump, and over at me sat out on the balcony.

"Did I do wrong?" she asked.

"Wrong?" I asked.

"Talking about you?" she shrugged.

"No – I'm sure you made their night."

"I just love you so much," she said.

"And me you," I said.

"I know what I'm going to call our baby," she said.

I smiled at her.

"You won't mind if I name it after an Arsenal player?"

"So long as it's not Sanogo, I'll be fine," I said.

I went into the bedroom and sat alongside her and watched as she fiddled with her ring.

"I really hope they do win for you tomorrow," she said.

"Me too," I replied.

My phone was absolutely manic Saturday morning, with Ginge the first to phone me.

"I love you man," he said as I'd eased his nerves by telling him that Arsenal would score at least three goals with one of the scorers being Aaron Ramsey.

"We'll have a drink over the phone after the match," I said.

"I'm a bag of frigging nerves," Freddy had stated. "Tell me what you told Ginge."

So I did.

I was like an agony aunt for Arsenal supporters, and even the postman had called me for guidance.

"You're in demand this morning," she smiled.

"The thought of failure and impending doom does that to you if you know Arsenal like an Arsenal supporter," I said. "It's the reason why they're so fickle – massive expectation, just to be let down at the final hurdle."

As I copped a shower Emily shouted me, alerting me to an unknown number that was flashing up on my phone.

"Answer it," I shouted out. "It could be important."

After I'd finally managed to squeeze some toothpaste

out of its tube and brush my teeth – as Emily brushed hers about ninety times a day and I was forever turning up to an empty tube – I walked out into the bedroom to see her sat crossed legged and as ever, barefoot and over on the balcony and talking on my phone.

"It's your mam," she said, smiling over at me.

"My mum?" I shrugged.

Emily passed me the phone.

"Hello?" I said.

It had transpired that Jeanette had let her know that we were to be divorced and that I was now living with an 'Emily Smith nee Orr' who was also going to be divorced, and who was having what would be her third grandchild. From what I could gather it hadn't been a 'shit-stirring' exercise as such, more a 'just how things stand' kind of phone call, and the fact that this, along with there being a marriage penned in for when we got back, had sort of instigated the call.

"The kids are in the other room," I said. "That's if you want to talk to them – they're five and six now."

I spent over an hour on the phone and had the kids both tell them what they had been doing and where they were. It was a bit upsetting if I'm honest, especially the bit when they asked about my dad – the granddad who I had always told them about and the one who had died when I was about their age.

Emily was handed the phone by my daughter, and words were exchanged, before I was passed the phone to say my goodbye.

"Are you okay?" asked Emily.

"No, not really," I replied.

I wasn't. I had not spoken with my mum in over three years as she'd had as much interest in my kids had she'd had in me. Jeanette never liked her, as much as she never liked

Jeanette. It was a mutual dislike, fuelled by the fact that Jeanette looked like some model and my mum definitely didn't.

"Girls like that are trouble," she had snapped. "You'll never be able to trust her, she'll have you running around after her all your life and she'll make your life a misery."

It was strange how she had been wrong on every count about Jeanette, but that was my mum. My mum only saw what she wanted to see. If she said black was blue, then there was never any argument. Black was blue.

"She wants you to send some photos of us and the children," smiled Emily.

I shrugged my shoulders. "Why now?" I said.

We all went down for some breakfast and I watched on as my two kids made the Moroccan chef earn his corn by having him fry up every conceivable omelette known to man and then secretly feed them to the thousand or so cats that lived within the hotel grounds – whilst an extremely concerned Emily watched me.

"Why would a parent not want to see her kids or grandkids?" I asked. "And then suddenly want to see them."

"I don't know, love," Emily replied.

As Emily took Lucy and my daughter to get pampered, I had young Mark and his dad come over and have a natter and a coffee with me in the lounge.

"I hope they win for you," said young Mark.

"Thanks mate, I replied. "I hope they win for me as well."

"So, where's the family?" his dad asked.

"All the girls are pampering themselves and my lad was on the terrace two minutes ago poking at a dead lizard."

Unbeknown to me Emily had called Jeanette – part of some reconnaissance for Emily, but to also to let Jeanette know that whatever had been said between her and my mum had resulted in a phone call and me being upset. However, it also transpired that it hadn't been Jeanette who had phoned my mum, it had been my mum who had phoned Jeanette. The upshot was that my mum was dying. She never said that to me during her sixty or so minute call, but she had told Jeanette. And as I sat in the lounge drinking my coffee, my future wife came rushing out of the salon with some badly applied green mud pack to her face, and I immediately knew that there was something wrong.

"I'm so, so sorry," she said whilst sitting at the side of me. "I had to tell you."

Within two minutes I had Libby and Sooty on the phone followed by Emily's mum.

"I'm really sorry, mate," Sooty had said – a feeling which was added to by Libby and by the kids' new Granny Sil', the latter whom who talked to me for a good hour, which did include some questioning surrounding my relationship with my mum, but more to offset it with the fact that everyone was behind me, including her aspiring nouveau-Londoner husband who was currently over at the coffee shop installing some electrics whilst a rather thickset Greek with a moustache was stood over him telling some rather tall tales.

"Everyone loves you," said Emily's mum. "And our M more than you'd ever know."

I knew that already. No one had to tell me how much Emily loved me.

After the call from Emily's mum I looked down at the number of the mobile phone that my mum had called off, and set off sending every photograph I had on mine. And believe me – there was a lot.

'Thank you, son x,' was the only message I got back. It wasn't a lot but it was something, and in life something is always better than nothing.

I got awoken from my sun bed slumber by a kiss from Emily about an hour prior to kick off.

"The children are in the park and the air-con is on," she said.

We went up to the room and I took the Maserati for a spin, and had it maxing out several times before the hand-cuffs eventually came off.

"Are you okay?" she asked as she washed my back whilst I was in the shower.

"I'm okay," I replied.

"We should go up and see your mam when we get back," she said.

"We should," I replied.

"I love you so, so much," she said.

As I walked into the lounge a rather proud Mr. Mohammed led me to the great big TV which had a rather pixelated stream coming in from ITV of the FA Cup Final. It was a shite picture but he was well impressed with the twenty-quid note I slipped him, and as such he did loads of clapping and finger clicking and had loads of staff running around making sure I was the most comfortable man in Morocco bringing me footstools and finger food such as cheese and olives and espresso and soda water. Young Mark and his dad joined me as well as Mr. Longbenton and a small contingent of my young teenage fan club, and the fact that our useless defence leaked two shite goals within seven or so minutes had all the lounge biting their nails.

"Aren't you worried?" asked young Mark.

"Not really," I said. "We'll definitely score three."

And within next to no time Santi Carzorla sent a 30-yard free kick into the top corner of their goal.

"What did I tell you?" I said, winking.

By then Emily and the kids had joined us, and as she sat on the huge Moroccan rug plaiting my daughter's hair and every so often looking over at me and smiling, Arsenal upped the tempo and had several stonewall penalties turned down.

"It looks like it could be one of those days," stated Mark's dad, who like Sooty and being a Leeds United supporter had seen more than a few of 'those days'.

"It's coming," I said. And then it came and all the lounge erupted. 2-2 Laurent Koscielny.

"What did I tell you?" I said, winking at young Mark.

There were a few more close calls as Arsenal battered on the door before the referee blew for extra time. And then I got my phone call from Ginge.

"I'm all over the place here," he said. "That referee must be effing blind or bent."

I calmed him down and re-mentioned the three goals and a certain Mr. Ramsey – which certainly wasn't Sir Alf.

Our French ferret walloped the crossbar with a tidy header before he laid on Aaron Ramsey with a nifty backheel to hit the winner, which had Emily and my daughter jumping up and down and young Mark giving me a hug. 3-2.

"It's just like you said," he said.

"I told you," I smiled.

"Nobody knows football like my dad," exclaimed my daughter.

Emily smiled over at me and winked.

Football? What a truly brilliant game. And life? When it's good, it is really good.

I slipped Mr. Mohammed another couple of quid and he had one of his staff kick up some music off my iPod, and our entourage went out on to the terrace and me and Emily and the kids had a dance to Steve Harley & Cockney Rebel's – 'Make Me Smile (Come Up and See Me)' and where we joined by nearly every one and any one and a sort of party that no-one expected ensued, which went on well into the night.

Again, life? When it's good, it is really good.

Chapter 27
Eddies Tales – Take 7

I had taken the early train down to King's Cross and had been met off the concourse by a rather excited Sooty. The documentary had been completed. His *other half* had just flown out to north Africa with his girlfriend and wouldn't be there for what would be its première, however for some strange reason, his future father-in-law was.

"Eddie, meet Mike Orr," Sooty said over at their offices. "It's Emily's father."

"You must be proud," I replied shaking his hand. "She's a beautiful young woman."

"I'm led to believe you've been working with her boy-friend?" Mike said.

"It's as good a time as I've ever had," I replied. "And yes, he's a lovely lad."

I could tell he liked that and we spoke at length for a good fifteen minutes before Faranha kicked up the documentary, and boom! Here was all their hard work.

It started with the intro of the Small Faces' 'Tin Soldier' and loads of press men flashing Sammy and his wife Angelé as they left Leicester City's football ground.

"One of Arsenal's longest serving players and England Under Twenty-Three schemer, and reportedly one of the highest paid players in British football, who has been the subject of recent enquiries from Leeds United, Chelsea, Newcastle United, West Ham United and a huge bid from Ipswich Town today signed for Leicester City for £100,000 sparking a massive transfer merry-go-round between clubs."

It continued.

"Just twelve months ago he had scored what was the winning goal in a major European final and more recently has picked up a League Championship medal and was a crucial part of the team that got them to Wembley, to complete only the second League and cup Double this century. One of the most gifted players of his generation had left the league champions, and he would be the first piece of the break-up of that famous Double-winning side, a side that should have been built on but which manager Bertie Mee destroyed – the following documentary shows unseen footage and follows the player everyone knew as 'Sammy' as his club came out of the dark days of mid-60s mediocrity to become what was the best club in England."

It then said, "History tells us a lot, but it never tells you everything."

The documentary showed a few goals which were scored by Sammy: A bullet header in a 2-0 win versus Liverpool in March 1970; a 20-yard drive in a 2-0 win versus Liverpool in August 1967; a 25-yard drive in a 1-3 defeat versus Leeds United in November 1964; and the famous 35-yard drive in a 2-2 draw versus Manchester United in September 1969.

I was hooked already, and the background music was lovely.

It then brought up a piece where in June 1970 England had gone crashing out the World Cup and questions were being asked about Sir Alf Ramsey – a rather deluded Sir Alf Ramsey.

"We have nothing to learn from Brazil," Ramsey had said.

We had everything to learn from Brazil, and over the next

few years we as a country would churn out player after player after player capable of playing for Brazil, however rarely did he use any of them himself, and this would be something that would come back and haunt him.

When Sir Alf Ramsey had to qualify for the 1974 World Cup – he failed. He didn't have to qualify in 1966 and 1970, but he did in 1974.

The country who would go on to win third place at that competition had knocked England out. It is said that it was the exploits of ŁKS Łódź goalkeeper, the 26-year old Jan Tomaszewski, the man who was nicknamed 'Tomek' and who was named Best Goalkeeper in the 1974 World Cup, and who had gone on to save penalties from both Malmo midfielder Steffan Trapper and Bayern Munich's brilliant forward Uli Hoeness in the competition that beat England, however Alan Ball being sent off and Bobby Moore gifting the Poles both goals in a 0-2 defeat in the earlier corresponding match over in Chorzow had a much more influential impact on the outcome of our failure, than Tomaszewski's exploits ever did at Wembley. And with over forty minutes left on the clock and two goals down, Ramsey sat in the dugout, twiddled his thumbs and did nothing.

The two players that helped lose that game were two of his boys from the success of 1966 and the failure 1970, however this was 1973 and there sat a deluded man.

Charlie George, Tony Currie, Stan Bowles, Alan Hudson, Peter Osgood and Rodney Marsh were all the sort of players that could have made the difference, however it was well noted that Ramsey didn't particularly like flair and it was also well noted that he didn't particularly like certain players from London clubs that much either, one of which was Arsenal, and the only Arsenal player to prosper under him post-1970 was Peter Storey: a cold, calculated, right back turned hard tackling midfield enforcer. A player thrust into midfield at the beginning of the 1970-71 season due to the injury of one of the most elegant midfield players in Britain at the time. Another player who Ramsey had ignored – Sammy.

Every team needs a ball winner in the centre of the park, and in 1970 it was Alan Mullery and Nobby Stiles who boarded the plane to Mexico. They were both players who were limited to what they could do, but they were players who had the managers back and in 1970 Ramsey was still King of the World.

However, a team doesn't need a spoiler when they are playing against other teams that come with the intention of doing nothing more than parking the bus. It is a position that is wasted.

"For a very average player he has a lot to say for himself," said Coventry City's manager Noel Cantwell about Alan Mullery in the *Daily Express*.

However this was nothing to what Manchester City's enigmatic assistant manager and coach Malcolm Allison said to him personally on television and in front of millions of viewers. "If you think you're world class – you're not. You are a one-paced player who has no acceleration and who is no good in the air."

A month or so prior to the 1970 World Cup, Arsenal had dismantled a team of internationals from Belgium 3-0 after coming from a 1-3 reverse, with three well-taken goals that any Brazilian would have been proud to claim as his own – the peach of which was a Rivelino- or Jairzhino-esque goal of epic proportions that involved a cross field pass which was aerially dummied by the player before being taken down on the chest, and then rifled in off the post from the edge of the box by that elegant player who divided opinion – Sammy.

That goal made sure of the club's first trophy since 1953.

A goal scored by the most misunderstood player of his generation. Why? Because his type of player had never been seen before. He was ten years ahead of his time, and only weeks early he had marshalled the centre of midfield against arguably the best team in the world in Ajax Amsterdam, another team they beat 3-0, and another team he had scored against.

The documentary showed the goals from the European final and the club lifting the trophy with jubilant fans ripping the shirts from the player's back. It was a euphoria the likes of which will never ever be seen again, and the man in the middle of all that euphoria was the nice, quiet and unassuming face and one of the faces of the 1960s – the David Beckham of his era. The beautiful looking boy from next door with all the skill, the money and the beautiful model wife. Life could only get better.

Sammy was an erudite, articulate and two-footed continental-type player, with one of the most ferocious shots in world football, however as much as Ramsey and Bill Nicholson, had dabbled with him in the under-23s, the delusion that was Sir Alf stuck with Nobby Stiles, a no frills player who was in decline, Alan Mullery, a Tottenham player and captain, like Ramsey himself some 15 or so years earlier and the player with the bald head who was 'that good' in 1970 that he would never pull on an England jersey again.

Failure was always on the cards, and as for Sammy, like the rest of the country, he had sat back and watched the nations hopes implode as a new era of quick thinking, quick passing and strong shooting from Brazil dismantled sides with ease. He was watching players such as himself be appreciated on the world stage. He should have been there. He should have been there but he wasn't. The player who had helped manufacture the destruction of the best team in the world and score the winning goal in a major European final was never even considered.

As for Brazil and Rivelino, the programme showed Sammy, five years younger in November 1965, hitting two brilliant goals against Corinthians of Brazil on a cold evening in London. Both were from around 20 yards, and both were brilliant. Sammy was a player who could play his best football against top continental opposition, and of that there was no doubt.

Corinthians had been second in their league behind Santos and had both Flavio and Rivelino in their ranks, and early on in the game the small 18,000 crowd witnessed Sammy hold off two tackles before hitting a shot from 20 yards which hit the back of the net like a rocket and then on 70 minutes saw him selling a dummy before racing into a gap and hitting a powerful swerving shot into the top corner – again from 20 yards.

This footage only cost £390 and had lain dormant in the ITN archives for years.

Sooty's *other half* had said at the time, "How can something so beautiful be hidden away from the public. A club like Arsenal should purchase the lot and put it all on show."

He was right. When it came to football and especially Arsenal, he was always right.

And then the programme showed more goals and more strikes from distance as the young Sammy dazzled us with 20-, 25- and 30-yard strikes, some going in, some cracking the woodwork, some being turned away by the goalkeeper. It was awe inspiring and quite unbelievable.

"He's bloody brilliant," stated Emily's dad, Mike. "I can't understand it?"

Sooty leaned over. "There was little media coverage back then," he said. "The only people who ever saw this were those watching in the ground."

"So where did you get all this film we are watching from," asked Mike.

"Ask your future son-in-law," smiled Sooty. "If he wants something that bad, he'll do whatever it takes."

I could see Mike's head ticking away like a clock.

Versus Stoke City in December 1964, a ball punted in from the left and Joe Baker dummied it for Sammy to place it home past Scottish international goalkeeper Lawrie Leslie; versus Manchester United in September 1965, Irish international goalkeeper Pat Dunne brilliantly saving from a vicious shot by Sammy after a smart one-two with David Court; versus Sheffield Wednesday in December 1965, Sammy putting it on a plate for Eastham to score for 2-0 and then walloping home the fourth for 4-0 in 55 minutes after some major indecisiveness from England U23 player and German-born Wilf Smith; versus Burnley in February 1966, a man of the match performance where he hit a 20-yard volley past Scottish international goalkeeper Adam Blacklaw after 16 minutes and in a match where Hugh McIlvenney had stated that he had operated with skill and exhaustive diligence as midfield orchestrator and it was just a shame that his midfield partner McLintock could not, which I am sure his comments would have 'pleased' the outspoken Scot; versus Newcastle United in October 1966, the game was only two minutes old when former England under-23 goalkeeper Gordon Marshall made a fantastic save from a vicious shot by Sammy.

There was more. Versus Fulham in October 1965 where Sammy had raced onto a pass from McLintock and hammered the ball in off a post and past goalkeeper Tony Macedo from 25 yards out and getting everyone of 33,324 crowd screaming his name; versus West Ham United in August 1966, where a last minute equaliser from a 20-yard strike past goalkeeper Jim Standon earned Arsenal a 2-2 draw against the former FA Cup Winners and European Cup Winners Cup champions and helped keep Arsenal top of the league; and versus Aston Villa in August 1966 where according to Hugh McIlvenney, he had been man of the match and had managed to beat goalkeeper Colin Withers with one of his ferocious shots, only to see it cannon off the foot of the post; and in late October 1966 against Manchester United where he forced a fantastic save from Alex Stepney before he unleashed another 25-yard screamer an inch over the bar.

There was even more. Versus Nottingham Forest at the City Ground In September 1965, a splendidly taken goal by Sammy after 59 minutes was the difference as George Eastham took a pass from Sammy and had a low shot forced down, but the ever-alert Sammy drove in a splendid shot from an acute angle past former England U23 goalkeeper Peter Grummit to make it 1-0; versus Sunderland up at Roker Park in April 1966 in a tedious game, Sammy helped break the deadlock after 56 minutes as he sent a long defence splitting pass to Alan Skirton, whose rising shot flew into the net, and just to wrap things up he made sure of the game after 82 minutes when he beat fellow U23 goalkeeper Jimmy Montgomery with a fine shot to make it 2-0; up at Maine Road versus Manchester City in September 1966, Sammy hit a beautiful 20-yard strike past Harry Dowd to help earn Arsenal a 1-1 draw; versus Blackpool in January 1967 where Arsenal travelled up to Bloomfield Road to play an out of sorts Blackpool who were heading for relegation, and with only four minutes on the clock, Sammy hit a shot from 25 yards which left the former England goalkeeper Tony Waiters with no chance. He added a second later in the game via a cannoned shot which ricocheted into the net to help make it 3-0; versus Manchester United in March 1967 where Arsenal played title-chasing Manchester United in front of the biggest crowd at Highbury since 1963, and in a match which for 45 minutes, Arsenal had given the visitors a horrific time with Sammy looking the best player on the park, totally orchestrating play in midfield. After 42 minutes his tenacity and flair was rewarded as he raced into the box in a move very similar to that of Johann Cruyff before being brought down by Denis Law. Then in the moment of complete silence and unbearable excitement he dusted down his shorts, placed the ball on the penalty spot, took four steps back and duly hammered the ball in off the right hand post and past Alex Stepney.

"Why didn't he take more penalties?" Sooty asked me.

Now here was a story – a few weeks later I had him seen down at The Valley in one of the most unfriendly friendly matches ever. Back then The Valley was a really strange looking ground, as one side of it – the East Stand was a huge terrace, which on its own was capable of holding around 30,000 spectators – and the ground itself at the time had a capacity of around 75,000, which seems strange looking at the club as they are now. Bearing that in mind, this match had a total attendance of 7,821 and there were pockets of concrete everywhere.

I had gone down with a mate who was a mate of Eddie Firmani, the Charlton inside forward, who earlier on in his career had played for Inter Milan and had been an Italian international. About ten minutes from time with the score 0-0 I was handed a Bovril by my mate and there was a shout for a penalty. I didn't see what happened as I was covered in gravy as some idiot behind me went berserk. Now when I said Sammy was like David Beckham, I really meant it. He hit the penalty that – well, it nearly took the corner flag out. He might have been able to hit 35-yard screamers on a regular basis but taking penalties was never really his strong point. When I saw him after the match he was really apologetic and said, "I've never been as embarrassed in all my life."

As for the documentary, it was brilliant. But I had never expected anything else. I had read the content and read of the narrative time and time again, however nothing could compare to when I saw him hit the goal against Austria. I have to admit, I became a bit emotional. I didn't know that he had got it. I really didn't know he had got it. I was one of the 20,000 plus at Boothferry Park that day and saw the goal. It was the only time I had ever seen it as it was a goal that had never ever been seen on British television before – and here I was, some retired old man watching a player who was exactly the same age as I was now, hitting the most sublime volleyed goal you could imagine, and for his country. I knew Sooty's *other half* had got this footage for me. And I knew when he had got it he would have been thinking about me. Why? Because that is just the person he was.

After the viewing Sooty took Mike and myself over to the coffee shop for some breakfast and it was there he enlightened Mike further about his daughter's fiancé.

"He never stops," Sooty said. "He always knew there was film footage and he's been scrounging it from anywhere and everywhere."

He had, however there was something we didn't know as we had sat watching it and that was that the majority of footage from Highbury had no sound; therefore he'd had Fred and Ginge back at the office superimpose the sound, but the 'noise' wasn't the crowd at Highbury in the 1960s – not all of it – a lot of the 'noise' was lifted from a seven-goal thriller between Liverpool and Newcastle during the mid-1990s.

"He wanted noise and a lot of it," stated Sooty. "And he knew he'd not get that from Arsenal."

"Did you know that Sammy played in front of the smallest first division attendance ever?" I said to Mike. "He also played in front of the biggest – over ninety-thousand."

"How's that one work?" Mike asked. "No club has that kind of capacity, do they?"

Sooty then recapped the bit within the documentary

where Sammy broke through against Manchester United and got upended to score the penalty that went in off both posts.

Mike nodded.

"It was televised at Highbury in front of sixty-three thousand and bounced up to Old Trafford via Viewsport for another twenty-eight thousand to see it."

They loved their football, and I loved them. Great lads – the pair of them.

We ate a Greek breakfast of Halloumi cheese and Lountza ham whilst drinking our coffees and I watched on as the proprietor came over, and as Sooty introduced him to Mike.

"This is 'you-know-who's' girlfriend's father," Sooty winked.

Fosis pulled a chair and sat down. "You let your daughter marry him?" he asked, looking sort of dumbfounded.

"Why, what's the matter with him?" Mike asked.

Fosis shrugged his shoulders. "Nothing, he great guy – spends a lot of money in here – not like tight fisted Greek who only want to bitch about other man behind their back."

He then pointed over to a frail looking Greek by the name of Ortheus (Theo) who was sat looking out of the window and then duly bitched about him before talking behind his back.

"He one of those – he spend less than ten euros a week in here."

Then Sooty explained what his *other half* had told him about the man we were to come to know as Theo and who was sat at the same table wearing a light brown and belted leather jacket with its big outdated lapels, always reading either the 'Ta Nea' or the 'Athlitiki Icho' Greek newspapers whilst drinking his coffee. He had been sat at the same table looking out of the same window and over at the same flat for the past twelve years and had consequently taken stalking to a whole new level. Constantina had jilted him, married his friend and they'd had three children, and there he sat, just waiting for one glimpse of her.

"That's sad," Mike had said to Fosis.

"No – he sad bastard," Fosis had replied. "The girl – big, lazy and fat."

"Really?" I said.

"She look like Demis Roussos but without beard – he want to get life."

"I think our inquisitive nature had got the better of us," smiled Sooty before pointing at Fosis. "For a fortnight after we'd heard that, me and your 'son-in-law' were both glued to the window trying to cop a look of this bird until this great idiot gave us a bit more info."

"They sat there two weeks," Fosis had stated. "You not see her, I tell them – she moved two years ago."

"Then why does he sit there still looking?" I had asked.

"I told you – he sad bastard," Fosis had replied.

I could tell that Mike was no different to me, and was in awe of who he was sat with – his future son-in-law's best friend and business partner.

"So how long have you two known each other?" Mike asked Sooty.

"Since school," he said. "He's a great lad and I'm not kidding when I tell you – he really thinks a lot of your Emily."

That was the first time I had seen Sooty show any true emotion about his best friend. I knew he loved him, but what he had just said was real, and not some form of practical joke that they continually played on each other.

"When my dad had died," explained Sooty, "he had been at my side all week – when my kids were born it was him who got me there to see it. How do you put a price on something like that? You can't."

I could see Mike liked that.

"What about his parents?" asked Mike.

Then Sooty explained that his father had died when he was just a young lad.

"I got on with his mother – although I haven't seen her in years," stated Sooty. "Smart looking woman, but very strict."

Sooty had some phone call and had to shoot off back to the office and Mike and myself were left to our own devices. We ate up and left the coffee shop and took a steady walk down to his future son-in-law's, and what was now essentially his daughter's, house, and whilst doing so we traded conversation. Mainly about his future son-in-law along with me telling him of the first time I ever saw them as a couple. Her, the little doll in the white dress with the blonde hair and the baby blue eyes, and him - the Armani-suited father with the million-dollar smile.

"I just can't work him out," Mike had said.

"You can once you know him," I said. "He really is a nice lad."

We sat in his house as Mike's wife made us a cup of tea whilst proudly talking up her daughter's new found life. I could certainly see where her daughter had got that smile.

I eventually stayed in London for five days with Pauline coming down, and as the two women did whatever they did through the day, Mike and myself utilised ourselves firstly over at Sooty's house and then over at the coffee shop. I loved being in his company. Mike was a hard working man with a lovely demeanour and I have to say, we got on like a house on fire – as did Pauline with Sylvia – or Sil' I should say.

I had picked Pauline up from King's Cross station and we were intending to book into one of the smaller hotels, but Sooty insisted that we stay over at theirs, and one night as the women drank wine out on the terrace down at their place in Holland Park we had chance to watch the programme again, and my so called 'wooden narration'.

"They both ribbed me like hell about that," I had said, with regards to the 'Mash gets Smashed' and the 'smash them all to bits' jibes I'd had to endure.

"Your son-in-law did the original narration," Sooty had said.

"Well, why is he not talking on it now?" Mike had asked.

"He said it wasn't good enough," I had replied.

"He's a stickler when it comes to perfection," Sooty had said. "And I mean with everything."

Mike saw some of that perfection when he had drove into Clerkenwell and tapped on the front door of a property.

"Oh, hello, you must be M's father," Jeanette had said. "Do come in."

He had been literally gobsmacked and said as much as I helped him run some cabling beneath floor boards and into the bedrooms of the two children he had recently met and who now referred to him as Granddad Mike.

I could see his mind continually ticking away as he thought of Jeanette and the children, the surroundings he was now in and the people that he had been with. However nothing would prepare him for the sight that would greet him as we sat in the kitchen drinking tea after he had done what he came to do.

"When was that taken?" Mike had asked, pointing at a photograph of his future son-in-law sat on a sun bed with both his and the owner of the property's children on either knee.

"Your M sent it me this morning," Jeanette had said, smiling.

"So do you all get along?" Mike had asked.

It was then we both saw Jeanette get a bit emotional. "There's a bit of a story, but yeah – we all try to get along."

"She still loves him," Mike had said after we had called off at a pub for a drink.

I knew he was right, but I never said anything.

"What ex-wife would have pictures of the ex-husband stuck on their fridge?" he had said shaking his head.

He then went on to tell me the second-hand story about their acrimonious break-up and also the breakdown in his daughter's relationship that sort of brought them together. It wasn't much different to what I had been already told, although I wasn't aware that he had gone from Jeanette to Emily. I was more aware of it going from Jeanette through a series of other parties before he got to Emily. I may have been aware, but I certainly never said.

That night I watched the documentary again and at the powerful way it portrayed Sammy's clubs rise towards the top of the pile, and the way it quickly broke up soon afterwards.

1967-68 had been a year of transition, 1968-69 a year when their league and cup form suggested they should have won honours and 1969-70 a year when they did, although for some strange reason, their league form faulted. Their negativity and focus on defence meant that they drew far too many games.

Sammy had been brilliant in Europe. I had seen him. The poise where he took the goal away in Moldova and pulled the trigger to set them on the way. Never had I ever seen a player hit a ball with such venom, and if it would have caught the goalkeeper in the face it would have most certainly have knocked him unconscious.

I'd seen Express journalist Desmond Hackett at the ground in Bacau and watched on with him as Charlie George first rattled the bar, and then Sammy who had been brilliant all night hammer the ball past goalkeeper Ghinte to put them 1-0 up, with Radford making it 2-0 later on.

"They might not be pretty to watch," Hackett smiled. "But they are damn hard to beat."

I hadn't been particularly fond of the guy, but he was

right. That season in Europe, Arsenal played a nice probing short-ball possession game, something which Bertie Mee for some strange reason negated the following season – telling the newspapers post-Mexico 1970 that the although the English supporter would like to see the individual flair of the Brazilians, they certainly wouldn't like to see the sort of possession football that Brazil had played. The latter of that was a comment that really did border on stupidity. Possession football worked back then and it still works now. Back then Leeds United were masters at possession football – Whenever one side has the ball the other does not, and it's obvious that you can't score if you don't have the ball.

Asked about Leeds United on TV, Malcolm Allison stated that the reason Leeds were so comfortable in possession of the ball was solely down to them regularly playing in Europe. The 60 minute documentary showed the individual skill and flair of Sammy in a game during the 1969 League Cup Final, where he dictated everything and got nothing, and as the final whistle blew, the haunting sound of Thunderclap Newman's 'Something in the Air' played as the Arsenal lads including Sammy dropped to their knees before trudging off the pitch to pick up their losers' tankards.

We all knew that Don Howe lost them that game the same as we knew that Bertie Mee ran the club into the doldrums after the Double season.

There was also individual skill during the 1970-71 Double season when in his second game back in the side after injury, he had suffered from an intense migraine in the first half and suffered some loss of sight but where his skill had been on show for all to see. Liverpool played football and Sammy played football. He may not have got the plaudits his play deserved, but his intelligence and hard work had made the first goal, which the rather pedestrian George Graham had hammered past Ray Clemence. He also came close on a couple of occasions.

An amazing 20-yard diving header from a throw-in against an extremely capable Wolves side in early December 1970 resulted in mayhem in the defence and Arsenal scoring.

The aerial bombardment that had served Arsenal so well, but which was being slowly found out, had now been temporarily replaced, firstly by Sammy's reintroduction back into the side, and then by Charlie George, and had given the club a 'Plan B' – and a plan which as long as Sammy was in the side, a visiting Manchester City could never handle.

Manchester City had the blonde mop-topped Colin Bell in their ranks as their hard working, all action, powerful and international box-to-box midfielder. Arsenal now had a central pairing of Storey the butcher and Sammy the surgeon, and just to spike it up a little bit more, the outgoing extrovert that was Charlie George.

Manchester City could never beat Arsenal just as Arsenal could never beat Leeds United. That was while Sammy was in the side, however. In the following 1971-72 season, Manchester City had picked up 2-1 and 2-0 wins against Arsenal. But Arsenal never had Sammy – Leicester City did. Arsenal by then had Alan Ball, a skilful member of the class of 1966 and former League champion with a contagious persona which at times bordered on toxic. If Sammy was the wrong player for the system, then what of Alan Ball?

Ball was a player in business for himself, and although he was initially part of the Arsenal team that threw away the League Championship in 1972-73 season, his personality was such that whilst the team itself floundered, he was its stand-out performer and playing some of the best football of his career. And as England found out in Chorzow in June 1973, Alan Ball wasn't the team player Bertie Mee thought he was.

The play was being orchestrated through him and the

results were dire. But Ball was okay. He was like 'that fantastic goalkeeper in that relegated side'. He was that main man.

I saw footage from Arsenal versus Everton in 1967 and of Sammy going through Alan Ball and listened to the turned-up noise from the crowd, and watched as the spiky red head with the squeaky voice failed to get some recompense as the big lads from the north London team, including Peter Storey, circled.

I remembered Sooty's *other half* laughing at it. "It's a bit like the little ginger tosser in the class trying to take a pop at the tall good looking lad."

That was exactly what it looked like.

Generally it was Sammy who was at the other end of those challenges, but if you watched the documentary he may have well been a nice guy, but he was certainly no angel – a fact emphasised by all the Rouen team wanting to hit the 'tall good looking kid' after he bundled their overly-elaborate and extremely acrobatic French under-23 goalkeeper into the back of the net.

I couldn't envisage Sammy as Nat Lofthouse the same as Sooty's *other half* couldn't envisage Georgie Best as Stanley Matthews, and he did pull me up on that after I had mentioned the former Blackpool winger a couple of times.

"Stanley fucking Matthews?" he had said. "That's everything that was wrong with the supporter of yesteryear. A few mazy runs in his pipe and cardigan and all the rattles were out – he was a right load of rubbish – it must have been like watching Bing Crosby on the wing."

He hadn't been that forthcoming about George Armstrong either.

"Ask yourself why Mee bought Marinello and this was after looking at John Connelly, Don Rogers and Willie Morgan and then he wanted Ralph Coates, Tony Green and Leighton James?"

I knew what he meant.

"There has to be some story there," he said. "Especially as Bertie Mee's daughter said that Armstrong was the only player to get regularly invited over to their house – he sounds a right creep."

Sooty's *other half* was indeed a 'reading between the lines' sort of person. Possibly a 'reading too much between the lines' sort of person. But he did have a point. I thought Marinello to be a lot better player than Armstrong, although history in their success would conclude otherwise.

It's sort of strange thinking about things like that and Sooty's *other half* always thought like that – always.

While we were down we went out for a meal with Mike and Sil' which concluded with a few shorts back at their future son-in-law's and daughter's house with Sil' telling us about the time her daughter came home.

"She had left," she had told Pauline. "She was heartbroken. She never said as much, but I think at the time she was wanting to come back home."

The obvious question of 'what happened?' was immediately raised by Pauline.

"You have to see him, mam," Emily had said in one breath whilst telling her mother that he was all over the place. "He's someone that is so busy with other things, that I don't think he'd ever have time for me."

"She was really upset and was in tears half the morning," a rather made-up Sil' explained. "And then he came and knocked on the door later that evening. It was really romantic."

Mike disagreed. "It weren't that romantic – he told half the street she was pregnant."

Sil' laughed while wiping her eyes. "He was lovely – there she was crying her eyes out and he sat there and told us that he thought our M was perfect and that he really loved her."

"Yeah," stated Mike albeit a bit cynically. "That had everyone really happy."

"Everyone was crying their eyes out," Sil' laughed, still sort of choked up. "And now they are having a baby."

I had to say that Sil' was the definitely the more emotional one out of the two and was really looking forward to their first grandchild.

"I can't bloody wait," she said, crying. "I really can't bloody wait."

That set Pauline off crying and had them both hugging each other and something was mentioned by Pauline that had never been said outside of ourselves, and that was of our 14-year-old daughter that had died over 30 years ago. Dawn had possessed a similar look to Emily – more the smile than anything else.

Chapter 28
My Mum

We had flown back into Gatwick and I'd dropped the kids off at Jeanette's who immediately kicked off because both kids were nicely tanned, which was more to do with the fact that she wasn't than the fact that I had disobeyed her command. I did get invited in and saw a few printed out photographs from Emily's phone of me and the kids, which had been stuck to the fridge and which was a bit weird if I'm honest.

"Sorry about your mum," she said as she pecked me. "And yeah, sorry about being a bitch as soon as I see you."

I smiled back.

"You look well," she added.

"Thanks," I replied. "So do you."

I managed a coffee and then shot off home where I got told the story of stories from Emily's dad.

He had literally loved being down here, but I'm sure the fact that he had a big house and a Maserati at his disposal, and the fact that everyone that he had come in contact with knew both me and their Emily, must have helped in his brief summary.

"It's not much different to being at home," he said. "Everything is just bigger and better."

"He's been taking me out every night," explained her mum. "He's a different man."

Morocco had been a great place to have a holiday, and as much as we loved it, so Emily's mum and dad had loved borrowing our lifestyle.

Lucy however, had cried her eyes out on ending her best holiday ever, and was as sick as a pig on having to return. Her and young Mark had been the archetypical lovesick teenagers and I was just surprised that with guitar in hand he had never tried to serenade her off. Perhaps it was the fact that he was balling his eyes out on us leaving that had stopped him. Young love, eh?

We saw them off at Euston Station and her mum, dad and sister were gone.

Emily linked with me as we walked off the concourse and on to Euston Road.

"We're still doing okay, aren't we?" she asked.

"Yeah, we're doing great," I said.

I knew how great we were doing next day when we had it confirmed that Emily's divorce would be finalised three days before our proposed marriage.

"Wow," she said on reading the correspondence. "That was quick."

"He can't have liked you," I quipped.

"I think you could be right," she confirmed.

I was told by my legal people – the same legal people as Emily that is – that mine would be extremely fast-tracked, so it came over as a bit strange that confirmation of hers had dropped through the letterbox first.

"It sometimes happens like that," explained my solicitor.

"Just make sure you don't bollocks all this up," I said. "All the parties are happy and I have a wedding penned in for next month – the last thing I want to be is still already married when I'm getting married – if that makes sense."

Solicitors? They were a strange breed.

"How's the lump?" I asked as I watched her humping it around the kitchen as I got in from my morning jog.

"Fine," she said. "A bit fidgety this morning, though."

"Good god – that must be my bad genetics," I said. "Just keep him away from the water gun and cats."

That brought a wry smile.

I went into work and had loads of hugs from everybody. Sooty had got the cheque from Tottenham Hotspur and Charlton Athletic had been sounding us out about doing their 2013/2014 season DVD, of which the billings would be nowhere near that of Spurs'. ITV had also had sent our legal people copies of the contract covering our proposed football programme.

"Just make sure ITV don't get sent my decree nisi by mistake," I told Sooty. "I think half the briefs over there are as thick as shit."

I called into the coffee shop around 1:00pm and noted all Fosis's new gaming machines and the way they were sucking his customers in – or not, rather.

"What's up, don't they work?" I asked.

"Greeks are tight bastards," he eloquently stated. "They don't want to piss money away on my machines. They rather drink coffee and bitch about politics or talk behind man's back."

I couldn't understand anyone wanting not to piss money away on his fantastic machines and totally placated him with that fact.

"How did you get on with Emily's father?" I asked.

"English Mike?" he replied. "Nice man. He like you a lot."

That was good to hear.

"I told him you no more whoring around and baby that come will nail your boot firmly to the floor," he candidly added.

"Thanks Fosis, I appreciate that," I said.

There was nothing like some idiot Greek to blow your soon to be bent trumpet.

Emily joined me ten minutes later and just to 'please' the proprietor of the establishment she won a thousand quid on one of his machines, which created a bit of dissension in the rank and file but also got them over to the machines fairly sharpish.

"I can't believe it," she said.

Nor could Fosis, who was now gritting his teeth sort of Jeanette-style as he'd already invested over £100 towards the jackpot on the said machine.

"That will buy our pram," she said.

I smiled. "Well, go buy it then."

"What, really?" she asked.

"If that's what you want."

"What about the 'not jinxing it' bit?" she asked.

"Do you feel jinxed?"

"No, do I heck," she smiled.

"Me neither – go buy your pram."

I got hit with lugging the carrier bag full of shrapnel around to the bank where I got asked loads of personal questions about the money I was depositing.

"It's a thousand quid in coins," I shrugged.

"Yes, but we need to know that it's not drug money," said the cashier.

"What, in coins?" I asked. "I'm a media executive from Euston Road, not some quid-a-pop crack merchant – my girlfriend's just won it on the gaming machines in the coffee shop around the corner."

They eventually took it, but I had to sign some form of declaration before they did.

The world my kids and our baby would be inheriting was a world going mad.

I got in that night to see Emily stood barefoot on some box out in the garden talking to the woman over the fence that we backed on to on the street behind us and who both kids now knew to not be a witch.

"I hope she knows you're not really that tall and gangly," I said as I let Giroud and Arteta out on the grass.

"Don't be daft," she said as she hopped off the box to show the woman we now knew to be Mrs. Soblierski (or Mrs Sosk as the kids called her, rather) one of the kids' ferrets.

"They're really lovely," said Emily passing Arteta over the fence, possibly hoping she could turn him into some handsome prince.

Inside the house I noticed that well over Emily's gambling winnings had been invested in some dead expensive big pram.

"It's a three-wheeler?" I immediately observed.

"They're all like that now," she sort of explained after washing her hands to rid the smell of ferret.

"So can't we take it on the motorway?"

"Don't be daft," she twanged.

"It hasn't even got a CD player," I stated whilst checking out limited slip differential, chrome rims and brakes.

"It's really well made," said Emily, trying to flog me the concept.

"I suppose it'll be handy for getting the coal in after he's outgrown it," I said.

"Did I do wrong?" she asked.

I smiled. "Emily – nothing you ever do is wrong."

I got a love and a cuddle as part-recompense for the extra seven and half hundred quid I assumed she had overspent on the said three-wheeled pile of shite my soon-to-be son would be being carted around in. However that price tag was suddenly offset when she mentioned the cot and loads of other rubbish she'd bought as part of her afternoon supermarket sweep in Mothercare.

"I couldn't resist," she said. "They're all so cute."

"Well if we're jinxed, I'll blame you," I stated.

"Shurrup," she twanged and pecked my cheek before dragging two Moroccan chicken and cous cous salads out of the fridge.

"Do you wish we were back there?" she asked regarding the holiday, as she poured me a dry white wine.

"Not really," I said. "I think our life's great wherever we are."

"Me too," she smiled.

We ate our meal and I watched her as she sat on the floor looking at all the kiddie clothes she had bought, none of which I knew would actually fit him a month after he started wolfing down the rusks.

"Do you like 'em?" she asked.

"What's not to like?" I replied.

"I'm dead excited," she said.

"You won't be saying that if laddo's a ten-pounder," I told her.

"How big were you?" she asked.

"I can't remember," I replied.

"Don't be daft," she twanged.

It was then that she reminded me of what was said that afternoon in the shower just prior to the Cup Final, and it was straight after that when Emily picked up the telephone and phoned my mum.

"You weighed eight-four," she smiled.

I had not been back up home in a long, long time and as I'd just had the kids for seven days, Jeanette had asked if she and Paul could take them somewhere at the weekend. Whether or not this was the fact of the matter or whether it was some ruse by her for my mum not to see them or them her, I couldn't say. Therefore after work on Friday night we drove up the

M1 to South Yorkshire and into some small cul-de-sac which housed the bungalow that belonged to my mother.

The greeting I got was more or less what I expected and nothing like we got when we were received by Emily's family. There sat what I assumed to be a bitter twisted old woman, who had both abused and neglected the only things that had ever loved her, and who was now grasping at what life she could get before she went wherever she was going.

"Mum?" I said.

"Son," she acknowledged.

"This is Emily," I said.

"You can call me M," smiled Emily.

"Where are the kids?" she asked.

I explained where they were although I knew I didn't need to explain anything to her. I owed her very little, and she knew I knew that.

"What are you calling the baby?" she asked Emily.

"We still haven't decided, really," she replied.

Mmm. She's having second thoughts now Sanogo was a no-go, I thought.

"He moves around a lot," she added. "Do you want to feel?"

And there it was. The pure intoxication that was Emily had my mum putting her hand on the lump that would become her third grandchild.

"He moved around all the time," said my mum with reference to me as she put the kettle on. "It was even worse when he came out – he was up and down like a fiddler's elbow."

"He's not much different now," smiled Emily, letting the cat out of the bag re my sexual prowess.

My mum passed us a coffee apiece and continued with bits of irrelevant conversation that was her life and failing to ask any relevant questions relating to the son or future daughter-in-law that was sat opposite her.

"Where are you going?" she asked, looking at the clock as we stood up to leave.

I was just about to say, "Emily's parents'" when Emily interceded and asked, "Why do you ask?"

"I thought maybe you could stop here," said my mum.

"If that would that be okay?" smiled Emily.

I had not stopped here in over twelve years, and there was nothing here that I had any feeling for, and my mum sort of knew that. I went out into the garden and looked over at a couple of the neighbours I didn't know, who were stood admiring the car.

"Evening," I said, acknowledging them with a nod.

Emily came out into the garden as I wandered around, and duly linked with me as she always did and pecked me on the cheek, which had the nosy neighbours now more intrigued into who we actually were, so much so that a couple more of them came out pretending to water their gardens, prune their flowers or whatever it was that they were pretending to do.

"It's ages since I've been home," I said.

Emily took her shoes off as she walked around the turf before sitting on a swing.

"So did your children never come here?" she asked, looking around.

I shook my head.

"So who's the swing for?"

"No idea," I replied.

"Seems daft having a swing with no children," she said.

She was right, it did seem daft her having a swing, and I looked up at the window to see my mum looking out at us.

"So when your mum saw the children where did she see them?" asked Emily.

"I can count on one hand when she saw them," I said. "A couple of times when we lived in Southgate."

"And that's it?"

I nodded.

I knew she knew that was terrible, although she never told me so. That was the difference between Emily and Jeanette – Jeanette always had to tell me so. Jeanette delighted in telling me so.

"Who's the swing for?" I asked as my mum came out to join us in the garden with some buttered malt loaf.

"Nobody," she said.

I knew she was lying as it was a fairly new swing.

"I thought you might have brought the kids," she said.

"Maybe if you would have asked me, maybe I would have," I replied after taking a slice of what was being offered.

"I know I'm not perfect," she said.

"None of us are," smiled Emily. "Me and your son included."

I just shrugged my shoulders. I was regularly led to believe by Emily that I was indeed perfect, so that comment was a bit of a let-down if I'm honest.

"You both look well," stated my mum.

"We make the best out of what we have," said Emily. "And what we both had a couple of months ago was nothing compared to what we have now."

"Your ring is nice," stated my mum.

"It's more than nice," stated Emily, smiling and giving my mum a better look at her ring.

"And so is the car," added my mum, looking over at it filling half the cul-de-sac.

As Emily and my mum went back into the house I sort of sounded out the nosy neighbours by introducing them to who I actually was.

"I've not been here in years," I said.

"She always said she had a son but we certainly didn't believe her," said the neighbour.

"My mum talked bollocks from time to time, but she never purposely lied," I nearly told him.

"She's got a couple of grandkids and one on the way," I said.

"I was wondering why on earth she'd had the swing put up," he replied.

I wandered back inside the house to see Emily sat on the floor cross-legged going through a carrier bag of photographs my mum had dragged out of some cupboard.

"Is that your dad?" Emily asked as she showed me a photo.

That was my dad, I thought. I felt like crying my eyes out.

"He was a smart man – just like him," explained my mum pointing at me. "My mother used to say to me, 'What's he doing with you – people like him don't marry the likes of you'."

I never actually knew my grandmother had said that.

"He died when he was six," she added.

I knew exactly how old I was as it was me who was with him. I could remember the day, date and time to the second. It had lived with me each day for the past twenty-nine years. A six-year old boy watching his dead dad being dropped into the ground in a scary box is something you don't easily forget. Nor is being blamed by your mother for not calling 999 quick enough – I was six years old.

That night I laid in bed with Emily and everything I had thought, I made verbal. And as she sat on the bed, I exorcised my past and told her absolutely everything, leaving out absolutely nothing.

I got up early Saturday morning anticipating a drive over the Pennines and into sanity, however the fact that Emily and my mum were in dialogue over cooking breakfast – which included bacon – made us stay that bit longer.

On us eventually leaving, my mum gave Emily both her white gold engagement ring and her gold wedding ring, which in itself told its own tale, and I was glad when I saw both sanity and true emotion after crossing beneath the River Mersey and on to The Wirral, where half the street again came out to greet us, with the exception of Lucy who was by all accounts upstairs on Facebook, and pining.

The exorcising of my demons had upset me and it took Emily literally thirty minutes to give her mum the edited highlights of our trip into South Yorkshire, which culminated in me being fussed over and pampered like some poorly, sick and wounded relative.

"Oh that's terrible, love," she said.

I knew it was terrible and I didn't have to be told, although Emily's mum, as ever, was just being overly concerned.

"It's made him who he is," stated her husband. "You need a few knocks in life to get where this lad has got."

I was getting to like the kids' new Granddad Mike. From zero to hero in one week. Good on him.

I left the Birkenhead tea-set to talk about what they wanted to talk about, which was most probably me, whilst me and young Stuart wandered down the street to see my sons green-fingered hero and fellow gardener – Emily's granddad.

"Hello Lee lad," he said before demanding that his wife Edie put the kettle on.

Bill wanted to know how we were getting on down there and asked literally loads of questions – everything from the business to football, about me and his granddaughter and of course his once-tearaway grandson who I had promised a job.

"I told him what's needed up here, and only he can do that himself, Bill," I said. "If he does that then I can help him most other ways."

"See, Stuart," he stated. "This is a man talking, not one of these idiots you've been hanging around with."

I then dropped it out that his job – providing he got the

right grades – would involve a couple of days a week at college to learn how media works – from the little things that we all think don't matter, through to the bigger things which we all know do.

"College?" he asked.

"Where do you think young Ginge, Abi and Faranha learned?" I asked. "This is a career you're being offered. You don't just take a car out of the showroom without learning to drive the thing first."

"It's just that you didn't say anything about college," he replied.

"Well I'm saying it now and you making it through college will tell me that you are up to scratch," I said. "However you bumming around will tell me another thing."

"That you're a bum," said his granddad.

"Exactly," I said. "Hard work equals big house, cool girlfriend and Maserati – no work equals nothing."

"Our M isn't cool," smiled Suart.

"I've told you before," I said winking. "Your M is very cool."

He listened to what I had to say, however I knew that more schooling was definitely not what he wanted.

I was then asked by Bill, my thoughts on England's chances in the World Cup.

"The same as they always are," I said, sipping my coffee. "We'll not even make the group stages."

"We've got a great set of young lads this time around though," he stated.

"We have," I replied. "A load of crash test dummies supplemented by a set of show boaters."

Bill shrugged his shoulders, not knowing what I meant.

"Hodgson will line up with the Liverpool lads," I said. "Which I can understand as Liverpool have a decent spine. Henderson is a good solid kid. He's not the best, but he's okay. Gerrard was okay this season, but internationally and like Lampard he is past it. Sterling – he's fleet-footed and unpredictable which makes us – the idiots back home – think that he's exciting. At the top level he'll be found out straight away, and we'll all get to see that he has no end product and is a bit of a headless chicken. Sturridge? He's your typical coloured lad from the city and will put more time into practising that stupid dance he does to show off to his bros than he ever will trying to get behind any opposition defence. And Rooney? He'll do what he always does when Theo Walcott plays and not want to pass to any of them just in case they do something decent and make him look bad."

Bill sat back. "What are crash test dummies, lad?"

"They're the players that are frightened to death about doing anything wrong so they stick to the easy pass all the time."

"Is Glen Johnson one of them?" asked Stuart.

"Johnson is a steady player – but he's in there because there are no other decent English right backs. I thought Sam Byram of Leeds would end up ousting him, but for some reason, be it injuries or whatever, he just never came on," I stated. "Sooty was a lot better right back than Johnson is."

"Is that your business partner?" asked Bill.

"Tim Sutton," I nodded. "He was being touted by Leeds and Blackpool all the way through university and Leeds even had our team from uni give one of their eleven's a game up at Thorp Arch."

Both Emily's granddad and Stuart seemed interested.

"He was like lightning – the best right back in the north of England when he was a kid – a bike accident did him of a career, but he got on with life and made the best out of what he could."

"He's really nice, granddad," stated Stuart.

"You're right Stu," I said. "He is really nice."

Bill asked me about the kids and the holiday in Morocco before asking if it would be okay if he and Edie came down some time.

"Sure – we'd love you to both come down," I said without offering their granddaughter a chance to knock it back. "Come down when you want."

This was an interesting one and when I got back to Emily's, what I relayed was met with some disquiet.

"What's up?" I asked.

"He never goes anywhere, everyone has to go to him," said Emily's dad, looking somewhat dumbfounded. "You must have made a right bloody impression on him."

"He really asked that?" asked Emily, smiling.

I shrugged my shoulders to confirm a yes.

"Wow," was her only reply.

And the room was still quiet as they all looked around at each other.

That afternoon we had a bit of a drive around the Wirral peninsula and over to West Kirby where Emily kicked off her shoes and invited me to walk with her on what at first glance looked like the beach.

"Come walk with me," she said, smiling.

I gritted my teeth and rolled up my trousers like some 1940s spiv in Blackpool and walked with her.

"I hope you know this is a fifteen hundred quid suit," I'd said as I slung my jacket, socks and shoes in the car.

It was hardly Morocco, but I didn't want to put a damper on her enthusiasm and as we walked she linked with me and told me about how she used to come here years ago and do the exact same, but it was me she was walking with now – her future husband.

"I made a right mess of it all," she said.

"No you didn't," I replied.

"I did," she said. "I could cringe now at what I put my mam and dad through."

I gave her a squeeze.

"We're alright though, aren't we?" she asked.

"Course we are," I replied. "We are dead alright."

"I love coming home," she said smiling whilst leaning into me. "But I loving going home better."

"I never knew there was a beach at Liverpool," I winked.

"You know it's not Liverpool," she said nudging me. "It's not much of a beach either."

I drove us back to her mum's for tea where I had to explain why my trousers were full of mud.

"He was throwing a ball for a dog," Emily grinned.

"There's potholes on that beach," I said.

"What beach?" asked her dad.

"Exactly," I replied as I stripped off to change. "I got asked to walk on a beach and all I ended up doing was trailing through half a mile of mud."

We stayed the night and set off back early Sunday morning. Life was flying by and I was enjoying every minute of it.

Chapter 29
Secrets

I'd had a right argument with the brief handling my divorce from Jeanette.

"So, smart arse," I snapped. "Where does this leave me?"

I had a massive wedding on the horizon – and at The Emirates, which we had already laid out fourteen grand for and as things stood I was still going to be married and possibly, post wedding reception, charged with bigamy. Jeanette had told me that she and her brief – who I was paying for – had signed everything off and I had no real doubt in my mind that they hadn't done so. Not that I didn't ask Jeanette if she was *really* sure that she had, which was met with some colourful superlatives slung in my direction along with a DVD. It could have been worse – it could have still been in the player.

I got home after a lousy day of arguing with the brief and sitting in on a load of boring interviews to a house full of kids, two of which were mine, two of which were Sooty's and two others which I knew I had seen before, but wasn't sure who they belonged to.

I got loads of hugs off the lot of them plus M which made me feel better, but I was still scratching my head as regards the other two. I put up with the horrible racket from the five lots of instruments as I ate my prawn and crayfish salad and did some work on my laptop, before the screeching stopped and Emily came into the kitchen.

"They're sounding better, aren't they?" she stated, whilst at the same time sort of asking an opinion.

"They couldn't sound any worse," I replied. "It sounded like a set of cats were fighting in the room last week."

Emily grinned. "They weren't that bad."

"Really?" I winked, before holding my hands up to the fact that there were two faces that I just couldn't quite put my finger on. "Anyway, who are the two fatties?"

"That's horrible," Emily whispered.

"Is it?" I asked. "They look like a pair of Russian shot-putters."

"They're Tim's nieces."

"Shit – I knew I'd seen 'em before," I said, whilst nonchalantly downing my shellfish.

I washed up and after being nagged by my daughter I went into the room to listen to some rendition the cats' choir elite were about to chuck out at me.

"That's one hell of a violin," I said to one of the overweight kids as I sat down. "Not even you will get that under your neck."

"It's a cello, you idiot," stated the kid.

Very nice, I thought.

Five minutes later I was scratching my head. "And you've taught them that?" I asked.

Emily nodded.

"Okay – do it again, just so I know the last time wasn't a mistake."

It wasn't. It was quite nice.

"What do you reckon, dad?" asked my daughter.

"It was lovely," I said. "What was it?"

Emily slumped at the side of me on the sofa. "I'm dead excited for them," she said.

"Why?" I asked.

"I want them to play at the wedding."

"What, a full gig or just that song?" I asked.

"Just the one they've practised," she said.

"How much do they want paying, because I refuse point blank to be shook down for more than one thousand per man – or woman."

"A thousand pounds?" asked one of Sooty's overly-erudite individuals.

"No, pence," I said before quickly asking, "So how much is that in real money?"

"Ten pounds," she answered back.

"Okay then, you've shaken me down," I said. "Two thousand apiece if you can do it this good on the wedding day."

"That's twenty pounds each," exclaimed Zooey, smiling.

"Not bad for a first gig," I said. "Even the Beatles didn't get paid that much."

"I'm a bit worried," I said, looking at Emily.

"What, about the music?"

"No, the wedding – my brief is adamant that I should have had my decree nisi sent out and that I'll be a free man before the wedding," I said.

"If he says they have – they have. Stop worrying."

"Why? Are you not worrying?" I asked.

"Of course I'm worrying," she replied. "But I never let on because I don't want to worry you."

I was glad that was cleared up. My head was a shed.

The parents came to pick up the 'Fab Five' and I managed a five minute conversation with Sooty about the ITV contract before the house emptied.

"Is everything okay?" asked Emily.

"Fine," I said. "It's just a big jump for us, but it's nothing we can't handle."

I collared Tony the postman on my jog around the block

the very next morning and was about to mention my missing post, however he immediately got on to the subject of telling me the great result he'd had on Cup Final day and that his wife had bought herself a car out of the winnings, which sort of sidetracked me a bit, and by the time I had got back in the house I had totally forgotten to ask him.

"How's the lump?" I asked.

"Uncomfortable," Emily smiled as she poured me a coffee. "Does it look big?"

"Massive," I said.

"Really?"

"It'll be ten times that size when we get married," I assured her.

"I hope I fit in my dress," she said.

"I hope he fits in the pram," I said, slurping my coffee.

"Are you purposely trying to annoy me?" she asked, smiling.

"Yes," I smiled back.

"Well, it's working," she replied.

"Sorry for being a git," I said. "And I love you very much."

"Thank you," she smiled.

At around 10:45am I went absolutely hairless with my brief. ITV did have my decree nisi. It was sent within the contract documents to their offices and a young girl called Simeone or Simon or Simona let us know. I got Faranha to nip down for it and to give the girl some flowers and about 1:30pm I got a message text through to my phone. 'Flowers were great. Fancy a drink x.'

"What does she actually look like – this bird who you dropped the flowers off with?" I asked – not as though any form of pre-marital adultery was ever going to take place.

"No idea – I just handed them over to reception and picked up the letter," stated Faranha.

"So you didn't see them get delivered?" I asked.

"I can't go demanding to see them actually dropped off, can I?" she stated.

She did have a point.

I was going to text back but I thought otherwise.

I let Emily know about the missing post and I let her know that we'd be good to go on the day, which resulted in a big scream down the phone. "It's really happening, isn't it?"

It was. It was really happening.

I went over to the coffee shop where Emily had started regularly meeting me for a drink and a natter, and a load of cheque signing.

"I'm sorry – this is costing you a fortune," she said.

It was. Emily had mentioned running away and getting married in the West Indies but I told her that there was no way on earth that I'd not help make Arsenal 'not' even richer by me 'not' having it at The Emirates. Anyway, we both had too many people who we loved not to share it with and make them part of what would be a really nice day, and when I told that to Emily, not only did I surprise myself, it made her cry. And her mum. And her gran. And strangely, Libby.

Emily had sent the wedding invitations out, in which we specified 'no presents'.

'Your presence, not presents is all we require'.

"What, you're not asking for any presents?" exclaimed her dad over the phone.

"No, dad," Emily had said. "We have everything."

Her dad still couldn't understand it.

Fosis came over and lifted the ban on Emily using the gaming machines.

"It is okay – Emily can use machine," he said. "I had it rigged."

"Then she's definitely not going to use it," I said.

"Andreas put in six hundred euros and he get nothing," he chuckled to himself.

"In which machine?" Emily asked.

Fosis pointed to the self-same one she had won the thousand quid on before and after putting in a fiver she won the lot, amidst screaming from her and crying from Fosis.

"I think we're going to have to send you away to get you out of this gambling addiction," I said.

"I can't believe it," she said.

Nor could Fosis, who booted one of his tables over.

I dragged the loot around to the bank but this time I had no problems depositing it, whilst Emily went and undertook another afternoon raid on Mothercare.

I stayed late at work as we were busy with some editing of a rush job that some other media company wanted, which was to sort of promote some sportswear when I received a phone call.

"Hiya love," said Emily. "I'm sorry to bother you and I know you're really busy but my gran and granddad have just turned up."

I looked at my watch which told me it was 7:45pm.

"Give me ten minutes," I said.

I let Freddy finish off and I put on my jacket and walked home where I met a beaming Bill and Edie, with a suitcase that had been packed as though they were leaving for South America.

"You haven't dragged that thing from Euston, have you?" I asked.

"They got the bus down," Emily said, shrugging her shoulders.

"Well, let me take your coats then," I said, smiling.

"They didn't want to take off their coats off until you were home," Emily sort of whispered to me.

"Sit down and make yourselves comfortable and I'll get this thing up to one of the rooms," I said.

The elderly couple dispensed with their garments and I

hung them up before carting the dreaded trunk into the west wing.

"You never said you were coming down," I smiled.

"We thought we'd surprise you," Edie said.

"Yeah, you did," I said. "It's nice."

"Have you eaten, Gran?" asked Emily.

"We had sandwiches on the bus," she replied.

Within two minutes Emily and her grandmother were working in unison in the kitchen and I knew there and then exactly who had taught her granddaughter how to cook.

"You both have a nice kitchen," exclaimed Edie. "I would have died for a kitchen like this."

Within twenty or so minutes we were all sat around all eating together.

"I try to feed him right, Gran," said Emily. "He's on the go all the time."

"He looks okay to me," she replied.

"He complains that I give him too many salads," smiled Emily.

"A little bit of something's not bad," said her grandmother. "Too much of something – I don't know."

"I'm not used to eating this late," stated Bill.

"And as I said," added her grandmother. "A little bit of something doesn't hurt once in a while."

I really liked her grandparents, they were old school but very self-sufficient and bounced off each other quite nicely.

Bill liked to talk football and spoke of the Liverpool teams of the 1960s and 1970s, a period in football that I was extremely familiar with and of Bill Shankly with an affection that I have only ever seen with Leeds supporters, when mentioning Don Revie.

Football – what a truly beautiful game.

"He can talk football all day, Granddad," stated Emily.

"There's nothing wrong with that," he said.

I sipped at my white wine whilst we spoke, and Emily gave her grandmother a guided tour of the house and showed off the three-wheeler and the mountain of other stuff her gambling winnings had helped procure, and in what would be our new baby's bedroom.

I was that mesmerised with the old lad that we didn't get off to bed until 1:00am, which had my future wife in awe of me.

"He really likes you," she smiled as she cuddled up to me. "I can't believe how perfect everything is."

"Me neither," I replied. "Life's great."

I was intending to tell her about the text message from that afternoon, but I knew that would have been a stupid mistake.

I got up a few hours later to have my jog around the block but got talking to the milkman for ten minutes who told me about his dog having parvo. I have absolutely no idea why, I just must have one of those faces. I got back in around 6:00am to Emily's gran frying bacon. I was well up for some of that, and just to spoil me she stuck an egg on top of it and made me a sandwich.

"I don't suppose you fancy living here full time?" I asked.

Emily came into the kitchen and poured herself a coffee whilst shaking her head and passing me a couple of 'tut tuts' about the calorie and cholesterol intake.

"A little bit of something doesn't hurt M," said her gran with her back to her.

Between them they were, like, telepathic, and I knew from what Emily had said previously that they were really close, and that when she was growing up as a child she had literally lived at their house.

"Is Bill still in bed?" I asked.

"No love, he went out for a paper," she replied.

I never bought a paper – everything I needed to read was online. In twenty years' time there would be no papers, nor magazines and Sting could sleep easily knowing the rain forests could grow unhindered. There would also be no music industry either. The internet was great for some things but rubbish for others.

Bill and Edie were all over the place while they were down here and it made my lads day when he saw him after school. "Granddad Bill, are we going to plant them strawbs?"

"Yes lad, when you come back up north."

Me listening to Violin Concerto No. 5 in D minor was put on hold as I had to go and pick up some seeds and compost in the Maserati, which I had to say I did through gritted teeth as the bag burst.

Jeanette came around to pick the kids up around 7:00pm and to see the two avid gardeners planting seeds in trays out in the back yard, as I'd told them point-blank that under no circumstances could the ferrets' tunnels ever be breached.

Jeanette's appearance was, as ever, extremely impressive and I got the same look from Edie as I had got from Emily's mum and two presumptuous albeit telepathic glances were exchanged between the granddaughter and grandmother.

"She's lovely," said Edie.

I nodded a confirmation, however there was no way I was wanting to explain myself for the one hundredth time, so I made myself scarce. Jeanette, though, spent a lot of time outside talking to Bill and on her leaving with the kids, Bill let Edie know that they were going over tomorrow for tea, which I could see that Edie certainly didn't fancy.

"She's really nice, Gran," stated Emily.

"She is," I said. "To your M – it's me she hates."

"She certainly does not hate you," Emily stated whilst smiling.

The empty house which had been gutted by the Russians and which was laid bare a couple of months earlier was not a bare and empty shell any more. It hadn't been for weeks.

Emily being there had helped fill it with wonderful people and children, two of which were my own. It is hard for me to stress the difference that a few weeks with the right woman by your side makes.

I got to bed that night and that is when more secrets were laid out on the mattress by the woman I was growing to love more and more each day, and who was sat cross legged on the bed wearing my 1971 Arsenal shirt which she refused point-blank to discard.

"It was the first thing you ever gave me," she had said.

"I doubt that very much," I had winked.

"You know exactly what I mean," she had smiled.

I did. I knew exactly what she had meant.

It turned out that her grandparents had had a big fall out with her mum and dad and never spoke for years, although that never stopped the kids from visiting. The cause of the fall out had been Emily and Emily's relationship with the son, or sons, of the man next door to Bill and Edie – Linton Fox. It was only recently that there had been any dialogue, and that I was told was solely down to me. My arrival along with my inquisitive nature had set the ball rolling, and totally unknown to me they were all talking again, although at times it was still a bit strained.

"Granddad threatened to kill Linton," she said.

"Really?" I said. "I hope he doesn't threaten to kill me."

"It was really bad," she said. "Granddad got on at my dad because he wouldn't go around there and thump him. The Foxes made my Gran and Granddad's life hell."

There was a bit more to it than that, which when it basically whittled down, was two feuding families in the same street arguing about respect, or indeed lack of.

Daft, really, but I would make it my mission to park my car a bit nearer her gran's house the next time I went up there, just to piss off the Foxes.

Bill and Edie grew on me the more they stayed. Watching Emily and her gran bake was – well, something else, and I couldn't wait to feast on all those carbs, which Emily would make sure I burned off by a thousand or so push ups before lights out, or in her case handcuffs off.

Her granddad was a really interesting guy and told me about the time his dad – Emily's great grandfather – had taken him to Anfield on New Year's Eve 1949 to see the great Billy Liddell score two goals to beat Arsenal in front of over 55,000.

"We beat them home and away," explained Bill. "But the buggers did us two-nil in the cup final the same season."

Old people are brilliant and this one never ceased to amaze me.

I got in around 6:00am the next morning to find the griddle on and my bacon crisp and Sky Sports on.

"You'd make someone a great wife, Edie," I said whilst drying myself off.

I got a great smile, sort of similar to Emily's, but not quite.

"Is it raining heavy?" she asked.

"A bit," I replied whilst wolfing down my bacon sandwich.

I had taught Bill the use of the internet the night before and he was in the front room having commandeered my laptop and going through 'Sporting Life' as I took him a cup of tea.

"I must admit lad, you both have life sussed down here," he said.

Me? I didn't want them to go home and I told them so.

Chapter 30
Goodbye

I had my auntie relay me the news at 3.30am on Friday the 6th June.

My auntie was a more miserable and vindictive version of my mum, but if I'm being honest at times there wasn't that much to separate the two – well, my mum of sort of around three weeks ago, that is.

It had been peaceful, and it had also been very quick.

Emily sat up in bed looking extremely concerned. "You okay, love?" she asked.

I nodded, but when I got a cuddle off her I can't deny the fact that I was very upset.

When you refuse to fight it, it is quick. Cancer takes very few prisoners.

My mum's decision was that she didn't want the chemotherapy, radiation, the tubes and all the morphine. My mum's decision was to die. At least she would see my dad again, if that's what really happens after you've gasped your last breath.

Emily and I drove up the north early the next day on a drive which culminated in me seeing her laid stone cold in a casket in the undertaker's. Anyone who has seen a corpse will tell you that they rarely represent the person it once was – this one in particular.

"Oi," I said to the undertaker. "This isn't my mum."

"Oh, I'm terribly sorry, sir," he apologised, before showing me into another room and telling me that he could get her in the ground by the end of the week.

This meant the reopening of my dad's grave, which was something else I certainly wasn't looking forward to.

Speaking with her for the first time in ages after we had been to Morocco had been strange, but not so much the few times after.

We had taken the kids up and I saw something that I had not seen since when my father was alive, and that was the gentle and caring nature of the woman, but what always got to me was the question of why leave it so late? Why now, and not then when it really mattered?

She had promised us both that she would be at our wedding. It was to be another thing she would let me down on.

Emily never said a great deal and just let me talk, but everything I did say was relayed to both her parents and grandparents and discussed in great detail then stripped bare and put back together and re-manufactured into pure sensitivity and love, and given to me whenever they saw or spoke to me. Just why my mum couldn't have been like that I didn't know. It was one of life's unanswered questions. I would walk over hot coals for any of my kids. It's what parents do, or in my eyes should do.

"Grandma, my dad says you are his mum," my lad had stated.

She nodded and smiled. It took her a bit but she smiled.

My daughter, however, being a year older had been a bit more wary, and therefore quiet.

"Do I look like my dad, when he was little?" he had asked.

"A bit," she had said.

She then burst out crying.

I have no idea what was going through her head, but my mum was never one you could easily read. This was something that my grandmother and grandfather – my dad's parents – had said as I was growing up. She had stayed in contact with them a couple of years after my dad had died before starting a process of deconstruction, whereby any relationship with them completely terminated. And by termination, I mean I was stopped from seeing them, which I was told broke my grandmother's heart. For six years I never saw them until one day they opened the door and I was there. The emotion they showed was very similar to that of Emily's family, which is perhaps something that makes me appreciate them as much as I do.

I remember the first time we drove the kids up to see my mum. She had been looking out the window as we had pulled up; however, that was where she stayed until we entered the house, and even then she made my kids work hard for any affection, so much so that they both spent the first half hour sitting on my knee thinking that they had done something wrong.

"Doesn't grandma like us?" whispered my daughter.

How does a parent answer that?

"She does, but she's old," I said.

"Grandma Sil' is old," she replied. "And she's always telling us how much she loves us."

They went in the garden and sat on the swing, but a swing in my mum's garden was not like the swing in their garden or that in Bill and Edie's garden. Those two gardens were full of love and happiness, and kids can tell. You might not think they can't, but believe me – they can.

After signing some papers. We left the undertakers and drove over see my auntie who was by now emptying my mum's bungalow.

"What are you doing?" I asked.

"Just taking some things," she explained.

"No you're not," I exclaimed, and I made her and the idiot who she was with cart it all back inside.

"Who's she?" asked Emily, re the accomplice.

"God knows," I replied.

"What's the matter with you?" asked my auntie. "You won't want any of this."

"Well if there's anything I don't want, I'll have dumped round at yours," I said.

Emily was shocked.

"It's my mum's elder sister," I said, shaking my head.

There was a story here that I never really understood, and that was that my mum had a sister who was three years older than her, but who had a different mother. I don't know much else as I was never told anything, and that being the case I never asked. It would be easy for me to find out, although why waste more time on someone who I considered both avaricious and self-centred? She was also a woman that beat me as a child, something that I would never ever do to any of mine. Hate is a strong word therefore I'll not use it, so I'll just say I had a dislike for her.

When she had phoned me there was very little emotion, if any.

"It's your Auntie Margaret," she said. "Your mother passed away at a quarter past two this morning."

My phone after that was littered with condolences and the like, so much so I'd had to turn it off and therefore the traffic got directed on to Emily's phone, which was already heavily trafficked with her concerned parents and grandparents asking if I was okay. I hadn't been initially, however I was now. It wasn't the death of my mum, more the emotion shown by the people around me which had moved me. At this moment in time my emotions were as hard as nails, and in my mind there was nothing worse than a plague of parasites rooting through another person's belongings hoping to get first dibs on it.

A couple of neighbours watched on as we went into the house and I immediately noticed all the print-outs of the photographs that I had sent her over from Morocco.

"She must have thought something of you, love," Emily said.

She did, in her own way, but for me that wasn't enough. It was nowhere near enough, and the fact that neither of my kids had got birthday or Christmas cards for the past two years made me more angry. She got sent them, why not return the gesture? But that was my mum.

Emily sat at the table and looked out of the window. "So what will happen to all this?" she asked.

I shrugged my shoulders. "I'll see if she's not done something stupid like leave it to someone or something and once that's sorted, sell it."

"Is there nothing you want?" she asked.

"Not really," I replied.

"What about the photographs we looked through?" she smiled.

I smiled at her. I certainly wanted the photographs.

I switched my phone on and got in touch with our legal people in London and asked if they would sound out my mum's solicitors re any will and rang up some locksmith out of the Thomson local directory to get the locks changed.

"How quick are you looking at?" the guy asked.

"Like, yesterday," I said.

I certainly didn't want this place leaving unattended.

Emily kicked off her shoes and made us a coffee as I looked through the stash which had been re-deposited on the kitchen floor, and which several minutes earlier had been making its way into the back of my auntie's purple car with the disabled sticker on it. That was of course before I marched them both back inside with it all.

"Wow," I said, looking at the contents of two savings account books before putting them on the table. "No wonder they were quick to come around."

Emily passed me a cup of coffee.

"Just over forty one thousand pounds in those," I said. "Two minutes later and she would have been the one drawing that lot out."

"That's terrible," she said.

She was right. It was.

One thing about my mum was that she was as organised as I was disorganised and it didn't take us long to get some order.

My phone rang. It was our legal people. I had to nip to my mum's solicitors and sign for it. I'd dropped for the lot. "Thanks," I said.

I phoned Sooty and gave him the runners and riders and hoped that he could hold the fort a bit.

"We're sweet," he said. "Ginge told me to tell you he was sorry."

"Tell him it's appreciated – he's a good lad."

"I've never seen you like this before," said Emily.

"Sorry," I said.

"Don't be," she replied. "I quite like assertive."

"Well, I aren't stringing you up in here for rule number one," I said.

I got a wry smile from her, which added a bit of levity to the situation.

"What do you want to do?" I said. "It seems daft you hanging around."

"Well, I'm not leaving you here," she said.

"This will take a couple of days to sort," I said. "Then there's probably the funeral on Friday."

Our life was that hectic in London, that the small matter of a death in South Yorkshire was a bit of an inconvenience, especially bearing in mind all the shite I had to sign for, which if I'm honest was a bit OTT.

"We'll stay up for a couple of days then," I said.

"Okay," she smiled.

And that was it, we got to work. I cancelled my workload for two days and Emily hers, one of which was a routine hospital appointment to check out the lump and another of which was a parent coming round to ours as regards the possible teaching of the piano to her daughter.

Emily sat on the floor sorting stuff out as I delved. My mother was one hell of a hoarder and I'd not seen this much shite since Arsenal had turned up to been turned over at Stamford Bridge.

The locksmith took less than an hour to sort the locks whilst I was over at the solicitors, and I got back to find him still there after two hours and talking about his twenty-six ferrets and his dog called 'Alf'.

"Thank god he's gone," Emily said after I'd managed to boot him out of the door. "He was possibly the most boring man in the world."

I had met loads of boring people and I had to concur that he was indeed up there when it came to being boring.

"I knew as soon as I'd mentioned the ferrets I shouldn't have," she said, shaking her head.

We had sort of made an itinerary of all the belongings and I had nipped into the garage to find even more plus a car I'd forgotten she had.

"Emily," I shouted, "Come and see this."

"Crikey, what's that?" she asked.

"An Austin 1100," I said.

I could tell she looked dead impressed.

"You can drive that back down," I smiled.

"It'd take me three weeks to get home in that," she said.

Just then one of the neighbours came over and sort of expressed his grief by offering me £200 for it.

"Does it even work?" Emily asked.

It did. I fired it up and it ran as sweet as a nut.

"I'm still not driving it down," she stated.

"These are classics," I said.

"And I'm still not driving it down," she said.

"It's cute – can you smell the leather?"

"And I'm still not driving it down," she confirmed.

"It can be our weekend car," I smiled.

"You'll look like Mr Bean in that thing," she grinned.

Mmm. Did I really want to look like Mr Bean?

"Okay then, we'll not drive it down."

I rang my auntie to ask if either she or her fellow looter wanted the car, which was met by a very eager, "Yes."

Therefore I told her that if she gave me a grand, she could have it.

"What's the matter with you?" I asked in reply to her calling me a quite nasty name. "I certainly don't need it."

I didn't. I had a £90,000 Maserati and sort of told her so.

I then got called an even nastier name and she hung up on me.

"I can't believe you did that," said a rather shocked future wife, shaking her head.

"Why? She was ready to go steal everything before we got up here," I said. "She knew damn well my mum had left me the lot – she had been on to the solicitors as soon as they opened."

"What, really?"

"Why do you think she was emptying the house?"

"God, that's awful," she said.

I agreed. It was.

We knocked off doing what we were doing and I looked at my watch, which told me it was sort of nearly tea time.

"You fancy nipping over to your mum's?" I asked.

"It's two and a half hours away," she said smiling.

"It's got to be better than staying here, M," I said.

"Really?" she asked, giving me an even bigger smile.

We shut up everything and got over to Liverpool within the allotted time-frame, mainly because we missed all the rush hour traffic around Leeds and Manchester.

Emily loved seeing her folks as much as I loved to watch her with them. There was nothing evil, underhanded, awful or plastic about them. You got what you saw and what you saw was nothing short of pure love.

Not telling them we were going over prior to us going over caught her mum a bit short and and after I had received a great hug and told how sorry they all were, she then stressed the question of 'why hadn't we told them we were coming over'?

"We thought we'd surprise you," her daughter replied.

"Yeah, you did, we've got nothing in the house," stated her mum.

That was easily sorted and I threw Emily the car keys and she ran her mum and their Lucy into Birkenhead town centre to get some shopping, which let me tell you now both didn't go unnoticed and went down like a bomb.

The kids' Granny Sil' had a gregarious nature, and as such spoke to anyone and everyone, and on pulling the car into the supermarket, who did she immediately come across? None other than Mrs Fox, and who just happened to be in her eight-year-old and slightly battered Vauxhall Corsa.

"My mam was dead glad you lent me the car," Emily had whispered afterwards.

"Have you seen my daughter and her fiancé's car?" she

had said to Mrs Fox.

"She was dead embarrassing," Emily had also whispered afterwards.

"It's a Maserati," she had said.

Lucy had confirmed the said embarrassment by stating, "Every time she sees her she's starts talking right posh."

"What, really?" I asked, smiling.

And then Lucy took her mum off with an exaggerated albeit quite aloof accent, "My daughter and her fiancé live in a five bedroomed house in north London, you know."

That made me smile.

"Her fiancé's company has just won a television deal from ITV, you know – you may have seen her fiancé while he's been up here – he drives a Maserati you know."

"I didn't know your mum was a snob, M," I whispered.

"Only when she's bragging you off," Emily whispered back.

"Her fiancé bought her a fifty thousand pound engagement ring, you know," continued Lucy. "They are to be married at The Emirates."

Lucy made us both smile, and if I wasn't feeling one hundred percent before, I certainly was now.

Stuart came into the house and gave me a hug along with one thousand questions as his mum and Emily put the tea on for the man of the house, who was shortly due in from work.

"I was told you were both up," stated Emily's father who gave his daughter a hug and me a hearty slap on the back, so much so it nearly took out two vertebrae.

"Wow - is that steak?" he asked, peering over at the hob.

It was, and this was something else which was going to hit me like a mallet.

After we had eaten and I had walked out onto the street with Emily and down to see her grandparents, she told me that both her mum and dad were finding things a 'bit tight'. This was partly due to the extra schooling that they were paying for their Stuart and the fact that they were always out to try and impress us, or me rather. Thirty pounds per lesson three or four times a week may not sound much when you spend money like we did, but when you're earning less than four hundred pounds a week and have a house, wife and two kids to support it is. Start paying for an engagement party with bouncy castles and the like, and start feeding the extra bodies and it soon takes its toll. I paid traffic congestion and parking fines like they were nothing. In Birkenhead, it is not nothing. It is something. It was a big deal. These were real people.

"I'm sorry M," I said.

"It's not your fault," she said, linking my arm and leaning into me before giving me a peck.

"So the food we just ate?" I said, shrugging my shoulders.

"My mam paid for it," she said.

"Didn't you offer?" I asked.

"Yeah, but she'd not take anything."

Bill and Edie were pleased to see us. They both loved Emily, especially the grandmother who immediately set about baking two apple pies, which less than an hour later I'd be having with ice cream, however my mind was some-where else. It was with both her parents.

"Excuse me," I said. "I just have to make a phone call."

I went out into the garden and rang Sooty – or Libby, rather – and explained what had been said. The answer was easy, however providing an answer and executing it were two totally different things. I could have given them the money, but these were proud people, and it could have looked demeaning, and in my mind they were far, far too good for that – so that could never happen. Therefore I took another route and Libby made sure that a company cheque would arrive at their house within the next couple of days, which would at least cover all Stuart's school fees.

The next day we drove back over the Pennines and I sounded out a couple of estate agents one of which duly under-valued my mum's property at £190,000 for a quick sale whilst taking a point and half off in commission in the process.

I looked at my mum's old car and didn't really want to sell it.

"Would I really look like Mr Bean in it?" I asked.

"Most definitely," she said.

Therefore I didn't really want to drive it either.

We filled the car with as much rubbish from within the house as we could, and that afternoon I dropped it all off at my auntie's and let her know that the house was now up for sale, that the locks had been changed and that I'd be up for the funeral on Friday .

"She was my sister, you know," she said.

"I know," I replied. "And I was her son."

I felt I had to say it, so I also told her that I would never treat my kids like my mum had treated me and nor would I ever treat any of my nieces and nephews like she had done.

"You're just like him," she snapped. "Your dad."

"Good," I said. "I'm glad."

I was. I was dead glad. My dad was nice.

It had been an interesting couple of days and in some respects a stark reminder of things past, and had been littered with a couple of corpses – one of which was my mother, a strangely pretentious future mother-in-law who I loved dearly and greedy underhanded relatives that I did not.

"I wouldn't fancy going through that lot again," I said as we drove down the A1(M).

"No, we have had better days," Emily smiled.

I got into the house and whilst Emily ran the bath I cleaned out the two mongoose along with feeding and watering them and rolling them about on the lawn for ten minutes, whilst having a chat on the phone with my two kids who both told me that they loved me. Oh yeah, and asked what had I brought them back.

I went upstairs to see Emily laid soaking in the bath.

"Are you getting in?" she asked.

I did and I had an hour long soak with her and the lump and we both copped an early night.

The next day I awoke around 5:10am and went for a jog and called into the 24-hour mini market for some milk on the way back, and when I got back in Emily was griddling bacon and had the percolator on. I loved being home.

"Sorry love, but we need some milk," she said.

"I know," I replied passing it her. "I'd given the ferrets the last lot."

She smiled as she took the milk and handed me a toasted bacon sandwich.

"I've been thinking about your auntie all night," she said, shaking her head.

"What about her," I asked, kicking up my laptop whilst listening to Sky Sports on TV.

"She's horrid."

"Yeah, I know," I replied.

"Your dad must have been a really nice man," she said.

That was a very nice thing to say, and I told her so.

"Wow," I exclaimed as I checked my last night's email.

Emily walked around and peered over my shoulder to see that the estate agent had received an offer of £175,000 for the house and from the daughter of the neighbour that had offered me £200 for my mum's car.

"That was quick," she said.

She was right. It was, and I wasted no time in accepting the offer provided that I wouldn't get pissed about with surveyors trying to shave more money off the said price offered.

I went into work to find Eddie and Sooty in conversation – firstly in regards to a phone call made to us from one of the suits at ITV whose father was an avid Arsenal supporter and secondly as regards to the expansion and a few of the ideas that I had bandied around and that needed work on.

"You okay mate?" Sooty asked me.

"Yeah, sound," I said. "Glad to be back though."

"Eventful?"

"Like you wouldn't believe," I replied, before asking about the guy from ITV whose father was the Arsenal supporter.

"His dad was on about the match at home to that French club in the European tie," he said.

"Oh yeah – what about it?" I asked as I poured myself a coffee.

Sooty then explained that the guy's father had watched the documentary and in particular the 1969/70 European campaign, with the only footage we never had being the two matches versus Glentoran. The fact of the matter was that he had been to every tie, home and away with the exception of the home tie versus Rouen where Sammy had scored right at the end – as at the time he'd been laid up with flu.

"The old man broke down crying," Sooty shrugged.

I can understand that, and as I have already said, football is a passionate game.

"He never realised how Arsenal actually scored the goal," added Sooty.

He had a point. Most newspaper reports at the time relayed the fact that it was some scrappy goal scored after 88 minutes that broke the deadlock, however it was anything but. It was true that there was a goalmouth skirmish with bodies everywhere, which could have affected the view of the sports journalists that had been present, however the camera that picked up the goal may have not been the best quality but had been perfectly positioned to see Sammy back heel the winner, sort of Christian Ronaldo-style – with him going in the opposite direction to where the ball was travelling. It had been a really fantastic piece of opportunism and skill.

There was also another thing that Sooty was about to tell me.

"Oh yeah – Sammy's been in touch and left his phone number," he said.

"Sammy who?" I asked. "I don't know any Sammy."

"Yeah, you do," he said. "The Sammy."

Wow. I had met loads of footballers, however this wasn't one of them. If anyone had asked me who I'd most like to meet, Lionel Messi or Sammy, I would have opted for the latter every time.

I sat down, smiling to myself. I had to tell Emily. And I did.

I got a scream down the phone which was followed by, "I knew – I knew he would be in touch."

How did Emily know?

"He sounds such a really nice man," she had said.

She was right. He did sound such a really nice man.

"So what are you wanting to do?" asked Sooty. "Should we get him down?"

In my mind Sammy was the ultimate 1960s football icon. He looked as good as he played, and his football was as good as some of the music that was around at the time. He defined that era – He was to the game in the 1960s what Brian Jones was to its music. Beautiful, stylish and totally misunderstood.

The only thing that could be construed as being different was that Sammy's personality matched his appearance, whereas the guitarist with The Rolling Stones certainly did not.

And Sammy had called for me. I had never felt as honoured – ever.

Around 1:00pm I called into the coffee shop for my daily insult, and saw Emily talking at the counter with the moustachioed Romeo wearing a sky blue checked shirt, which was unbuttoned down to the naval, and who if I read it right, was looking a touch emotional.

"Thank you for invite to wedding," Fosis said. "I honoured."

"Yeah, no problem," I said. "Just don't go arguing with any of the other guests or kicking over any tables."

We sat down with an espresso and Perrier – well I did, Emily just had a coffee as the last espresso she'd opted for in here was sort of lost in translation and ended up being a Greek coffee and that being the case it took her half a dozen teeth brushing sessions and half a bottle of Listerine to get shut of the taste.

We talked and the subject of my mum got brought up.

"I hope you don't mind but I've dropped a couple of the photos in at Boots to be blown up and framed," she said smiling.

That was nice, I thought.

"What's in the bags?" I asked, noticing the big Debenhams logos.

"A dress for Friday," she said. "And some shoes."

"Friday?"

"Your mam's funeral."

"Why, are you wanting to go?" I asked.

"Course I want to go – it's your mam."

She was right. It was my mum.

The funeral was exactly what I thought it would be with

only a handful of people to see her off, which in itself tells you everything you need to know about the person who is being laid to rest.

It was short and it was sweet, and the vicar did a great job of explaining someone who definitely couldn't have been my mother.

"Have you thought where you want to be buried?" Emily asked as she linked my arm as we walked away from the grave.

"Not particularly," I replied. "Have you?"

I got a nudge. "I didn't mean it like that."

"Good – I haven't even married you and you're already after scattering my remains," I said.

"I am not," she said, again leaning in to me.

We left the cemetery and drove firstly to the house to pick up what belongings I could relate to, and then over to the estate agents with the keys and details of our legal representatives.

"I want completion in three months," I said.

I never wanted to step back in South Yorkshire ever again.

Chapter 31
The Wedding

Mine and Emily's life over the last couple of months had been a whirlwind, and nothing would prepare either of us for a couple of days after our degree absolutes had come through – mine one day before the event itself. There was nothing in life like cutting it fine.

June 21st was certainly not the day we initially planned to get married, however we both knew we couldn't have done it any sooner as our divorces would never have been finalised in that short period of time. The upshot was that Emily was now a couple of days short of being 30 weeks pregnant.

The days preceding the event were littered with two World Cup defeats for England along with other niceties, such as none of the 120 people we had invited had turned us down. My best man was always going to be Sooty and both he and Libby had done a lot of running around to help make sure that the day ran smooth. As had both Jeanette and Paul.

The house was always busy with someone or someones staying over and people popping in and out. A bit like Emily's mum's house in Birkenhead, really. The future wife was insistent everything was under control, however I'd be lying, or she would rather, if she'd had really thought that. Ask anyone – a wedding is an extremely stressful time because nothing ever goes to plan and there is always someone pulling in the opposite direction.

Stuart was up on the Wirral both enjoying his sixteenth birthday and literally shitting himself that he hadn't flunked his exams, and every now and then he'd phone me to try and reassure me – or himself rather. He also took time out to thank me for the two Liam Gallagher 'Pretty Green' shirts that we'd sent him up.

As did his mum, who never ceased to stop bragging me off, and prior to her banking the company cheque Libby had sent her for £1200, had shown it to everyone in the street.

"Oh, he's such a gentleman," Emily's mum had said. "And he's so thoughtful."

It did make me wonder if it had been Sil' who had written my mum's eulogy that the vicar had garbled at her funeral.

As for Stuart, I told him, "Only you can do this, no-one else can." And therefore the ball was firmly in his court.

To say we were busy didn't stop the steady traffic of kids in the house, my two especially. I thought they had moved in on a permanent basis over the last two weeks, so much so Jeanette offered to waiver maintenance. I don't know if she actually meant it, but it was a nice gesture all the same.

Lucy had been down the last two weekends and she had sussed out the use of her big sister's flash laptop and was talking at length over the internet to young Mark from Drighlington, who – believe it or not – with his family, plus Mr and Mrs Longbenton and their family, was coming down for the night-do. For me it was always a case of the more the merrier, and if I'm being honest, Emily thought that too.

"Good god," she said, "That's nearly three hundred people for the night-do."

"I know," I smiled. "I bet you wish you'd asked for presents now, eh?"

I could see she was certainly thinking about it.

"It's great being popular though, innit?" she twanged.

"Yeah. Great," I said.

"I'm dead excited," she smiled.

"Me too."

Her weekly music classes were running at three and four days a week, with her six regulars plus a couple of kids from the same all girls school as Sooty's kids, and that being the case she had sort of got back into teaching with me constantly being told it was something that she, "Really, really enjoyed." I don't know if she actually pre-planned it the way it panned out but she succumbed me into buying her a piano, by firstly wanting to buy some crappy looking fifty quid organ off Ebay.

"Are you really serious about this?" I asked.

She gave me an affirmative nod and smile.

"I'm only asking as you've got the house really nice and we really don't want anything like that pile of shite you're looking at stuck in the conservatory."

"I really am serious," she said.

"And it'll make you happy?"

"So can I get it?" she smiled.

And that's when I told her "definitely not" and to leave it with me, and I got Bondy's dodgy mate from Hammersmith on the blower.

"I only want to pay a couple of grand," I said. No, I didn't say – I frigging stated it, as the last 'four grand tops' for the ring turned out to be two and half grand more than I'd asked for, plus another five hundred for the receipt plus another five hundred for the kosher insurance documents.

"He really likes you," Bondy had told me when I'd seen him over in Marrakesh.

"He would do," I replied. "I give him money."

Bondy's mate didn't disappoint and four days before the

wedding I got a telephone call from some unknown number talking garbage in some foreign dialect that I couldn't decipher, sort of asking if I had a 'block and tackle'.

"I have piano for you."

"Yeah, just wheel it in the house," I had said.

"No, we need block and tackle."

We? Who's we? I certainly wasn't doing any humping as the last thing I needed was a bad back for Saturday.

"We need maybe five or six bodies," stated the voice.

"How big is this actual piano?" I had asked, as either it was the size of a Ford Focus or the guy on the other end of the phone was some sort of weakling.

"It's big," he had said.

"How big?" I had asked.

"Big," he had replied.

I got Bondy's mate on the phone just to clear a few things up.

"How big is this frigging thing?" I asked him.

"Huge," came his reply.

"Huge as in how huge?"

"Fairly huge," he replied.

"What, like Ford Focus huge?" I asked.

"It's great value for five grand," he said.

"Five grand? You said two?" I stated.

"I know but this is a really good piano."

It was a really good piano. It was also a really big piano.

"God, that's a big one," chuckled Emily.

"Don't you start," I said, looking at the giganticness of the thing.

"Will it fit in the room?" she asked.

"Believe me, for five grand it'll fit in the room," I said.

From 9:45pm until 12:30am we struggled like hell to get it over Mrs Sosk's and into ours, hoping we never crushed the ferret tunnels as it went in through the rear patio doors.

I had to hand it to Mrs Sosk: she was as strong as both removal men put together and she swore like a trooper when they dropped it on her foot.

"Are you sure you want it there?" I asked Emily.

She said very little but I could see her bottom lip going as I got a great hug.

"I gather you like it then?"

I may have got a massive hug but something was narking me a little bit – especially when I saw the two removal men scarper when a patrol car turned in off Grays Inn Road.

"You better get me a receipt for this thing," I told Bondy's mate.

"Do you want it insured as well?" he asked.

That was another thousand quid up in smoke.

Bondy's mate nearly gave me a heart attack a couple of days later when I nipped out for a jog at 5:10am.

"You been out here all night?" I asked.

"We work a lot of unsociable hours," he replied.

"I believe you," I said. "Looking around."

We went inside and he handed me the receipt from a music shop in Leicester and the kosher insurance documents.

"Is this right?" I asked. "A piano worth thirty-five grand?"

"Yeah," he replied. "That's what the man said."

I took his word for it and he left.

Emily had been besotted with the thing and spent half the day polishing it and the other half wheeling it around. Not that it did anything as no matter where she stuck it, it still filled half the room.

"What do you reckon?" she asked on me coming in from work.

"It's really big, M," I said.

"It is a bit, isn't it?"

"Yeah, a bit."

"I think we'll get used to it," she convinced herself.

"I'm sure we will – just don't go wanting a snooker table or we'll never be able to get in the house."

A great smile lit up her face. "Stop being daft," she twanged.

She tinkled around on it a bit, but I never heard her play on it although Mrs Sosk came around and had told me that she had walked in on her playing and singing, which was a new one. I'd not heard her sing either. I'd heard her whistle when she was in the bathroom with the dodgy handle, but never sing.

As for Mrs Sosk, I got Adebayor and his mate to call off at ours one evening and make part of the fence into a gate so she could get easy access to our house, seeing as though we knew she wasn't a witch. She was also pretty good at both handling and cleaning out the ferrets and even dragged our bin out for us on dustbin day.

"'You've got a Steinway," stated Sooty as he picked his kids up from a music lesson.

"What's one of them?" I asked.

"That great big piano in the room," he answered.

"Yeah, I bought it for M."

"They're over thirty grand," he whispered, sort of shrugging his shoulders.

"I got it off that big Asian kid who used to work with Bondy – five grand plus documents," I said.

"Whose house did that come out of?" he asked.

"A really big one, probably – it took a dead long time getting in ours," I replied.

I could see him pondering.

"Do you think he'll get me one?" asked Sooty.

"Sure. He'll probably steal you ours," I replied.

Since Emily's grandparents had been down I had kept in daily contact with them and after he'd had his suit measured I had their Stuart take Ginge's old laptop back up north after it took me seven hours to wipe all the porn off it.

"It's only a year old," I told Bill. "It'll be great for the internet."

It was. And within a day or so he had about twenty different email addresses, an Ebay account and Facebook page, the latter of which he could keep in touch with my lad regarding gardening tips, but more importantly for my lad – toys for Christmas from all his new grandparents. Some of the old ones miss out so much because they get stuck in their ways and refuse to embrace technology – not this one, though.

So two days before our big day I got home from work and refused point-blank to work until next Tuesday.

"Five days off," I said as I slumped on to the couch in the room with the big screen TV which was followed by M, and of course the ever growing lump with my name on it sat in my lap.

"I can fit in my dress," she smiled. "I tried it on again."

"You're not that big," I said.

"Really?"

"Yeah, really."

That pleased her.

"You fancy doing anything?" I asked.

"I'd like some 'me and you' time," she said.

"We have loads of me and you time," I said. "That's why I'm always knackered – even with the lump you're still loads fitter than me."

She smiled. "I don't mean like that."

"Okay – what do you fancy?"

We went out for the night, and were on our own for the first time in ages. We had a nice meal and went to that bar where they played indie music and we talked until throwing out time.

"I've got a surprise for you on Saturday," she said, linking my arm whilst leaning into me.

"What – you're not going to turn up?" I asked.

"Don't be daft," she twanged.

"Okay," I said. "I'll look forward to it."

"I think Tim's got one for you as well," she said.

"No doubt – I'll certainly not look forward to that one."

We got back to the house and there were loads of emails and missed phone calls.

"I need a secretary for this lot," I said.

"You have one – me," she smiled.

I poured us a wine each and we snuggled up on the couch and watched a film into the early hours and got knocked up by Tony the postman at 6:30am with a load of special deliveries.

"You didn't change your mind and tell everyone that you wanted presents, did you?"

"Wow," she exclaimed.

I needed a barrow to get them all in the house. There were loads of the things.

We ate breakfast together which was strangely smoked salmon and scrambled egg on toast, which I'd never had – ever, and within minutes of being seated the phone calls started.

"We're still dead important," she smiled.

"I think you like all the attention," I said.

"I definitely do," she smiled.

As we were the age we were we sort of negated the general stag- and hen-dos and it was just a meal over at Sooty's for the men and the same for Emily and the women over at ours, with all the family coming down and sort of separating into males and females. In short it was organised madness as nothing went to plan and after an hour or so I had a rather emotional M on the phone telling me that everyone over at ours was upset and crying.

"What have you done?" I whispered. "You haven't thrown them all out, have you?"

I was waiting for an answer and suddenly got, "Paris, the piano, my ring …" and I couldn't make out the rest as she started crying, although I caught the, "I really love you so much," bit at the end though.

"Are they okay, mate?" asked Sooty.

I shrugged my shoulders. "I think so."

Young Stuart had taken to Ginge, and his northern upbringing helped him negotiate his way around Sooty's pool table like a good 'un, so much so that not even Sooty could beat him, so while they played pool we watched TV as France thumped Switzerland 5-2 with Giroud looking particularly impressive.

Sooty had a massive Chinese takeaway delivered and Emily's dad explained that his father-in-law, Bill, had never had Chinese food before.

"He's a 'meat and two veg' bloke," exclaimed Mike.

I had seen it while he was down at ours for the seven days he and Edie had stayed. Nothing flash, but good healthy stuff all the same. Well apart from the bacon, that is. And eggs. And sausage.

I watched as Bill picked at some battered chilli prawns and spoke with Sooty, with the latter explaining to him how we used to make DVDs when we left university, and how his dad, god bless him, had helped set us up. This impressed Eddie quite a bit as well.

"My dad used to always be on at him to slow down," said Sooty, pointing at me with his chopstick.

He did. Pete was a great bloke and it was really sad when he passed away. He and his wife, Jill, were as good as any parents to me. Sooty was a lot like his dad. Nothing like his mum, but loads like his dad. His mum had been a great source of advice when we were growing up.

"Men always go for great ankles," she said, sort of meaning 'legs' but sort of also stating the fact that she herself had nice ankles. She did, and that must have stuck with me as I've never had any women with horrible looking ankles. Well, to be honest I've never had any horrible looking women.

There was the odd exception, though. When we were fifteen Sooty had been on holiday to Skegness and had sort of got off with this girl from Tideswell in Derbyshire and obviously sounded me out about making a foursome with one of her mates a couple of weeks later. We met up and got them back to Jill and Pete's and on copping them, Jill candidly stated, "What the hell are you doing with them?"

It was a bit of a reality check really as they were, if I'm being honest, pretty rank. Well, not for Sooty but definitely for me. So much so, when we buggered them off I had both girls stalking me over the phone for weeks after that, with Sooty's ex threatening suicide if I didn't marry her and give her babies. I had that quite a lot when I was growing up. Girls' hormones are all over the shop when they are at that age, and the last thing they need is some young kid who doesn't give a shit to take advantage. I saved the taking advantage bit for when I was a bit older and when the girls knew a bit more. Not that it ever stopped me from being a git.

It was a great night, and I saw Stuart and Ginge talking at length to one of our mates who was one of the technical boffs on Sky Sports Saturday.

"He's a top lad – him, Stu," I said. "It's the likes of him you learn from."

Stuart was in awe of everything around him and if he looked after it and did the ground work, he had a great life waiting for him.

I walked outside with a wine in my hand, sat on the terrace and had Sooty come out and sit with me.

"Big day tomorrow," he acknowledged.

I nodded.

"I can't believe how quick this has all happened," he said.

"Me neither," I replied.

"Everyone's rooting for you both," he said.

"Even Jeanette," I winked.

"Jeanette only bollocks you because you need it – it's the same with Libby," he said. "You know they both love you."

I did. "Thanks mate," I said.

We had a few taxis arrive to take the certain people off to where they were going and me, Sooty and Ginge cleared up all the shite and drank and talked into the early hours. It was one of those nights you have where you feel very good about yourself the next day. Company with great friends is always like that. Company with great friends is fantastic.

Emily's grandfather and dad were the first up the next day and were sat at the big kitchen table drinking tea when I got up.

"Did you both sleep well?" I asked as I poured myself a coffee.

"He's got a right place here," said Emily's dad.

"He married well," I smiled. "But he deserves it."

"We've just been talking about you, lad," said Emily's grandfather.

"Really?" I replied.

"I've had Edie on the phone the last half hour crying," he said.

Mmm. I didn't like the sound of that.

"Have you any family coming down?" asked Emily's dad, sort of side-tracking the conversation a bit.

I shook my head.

And that was that. Any would-be conversation just hit a brick wall.

I got a message text through. 'Really really love U x M ps. Plz turn up.'

I text back. 'Def will do x.'

We had both been married before but in totally different

circumstances. I'd had a fairly big white wedding and Emily had had a register office do, with only a few family attending and that being the case I let my emotions make the decision and went totally over the top making sure that this would be a day she would definitely remember.

She never overplayed her hand and knew what sort of dress she wanted. First one that would fit her, but more one that she would feel comfortable in.

"You don't want a wedding dress, then?" I had asked.

"It is a wedding dress," she had smiled. "Just not a big frilly wedding dress."

It looked like just a posh cream dress to me.

I had it relayed to me by Sooty that over at our house things were manic, with violin playing bridesmaids on the Xbox and two ferrets loose in the house.

"I told my lad not to have the ferrets in the house today," I said.

"What – aren't they coming to the wedding?" asked Sooty.

"I don't think they're on the guest list," I said.

"Maybe they'll gatecrash," said Sooty.

Mmm. Now there was a thought. My lad was great at putting things in his pocket, especially when we were out shopping. I nipped into B&Q the other month for some drill bits and found that he had come out with a spanner and a pair of pliers. Jeanette said that she was always telling him off about it. She had gone in TK Maxx only the other week and he'd managed to come out with three pairs of sunglasses.

"Did you have to take them back?" I had asked.

"You're joking," she had replied. "They were Fendi."

I had been thinking about taking him down to Hatton Garden.

We all jumped in a cab and went over to Tony the Barber's who treated us to a shave and a trim whilst also trying to talk up Greece's chances in the World Cup.

"Tony, they are rubbish, mate," I said. "They were even rubbish when they won the Euros in 2004."

"No, this team good," he said.

"No, that team very shit," I said.

I hated international football, although Sooty loved it – possibly because his team, the Mighty Whites, were more recently found floundering in the mid to lower reaches of football's second tier.

Emily's dad and granddad loved getting a shave with a cut throat razor and the fact that Tony was just as meticulous and removing nasal hair with it as he was at scraping your chin gave them the thrill of some roller coaster ride thinking that at any minute it could derail.

Tony may have not been a big talker but he was certainly a big Arsenal fan and was the worst loser you could ever imagine, and over the last few seasons he'd had plenty of practice at it, and that being the case I always made sure I never had a shave after a defeat. I expected ears and noses missing after Chelsea had humped us 6-0, but he surprised me and just shut the shop up for a couple of days and grew a beard.

Stuart had never been to The Emirates before and it really is a nice place if you take away the fact that they only open the turnstiles two hours before kick-off and that the food on offer inside is crap.

I remember my dad taking me to a night match at Doncaster Rovers not long before he died and introducing me to a drink of Oxo and his mate from work who was called 'Zig-a-Zagger', and who stood shouting it on the terraces of Belle Vue long after my dad had gone.

"Not bad is it?" I said to Stuart as regards The Emirates; I must say he looked really grown up in his new suit.

"It's brilliant," he replied.

I remembered the first match here against Aston Villa

where Gilberto had equalised in the last few minutes. I also remembered the Villa match earlier this season when the atmosphere was pure toxic and where Kieran Gibbs went off after being elbowed by Christian Benteke.

"What's he gone off for?" I had screamed. "It's only a lousy cut."

I always considered football a man's game – a contact sport, and after being kicked up in the air a few times by Sooty you realise how hard it can actually be. Gibbs was a player who for me could have it all, but one who just lacks that extra something. Leaving the field of play for a bit of a scratch was pretty gay if you ask me and sort of sums his attitude up.

When Sammy had been playing up at Elland Road in the same game he'd hit home the 25-yard drive against Leeds he got heavily clattered by Norman Hunter – Elland Road was a violent place. Sammy however had picked up a nasty ankle injury and it was Don Howe who was captain at the time – who'd had to physically throw him off the field.

Sammy was a player who would hobble around on a crutch if it meant him getting a game. He was in good company as Peter Storey was exactly the same. Kieran Gibbs needed to add that certain something to his game, and I'm sure if he did that he would now be the one over in Brazil rather than the crash test dummy that is Leighton Baines.

Wedding days tend to go quickly as there are so many people you know wanting to speak to you and congratulate you.

A civil service beats the hell out of a church service as it's much more laid back and a damn sight more comfortable and on seeing me, my lad ran up to me and gave me a hug and firstly complained about the horrible suit his mum had made him wear and then about him not being able to fetch Giroud and Arteta.

"You can't have the ferrets running around The Emirates," I said. "Arsène Wenger hates them."

"Why – is he scared of 'em?" he asked.

"Petrified – like your mum is with spiders."

Jeanette came up to me and gave me a peck and straightened my tie. "Come on, leave your dad alone and come sit with me," she said.

"Leave him – he'll be okay," I said.

"Are you sure?" she asked.

"Of course."

"She looks lovely," stated Jeanette with reference to Emily.

"So do you," I said whilst patting my lad's hair down.

"M says he's been in your hair gel," she smiled.

I managed a natter with Emily's mum and Edie, who were both really emotional, and by then the music kicked up and Emily walked in with her dad and her bridesmaids – a beaming Lucy and my daughter who was yacking to both Sooty's kids.

"You look nice," I said as she walked up to me.

"So do you," she smiled.

"I told you I'd turn up."

"Yeah, you did didn't you," she said.

A couple of 'I will's later and we were in the reception area where my lad dispensed with half his suit to go play with the other kids before being summoned back by his mum to watch his sister play her violin along with Sooty's two kids and both his portly nieces.

£100 that cost me, and I have to say it was well worth it. Especially when one of his nieces fell off the stool. She rolled over as good as any stunt man and was so professional in the way she got straight back on the horse.

Everything looked immaculate from the venue down to the people, who incidentally were being chaperoned by some fleet-footed and very camp wedding coordinator who was a dead ringer for Gervinho – something which certainly didn't go unnoticed by my lad.

"Dad, is that Gervinho?" he asked.

"Definitely," I replied.

"Can I go get his autograph?"

"Sure," I said as I watched 'Autograph Albert' chase the Ivorian around three tables with a pen and a place mat.

"What's he doing?" smiled Emily.

"Trying to get an autograph off that gay bloke with the daft hair," I said.

Most players will give you time to sign their autographs, and one of the things that struck me was about something that Jeanette's Paul had said when he was at our house the other month – and about Frank Lampard of all people. After a cup game, where Chelsea had only managed a draw away at Brentford, Lampard took time out to go into the crowd and sign autographs.

"Sheer class," Paul had said.

He was right – it was.

There is always the exception however, and I always remember an old mate of my mate 'Millwall John', who had told me that when he was a kid he was absolutely Chelsea nuts. He still is as it happens! This day he had been stand-ing outside Stamford Bridge in the freezing cold in Janu-ary 1967 after his team had beaten Southampton 4-1 and he'd asked Southampton's Welsh international striker Ron Davies for his autograph. Davies duly told the young lad to, "Go get yourself fucked."

The player was the subject of some £200,000 transfer speculation a couple of years later, however he never got the big move, however his team mate and fellow striker Martin Chivers did. They may be a bit of irony in that. True story, that.

Sammy certainly wasn't like that.

Saying that, I doubt David Beckham, Luis Suarez or any other world superstar footballer who has played in the Premier League would ever do that. Why hurt a young lad's feelings, when the only feeling he is showing is the total adoration for the god like person he is handing the pen to?

My lad got his autograph, but he was disappointed as hell that Gervinho had signed it 'Martin'.

We ate a nice three course meal and Sooty got up to speak on our behalf and was as eloquently spoken as ever as he told Fosis, Andreas in the green suit, Turkish George and a couple of lads from BSkyB to stop playing cards on the far table while he was talking. As I said, I liked informal.

Sooty offered us a toast and did a bit of rambling amidst a bit of sniggering from the guests before he stopped and whispered Emily something. I don't really know what but he got a nod and a smile in response, and I have to say her bottom lip started wobbling a bit – again.

"Are you okay?" I whispered.

She nodded. "I just love you so much," she whispered back.

And then the horror of horrors came.

"I know the star of the show is going to hate this," stated my best man. "And don't think I don't know who had the old ice cream van dumped outside my house or put my wife's details in the Free Ads as some escort."

That bit had everyone laughing. That was everyone apart from Libby, who'd had to change her number.

And then Jeanette stood up as he took her over the mike, and it was then that you could hear a pin drop.

"Hello – for those who don't know me – I'm the groom's ex-wife."

That may have got everybody's attention but my heart immediately sunk to the floor and my palms were as clammy as hell, although Emily did put her head on my shoulder and gave me a firm squeeze.

"I am also his friend, and Emily's friend too," she said, before sort of semi-breaking down under some emotional stress only to be propped back up by the rod of iron that was Libby.

"Go on, love," Libby said.

"We all love him so much," she said wiping her eyes. "He's a fantastic person – totally bloody stupid – but a great person."

Thanks for that, I thought.

"M didn't know this at the time – but she sent me a photograph when they were on holiday in Morocco that had me literally crying for hours," she said.

She then held up the photograph she'd had on her fridge of me and my two kids who were both sat on my knee. The bare chested me, that is.

"Before we were married he used to tell me that was all he ever wanted to do ..."

Emotion took over and she started crying, which set everyone off until Libby propped her up again.

"All he ever wanted was to have his child on his knee, and on this picture he has two."

She showed the photograph around to everyone and then I understood what was going to come next.

"Lee loved his father very much and when he was six years old his father had died while they were on holiday in Bridlington. Both of them had gone out on a boat trip on the Yorkshire Belle – it was there that he had sat on his father's knee whilst an accordionist had played some music and where his father had told him that there was no better feeling in the world than a dad to have his son sat on his knee."

I felt everyone looking at me and my back was wet through as Jeanette turned to me.

"Can you remember what music they were playing, Lee?" she asked me.

I could.

"Train whistle blowing makes a sleepy noise," I mumbled wiping my eyes. "Morningtown Ride."

She nodded.

"They got back to the hotel and that's where Lee lost his father – all Lee ever wanted to do after we'd married was bounce his own children on his knee on the self-same boat trip that he and his father had been on – and you know what? He did – and with both of them."

Nearly everyone was in tears. My dad had had a heart attack in the hotel straight afterwards and he couldn't be revived, and I'd been rooted to the spot scared stiff when my mum walked in on him dying. It was horrible and it is something that never left me.

"And I know when M has her baby boy," added a rather emotional ex-wife, "That he'll do exactly the same – because he really, really is the nicest man and the best father any child could ever have."

It took a while for everyone to calm down as there were lots of nose blowing on serviettes and such like, but she still wasn't done.

"And what everyone keeps asking me," she said wiping her eyes. "Is what they are both going to call the baby that I know will sit on his knee? And that includes M's mum and dad and both her grandparents, both our kids, Tim and Libby and theirs, and even my mum and dad." She shook her head smiling whilst still very much emotional. "I'm asked it every day."

Sooty took the mike off Jeanette and passed it to Emily who was no less emotional as anyone else in the room. "So, do you want to put everyone out of their misery?" he asked, smiling.

She stood up and looked down at her lump before thanking Jeanette for upsetting everyone and making everyone cry – she actually even said that – and then turned her attention to me.

"I loved him from the very first day I met him," she said smiling.

"What, really?" asked Sooty, which sort of brought a few laughs.

"Shurrup you," she twanged smiling before continuing with what she was going to say. "And even when we were together I always thought that I could never have him – and I was never, ever as happy as when he drove all the way up to my mam's to see me and meet all my family – every one of whom love him so, so much."

I had to admit, this bit was brilliant. She was making me sound great.

"And all the time when I was falling more and more in love with him there was something else – and it wasn't just the baby. There was this football player both he and Tim were doing a documentary on, who Lee came to think the world of and who he was so insistent that he was so nice a man that it stopped him reaching the heights he should have."

Everyone was listening.

"I feel there's nothing wrong with that. I like nice. I love nice. Nice is just nice. You can't get better than nice. And I've married such a nice man."

"So?" asked Sooty, smiling and shrugging his shoulders.

"I want us to call our baby Sammy," she smiled.

And there it was. The lump with my name on it was going to be named after a big-chinned, one-eyed coloured tap dancer who was a dead ringer for the Brazilian spoiler Gustavo. I certainly hoped it wouldn't look like him.

There was loads of clapping and cheering as Emily sat down and passed me the mike.

"How can I follow that?" I said. "I can't, so I won't, but you've all made us happy for coming – even though nearly everyone is crying."

I therefore passed the mike over to Sooty who did a great job of cheering everyone up before the reception broke up and every woman in the place had to go and re apply their smudged make up for the photographs.

I had to hand it to Sooty, this had been one hell of a speech – although I'd seen happier contingents at funerals.

And as the band set up for the night we had loads of photographs taken and more and more people turned up and that was when we became one bridesmaid short. Lucy and young Mark from Drighlington were sat on a couch with their mobile phones out swapping music and photos and being chaperoned by a more diminutive 'Michaeleen Oge Flynn', or the gooseberry that was in fact my lad who was by now down to his vest.

"He's so cute," said Emily.

"If he takes any more clothes off he'll be so nude," I said before summoning him over.

"Where's your shirt?" I asked.

"Which one?" he asked.

"The one that you were wearing."

I got a shrug of his shoulders and an, "Uh, uh," before he ran back over to the couch to re-play being the gooseberry.

"I'm glad that's sorted then," I said.

We mingled and shook loads of hands as the room filled up more and more and that is when Sooty played what he thought was his ace card, while I was having a natter with Ginge about us trying to sneak off to cop a bit of the Germany versus Ghana game.

"M wants to tell everyone something," he said. "You've got to get up there."

I looked up at Emily, who was stood on the small stage

with a mike in her hand, and as I walked over I noticed a great big grin emanating on his face as he traded a bullshit comment of us having to thank all the guests for coming etcetera, etcetera.

As I walked onto the stage everything went quiet and I had around two hundred and fifty faces glaring at me as the lights were dimmed amid the flashing of cameras.

As I expected Emily to kick off some kind of toast, I got the shock of my life when the band rose from its slumber behind me with one hell of a 'tada' in the way of loads of trumpets or violins. Whatever it was, it was loud.

And then my worst nightmare happened. I got the intro of a song from David Lynch's rather strange 'Mulholland Drive' flick, which was followed by a rendition of Connie Stevens' 'Sixteen Reasons', by the band and my new wife, the latter of who was ready to tell all these two hundred-plus faces looking up at me of the 'Sixteen Reasons' why she loved me.

Believe me when I say it, when she kicked it off those sixteen reasons felt like three hundred and sixteen reasons and I hoped that the ground would swallow me up.

However there was a twist in the tale and my mood changed when I realised that she could actually sing and without any real effort – even though she was wrong in assuming that I had a freckled nose or indeed wore crazy clothes, although the latter part was rather nice where she told me, "You say we'll never part, our love's complete," was sort of spot on, and I told her as much afterwards.

"I didn't know you could sing?" I said amidst everyone clapping.

"I didn't want to do it," she said. "Because I thought I'd embarrass you, but Tim said you'd love it if I did."

"Yeah, I bet he did," I said. "Remind me on Monday to get ten cubic metres of concrete dropped off at his house."

"Is he having some work done?" she asked.

"Nope," I replied.

We walked off the stage to more and more clapping and I could see that Sooty's immense disappointment concluded the lack of my embarrassment.

"Will the bride and groom set us off dancing?" stated the band leader before he kicked up some more trumpets.

Then as soon as we walked on to the dance floor my lad came over and took both mine and Emily's hand which was followed by my daughter doing the same. Four turned into six as Emily shouted Jeanette over, who initially tried to stand her ground as 'just' a spectator, but Sooty and Libby encouraged her to join us.

And there we were – me, Emily, my kids, Sooty, Libby and theirs and both Jeanette and Paul dancing to what I could make out was the Beach Boys' 'God Only Knows'.

Everybody I loved more than anything in the world – all together.

Life was nice. I liked nice. Nice was nice.

Chapter 32
What if?

So that was that: a few months of madness with the rest of my life to look forward to. I looked in my phone at the number that I had. Not the woman who had thanked me for the flowers thirteen times as I knew that was Sooty – I'd actually caught him sending me a text and he put his hands up straight away.

"What if I'd have texted back?" I asked.

"Yeah, but you didn't," he said.

No, I didn't. I certainly might have done before, but I wouldn't now. I was happy with what I had. What I had was great.

The number in my phone that I was looking at was that of Sammy.

Arsenal were happy with what they got in 1970/71. It certainly wasn't planned how it turned out, it just happened how it did. During the early tenures of the George Graham period and more often with the latter tenure of the Arsené Wenger period, their Arsenal sides hit an inconsistent patch during the winter months. It is always a case of form and the fact that form is generally temporary. Class is something that is permanent and when the rest of the side hit an inconsistent patch it is the top players – the class players, who the team look up to in order to help them ride it through.

Arsenal's form was steady in the early part of the 1970/71 season, not brilliant as the history books would have you believe. Defeats away to Chelsea, Stoke and Sturm Graz of Austria and at home to Crystal Palace was hardly the form of Champions, however three big players came back in the winter months and gave the team a push, two of whom stayed the course right up until the end and one of whom did not.

In the preceding 1969/70 season Leeds United went for the lot and got nothing. Pipped to the post by Alan Ball's Everton in the League, knocked out of the European Cup 3-1 on aggregate by Celtic and beaten in the 1970 FA Cup Final by Chelsea after a replay. It was a story of what could have been. Life is full of 'what if's.

Arsenal could have gone the lot in the following season. Why not? They certainly had the squad.

On February 19th 1971, journalist Norman Gillier ran a story in the *Daily Express* titled 'Mee's Everest', where it was said that the club were chasing the treble. There was even talk of emulating the points tally, which was wrestled from Arsenal and held by Leeds since 1968/69.

"It may be an impossible dream, but we are going all out to make it a reality," Mee had stated. By March 23rd the impossible dream was over and gunning on three fronts was reduced to two after a contentious 0-1 reverse over in Cologne – a team that they should have really beaten quite easily.

I watched the part of the documentary where Arsenal put the Belgian team of Beveren to the sword 4-0 in the third round of 1970/71 European Inter-Cities Fairs Cup. It was hardly top rank opposition, but Beveren to their credit had already knocked out Valencia in the preceding round and at the end of the day you can only deal with what gets put in front of you.

The season before, Arsenal may have disposed of Sporting

Lisbon, Ajax and Anderlecht – all teams packed with internationals – but they made very heavy work of a Glentoran side in the early rounds. They also made very heavy work of Sturm Graz in the second round of this competition and Beveren were very much on par with them and they needed disposing of, and it was Sammy who provided that much needed spark.

Just back from his pre-season injury he had only played in the wins against Ipswich Town and Liverpool and was strangely given the number four shirt, as Peter Storey was clinging onto his favoured number eight.

It took him exactly that number of minutes (eight) to race through on goal and get upended for the number eight to have his penalty saved by the former Hajduk Split goalkeeper Lukas Poklepovic.

Sammy stated afterwards that Storey was demonised as just being some cynical hatchet man, however there was much more to his game than that.

"He may not have been the most adventurous of players," explained Sammy, "But his distribution was flawless."

Putting the eighth minute setback behind them, the butcher and the surgeon ripped the heart out of Beveren and Sammy had a great shot saved by Poklepovic before half time, but after 56 minutes he raced onto a Ray Kennedy knock down and hammered the ball into the top corner from 25 yards.

Up against European opposition was where his kind of football could thrive and next up were Cologne.

The footage we had got was quite poor but we cleaned it up to make it on par with the Final against Anderlecht the year before.

There had been three league defeats in between Beveren and Cologne. One against Ian Greaves's Huddersfield Town

(1-2) at the old Leeds Road, which was as contentious as you could get as the referee awarded the West Yorkshire club a penalty for handball on McLintock when it was clearly over a yard outside the area, if it was a handball at all. To make matters worse McLintock had his nose broken in the first minute of that game. The other defeats were against Bill Shankly's Liverpool (0-2) and Brian Clough's Derby County (0-2) and the only person to come out of either game with any credit was strangely Bob Wilson, even though Tommy Smith beat him with a 25-yard drive. The upshot was that the team had hit an erratic patch of form prior to the Cologne game, even though Manchester City (1-0 and 2-1) had been capably despatched in both the League and FA Cup as well as Manchester United (3-1) over at Old Trafford and up at Molineux a very good Wolverhampton Wanderers side were put to the sword (3-0), with Charlie George twice hitting the woodwork.

Cologne came to Highbury and sat back and played their methodical and cautious European game and were reliant on 81-cap German international Wolfgang Overath, who had delighted the pundits at the World Cup in Mexico and had previously helped Cologne to the DFB-Pokal (German Cup) two years earlier and the Bundesliga title four years before that. As stated, it is your team's class players that help get you get through the tough games. Arsenal on the other hand negated their European game that had served them so well the season prior, when they had capably swept everyone aside including Cruyff's Ajax to lift the trophy in favour of hitting the German side, like they had done their opponents in the League. It was basically a case of poor tactics and their approach play left a lot to be desired. McLintock had opened the scoring hoping that the floodgates would open but the Germans kept to their game plan and caught Arsenal several times on the counter, with their most unlikely attempt at goal beating Bob Wilson – and direct from a corner. 1-1. I had watched the match and it was patchy at best. Wilson was culpable for their goal, but in fairness he had kept out a couple of efforts. Don Howe's Division One tactics weren't working and he needed a fall guy and as history would state, he played his hand and replaced Sammy at half-time for George Graham, and Arsenal scored a goal fifteen minutes from time through Peter Storey to make it 2-1. But as history would also tell you – it wasn't enough.

How would things have worked out if Don Howe had not withdrawn Sammy, no-one knows, but a lot of things can happen in 45 minutes. Maybe he would have scored and made a goal like he had done against Beveren. The only person to come out of that tie with any real credit was Storey, who had undertaken his duty of shackling Overath. No one else did.

Don Howe certainly wasn't perfect and he had been wrong on lots of occasions.

'Yeah, but he was part-orchestrator of the Double,' is the sentence to end that argument.

He was also the same part-orchestrator that lost them the 1969 League Cup final when he urged on a 'dying' side to go all out for the win on the quagmire that was Wembley, and got caught on the counter, exactly as they did versus Cologne. There was nothing good about that. It was a decision that bordered on stupidity, as was his leaving Arsenal the way he did, taking half the back room staff with him in the process. He may have thought he was being cute posing for the national press looking like Noël Coward in his dressing gown and slippers and holding the telephone for the camera and telling the hacks that 'he didn't feel wanted' – however he wasn't. He was just being Don Howe.

His man-management strategy at West Bromwich Albion was firstly to keep an unhappy Jeff Astle and Colin Suggett and flog Asa Hartford to Leeds before getting him handed back as 'goods not worthy', and then get them relegated – although in March 1973 his bottom-of-the-table team did beat Arsenal 1-0 at The Hawthornes to derail Arsenal's hopes of winning the League Championship.

It could have been different for Sammy too, as Howe had been playing footsie with the Leicester City board over the vacant manager's position at Filbert Street before he took over at West Bromwich Albion. Looking back at it, maybe West Bromwich Albion wished he had taken the Leicester job – who knows, but what is known is that there would be no way at all that Sammy would have ever signed for Leicester City if he had.

"You're reading too much into this," Eddie had told me.

"I am a naturally inquisitive person – that's what I do," I replied.

"Yeah, but you don't know that," Eddie had said.

I knew I didn't but I always put loads of twos together and maybe from time to time I never got the right number at the end, but one thing I never ever got was an odd number. Somewhere in there is the right answer.

There was a problem with Bertie Mee and Don Howe in much as there was Joe Mercer and Malcolm Allison at Manchester City. It was a winning combination in both respects, however both coaches wanted more, and by more, I mean more power.

It is well-noted of Howe's coaching style that it is based on defensive stability and is very route-one, something which Arsenal found to their credit for much of the 1970/71 season, as did a piss-poor Wimbledon side in 1988 when he was coaching it, and when his long-ball tactics won them the FA Cup against what was a brilliant Liverpool side.

Sammy certainly didn't fit into that style of play, but whereas Howe said he felt unwanted, Sammy did not.

Denis Hill-Wood pleaded with Sammy to stay, and there was a time when he was indeed wavering to stay. It was the same with Bertie Mee. Why not? Sammy was a brilliant footballer and the team would go into next season along with Leeds United as title contenders. However where would he play? The same place Alan Ball would go on to play, most probably.

When Ball had arrived he upset just about everyone and came in as top earner. John Radford had specified that he was the wrong player for the club, which immediately tells you about Arsenal's stance on midfield skill. Radford also said that the Double side would have been better if he had played up front with Charlie George rather than Ray Kennedy, which again gives history another angle. Kennedy was thrust into the Arsenal side as some raw battering ram, much the same as was Kevin Campbell in the 1990/91 season, both players of who were targeted by sections of the Highbury crowd.

The irony was that Ray Kennedy was by far the most successful player of the Double side even though his inclusion throughout the Double year, although highly positive, messed with the overall dynamics of the side, as Charlie George was shifted back into midfield.

George was an extrovert, the big mouth, the crowd's favourite – Sammy was not. George played with an arrogance that Sammy didn't have. The crowd loved it. Even when he made the suicide back pass that led to Arsenal going 0-2 down in the semi-final against Stoke City the crowd still loved him. Sammy had come on as substitute and Arsenal had begun a rhythm. Passes were being made which had Stoke City struggling to deal with them. Stoke should have been out of sight, but they weren't. Arsenal were knocking on the door. George was off injured and Sammy was on. Arsenal were going to get back in the game and they did. History tells you that it was Peter Storey who got the credit, but that's not the whole story. The game was lost until Sammy got on the field. Maybe that corner that preceded the penalty in the dying seconds wouldn't have happened if it hadn't been for Sammy dragging John Radford away from arguing the toss with the referee whilst the clock was still ticking. Who knows? His reward? Bar an appearance as substitute against what would become Don Howe's new team, Sammy never played another match for Arsenal.

It is well documented as to the reason Sammy left, but as I've said before football fans are fickle, and when it comes to Arsenal, they are among the worst. I know, as I'm one of them.

When George got the jeers from the crowd he stuck two fingers up at them and told them to 'bollocks' and then got on with it. Sammy was a thoughtful guy and took it to heart. He shouldn't have but he did.

Emily said to me, "I like nice – there's nothing wrong with nice."

She was right, there isn't, but sometimes the nice guy doesn't always win, as was the case with Sammy.

Maybe if he had stayed things would have been different. With Howe gone, maybe his game would have thrived. It has been well-documented that during the 1972/73 season, Bertie Mee dabbled with Ajax's all conquering total-football, but his lack of ball players made him revert back to type. Sammy was one of those players. Sammy, Storey, Ball and George in a midfield? What a combination.

I sat back on the couch in the big room and at everything I had around me – my new wife with the lovely smile and bundle up her jumper that would come into a world full of love and in a home that she had helped make.